Hidden Heirs:
One Night...to Wife

SUSAN MEIER

SHARON KENDRICK

JENNIFER FAYE

MILLS & BOON

First Published in Great Britain 2023
by Mills & Boon, an imprint of HarperCollins*Publishers* Ltd,
1 London Bridge Street, London, SE1 9GF

www.harpercollins.co.uk

HarperCollins*Publishers*
Macken House, 39/40 Mayor Street Upper,
Dublin 1, D01 C9W8, Ireland

HIDDEN HEIRS: ONE NIGHT...TO WIFE © 2023 Harlequin Enterprises ULC.

Pregnant with a Royal Baby! © 2016 Linda Susan Meier
Crowned for the Prince's Heir © 2016 Sharon Kendrick
Heiress's Royal Baby Bombshell © © 2018 Harlequin Enterprises ULC

Special thanks and acknowledgement are given to Jennifer Faye for her
contribution to the *The Cattaneos' Christmas Miracles* series.

ISBN: 978-0-263-31864-7

MIX
Paper | Supporting
responsible forestry
FSC™ C007454

This book is produced from independently certified FSC™ paper
to ensure responsible forest management.

For more information visit: www.harpercollins.co.uk/green

Printed and Bound in Spain using 100% Renewable electricity at
CPI Black Print, Barcelona

PREGNANT WITH A ROYAL BABY!

SUSAN MEIER

To my own Prince Charming, and our marriage – a journey of ups and downs that surprises me every day. Usually in a good way. :)

CHAPTER ONE

WHEN THE DOORBELL to her condo rang, Virginia Jones, Ginny for short, had just gotten out of the shower after a long, long day at Jefferson High School in Terra Mas, Texas. Her school was the last on a list of places Prince Dominic Sancho of Xaviera, a small island country between Spain and Algeria, was visiting on a good-will tour. As guidance counselor, she'd shown him the school and introduced him to staff, then herded the kids into the gymnasium, where he'd given an hour-long talk on global economics: how the world was a much smaller place than it had been before the internet.

She'd loved the talk, but she'd liked looking at Prince Dominic even more. Tall and broad shouldered, he filled out the formal uniform of his royalty like a man meant to be a king. His dark eyes sparkled with amusement at the antics of "her" kids. His full lips had never stopped smiling.

If it were permitted for grown women to swoon, she would have made a fool of herself with him that afternoon. As it was, common sense had kept her pro-fessional. And now she was tired. Not up for a visitor.

Her doorbell rang again.

She gave her glass of wine a longing look before she rose from her sofa.

"I'm coming." She said it just as she reached the door. Going up on tiptoes, she peeked through the peephole. When she saw Prince Dominic, she gasped and jumped back.

Her doorbell rang again.

She peered down at her sweatpants and tank top, ran a hand along her still-wet long blond hair and knew this would go down in the annals of her life as one of her most embarrassing moments.

With no choice, she pasted a smile on her face and opened the door.

He laughed. "I caught you at a bad time."

"Unfortunately." Just looking at him made her heart speed up. He'd removed the royal uniform and replaced it with a lightweight white V-neck sweater and jeans. Not a hair of his shiny black curls was out of place. His dark eyes sparkled with amusement.

"You probably think all Americans are idiots."

"No, I think the United States is a very comfortable country." He paused long enough to lift his perfect lips into a warm smile. "Are you going to invite me in?"

She motioned for him to come in with a wave of her hand and kept hyperventilation at bay only by a miracle of self-discipline. She had a *prince* entering her house. A good-looking, good-natured, good *everything* prince.

As she closed the door, he said, "I'd actually come here tonight to see if you'd like to have dinner with me." He shrugged. "And show me your town."

She had to work to keep her eyes from bugging. He wanted to take her *out*? Then she realized his request made sense. She'd shown him the school. Of course, she was the prime candidate to show him the town. He was not asking her out.

"Then I thought maybe we'd fly to Los Angeles and go to a club."

She let her eyes bulge. Okay. He *was* asking her out. "You want to go clubbing?"

"Don't you like to dance?"

Her heart tripped over itself in her chest. "I love to dance."

He smiled. "Me, too. I'm afraid I don't get to dance often, though. Duty supersedes fun. Please say you'll come with me."

"I'd love to."

Though he was in jeans, he looked good enough to eat, so she slithered into her prettiest red party dress, put on her best makeup and slid into tall black sandals.

They had dinner at the local Italian restaurant, with his bodyguards unobtrusively eating at the tables beside theirs, then they actually got on his royal jet and flew to LA, where they'd danced until three. He should have dropped her off at her building lobby. Instead, he came up to her condo, and the few kisses they'd shared in his limo turned into passionate lovemaking. The best sex of her life. She'd kissed him goodbye at the door in her one and only fancy robe—which she'd retrieved from her closet when he made the call to his driver that he was ready. Then just when she was about to shower for school again, he called her.

"Thank you."

The sweetness of his words caused her throat to tighten. Her voice was soft and breathless when she said, "You're welcome."

"I'm sorry we'll never meet again."

"Me, too."

But in a way she wasn't. She'd had a wonderful fairy-tale night with a prince, something she could hold in her heart forever. There would be no need to worry if he would be a good king or a bad king; no need to know if he did stupid things like hog the bathroom; no need to worry if the stress of his job would make him an alcoholic, as her dad had been. No need to know the real Prince Dominic Sancho.

There had been one glorious, wonderful night. No regrets and no worries about the future. The way she liked all her relationships.

They hung up on mutual sighs. In the process of setting her phone on her bedside table, she realized that because he'd called her, she had his number. She clicked a few buttons and when the digits came up caller ID said private line. She smiled. She didn't just have his number she had his *private* number.

That pleased her enormously. If she ever got curious or lonely, she could call him…

Or not. Best to sit and stare at his number and imagine good things. Not bad. Never bad. She'd had enough bad in her life.

Knowing there was no time to sleep, she dressed for school, hugging her secret to herself. For two weeks she walked on a cloud of happiness, then one morning she woke and realized she hadn't gotten her period, and she knew there *really* was a good reason to have his private number.

"Thank God our country isn't like Britain used to be where the future king had to marry a virgin."

Prince Dominic Sancho held back the anger that threatened to rise up in him. He'd been the perfect royal for nearly thirty years and one slip, one reckless night in America, had wiped all that away. His father might be angry, but it was *his* life plan that had been changed.

In order to ensure the integrity of the line and the safety of his child, he had no choice but to marry Ginny Jones, a woman he didn't know.

"Yes. Thank God I'm permitted to marry the mother of my child."

"I was being facetious." Short and bald, with a round belly, his father, the king of Xaviera, was an imposing, strict man. He hated mistakes. Couldn't even tolerate slipups. Especially not from the son who was his successor.

"And I was being sarcastic." It wasn't often that he got smart with his father. In fact, he probably hadn't done it more than five times in his entire life, including his teen years. But discovering a simple one-night stand had resulted in a pregnancy had pushed him over the edge. His brother was the king of playboys but did he ever suffer a consequence for his actions? No. Yet the first time Dom stepped out of line, he was punished.

"I've arranged for you and Ms. Jones to meet with the protocol officials whenever you're ready. But no later than tomorrow morning." King Ronaldo caught his gaze. "Prepare your *bride*."

The insult in his father's voice cut through Dom like a knife. He just barely succeeded in not sniping back.

He rose from his seat across from the ornate desk that was the seat of power for the king. He should have said, "Thank you for your time, Your Majesty." A good prince would have done that. Instead he said, "I'll get back to you."

"See to it that this wedding is done right. I will not be so easy on you if you screw up again."

He bowed and headed out of the room. *I will not be so easy on you if you screw up again?*

Anger coursed through him. He stifled it. His father

was the king. Dominic was heir to the throne. He *knew* there were protocols and rules. He'd broken them. He deserved this.

Still…the penalty for one misstep was marriage? *Marriage.*

After the way his father had fallen apart when his mother died, Dominic understood why his dad was careful, rigid now. His grief had been so intense that he hadn't come out of his quarters for six weeks and in that time the country had begun to crumble. Parliament nearly took his crown, and, watching it all unfold, Dominic had promised himself he would never marry, never soften so much that a loss nearly destroyed him.

When an opportunity for a treaty had arisen, the price being his marriage to a princess of a country that had been an enemy for centuries, he'd thought why not? Not only was the feud between their kingdoms old enough that it was time to retire it, but also there'd be no real emotional ties in a marriage that was part of a treaty, and he'd get an heir who would be a prince in two countries. But now here he was. Forced to marry a woman he didn't know, ruining his design for a double royal heir, because of his own carelessness.

His life plan really had gone to hell.

He sucked in a breath and walked to the back stairway that led to his private quarters, buying time before he had to talk to Ginny. If he was angry, he couldn't imagine how she felt—

Unless she'd gotten pregnant deliberately?

The horribleness of the thought froze his blood, stopped his breathing, and he told himself to calm down. Too many things had to align for her to have orchestrated the pregnancy, including the fact that he was the one who had gone to her condo that night. And she'd been a cute mess. Wet hair. Sweatpants. She obviously hadn't been planning on seeing him that night.

Reaching the top floor of the east wing of Xaviera's palace, he strode in the direction of the white double doors with intricate scroll designs carved down the sides. The huge square "waiting" area between the top of the stairs and his apartment had scant furnishings, though the walls were adorned with art. Picasso. Rembrandt. Monet. Hidden treasures. Mostly for his viewing. Because that's what his life was. Special. Honored. In spite of the awkward meeting with his father, he knew that he was different. Some day he would be a king.

The click of his heels echoed as he walked along the marble floor. When he reached the doors, he took both handles and opened them onto his home, his haven.

Virginia Jones rose from the tufted bench seat in what served as a foyer for his apartment. Medium height, with long yellow hair and the kind of body that tempts a man to do exactly what he had done the night he met her, Ginny was every man's fantasy. When her striking blue eyes met his, he remembered how adorable she was at the Texas high school, a guidance counselor beloved by her students. He also remembered the hot little red dress she'd slipped into when he'd persuaded her to go clubbing with him. The dress had brought out the best of her figure, almost made him drool and turned him into a real live Prince Charming. Seducing her had been second nature. The sex had been amazing.

It seemed that was all he could think about when he looked at her. And now he was about to make her a princess.

"So?"

"So, my father and my kingdom wish for us to marry."

Those bright blue eyes met his. "Wish?"

He motioned for her to follow him into his formal living room. More marble floors greeted them, except these were covered by rich red Oriental rugs. White sofas flanked a white marble fireplace. Red pillows gave the room some color. He gestured for Virginia to take a seat while he strode to the bar and grabbed the decanter of Scotch.

"Can I get you a drink?"

She gaped at him. "I'm pregnant."

He winced. "Right." He took a breath. "How about some orange juice?"

"I'm fine." She held his gaze. "I'm more anxious to learn my fate than to pretend we're having a tea party."

He had no idea where the attitude had come from, but that was the truth of getting intimate with someone you didn't know. She could be the Wicked Witch of the West, or a woman who wanted to save the whales, or a woman who had no loyalties at all, a woman who was lazy, crass or stupid, and he was stuck with her.

"All right." He walked to the sofa across from the one on which she sat and set his Scotch on the glass table between them. "Maybe the better way to put it is that they are *requesting* that we marry."

"So I have a choice?"

"Not really. You are pregnant with the heir to Xaviera's throne. If you decide not to marry me, your child will be taken from you."

She gasped. "What?"

"He or she is the heir to our throne. There isn't a country in the world who'd dare supersede our laws with their own when it comes to royalty, especially royalty in line to rule the country."

She bounced from her seat. "That's not fair!"

He sat back, watching her long legs as she paced. Though she wore jeans and a snug sweater, he pictured those legs beneath the shiny red dress. "Try suing. Waste time. Ruin the chance for us to have a royal wedding. Ruin the chance for the gossip to die down and our child to be brought into the world with a celebration instead of whispers."

She stopped pacing and caught his gaze, obviously thinking through what he'd said.

He took advantage of her weak moment. "You won't win and you'll bring our child into a world of chaos for nothing because I have a plan."

"A plan?"

Ginny stared at the gorgeous man on the sofa. With eyes so dark they almost looked black and onyx hair, he was every inch a prince. A royal. A future ruler who lived a life of privilege. A man just a little bit above everybody else.

As they talked about a situation that would totally change her life, he very calmly sipped Scotch.

"My father wants the next king to be born in wedlock." He held her gaze. "Our subjects will, too. But that doesn't mean we have to stay married."

Relieved, she sat on the sofa across from him again. "It doesn't?"

"No. But it does mean we have to play a part for a while." He glanced at his Scotch then back up at her. "Over the next couple of days, as the protocol office begins planning our wedding, we'll be seen together in public."

Her heart thumped when he said *wedding*. She would be married to a guy who would someday be a king. Did that mean sleeping with him? They might be at odds now, but the night they'd gone out, they'd had a really good time. She had no idea how *that* factored into his plan, so she kept her face calm, simply kept her gaze locked with his, hoping to appear cooler than she was.

"Next week we'll announce our engagement, quick wedding and pregnancy all at once."

That didn't sound fun. "Oh, boy."

"Don't worry. I've thought this through. The people of Xaviera will be thrilled to see me getting married. But the only thing they love better than a royal wedding is a royal pregnancy. If we play this right, the next few months could be a wonderful time for the people of my kingdom."

"Okay." Her nerves popped and jumped, but she resisted the urge to bounce off the sofa and pace again. If he could be calm, she could be calm. And really what he said made sense. They were doing this for his people and their child, a future king, who deserved to be born amid celebration.

"So we'd get married next month and after that we'd spend the rest of your pregnancy making appearances as the happy couple expecting the next heir to the throne, then the baby will be born to a country excited and happy about his birth."

She could picture it. She'd seen enough of Britain's royal family's weddings, as well as their pregnancies, to have a pretty good idea of what she was in for. Except Xaviera was a small country, much smaller than Britain, so she could probably cut the exposure in the press and even in Xaviera itself in about half. Which wouldn't be *too* bad.

"After that we should stay married until the baby's about two. At age two, there's a ceremony that would induct him or her into the line of reigning Sanchos. We can be cool to each other at that ceremony, and then we can divorce without causing too much of a stir because after that nothing press worthy happens in his life until he turns twelve." He sat back. "If people want to say we married hastily, or even if they say we only married for the baby, we agree. But waiting until he or she is two shows we gave the marriage a good shot. Because we'll be fair and calm about it, everyone will support us."

"And what about the baby?"

"What about the baby?"

"Who keeps him? What kind of custody arrangements are we talking about here?"

"There are a few scenarios. I was hoping you'd let the years we're married go by without making any final decisions, but if you choose to take our child back to America, a contingent of bodyguards will be sent with you. Xaviera will purchase a home with suitable security."

"What about my job?"

"Your job will be mother to Xaviera's heir. At least until he or she is twelve."

"Twelve?"

"Up until twelve he can be homeschooled. After that there are mandatory boarding schools. He or she has to have a certain kind of education."

"No public school, huh?"

"Mock if you want, but that is the situation." He rose from the sofa. "Once he goes to boarding school, your life is your own again. Except you will be expected to attend all of his public functions."

She could see it. She could picture herself as the future king's mom, wiping grape jelly from her little boy's chin in private, and way, way out of the view of cameras when he was in public. Knowing that she'd easily slip out of the limelight settled some of her nerves. Still, there was more to it than grape jelly and hiding from cameras.

"I'll give you a week to think about it."

"A week?"

"The week you're at the palace. The time we're getting out. Being seen in public. Having a date or two."

Their eyes met. Their last date had been fantastic. But it was also what had gotten them into this mess.

"I think I still have some more questions."

"About the dates?"

She nodded.

"Like, will we kiss?"

A starburst of tingles exploded in her stomach. She nodded again.

"Yes. We have to pretend we adore each other. That we met and swept each other off our respective feet." He held her gaze. "Which we sort of did."

Memories of holding hands, intimate touches and those unbelievable kisses rippled through her, tightening her chest, sending her pulse into overdrive.

"But sex is off the table." He smiled. "Unless you're interested."

Her heart thumped. She tried to imagine herself resisting that smile, that charm—

Actually, he hadn't been all that charming in this chat, except when it suited him. That was the curse of getting involved with someone she didn't know. She'd met and made love with Prince Charming. She had no idea who the real Prince Dominic was. What if he was like her dad? Only pulling out the charm to get what he wanted?

Oh. No brainer. She could resist that like sour wine at a bad dance club.

"Ginny, this relationship can go any way you want."

And the stoic, respectable prince was back. "Behind the walls of this palace we can be as distant or as intimate as you wish. But make no mistake. If you marry me, it's temporary. Don't get stars in your eyes. Don't get any big ideas. This marriage will not become permanent. I had been promised to a princess as part of a treaty and that was what I wanted. A marriage that meant something, accomplished something. A real marriage doesn't work in my world. So this little arrangement will not turn permanent. You need to know that, too, before you decide."

CHAPTER TWO

"So it will be totally a marriage of convenience?"

Ginny lay on the bed in the suite across the great room in Dominic's palace apartment. Cool silk caressed her back. Fluffy pillows supported her. Rich aqua walls brought color and life to the cavernous space.

"That's it. Nothing but a marriage of convenience to bring the heir to Xaviera's throne into the world legitimately."

"Oh, sweetie, that's weird."

"I know, Mom. But you have to remember the child we created will be in the public eye his entire life. How selfish would it be for me to refuse to marry Dominic, and have the heir to Xavier's throne born in a way that causes whispers and gossip that follow him forever?"

"True."

"Besides, this might just be the best thing for me, too. I mean, seriously, I don't know Dominic. What he said today about not wanting to be married proves it. He was such a sweetheart when he came to the school that day that I thought he really was a Prince Charming."

"They're all Prince Charming on dates, Ginny. It's real life that brings out their bad side."

Ginny winced. Though Dominic and her alcoholic dad seemed to share the charm gene, her dad had been mean and emotionally abusive. Dominic just seemed formal. It wasn't fair to compare the two—even if she would be wise about the charm part.

"He's not a bad guy, Mom. He's just not the happy-go-lucky guy he was on our date. And, you know what? I'm probably not the starry-eyed, flirty girl I was that night, either. We were both just having fun. But this pregnancy is real. And that's why he's serious."

"Okay. You're right."

"I know I'm right, but I still don't know what to do."

"It sounds like you think you should marry him. What are you giving up? A year, a year and a half of your life?"

"About two and a half years, and my career. Apparently, my job for the next twelve years is to be the heir's mom."

Ginny's mom laughed. "Even if your child wasn't a prince or princess, your priorities would switch from your job to this baby." She sucked in a breath. "You know what? This isn't all that much different from having the baby of a commoner."

"Except for dealing with the press."

"Yeah, well, the press is different."

"And boarding school."

"There is that."

"And living in a palace."

"Right, palace." Her mother sighed. "But the situation is done, Ginny."

"I suppose."

"So what concerns you?"

"Well, I have to see if I can handle it. Dominic's given me a week to make up my mind. He said we'd go out in public a few times." She groaned. "Oh, damn."

"What?"

"I brought jeans and T-shirts. One sundress." She dropped her head to her hands. "I'm going to go out with a prince, in public, in my junky clothes?"

"Your wardrobe is fine. *You'll* be fine."

"Right." She hadn't even told her mom about kissing Dom, possibly sleeping with Dom. All she'd mentioned was not knowing Dominic and changing her life to suit a baby, and just that had scared her silly.

This was a mess.

Two quick knocks at her door brought her head off the pillow. "Yes?"

"It's me. Dominic. My father requests our presence at dinner tonight."

Ginny turned toward the wall and whispered, "Gotta go, Mom," into the phone before she rolled off the bed and said, "Sure. That's fine. What time?"

"Seven." He cleared his throat. "It's semiformal."

She gaped at the door, as discomfort swamped her. Not only did she not have a semiformal dress for dinner, but her suite had a private sitting room outside her bedroom. He had to be in that room to be knocking on her bedroom door. He might have knocked on the door to her suite before inviting himself in, but she wouldn't have heard him. The darned place was so big and had such high ceilings that sound either echoed or disappeared. He wasn't infringing on her privacy. She hoped.

"Semiformal?"

"I took the liberty of having the staff get some suitable clothes for you."

Pride almost caused her to say, "I'm fine." But when she looked down at her jeans and considered the contents of her suitcase, she knew this was the first step in many toward giving up her real life.

"You're right. I have nothing acceptable to meet a

king." She walked to the door, opened it and watched as four men brought in bags and boxes and armloads of dresses, including gowns.

"Oh, my God."

Dominic walked in behind the parade of men. "Even if you decide not to marry me, you're here for a week."

Her mouth fell open at the ease with which he spoke in front of staff, but the expression of not a single man even twitched. This was one well-trained staff.

She took a quick breath. "So I need to be semiformal."

He nodded. "Yes."

"Okay. Scram. I have some work to do to be presentable."

"I can have a hairdresser sent up. Manicurist. Masseuse."

"Why would I need a massage?"

"Maybe what I should get you is a rundown on my dad. Then you'd very clearly understand why you want to be Zen and you'd get the massage."

"Great."

She took advantage of the hairdresser and manicurist, and ten minutes before it was time to leave for dinner she wished she'd agreed to the masseuse.

Dressed in a lightweight blue dress that stopped midcalf, with her hair in an updo suitable for a woman of seventy and old-fashioned pumps dyed to match the dress, she stepped out of her bedroom.

Standing in the great room, Dominic smiled. Unlike her ugly blue dress, his tux appeared to have been made for him. Again he was every inch a prince. Handsome. Debonair. Regal.

While she looked like a frumpy old bat.

"You look lovely."

"I look like the Queen of England. Get me a hat and one of those sedate purses she carries all the time and people would probably get us confused."

He laughed. "You are meeting a king."

"Who wants to be reminded of his grandmother?"

"You do not look like a grandmother."

"Well, I sure as hell don't look like a twenty-five-year-old guidance counselor in the coolest school in Texas."

"Trust me. You will want the armor of a grandma dress when you meet my dad." He took her elbow and led her to the door, out of the apartment and through the echoing lobby to the waiting elevator.

As they stepped inside and the door closed behind them, she said, "You have some impressive art."

"We are royalty."

"I guess I'd better get used to that." That and ugly clothes.

"That's why we're giving you the week. To get accustomed to us."

She released her breath in a slow sigh. She knew that, of course. She also suspected the clothes weren't ugly as much as they were dignified.

"Who picked out these clothes anyway?"

He stared straight ahead at the closed elevator door. "I did."

She pulled the skirt of the too-big dress away from her hips. "Because you think your dad will like me better in baggy clothes?"

"I was a bit off on your size. But it's better to be too big than too small."

"Couldn't you at least have gotten something red?"

"Blue matches your eyes."

The sweetness of that caught her off guard. For a

second she'd forgotten he knew the color of her eyes. But thinking about it, she remembered that gazing into her eyes, making her feel special, had been his seduction superpower.

"Besides, red would have reminded me of that night."

Her lips lifted into a smile. "Oh?"

"You were devastatingly beautiful."

Her heart skipped a beat. He'd made her feel beautiful. "If you hadn't been staring straight ahead when you said that, it would have been romantic."

"We don't want to be romantic, remember?"

"So that means you're not going to look at me?"

"I'm not going to make eye contact. I'm pretty sure that's what got us into trouble on our date."

She laughed, but happiness bubbled inside her. He *liked* her. A *prince* liked her. At the very least, he liked her looks.

It was heady stuff.

The elevator bell rang. The doors opened. Dominic led her out. "The family dining room is this way."

They walked across a short hall to open doors that ushered them into a formal dining room. A table that could have seated forty dominated the space. Four places were set near the head. An older man dressed in a royal uniform and a younger man in a tux like Dominic's rose as they entered.

"Virginia Jones, this is King Ronaldo Sancho and my brother, Prince Alexandros. We call him Alex."

Ginny froze. What was she supposed to do? Curtsy? Bow? Damn it. Why hadn't she paid attention to etiquette—

What etiquette? Guidance counselors knew the basics but nothing else. And she certainly hadn't expected to someday meet a prince, let alone a king. She hadn't attended etiquette classes. Was there even such a thing anymore? She couldn't be mad at herself for not knowing something she'd never been exposed to.

"You hold out your hand," King Ronaldo said irritably. "And it's my choice to kiss it or shake it."

"Oh." She held out her hand. The king shook it.

Great. She'd already blown her first introduction.

Dom turned her in the direction of his brother. As tall as Dominic and every bit as good-looking—though his face had a roundness to it that made him appear kinder, with eyes that sparkled—Alex smiled warmly at her.

"It's a pleasure to meet the woman who snagged my brother."

King Ronaldo growled. "We do not speak that way in this house."

"Really, Father," Alex said, as he took his seat and opened his napkin. "This house is the only place we can speak like that." He smiled at Ginny as Dominic seated her. "It's a pleasure to have you in the family, Ginny, even if my brother does intend to dress you like a grandmother."

With a gasp, she faced Dom. "I told you!"

He almost smiled, but his father let out one of those low growls of disapproval again, and Dominic's face shifted, returning to his formal expression.

As a servant brought in salads, King Ronaldo said, "So, Miss Jones, tell us about yourself."

She swallowed. "Well, you know I'm a guidance counselor at a high school."

"Which is where you met Dominic."

She nodded. "My mother was a teacher. I loved the relationships she had with her students."

Alex said, "So why not teach?"

"I wanted a chance to meet all the kids, know all the kids, not just the ones I was teaching."

The king said, "Ump," but his tone of voice was positive.

She relaxed a bit. But when she glanced at the row of silverware, sweat beaded on her forehead. Seven forks. Just what in the name of all that was holy were they about to eat?

Remembering the rhyme she'd been taught in grade school, she started with the outside fork.

"What else should we know?"

"Actually, Your Majesty, since you've already decided the answer to our problem is to marry, and I'm the one who hasn't made up her mind, I think I should be the one asking questions."

Alex burst out laughing. "I like her."

The king growled again.

Dominic shot her a look of reprimand.

So she smiled and rephrased the question. "It's an honor to have been asked to join your family. But in America we have a saying about not buying a car unless you kick the tires."

Alex laughed again. "Now we're tires."

Not sure if she liked Dominic's brother or not, Ginny shrugged and said, "Or you're the used car. Be glad I didn't use the don't-buy-a-horse-without-checking-its-teeth analogy."

Alex laughed. Dominic groaned. But the king quietly said, "Fair enough. What would you like to know?"

"I don't really have to dress like this for the entire time Dominic and I stay married, do I?"

"You need to look respectable." King Ronaldo inspected her blue dress and grimaced. Even he thought it was ugly. "If we let you choose your own wardrobe, can you do that?"

"Of course, I can do that!"

"You also need to behave with the utmost of decorum in public."

"I can do that, too. Though I might need some help with protocols." She answered honestly, but she hadn't missed the way the king had turned the tables on her again, and she retook control of the conversation. "So what was Dominic like as a child?"

The king said, "Headstrong."

Alex said, "A bully."

Dominic said, "All older brothers bully their baby brothers. It's like a rule."

And for the first time, Ginny felt as if she was actually talking to people. A family.

Alex shook his head. "Do you know he agreed to marry the princess of Grennady when he was only twelve?"

She faced Dom. "Really?"

Their eyes met and memories of holding him close, whispering in his ear, being held and touched and loved by him rolled through her, and she understood why Dominic had been avoiding eye contact in the elevator. Looking into someone's eyes was intimate. In those few seconds, he wasn't just a name or a problem or a memory, he was a real person. The guy she'd made love with. Father of her child.

"My mother had just died. Our kingdom was in a state of mourning from which we couldn't seem to emerge. It was appropriate to do something that didn't just ensure peace—it also brought up morale."

She continued to hold his gaze as he spoke, and something warm and soft floated through her. At twelve, he had been mature enough to do his duty. Hell, he was mature enough to *know* his duty. It was remarkable, amazing.

Alex sighed. "Now I'm stuck marrying her."

She faced Dom's younger brother with a wince. "Really? You have to marry the princess Dom was supposed to marry?"

The king said, "You can't just back out of a twenty-year-old treaty. We promised a marriage. We will deliver a marriage."

Alex batted a hand. "Doesn't matter. The princess and I will have a marriage of convenience." He shrugged. "I'll run around on her. She'll run around on me. Nobody will really know who our babies belong to and we won't allow blood tests. It'll be fine."

The king scowled. "Once again, Alex, I won't have you talk like that at the table."

Silence fell over the foursome. Dominic didn't defend his younger brother, who seemed oddly cowed by the reprimand. Hoping to restart the conversation and shift everybody's attention, Ginny tried to think of a question to ask, but couldn't come up with one to save her soul. She wanted to. She wanted to lift the gloom of talking about a dead queen, mourning subjects and a younger brother resigned to a loveless marriage— his life made tolerable by affairs. But nothing came to mind, except an empty, hollow feeling that *this* was the family she was marrying into.

But even as she thought that, she realized there was a human side to this story. A man had lost his wife and raised two boys alone. One son had become a slave to duty. The other rebellious.

Was the pain of losing a wife and mom any less because they were royal?

In some ways she thought it might have been worse.

Dominic started a conversation about the country's budget and a quiet discussion ensued. When the dinner was over, the king took her hand, bent and kissed it. An apology, she supposed, for the long, difficult dinner. Or maybe an acknowledgment that the next few years of her life would be like this, if she chose to marry Dominic.

They walked back to Dominic's apartment in silence, her blue dress swishing against her calves, mocking her, reminding her just how out of her element she was and just how much she wished she were back at her condo, sitting by the pool, sipping something fruity.

When they entered Dom's apartment, he said, "We'll meet the minister of protocol tomorrow morning."

"Okay." She headed for the double doors of her bedroom suite. "Great."

"Don't let my family scare you."

She stopped, turned to face him. "I'm not afraid of you." She almost said, "I feel sorry for you." For as difficult as the beginning of her life had been, she'd redeemed it. She'd built a world of friends and meaning. Dominic, his brother and the grouchy king were stuck.

But the strange look in his eyes kept her from saying that. He didn't seem embarrassed by his family as much as he appeared interested in what she thought of them. He wanted her to like them. Or approve of them. Or maybe just accept them.

She walked over to him, her ugly dyed blue pumps clicking on the marble floor, echoing in the silence. "I'm very accustomed to dealing with ornery dads. I was fine. Your father and brother might be a little grouchy or stern or even too flip, but I'd have paid to have family like them."

He sniffed a laugh. "Right."

"I'm serious." She smiled slightly. "Your brother needs a week of time-out in his room to get his act together, or maybe a good friend to talk through his life. Your dad lost his wife and lived his grief in the public eye. And you just want to live up to what your dad wants. You're actually a very normal family." Something she'd longed for her entire life. Something that could suck her in if she wasn't careful. "Good night."

As she turned to walk back to her bedroom suite, Dominic whispered, "Good night," confused by what she'd said. From what his investigators had dug up, her father was dead. Her mother adored her and she had a billion friends.

So what was that sad note he heard in her voice?

And why the hell would she have wanted *his* family?

He told himself it couldn't matter and walked to his suite, removing his tie. But the next day when she arrived at the table for breakfast, he jumped to his feet, feeling something he couldn't quite identify. He didn't see her in the red dress, dancing provocatively, happily seducing him. He saw a fresh-faced American girl who had something in her past. Something his private investigator hadn't dug up, but something that made her more than accepting of his stiff and formal father, and sometimes-obnoxious playboy brother.

He pulled out the chair beside his. "What would you like to eat?"

"I'd like one of those oranges," she said, pointing at the fruit in the bowl on the buffet behind the table. "And some toast."

"That's it?"

She shrugged. "It's all I'm hungry for."

He rang for a serving girl and made her request for toast and a glass of water. She plucked an orange from the bowl and began to peel it.

"Did you sleep well?"

"Yes."

"You remember we meet with the minister of protocol this morning?"

"Mmm-hmm."

His nerves jangled and he cursed himself. They were entering into a pretend marriage for the sake of their child. It was her prerogative if she didn't want to get too chummy with him.

Still, it didn't seem right not to say anything while they ate breakfast.

"If you decide to stay and marry me, we'll have your mom flown over, not just for the wedding but for the preparations."

"My mom still teaches."

"Oh."

"I'm twenty-five. She had me when she was twenty-five. That makes her fifty." She peeked up from her orange and smiled at him. "Too young to retire."

"You said she likes teaching."

"She loves teaching."

And the conversation died. Frustration rolled through him. As her toast arrived, he tried to think of something to say; nothing came to him.

She pulled one of the many newspapers provided for him from the stack on the end of the table and began reading. Even as he was glad she was a smart woman who appeared to be up on current events and most likely wouldn't embarrass him, he scowled internally, realizing reading the paper was a good way to avoid talking to him.

After breakfast, they walked along tall-ceilinged corridors to the first floor of the palace and the office of the minister of protocol, their footsteps the only sound around them. If a servant caught a peek at Dominic, he or she froze in place and bowed as he passed by. He barely noticed until he caught a sideways glance at Ginny's face and saw it scrunch in confusion.

"I don't like the fuss."

She peeked over. "Excuse me?"

"I don't like the fuss. But respect is part of the deal. To be an effective leader, your subjects must respect you. Trust you to rule well. Bowing is a sign that they trust you."

"Interesting."

Annoyance skittered through him. "It's not 'interesting.' It's true."

"Okay. Maybe I said that wrong. What I should have said was it's interesting that it's true because it gives me a whole different perspective of you as a leader. It helps me to see you as a leader."

It shouldn't have relieved him so much that she agreed. But he told himself it only mattered because he needed for her to respect him, too, for the years they'd be married.

Finally at the back of the building, they took an elevator to the first floor to the working space of the palace.

"Holy cow. This is big."

"It's huge." He pointed to the right. "The king's offices are over there. My offices and my brother's are near his. To the left," he said, motioning toward a long hall, "are the general offices. This is where our ministers and staff work."

* * *

Not able to see the end of the hall, Ginny blinked. It went so far it was almost like looking at an optical illusion.

He smiled. "I know. Impressive."

She said, "Right." But when her gaze swung around to his, she was no longer talking about the size of the palace. Everything about being royalty was bigger, better, grander than anything she'd ever seen or experienced. The truth of being a commoner washed through her again. His family might have normal bickering siblings with a traditional disciplinarian dad, but she couldn't forget they were rulers. Rich, powerful. The kind of family she shouldn't even cross paths with, let alone marry into.

"This way."

He took her elbow to guide her and sparkly little pinpricks skittered up her arm. She didn't know which was worse—being incredibly attracted to him or her good reaction to his brother and dad. Either one of them could get her into trouble. She shouldn't have admitted the night before that she'd have loved to have had a family like his. She could see it had made him curious. She'd tried to downplay it by being distant that morning, but she knew they were going to talk about this and she knew he had every right to ask. The question was: How did one explain living with a cheating, lying, thieving alcoholic to someone raised with such structure, such finery?

The minister of protocol turned out to be a short older woman whose green eyes lit when Ginny and Dominic entered the room.

She rose from her seat. "Prince Dominic!" She

rounded the desk and hugged him. "I hear congratulations are in order. You're about to have a baby!"

It was the first time anybody had actually been happy about her pregnancy or spoken of her baby as a baby, instead of a ruler or a prince or the guy who would be king. Ginny's heart filled with warmth and she forgot all about her dad, her past, her rubbish upbringing and the fear that someday she'd have to explain it all to Dominic.

The minister turned to Ginny. "And you." Her smile was warm, but didn't reach her eyes. "Congratulations on your upcoming wedding. Welcome to our home."

Stifling the urge to curtsy and the vague feeling that the minister didn't quite think her good enough, she said, "Thank you. But I still haven't made a decision on the marriage."

Dominic took over the introductions. "Virginia, this is Sally Peterson, our minister of protocol."

"You may call me Sally." She motioned to the chairs in front of her desk.

"Because Virginia is on the fence, I thought perhaps you could better explain to her why our getting married is a good idea."

"Okay." Sally folded her hands and set them on the desk. "What's the best way to explain this?" She thought for another second, then said, "Because your child will someday be our ruler, there isn't a court in the world that would refuse us the opportunity to train him, to bring him up to be our king. Which means you have four choices. First, marry Dom." She smiled at Dominic. "Second, don't marry Dom but live in the palace with your child to help raise him or her. Third, don't marry Dom, move back to the United States with a contingent of bodyguards and household servants until the child is twelve and will attend boarding school, and fourth, give up all rights."

Her voice softened. "I'm certain you don't want to give up all rights. Not marrying Dom, but living in the palace and helping raise your child makes sense, but will expose Dom to all kinds of gossip. He could be perceived as being unfit as a ruler if he couldn't even persuade the woman he'd gotten pregnant to marry him."

The thought of the ramifications for Dom made her blood run cold. She might not really know him, but she knew him enough that she could not let that happen to him. "What would happen if we got married?"

"You would need to be seen in public together at least twice before you would announce the quick wedding. We will also announce the pregnancy at the same time so that the rumors of a pregnancy don't take the sheen off your wedding day. The theory is if we get it out immediately it won't be 'news' anymore."

Exactly what Dom had told her.

He caught her gaze and smiled at her.

Once again she saw a glimpse of the guy who had whisked her away the night of their fateful dalliance. Stiff and formal or not, almost-complete stranger or not, he was the father of her child and his needs had to be considered.

"Plus, if you marry Dom, your position gives you a bit of power so to speak. You can use your celebrity to support causes. As someone who'd worked in education, you may wish to host events to raise awareness or to build schools anywhere in the world."

"Oh." That was amazing. Something she hadn't considered and something that would give her a chance to impact the *world*. Just the thought of it stole her breath. "That would be great."

"Plus," Sally said with a chuckle, "a royal wedding is fantastic. Your gown would be made by the designer of your choice." She laughed. "And money is no object. The guests will be royalty and dignitaries from every country in the world. You would get to meet your president."

"The president of the United States would be invited?"

"And he'd attend." Sally smiled. "Our royal family is influential. We don't just control waterways. We have oil, which gives us a seat in OPEC."

It was hard enough to adjust to the knowledge that Dominic was a royal. Now she was being told his small, seemingly insignificant country was powerful?

Oh, boy.

Dominic's hand stealthily slid from the arm of his chair over to her hand. He caught her pinkie with his, linking them.

She swallowed. He'd done that in the limo on the way to the club in Los Angeles. A small, sweet, simple gesture that made her heart catch and her breathing tremble. He recognized that all this information was becoming overwhelming for her. And the pinkie knot? It told her he was there for her.

Damn, but he could be sweet.

"But, as I mentioned, you have choices. And as I understand the situation, you and Dominic plan to divorce two years after the baby is born."

Dominic quietly said, "Yes."

The small, sweet gesture suddenly felt empty. Pointless. There was no need for them to be close. They just had to be friendly.

She pulled her hand away.

"In that case, most of your options still apply. Except

Dom wouldn't suffer the negative press of being unable to persuade you to marry him."

"I could return to the United States."

Sally laughed. "If, after years of being influential in education, of being someone known to the entire world, someone impacting the world, you still want to go back, then, yes."

Ginny smiled. Something about the way Sally kept highlighting the good part about staying in the country told her there was a catch, and she knew it had to have something to do with her child. "But the baby would go with me?"

Sally rose from the desk and walked to the front where she leaned against it. Her voice was soft, gentle. "Yes. As I'd said, that is an option. But it will require heightened security and teachers for home schooling unless you can find a private school that passes our tests. Then every time there was a ceremony, a formal dinner, a holiday, he'd have to be flown home." She shifted against the desk. "Ideally, our future ruler should be raised here. In the palace. It just makes things easier."

"Right."

Dominic faced her. "Our child needs to be acclimated into the life of a royal. Not rigidly, but to realize all monarchs and leaders are people, too. Countries are made up of people. Troubles are borne by people. Ruling is about people."

Caught in the gaze of his dark, dark eyes, she remembered why she'd fallen so hard for him the night she met him. He always knew the right thing to say.

Even if it was a modification of the truth.

Yesterday, he'd been smart enough to let her believe

returning home would be possible, when in reality it sounded as if it would be very hard on their child.

He hadn't out and out lied. In fact, if the option really was available for her to return to the United States, then he hadn't lied at all. But he was counting on her love for their baby to help her to see that returning home might be an option but it was a poor one.

She couldn't decide if he was manipulating her or trusting her, but after eighteen years of a bullying, manipulative father, that misstep made her stomach roil.

She rose. "You know what? I'm a bit tired. I think I should go back to the room."

He bounced to his feet. "Of course."

She faced Sally. "I'll need some help with etiquette. I know the basics but the specifics are way beyond what a high school guidance counselor needs to know. Even if I decide not to marry Dominic, I have an entire week here and I don't want to embarrass him."

Sally grabbed her calendar. "I'll make appointments for you."

"Just let me know when to be where."

Dominic laughed. "The teachers will come to our apartment. You're not just a guest of a prince. You're pregnant. We want to take care of you."

She ignored his laugh. Ignored the smile on his face. Ignored that he was solicitous about her pregnancy. Her dad had been exceptional at being sweet, being charming, when it suited him. She didn't want to think Dominic was like her dad, but the facts were out there plain and simple. He'd told her a half-truth the day before.

Still, she could deal with this. She was unfortunately good at dealing with people who told her half-truths.

She straightened her shoulders. "That's fine. I'm happy to have the sessions in your apartment."

She held her head high as she walked out of Sally's office, but her stomach churned.

Why was she even *considering* marrying a man who was a manipulator like her father?

CHAPTER THREE

DOMINIC HAD TO run to catch up to her. "What was that all about?"

"What?"

"Your sudden need to leave as if Sally had done something wrong."

"It wasn't Sally." She turned on him. "*You* led me to believe I could go home."

"The option is yours."

"Oh, sure, if I want to make our child's life a miserable succession of plane rides between Texas and Xaviera."

Not waiting for a reply, she raced to the elevator, punched the button and was inside before Dom had wrapped his head around what she'd said. He jumped into the plush car two seconds before the door would have closed.

"I'm sorry if the truth offends you."

She turned on him again, poking her index finger into his chest. "The truth? You told me half the truth, so I would get false hope. When the situation looked totally impossible, you held out the offer of being able to return home. Now that I'm adjusting to you, to your family and to people bowing to you, I'm told the option exists, but, oh, by the way, it will make your child's life suck."

He caught her finger. "What did you want me to say? No. You can't ever go home again?"

"Yes! I'm twenty-five years old. I handled two thousand kids for three years. I can handle this!"

The elevator door swished open. She yanked her finger from his hand and headed across the big square marble floor to the regal double doors of his apartment.

He ran after her, but didn't reach her until she was already in the sitting room of their apartment. When he did, he caught her arm and forced her to face him. "I will not have you be mad at me for something I didn't do! We didn't talk a lot yesterday. I gave you your bare-bones options because that's all you seemed to want to hear. Sally expanded on those options today. If you'd wanted the entire explanation yesterday, you should have stayed for it! Instead you said something about wanting to go to your room. I was fully prepared to talk it all out. *You* left."

He could see from the shifting expressions in her blue eyes that she knew what he said was true.

She dropped her head to her hands. "Oh, God. I'm sorry."

"It's okay."

She shook her head. "No. It isn't." She sucked in a breath. "Look, my dad was a hopeless alcoholic who was always lying to me. I have trust issues."

Glad to have his real Ginny back, Dom breathed a sigh of relief. "We all have trust issues."

He motioned for her to sit, so they could talk some more, but she shook her head. "I'm fine. Really. Tired, but fine."

A trained diplomat, he read the discretion in her answer and knew she didn't want to talk about this. Who would want to talk about a father who drank so much he'd clearly made her miserable? But at least he understood why she'd absurdly said she would have taken his family when she was a child.

"I probably also should have told you that all of this will be set out in an agreement."

"An agreement?"

"Yes, the legal office will draw up an agreement that sets out everything. Your responsibilities. Our responsibilities. What's required of you as mother to our future heir."

"You're going to put all this into an agreement?"

He chuckled. "You wouldn't?"

She considered that. "A written agreement would make things easier."

"It's one of the few documents that will remain totally secret. Because it's considered private, no one but you and I, the king and both of our counsels will even know it exists. But your jobs and responsibilities will be spelled out and so will mine. Plus, we can provide you with counsel who can assure you the agreement is fair. If you don't like who we provide, you can choose your own counsel."

She nodded.

"We're not trying to cheat you."

"Right."

"Really. And we don't sign the agreement until the day of the ceremony. So right up until the day we get married, you can change your mind."

"I'll just be doing it publicly."

He shrugged. "Sorry. The press sort of comes with the territory."

She didn't answer, but she'd definitely calmed down.

A written agreement seemed to suit her, but she still looked tired, worn. "Why don't you go lie down?"

She nodded and walked into her suite, closing the door behind her.

He gave her the morning to rest. When she came out at lunchtime, he pulled out her chair and she smiled.

Relieved that she really was okay, he said, "A simple coffee date has been arranged for us this afternoon."

"Then you'd better get someone up here to help me with wardrobe because I went through the clothes you had sent up yesterday and there isn't anything in there that I'd actually wear out in public."

"What about the white pants with the sweater?"

"Seriously? That blue sweater with the big anchor on the front? My mother would wear that."

"Okay. Fine. Right after lunch I'll have a clothier come up."

"Great." She looked at the food, then sat back as if discouraged.

"You don't like ham sandwiches?"

"They're great. I'm just not hungry."

He sucked in a breath. They'd had a misunderstanding but worked it out, and she'd taken a rest. When she'd come out of her suite, it was to eat lunch. Now suddenly she wasn't hungry?

"You had an orange for breakfast. You have to eat."

"Maybe I can get a cookie at the coffee shop."

He laughed, thinking she was joking. Seeing she wasn't, he frowned. "Seriously? That's going to be your food for the day? A cookie?"

"I told you. I'm not very hungry."

He supposed their situation would be enough to make a normal woman lose her appetite, but being married to him wasn't exactly the third circle of hell. Everything and anything she wanted could be at her disposal. There was no reason for her to refuse to eat.

"Okay. From here on out, you choose our menus."

She nodded. He felt marginally better. But what man in the world could possibly like the idea that just the thought of marrying him had taken away a woman's appetite?

Was she subtly saying he made her sick?

After a visit from the clothier, an hour's wait for clothing to be delivered and an hour for her to dress, they left the palace in his Mercedes. He drove, surprising her.

"We don't need a bodyguard?"

"They're discreetly behind us. This is supposed to look like a casual date."

"Ah."

He tried not to let her one-word answer grate against his skin, but it did. She wouldn't eat around him and her conversation had been reduced to one-word answers. He'd thought they'd resolved their issue, but maybe they hadn't? Or maybe the reality of marrying a prince was finally sinking in?

"You know you're going to have to say more than one word to me when we get into the coffee shop."

"Yes."

He gritted his teeth. "We could also use this time to chitchat so that when we get out of the car, we'll already be engaged in conversation the way normal people would be."

"I know all about being a normal person." She flicked her gaze to him. "You, on the other hand, are wearing a white shirt out for coffee."

"I'm a prince."

"You're also a person, supposedly out with a woman he likes. A woman he's comfortable with. White shirt does not say *comfortable*."

"Oh, and scruffy jeans does?"

She laughed. "Are you kidding? Scruffy jeans is the very definition of *comfortable*."

"You look like you're going to the trash yard."

"I look like an American girl on a date with a prince she just met. I am playing the part. As our dates get more serious so will my wardrobe."

Unexpectedly seeing her reasoning, he sighed. "Okay. I get it. Just don't make fun of the white shirt."

"Fine."

He glanced in the rearview mirror and saw not just the Mercedes with his bodyguards, but also the usual assortment of paparazzi. Satisfied, he finished the drive to the ocean-side coffee shop.

Xaviera's warm sun beat down on him as he walked around to the passenger's side and opened the door for Ginny. He took her hand and helped her out, to the whir of cameras. She stepped out, one blue-jeans-clad leg at a time, wedge sandals, short blue T-shirt and big sunglasses, all looking very normal to him in the parking lot of a beach café.

She really had been right about her very casual clothes.

Standing in front of him, she caught his gaze and smiled, and his heart—which had been thundering in his chest from fear of the first step of their charade—slowed down. He hadn't forgotten how beautiful she was, but somehow or another the sunlight seemed to bring out the best in her rich yellow hair and tanned skin. She might not be royalty or someone accustomed to the public eye, like an actress or model, but she was every bit as beautiful—if not more beautiful because she was genuine.

The cameras whirred again.

She whispered, "What do we do? Do we wave?"

"We ignore them."

She peeked up at him. "Really?"

He laughed, took her hand and led her to the café door. "Yes. We know they are there. But we also know they are always there, even if, for us, they have no purpose. Unlike an actor or actress, we don't need them to enhance our visibility. We tolerate them. Thus, we ignore them."

"Got it."

He held the door open for her. The press rushed up behind them, but his bodyguards closed the door on them. Two things happened simultaneously. The press opened the door and crammed in behind the bodyguards, their cameras whirring. And Marco, café owner, greeted them.

"Prince Dominic!" He bowed. "It's an honor."

"Can I have my usual, Marco? And—" Oh, dear God. First complication. He could not order coffee for a pregnant woman. He faced Ginny. "What would you like, Ginny?"

As soon as he said her name, the reporters began shouting, "Ginny! Ginny! Look here, Ginny!"

She slid off her sunglasses. Doing as he'd told her, she ignored the press. "How about some water? It's hot."

The press laughed. "Did you not know our weather was hot?"

"Where are you from?"

"How old are you?"

"How did you meet?"

"How long have you been dating?"

Dominic also ignored them. "Just water? What about that cookie?"

Marco said, "I have a cookie that will make you happy to be alive."

Ginny laughed. "That'd be great."

"You sound American."

He saw Ginny waver. The questions directed at her were hard for her to ignore. And the press began closing in on them. Even with his two bodyguards standing six inches away, the reporters and photographers bent around them, shouted questions and took pictures as Marco made Dom's coffee, retrieved a bottle of water and wrapped a cookie in a napkin.

Dom took their items and turned to say, "Let's go out to the deck by the dock," but, as he turned, he saw her sway. Before he could blink, she began to crumble.

He dropped his coffee, the water and the cookie to the counter and just barely caught her before she hit the floor.

The cameras whirred. A gasp went up from the crowd. Dominic's bodyguards turned to help him as Marco came out from behind the counter, broom in hand.

"Get out of here!" He waved the broom at the paparazzi. "Get out, you brood of vipers!" He glanced behind the counter. "Antonella. I chase them out. You lock the door!"

Down on one knee, holding Ginny, Dominic cast Marco a grateful look as the coffeehouse owner and Dom's bodyguards shooed the press out of his shop and Antonella locked the door behind them.

Ginny's eyes slowly blinked open. "It's so hot."

He sort of smiled. She was so fragile and so beautiful, and holding her again took him back to their night of dancing in LA and making love in her condo. A million feelings trembled through him. Brilliant memories. A sense of peace that had intermixed with their fun. The wonderful, almost-overwhelming sensation of being able to be himself because she was so comfortable being herself.

"You're adding to the heat by wearing jeans."

"Trying to look normal."

Her skin was clammy. Her eyes listless and dull. His happy, beautiful one-night stand memories dropped like a rock, as his heart squeezed with fear. "We need to get you to the hospital."

"You're sending a pregnant woman to the hospital for fainting? You haven't been around pregnant women much have you?"

"That's all this is?"

She drew in a breath and suddenly looked stronger. "Heat. Pregnancy. Nerves. Take your pick."

He said, "Right." Then nodded at Marco. "Open her water."

The solicitous shop owner did as he was told. He handed the opened bottle to Dominic, who held it out to her. She took a few sips.

Dominic sighed, grateful she was coming back but so scared internally that he shook from it. His heart had about leaped out of his chest when he saw her falling. "You should probably have a bite or two of the cookie. I told you to eat lunch."

She smiled. "Wasn't hungry."

Antonella brought over the cookie. "You eat."

Ginny sat up a bit and took the cookie from Antonella's hands.

"Maybe we should get you to a chair?"

She laughed. "I feel safer down here. No cameras. No one can see me through the windows."

He felt it, too. Behind the tables and chairs between them and the doorway, he felt totally protected from the press.

She ate a few bites of her cookie, drank the entire bottle of water and held out her hand to him. "We can stand now."

"We're going to have to go back to the car though a crowd of reporters and photographers who just saw you faint. If you thought their questions were bad before this—" he caught her gaze "—now they are going to be horrific. A tidal wave of jumbled words and noisy cameras. Are you up for this?"

"I'm fine."

"Right. As soon as we get home, I'm having you checked out by the doctor."

"I would expect nothing less from a man accustomed to bossing people around."

His fear for her wouldn't recede and she didn't seem to be taking any of this seriously. "Stop joking. You fainted."

"On a hot day, after not eating." She smiled suddenly, pushed herself to her tiptoes and kissed his cheek. "I'm fine."

The unexpected kiss went through him like a warm spring breeze. He told himself not to make too much of it, but how could he not when color was returning to her cheeks and she was smiling, really smiling, for the first time since their argument that morning.

Wanting to get her home, Dominic said, "Let's go."

But before they could walk to the door, Marco hugged her and then Antonella hugged her. Dominic finally noticed the few stragglers sitting at the café tables, necks craned to see what was going on. One or two whispered, but in general, they'd given them privacy.

Leading her to the door, he addressed them, "Thank you all for your consideration."

People nodded and smiled and a few said, "You're welcome." Then they reached the door. The lock clicked as Antonella sprang it.

He said, "Ready?"

Ginny nodded.

He opened the door to the whir of cameras and shouts of questions. "How are you?"

"Why did you faint?"

"What's your last name?"

"Are you pregnant?"

Dominic's steps faltered.

But Ginny slid her sunglasses on her face and smiled at them. "I didn't eat lunch." She turned to Dominic and entwined her arm with his. "Dom told me to eat lunch but—" She held out a leg. "Look at these jeans. They are to die for and I wanted them to fit." She smiled again. "American girls, right? We love our jeans and we want them to look perfect."

Then she turned them in the direction of his Mercedes. His bodyguards created a path for them to walk.

He opened the door for her.

She slid inside. Before Dom could close the door, she gave a final wave to the press. "I'm fine," she called out to them. "And, I swear, I will eat before we come out again."

Walking around the hood of his car, he heard the rumble of laughter. He peeked up to see the smiles of approval on the faces of those in the crowd. And why not? She was beautiful, approachable, *likable*.

But he also saw a few reporters frowning in his direction. He saw the ones on their cell phones talking feverishly.

He slid into the car. "You know your pregnancy's out now, right?"

"Yup." She caught his gaze. "Looks like we won't need a second date."

"You're saying yes?"

She nodded.

He took her hand and lifted it to his lips. "Thank you."

"Oh, don't thank me. I have a feeling we're in for one hell of a ride."

CHAPTER FOUR

THEY SCHEDULED A press conference for nine o'clock the next morning in the press room of the palace. The king announced his son's marriage to Virginia Jones of Texas in the United States, a former guidance counselor. Then he gave the podium to Dominic.

As Ginny expected, the resounding cry that rose from the crowd was… "Is Ginny pregnant?"

Another man might have been cowed, embarrassed or even unprepared. Ginny knew Dom had rehearsed every possible scenario of this moment into the wee hours of the morning with someone from his staff.

So she wasn't surprised when he smiled and said, "Yes."

The swish and whir of cameras filled the room. Several people called, "Ginny, look here."

But she kept her eyes trained on Dominic because that's what *her* two hours of training the night before had been about. That and choosing something to wear. After a doctor had seen her and pronounced her well, a clothier had arrived with swatches and catalogs. Sally from the protocol office had wanted her in a raspberry-colored suit. The king had thought she'd look more dignified in a white suit. But she'd reminded them that she'd fainted because she was *pregnant* and had gotten too hot. Her choice for the press conference had been a simple green dress with thin straps and a pale green cardigan—which she could remove, she reminded the king—if she got too hot.

The king had scowled, but Dominic had suddenly said, "I think she's right."

All eyes had turned to him. He'd shrugged. "You're not the ones who had to watch her fall. I barely caught her. I don't think we want to risk having that happen again."

Nope. If there was one thing Ginny knew, it was that she did not want to faint again. Seeing ten pictures of herself crumpling to a coffee-shop floor in the newspapers that morning had been enough to cure her of ever wanting to faint in public again.

But Dominic standing up for her choice had caused her breath to quietly catch. Her simple pregnancy might impact an entire kingdom—and maybe someday even the world—but this was her *baby*. And Dom's.

When he stood up for her, he caught her gaze, and in that second a wave of feeling had almost made her dizzy. They'd created a child and were getting married—temporarily. He'd warned her not to spin fantasies of permanency with him, and she wasn't, but with a baby on the way and so many people telling them what to do, she didn't see how they could get through the next few months without forming a team.

Which made it a terrible, terrible thing that she'd compared him to her father. Because no matter how hard she tried, she couldn't stop doing it. Not because she genuinely believed Dom was like her dad, but because she was so afraid. Living with her dad had been a nightmare. Only a fool would deliberately enter that kind of situation again.

So he couldn't be like her dad. He *couldn't.* Yet something about this situation, and Dom, set off warning signals that would not let her relax.

Watching Dominic speak now, she waited for his signal for her to join him at the podium. He fielded a question or two about how they met, then, just as they'd practiced, he turned to her with a smile and said, "Why don't we have Ginny join us to help answer some questions?"

In her high-heeled white sandals that perfectly offset the pretty green dress, she carefully walked to the podium. He slid his arm around her waist, bringing her closer to the microphones. Questions filled the air.

"Have you found a dress?"

"Are you having morning sickness?"

She heard the questions, but looking up at Dominic, all she saw were those onyx eyes filled with expectation. Could she stand up for him? Would she stand up for him? Would she protect his reputation as the future king the way he'd stood up for her the night before? Was she willing to fully commit to the charade?

Just as she couldn't quite get herself to trust him, the question in his eyes told her he didn't entirely trust her, either.

Which made them even.

If there was one thing she'd learned about partnerships, it was that they ran best when the partners really were even. Oddly, this deal would work not because they trusted each other, but because they didn't.

"Are you a real live Cinderella?"

That question made her laugh and brought her out of her reverie. She faced the sea of press crowded into the small room.

"Yes. I do feel like Cinderella. No, I haven't even

chosen a designer to make my dress. So I'll need all four weeks before the wedding just to find something to wear." When the reporters laughed, she smiled. "And no morning sickness."

She paused long enough to give Dominic her best fake loving smile, deferring to him, the way she'd been taught to the night before. When their gazes met, she could see he was pleased with how she handled herself. She recognized that his happy expression was part of their act, but he'd looked at her exactly that way the night they'd gone clubbing. The night they'd created their baby.

Her heart kicked against her ribs. A flash of memories flooded her brain. Kissing in the limo. Laughing at stupid things. Not a care in the world. And for one foolish second, she wished they could be those two people again. Two people just having fun. Not making a commitment—

She quickly looked away. Things like that, staring into his fathomless eyes, longing for a chance just to enjoy each other, would get her into trouble.

She faced the reporters. "So I won't faint again." She winced. "That is if I listen to Dom and actually eat breakfast and lunch."

A quiet chuckle went up from the group as they scribbled in notebooks.

The questions started again.

"What about your job?"

"Will you miss working?"

"What was it like growing up with an alcoholic dad?"

"Did you spin daydreams as a little girl that you'd someday marry a prince?"

The room suddenly got hot. She hadn't expected her

dad's life to escape scrutiny. She simply hadn't expected it to come up so soon.

She pushed her hair off her face, buying time, hoping to cool her forehead a bit before sweat began to bead on it. "I love my job." She answered the first and second questions together since they were easy, as she dreadfully scrambled in her head to think of how to answer the third. "If it were possible to be a princess *and* be a guidance counselor, I'd do both. As it is, my duty lies with Xaviera and our baby." She laughed. "My mom reminded me that even if my baby wasn't a future king, he'd still take up all my time and shift my priorities."

Before she could deal with question three, two other reporters raised their hands and called out, "So you've spoken to your mom and have her blessing?" and "Where is your mom?"

"My mom is finishing out her semester," she said, then suddenly wished her mom didn't have to work. Being alone in a strange country, in a white-hot spotlight with a guy she'd liked a lot was making her crazy. She had to remember he wasn't fun-loving Dom. He was Prince Dominic. And this marriage wasn't real. Hell, this whole situation was barely real.

"She has a few more weeks of school, but she'll be here for the wedding."

"I'm still waiting for an answer about your childhood with an alcoholic father."

The sweat arrived, beading on her forehead. A hot, dizzying wave passed through her, weakening her knees, just as it had two seconds before she'd fainted the day before.

"My father was sick," she said quietly, praying her legs would continue to hold her. "He also died when I was eighteen. I barely remember that part of my life."

That wasn't really a lie, more of an exaggeration. She didn't want to remember, so she spent her days refusing to even think about those years.

"As for whether or not I spun fantasies about marrying a prince." She smiled. "I hadn't. I was a very pragmatic child, enamored with my mom's love of her classes and students. But I'm glad I met Dominic."

Again, not a lie. She *was* glad she had met him. She'd loved their night out. It was being in cahoots with him, putting so much of her life into another person's hands, that caused fear to course through her. Especially after the mention of her dad. After being reminded that trusting the wrong person could suck the life out of your soul, reduce you to someone who suspiciously weighed every word and soon didn't trust anyone. Someone who protected herself by staying in her room, alone and lonely.

She did not want that to be her life again.

This time when she turned to smile at Dominic, she knew her eyes were dull and listless.

She wasn't surprised when he said, "And that's all for this morning. Our press office has issued a release with all relevant information."

He led her off the podium and then out of the room, behind the king, who turned to her with a satisfied look. "You lasted much longer than I predicted."

She winced. "Thank you, I think."

"Well, it's a compliment to an extent. I'm still not sure I trust your fashion sense. And I'm not at all pleased that you didn't warn us about your dad."

Her stomach churned. She'd buried her dad seven years ago, but here she was hiding him again, protecting him again— "I…"

Dominic stepped up. "I knew about her dad. My

security detail investigated everything." He caught Ginny's gaze. "I admit we glossed over his alcoholism because he's been dead for seven years. But no one kept it a secret."

She swallowed. Every time she looked in his eyes, she had no question about why he'd so easily been able to seduce her. But every time he talked he reminded her that she didn't belong here in his life, and how difficult the next years would be. "I guess you did that while we were waiting for the paternity results."

"Actually, we investigated you when we were told you would be my liaison at the school." He faced the king. "And you have a full report on Ginny's life in your office. Her father is in there."

King Ronaldo said, "I don't know how I missed it."

"You missed it because he's barely a footnote. He was never arrested. Never in the papers. Never anything. And now he's gone. Ginny and I talked about this a bit yesterday and the end result was I decided there's no real reason to put her through the memories by insisting she give us details."

He smiled slightly at her.

She tried to smile back. But an odd feeling tumbled through her. Not quite a nudge that she should trust him, the feeling told her at the very least she should appreciate the way he'd saved her from having to relive a part of her life that was gone. Past. She shouldn't have to explain it.

Sally said, "Yes, well, Prince Dominic, you should have bought this to your father's attention instead of expecting him to find it in a report."

Dom faced Sally, who stood with her arms crossed, clearly unhappy with him. He said, "I'll remember next time," but when he turned to Ginny he winked.

The weird feeling tumbled through her again.

Sally lifted her clipboard. "Okay, Ms. Jones, you have a few people coming to the apartment for lessons today. Mostly protocols and etiquettes. At four, the clothier and I will be bringing catalogs of various designers' work so you can begin the process of screening designers for your dress." She flipped a page. "Dom, I believe you're due in parliament this afternoon."

Dominic caught Ginny's hand. "Then I guess we better get back to the apartment and arrange for lunch."

Sally said, "Fine—"

But Dominic didn't wait for the rest of her answer. He turned and walked away, leading Ginny down several halls. He walked so fast, she had to skip to keep up with him in her high, high heels, but the air that whooshed past them was cool, and she suddenly felt like laughing. Not only had they survived the press, but Dominic had taken her side—again.

When the elevator door closed behind them, Ginny said, "That was awesome."

"What? You liked being interviewed by reporters?"

She batted a hand. "I could take that or leave that. What I loved was you walking away from Sally."

Dom spared her a glance, then he grinned. "She's protocol office so she basically runs everything. It's fun every once in a while to remind her that she works for me."

"Oh, so you're a tough guy now?"

He laughed. "I told you being a king is all about being respected."

"Well, in that case, let me say you got some votes of confidence from me."

He turned. "Really?"

"Yes. Last night when you said we should use my

dress choice and this morning when you let me answer my own questions from the press—those were good. But not letting Sally push me around? Or your dad? Those were better. I... Well, I felt like a real person."

"You are a real person."

She laughed, but something inside nudged her to talk, to at least trust him enough to tell him the basics. "I know that. But my upbringing was awful. There are more chances that I'm going to embarrass you than make you proud."

"Are you kidding? Your first public act was to faint, then pretend it was no big deal when you walked back into the fray of reporters to get to the car. You waved and told them you were fine as if they were a bunch of friends hanging out on a street corner." He laughed. "I think they don't know what to do with you."

"So confusion is the way to go, if I can't beguile them with my good looks and charm?"

He sneaked another peek at her as the elevator door opened on the big square foyer before his apartment. "Oh, I wouldn't discount your charm just yet."

She looked up at him. He gazed down at her. With the huge hall just outside the door empty and quiet, the tiny elevator suddenly felt intimate.

Gazing into his eyes, she remembered how he'd pulled her to him outside her apartment door and kissed her like a man so crazy about a woman he couldn't resist her.

So maybe he did think she had charm.

The elevator door began to close and without looking away Dominic caught it, forcing it open again.

"We better go."

"Yeah."

Neither of them moved. Something hummed between

them. She'd say it was the same something that had brought him to her condo door all those weeks ago, the same something that drew them to her bed, except in the past two days she'd made him laugh and he wasn't going to make her talk about her dad.

He took a step closer to her and her breath shivered. Her lips tingled from wanting to kiss him. But he stayed where he was, close enough to touch, but not making a move to kiss her, though his eyes shimmered with need.

The air filled with something hot and tempting. She knew she could easily label this lust, but she knew something else was at work here. They really were forming a team. And the pull of that, the longing not to be alone in this deal, fighting for herself and her rights, but having somebody fight with her, was even stronger than the lust that had driven them that night.

That scared her silly.

But his gaze held hers.

And everything inside her trembled with yearning.

She longed for the day she'd met him, when she didn't fear their future because she didn't think they had a future, and she wondered what it would be like to let her guard down again—

But Dom had warned her not to spin fairy tales. And life had taught her that good things could turn bad in the blink of an eye. Not more than twenty minutes ago, she'd been worried about comparing him to her dad. Now she wanted to kiss him? To trust him?

Everything was happening too fast.

This was a ruse. Nothing more. And she was going to get hurt if she didn't stop trying to spin that fairy tale.

She turned and walked out of the elevator to the apartment and to her suite.

CHAPTER FIVE

DOMINIC ATE A very quiet, disappointing lunch. No matter how he tried to engage Ginny, she'd smile distantly and pop a bite of food into her mouth so she didn't have to talk to him. Glad to see her eating for the sake of the baby, he couldn't allow himself the luxury of being upset that she wasn't talking to him.

Still, it made him nuts.

They were perfectly fine in that elevator until the conversation about her charming the press. She *could* charm the press. And without effort. But something about that one simple comment had made her quiet. Distant.

He probably shouldn't have mentioned it. Her ability with them was so natural that if he hadn't pointed it out to her, she would have used it without thought. But he liked talking to her and he liked it when they were getting along. Their natural connection would be what would make the charade work.

Then they'd had that moment of looking into each other's eyes, and for twenty seconds he'd thought he wouldn't be able to resist kissing her. But he *had*. He'd remembered his dad, the weakness that plagued him after Dom's mother's death. He knew he couldn't afford a marriage with real emotion. And when he kissed her, he felt things he couldn't define or describe. So he stepped back, away from a kiss he wanted, to prove he didn't *need* it.

That should have made her happy. God knew it made him happy to see he could resist her. She should be happy, too. Instead, she was distant.

He left her after lunch and spent four grueling hours in parliament. Tired and somewhat disgusted, he returned to his palace apartment to find Sally and Joshua, the clothier, sitting on one sofa with Ginny alone on the sofa across from them. Though Sally was frustrated, Joshua looked to be the picture of patience as he ran down the benefits of a list of designers.

Ginny frowned. "I know what I like. I know what I look good in. It just seems so sterile to be picking a gown this way. I always imagined myself trying things on."

Joshua smiled patiently. "Most women would kill for the chance to choose a designer to make a unique gown."

Ginny only sighed and glanced at the photo array of designers and their creations.

Sally shook her head. "What difference does it make? For Pete's sake. This wedding is just for show. It's not real. The gown doesn't have to reflect *you*. It just has to be beautiful. Something fit for a princess."

Ginny finally noticed Dom standing in the foyer by the door, but she quickly looked away. Still, he'd seen the naked misery in her eyes.

She straightened her shoulders, as if seeing him reminded her of her duty to him, and she pointed at one of the photo arrays. "This one. I'd like this designer."

Sally sighed with relief and rose. "We'll contact him."

Joshua rose, too. He bowed. "I am at your service."

Sally said, "Good because she still has a wardrobe to choose. Two pair of jeans and a green dress with cardigan won't be enough clothes for two days let alone over two years."

Joshua on her heels, Sally headed for the white double doors. "You'll be required to meet with Joshua again tomorrow afternoon, Ginny."

"That's Ms. Jones," Dominic said, suddenly annoyed. "She may not be a princess yet. But she will be. And when she is she will be your boss."

Sally quietly gasped and stepped back, but she quickly recovered. Bowing to Dominic, she said, "Yes, Your Majesty."

Joshua all but quivered with fear. New to the palace, because the king and the two princes rarely required help in choosing suits or having them made, he glanced from Dom to Sally, wide-eyed.

Sally opened the door and left. Joshua scampered after her.

Ginny blew her breath out on a long sigh. "You shouldn't have yelled at her. It wasn't her fault that I'm having trouble choosing. And our time is running out. She's right to be annoyed with me."

He walked to the bar and poured himself a Scotch. "Oh, sweetie. You have so much to learn about being a princess."

"I'm not going to be vapid and spoiled."

"Of course, you're not. But you can't let staff belittle you."

"As I said, she was right to be annoyed with me."

"Again. No. You are the member of the royal family here. If you want to take until the day before the wedding to choose your dress, that's what you do. Then *they* scramble."

She laughed.

He sat beside her on the sofa. "So, are you really happy with the designer you chose?"

She shrugged. "He's as good as any."

He caught her chin and nudged her to face him. "As good as any isn't good enough. I want you to be happy the day you get married. It may not be forever, but it's your first wedding."

"That's what I keep thinking."

"So what would you do if you were getting married for keeps?"

"I'd have a lot of pink roses."

"What else?"

"My two friends would be bridesmaids."

"You can have that." He sipped his Scotch. "What else?"

"I don't know. I always imagined my mom and me picking things out." She peeked up at him. "She has great taste."

He laughed. "Really?"

"Well, actually, we have about the same taste. But picking a gown is just something a girl wants to do with her mom. You know. Second opinion and all that." She took a deep breath, blew it out, then looked Dom in the eye. "My picture is going to go around the world. I'd like for it to be a good one."

He nodded. "That's something I'm so accustomed to I forget that others aren't." He rose from the sofa. "I have a dinner meeting tonight that's going to segue into a bigger meeting with several members of parliament. Why don't you call your friends on Skype and invite them to be your bridesmaids?"

She looked up at him, her eyes round and blue and honest. She was one of the most naturally beautiful women he'd ever met. She was also being a much better sport about this marriage than a lot of women would be. She hadn't asked for anything. She just did as she was told. And if she didn't talk to him, maybe that was his fault? He'd told her not to expect a long, happy marriage. If she held herself back, maybe that's what she felt she needed to do.

"Really? I can have bridesmaids?"

"As many as you want." On impulse he bent down and kissed her cheek. "Would a wedding without bridesmaids really look authentic?"

She shook her head.

"So call them."

Ginny watched Dom leave the sitting room and head for his bedroom suite, fighting that feeling again. Except this time, she named it. She wasn't worried about liking him or even being attracted to him. What she was feeling—or maybe recognizing—was that he was a nice guy. A good person. She thanked God he'd reminded her that the wedding needed to "look" authentic to serve his purpose. Otherwise, she might have melted right there at his feet.

She could resist the solemn guy, the one who would be king someday, who wanted everything to be perfect. The other guy, the sweet one who tried to make her happy? That was the guy who had been staring at her in the elevator. The one she'd wanted to kiss. He was the one she had to watch out for.

She returned to her room, found her laptop and connected with her two best friends on Skype. They knew she was pregnant, of course. She'd gone to them for guidance. She'd also called them the day she'd fainted, when she'd agreed to marry Dom. They were not surprised to be receiving invitations to be bridesmaids.

That little piece of normalcy lifted her spirits. It wasn't going to be a real marriage but it was going to be a real wedding, and she was going to look pretty and have her friends with her. They would keep her occupied the week before the big day. And, in a good mood, she'd be better able to look happy for the ceremony.

The next morning at breakfast, she showed her appreciation to Dominic by asking him how his meetings had gone the night before.

He winced. "There are one or two people who fear we are making an alliance with the United States by bringing you into the royal family."

She laughed. When he didn't, she said, "Really? Seriously? They think marrying a commoner from the United States is a lead-in to a treaty?"

"My brother will be marrying a woman as part of a treaty. Why would you be surprised our government is questioning my marriage?"

She shook her head and went back to her oatmeal. "I forget that your country looks at marriage differently."

"It's not really my country that looks at marriage differently. It's the royal family and what's expected of us. I'll be spending weeks alleviating the fears of several members of parliament, assuring them that our marriage is not part of a big master plan."

Taking a bite of oatmeal, she nodded. "I get it. It's something you shouldn't think you have to do, but you will. Just like I'll be spending two hours with Sally's staff today, learning how to curtsy."

"I thought curtsying was out. Old school. Something nobody did anymore."

"According to Sally's morning memo, there are some

small eastern European countries that still believe in it. I just hope we don't run into any of those royal families when I'm big-as-a-house pregnant. I can't imagine curtsying and balancing twenty-five pounds of stomach."

He laughed. "You're going to make an interesting princess."

"Lucky for you, it's only for a little over two years."

He said, "Uh-huh," and went back to reading his newspaper.

Ginny didn't care. Their conversation proved that she could talk to the "nice" Dominic and not get carried away. They did not have to be best friends. But they did have to get along. They had to look good together in public. They needed to know enough about each other that their charade appeared to be real. And this morning it was clear they were succeeding.

If there was a little rumble in her heart about wasting her wedding, a beautiful wedding, on a fake marriage, she silenced it. She'd never imagined herself getting married. Living with her dad had scared her off that. She'd never allow herself to let her guard down with a man enough to get serious enough to get married. So this was her wedding. Her one shot at being a bride. She'd be a fool not to make it as perfect as she could.

At four o'clock that afternoon, Dom unexpectedly returned to the apartment. As they had the day before, Joshua and Sally sat on the sofa across from her. The photo arrays and designer lists were with them.

She faced the door with a smile. "I thought you had more glad-handing to do."

He walked in and said, "I do. But I was the one who told Sally and Joshua to bring the designer lists up to you again. I wanted to make sure we were all on the same page."

"They told me you said I wasn't sure about the designer." She bit her lip, not happy that something she'd told him had become an issue.

He caught her gaze. "I want you to be sure."

The feeling whooshed through her again. The one that told her he was looking out for her because he was a nice guy. He might not love her. He might not even know her well enough to like her. But he was a nice enough guy that he wanted her to be happy.

"Okay."

Even as she said that, the big double doors of Dominic's apartment opened. "Ginny?"

Ginny's head snapped up. "Mom?"

She blinked as she saw her tall, slim mother race into the sitting room from the echoing foyer. Wearing a tan pantsuit that the king probably would have loved for its dignity, she ran over to Ginny.

Ginny rose and was enfolded into her mom's hug. After a long squeeze, she said, "Let me look at you!"

"Why aren't you in school?"

"Dom called. He said you needed help with your gown."

Her throat closed and tears welled in her eyes. This act of Dominic's was a little more difficult to call the actions of a nice guy trying to keep her happy. Having her mother flown to Xaviera was so kind it made her chest tight.

"I don't exactly need help. I just love your opinions."

Her mom said, "Even better." Then she faced Joshua and Sally, both of whom had risen. "And you must be Sally and Joshua."

Sally bowed slightly. Joshua said, "She's actually very clear about what she wants. I think she just needs your reassurance."

"Joshua, Sally, this is my mother, Rose Jones."

Ginny's mom smiled broadly. Her pretty blond hair had a hint of pink in it, because—well, she was a Texas girl, who'd grown up dancing to the Beach Boys and riding horses, and that crazy part of her had no intention of dying. "Let me see the designers and the dresses."

Joshua immediately handed over the photo array panels, but Ginny stepped away and slid around to the back of the couch where Dom stood.

He raised his eyebrows in question. "What?"

"You told my mom I needed help?"

He shook his head. "No, I called her and said I wanted you to be happy planning this wedding."

The sweetness of the gesture filled her heart. "I would have been okay."

"And the wedding would have looked fake."

This time the reminder that he didn't want the wedding to look fake didn't go through her like a knife. It was their deal. He'd always been up-front about their deal.

The crazy feeling she got around nice Dom morphed into something soft and happy. "We're going to have a beautiful wedding."

He smiled. "Yes, we are."

The air between them changed. For a few seconds, she debated springing to her tiptoes and hugging him, but that wasn't really acceptable, either.

Holding his gaze, she took a step back, then another, suddenly realizing why she kept getting odd nudges. After decades of surface relationships that she'd ended before she even knew the guy she was involved with, she'd managed to never really know anyone, never get beyond platitudes. But planning a fake wedding? Living in the same apartment with Dom? Coconspirators to protect their child? She was getting to know him. And she liked him. A lot more than she'd ever liked any man.

And he'd warned her not to spin a fairy-tale fantasy because he didn't want a marriage with emotion.

CHAPTER SIX

Two days later, Dom strode down the marble-floored hall to the double doors of his apartment. Since Rose had arrived, his home had become like a beehive. Where Ginny might be shy about creating a wardrobe, Rose had taken to the task as if she was born to it. Designers had been called in. Dresses and pants arrived for fittings. Two styles of wedding dresses had been chosen and Alfredo Larenzo, an Italian designer, had been hired to create them.

With a wince, he partially opened one of the two double doors, sticking his head in far enough to see into the living room. Which was, mercifully, empty. For a second, he hoped that Ginny and her mom had gone out for lunch, but his chest pinched. Since Rose had arrived, he'd also barely seen Ginny.

Not that he missed her. He didn't really know her. They were in a fake situation. There was nothing to miss. The thing was, he liked seeing her. Usually, she was funny. After four-hour sessions in parliament, funny was welcome. So he didn't miss her. He missed her silliness.

Comfortable with that assessment, he walked past the double sofas, over to the bar. When he turned to pour his Scotch, he saw the door to Ginny's suite door was open. And there she stood, in little pink panties and a pink lace bra. A short man wearing spectacles and a white shirt with the sleeves rolled to his elbows had a tape measure around her hips. Her mom stood with her back to the door, obviously supervising.

Dom stared. He'd forgotten how perfect she was. With full breasts, a sweet dip for a waist and hips that flared just enough for a man to run his hand along, she had what most men would consider a perfect figure.

The short, dark-haired guy raised the tape measure to her waist and Dom followed every movement of the man's hands, remembering the smoothness of her shape, the silkiness of her skin. The tailor whipped the tape around and snapped the two ends together in the middle, right above her belly button and Dominic's head tilted.

Right there…

Right below that perfect belly button…

Was his child.

His child.

His hand went limp and the glass he was holding fell to the bar with a thump.

Ginny's head snapped up and she turned to see him standing there, staring. Their eyes met. And it hit him for the very first time, not that she was pregnant, but that the baby she carried was *his.*

His baby.

He'd created a life.

Rose turned, saw him and walked to the door. "Sorry, Dom. Didn't realize you were home."

And she closed the door.

Dominic stared at it. The whole thing about the baby didn't floor him as much as the realization that the baby was in Ginny's stomach. In a few weeks that flat tummy of hers would be round. She'd gain weight. Be miserable. Probably grouchy. Her feet would swell. She'd be clumsy—in front of millions. And then she'd spend God knew how long in labor.

Because of his baby.

Ginny's suite door opened and she walked out, tying the belt of a pink satin robe around her.

"Was there something you wanted?"

He stared at her, his chest tight, his mind numb. Up until that very moment he hadn't really considered how much Ginny was doing for him. Oh, he understood the loss of her job, but he suddenly saw the other things— losing her friends, living away from her mom, stretching her tummy to unknown limits, changing everything.

For his baby.

"Dom?"

He shook his head to clear it. "Sorry. I'm taking a break and thought I'd come up and see if you're ready for the formal dinner tonight with the ambassador."

She angled her thumb behind her, pointing at her suite door. "That's what the little guy with the moustache is doing. Final fitting for a dress Sally tells me your dad is going to have a fit over."

A laugh bubbled up, but he squelched it. "You can't always push my dad's buttons."

She shrugged. "I'm bored."

His laughter died. "Really?"

"No! Absolutely not. I'm getting fitted for a billion dresses and three-point-five-million pair of jeans. I never realized how many clothes a princess was expected to have."

"So you're not bored?"

"No. I just have a style." She shrugged and the pretty, shiny pink robe shifted over her sun-kissed shoulders.

He remembered biting those shoulders, nibbling her

neck, rubbing his entire body over the length of her entire body.

"And, I swear, I'm not going overboard with sexy clothes. I'm just not going to dress like a grandma."

He cleared his throat. "I get it about not wanting to dress like a grandma. But be careful."

"You don't think it's time for someone to bring your dad into the twenty-first century?"

"If you can bring him in without the press having a field day, then give it your best shot."

She smiled, turned and walked back to her room. He watched every swish of the satin over her round bottom.

"Dinner's at eight, right?"

She called the question over her shoulder, her shiny yellow hair flowing to the middle of her back, accenting that curved waist that led to her perfect butt.

Dominic licked his suddenly dry lips. "Yes, eight. But we need to be in my dad's quarters at seven so that we all arrive in the dining room together, long before the ambassador so we can greet him."

"Piece of cake."

She opened the door to her suite and walked inside, leaving him alone in the living room again.

He tugged his tie away from his throat. A year of celibacy with her was not going to be easy.

He threw back the shot of Scotch and returned to his office for a few hours of admin work. When he entered the apartment again, Ginny's door was closed. He suspected she was getting ready for the dinner, so he went to his quarters, showered and put on the trousers and white shirt of his tux.

He managed the bow tie the way he could since he was eight, but the onyx-and-diamond cuff links, heirlooms with tricky catches, wouldn't lock.

He looked at his door and smiled. For the first time in his life he had a woman. In his quarters. About to marry him. Why shouldn't he take advantage?

Walking past the white sofas in the sitting room, he reminded himself that another man engaged to a gorgeous woman would find much better ways to take advantage of the situation, but he sought only help with cuff links. He was insane.

He knocked on her door.

"Yes."

"It's me, Dom." He sucked in a breath, suddenly feeling like a teenager trying to ask a girl to a dance. Idiocy. He cleared his throat and strengthened his voice. "The cuff links I'm wearing were gifts from the ambassador we're dining with tonight. They'd been in his family for a century. The clasps stick."

Before he could finish, her door opened. She stood before him in a pale blue satin dress. Sleeveless—strapless—it should have given him a delightful view, but she wore a little lace thing over it—sort of a jacket, but not quite long enough.

Her hair had been put up, but not in the grandma hairdo. It was more like a long, silky, braided ponytail with flowers woven through it.

She lifted her pretty face and smiled at him. "Heirlooms, huh?"

He said, "Yes," but his voice came out rusty again. Except this time he knew why he was dumbstruck. She wore almost no makeup, yet she was still the most beautiful woman he'd ever met.

"Let me see."

He held out his arm and she examined the cuff links that he'd slid through the buttonholes but hadn't locked. She took the first in her nimble fingers, her face pinching in concentration, and something warm and wonderful swished through him.

He told himself it was nothing but attraction, but when she finished closing and locking the cuff links, she glanced up and smiled at him, and he realized how nice she was. It was no wonder she was so good with the children of her high school. She was just plain sweet.

And he was a pampered ruler. Somebody so accustomed to getting his own way that he'd persuaded her to marry him. It was for the best, of course, but that was his pathology. Even if it hadn't been the best for Ginny, if it had been the best for his country, he would have tossed her feelings aside and worked things to his benefit anyway.

The warm, fuzzy feeling she inspired shifted into cold, hard steel. Because that's who he really was, and even as much of a bastard as he could be, he didn't want to hurt her.

Not after she was doing so much for him.

Dom and Ginny left their apartment at ten to seven. He was the picture of kingly gorgeousness in his black tux.

When she told him that, he cast a sideways glance at her. "Thank you. You look lovely, too."

Not twenty minutes before they had shared a happy moment over his cuff links. Now he was cool and distant? It didn't make any sense.

They walked to the elevator, which opened as soon as they arrived. Neither spoke as they stepped inside and Dom pushed the button for the second floor.

A guest of the palace, Ginny's mom was invited to join them for dinner, and she waited for them in the second-floor lobby beside the elevator.

When they stepped out, she hugged Ginny. "Very pretty."

Ginny displayed her newfound curtsy skills. "Thanks. Your outfit is gorgeous, too."

Rose smoothed her hand along the soft beige satin. The king had offered the services of their clothier, and her pragmatic mom hadn't had a qualm about using them. She had the tailor whip up a simple satin skirt and sequined top that sort of looked like a tank top. She'd swept her yellow and pink hair into a neat French twist. She looked simple, but elegant. More elegant than Ginny had ever seen her.

As Dom guided them in the direction of the king's quarters, Rose whispered, "I could get used to this."

Ginny's eyes widened in horror. She had no idea why Dom had suddenly become distant, but hearing her mom say she could get used to luxury wouldn't help things.

"Do not say that!"

"I was kidding! It's stuffy here." She glanced around at the paintings on the elegant walls. "Almost like a really fancy prison."

Though Dominic hadn't appeared to have been listening, he turned and said, "Protocols and security are necessary."

"For protection and respect," Ginny quickly told her mom, wanting Dom to see her mom hadn't meant any harm. She simply wasn't up to speed on the lives of royalty. "If somebody's going to rule a country in a part of the world that isn't always stable, they need to command respect."

Dominic gave her a look of approval that helped alleviate the sense that she'd somehow caused his bad mood.

But her mom waved a hand. "Give me the good old-fashioned life of a commoner any day of the week."

Ginny smiled nervously, as Dom shook his head. He'd been so cute when he'd come to her suite, asking for help with his cuff links. Now a world of distance seemed to be lodged between them. She wouldn't tell him, but it had been nice to have a chance to touch him. And there was nothing more intimate than fixing a guy's cuff links or his bow tie—as a wife would.

She told herself not to go overboard with those thoughts and knew she wouldn't. She didn't want to get hurt by spinning fantasies. Still, though she might be a fake fiancée about to be a fake wife/princess, she and Dom were in this together. She didn't like the fact that he was unhappy. Especially if it might be because of something she'd done.

Security guards opened the gold doors to the king's quarters and Dom invited Ginny and her mom to enter before him. The foyer ceilings had to be three stories high. Everything from lamps to picture frames was trimmed in gold.

Her mother immediately recognized a Monet. She gasped. "Oh, this is delightful! One of my favorites."

"I'd be happy to give it to you as my wedding gift to you."

All heads turned as the king entered the foyer.

He kissed Ginny's hand, then Rose's.

Rose frowned. "First, I do not have the kind of security I'd need to put that in my home. Second, I'm not the bride. I don't get gifts."

"It's our custom to give parents of people who marry into our family a gift…something like a welcome to the family."

Her mom's eyebrows rose as she glanced over at Ginny, who shrugged slightly.

She leaned toward the king and whispered, "We're really not going to be in your family long."

He bowed. "A custom is a custom."

Rose nodded. "Point taken. Do I have to get you a gift?"

King Ronaldo unexpectedly smiled. "Do you wish to welcome me to your family?"

Rose laughed noisily. "Well, honey, I guess I do. Except you have to come to my house to get the gift."

The king directed everyone to the door again. "Maybe I will. But right now we're going to the formal reception room to meet the ambassador."

The king took Rose's arm as Dominic tucked Ginny's hand in the crook of his elbow.

She'd never seen her mom flirt. Not even after her dad had died. Not with anyone. Ever. The sight of her mom and the grouchy king—well, flirting—made her want to say, "Aw," and shiver with revulsion simultaneously.

King Ronaldo peeked over his shoulder at Ginny. "By the way, Ginny, I approve of the dress."

"This old thing?"

He smiled patiently. "I know you're coming to understand our customs and our etiquette, so you can't tease me anymore by pretending you don't understand. Were I you, I would have said thank you."

Dominic gave her a look and, suddenly, desperately wanting to please him, she took a quick breath and said, "Thank you."

"I'm hoping your entire wardrobe and wedding apparel will follow a similar pattern."

"Yes, Your Majesty. I appreciate that you're allow-ing me so much say in the wedding plans."

"Thank your future husband," the king said as the reached the door of the reception room. "He pleaded your case. Something about pink roses and your friends as bridesmaids lending authenticity to the whole thing."

Two guards opened the doors. The king walked into the room and led her mother to a discreet bar.

Ginny turned to Dom. "So, you pleaded my case?"

He glanced back at his father. "Saving an argument."

She reached up and tightened his bow tie. "Well, I appreciate it."

He caught her hand. "That's fine. My tie is fine."

She nodded quickly, annoyed with herself for the in-timate gesture and for upsetting him again. "I guess I'm just getting a little too comfortable with you."

He caught her gaze. "You shouldn't."

Ginny stared into his dark, dark eyes, suddenly real-izing he wasn't angry with her. But if he wasn't angry with her, that left only himself. Was he angry with him-self? For asking her for help with cuff links? Or because asking for help with his cuff links proved they were getting close? Becoming friends?

She saw that as a good thing. Within the cocoon of their conspiracy, for the first time in her life, she was taking the initial steps of trusting a man. She didn't have to worry about consequences. There were none. She knew they were getting divorced. There was no way he could hurt her. And the little bit of intimacy with the cuff links had been warm and wonderful.

But obviously, he didn't feel the same way.

The ambassador arrived and Ginny played her role exactly as Dom wanted her to play it. They had a toast with the ambassador and his wife, Amelia, who then toasted the newly engaged couple and wished them happiness.

The ambassador then handed them a small box. Dominic opened it, smiled and handed it to her.

She glanced inside and her gaze jerked to the ambassador. "Emerald earrings."

Amelia said, "Our country's gift to you on your engagement."

She said, "Thanks," but her stomach tightened. She hadn't considered that kings and ambassadors and entire countries would give her gifts. But really? What wedding didn't attract gifts?

At the end of the evening, when the ambassador and his wife retreated to their suite, she and Dom also took their leave. Rose had decided to stay and have one more drink with the king, and Ginny's head spun.

When they got into the elevator and the door closed, affording them their first privacy of the evening, she turned to Dominic. "I don't know if I should apologize for my mom flirting with your dad or groan over the fact that we're going to get expensive wedding gifts that we have no right to."

"We're getting married. We have every right to get gifts and well-wishers have every right to send us gifts." He frowned slightly. "Haven't you seen the stack of presents that already arrived?"

Her mouth fell open. "We've already gotten gifts?"

"Many. The protocol is that they stay with Sally until she has an appropriate thank-you card printed up on the royal family's stationery."

"We don't write our own thank-you cards?"

He smiled briefly.

Ginny held back a groan. No wonder he didn't want

to be friendly with her. She was more than a commoner. She was a bumpkin.

She swallowed. "What are we going to do with the presents?"

"What do you mean, what are we going to do with the presents? The same thing other newlyweds do."

The elevator door opened and he walked outside. She stood frozen, feeling odd—feeling horrible, actually. While she was learning to trust him, he was walking away from her. She might be a bumpkin, but he was the one who had his protocols out of order if he wanted to keep gifts they didn't deserve. Technically, they were at the center of perpetuating a fraud. They would benefit from a lie.

She scrambled after him. "So we're going to keep these things?"

He stopped, spun to face her. "What would you suggest? That we tell our guests no gifts? That we all but let them know we plan on divorcing. Get your head in the game, Ginny!"

His tone was like a slap in the face. She took a step back, then another. "I'm sorry."

He cursed. "Why are you saying you're sorry! I'm the one who just yelled at you! Do you have to be so nice? So honest?"

"You'd rather I be dishonest?"

"I'd rather that your sanctimonious attitude not make me feel like I'm doing something wrong all the time."

He turned to the white double doors, marched over, opened them and walked directly to the bar.

She scampered after him. "Wait! What?"

"You're so nice. You spar with my dad, then say something so respectful, he knows you're coming around. You didn't want a new wardrobe until we insisted. You're nice with Sally. You're happy your mom is here and it's clear she loves you." He stopped, sucking in a breath.

"You're mad at me because the situation is working out?"

"I'm mad at you because every day it becomes clearer and clearer that I'm going to hurt you."

She tilted her head, not quite understanding what he was getting at.

"You say you don't want to get drawn into this life and I believe you. But you and I…" He downed the shot of Scotch and poured another. "We sort of fit. You feel it as much as I do. It's not something we plan or intend to do. It's that thing that happens at odd moments. The times we're on the same page or thinking the same thought and we know it with just a glance." He walked from behind the bar to stand directly in front of her. "And pretty soon we're going to start remembering how good we are together in other ways and then we're going to be sleeping together."

Her heart thumped. He *was* feeling the same things she was. That unexpected trust. That sense that everything was going to be okay. "You thought we were good together?"

"You *know* we were good together."

"And you think we fit?"

"I see those little things happen every day. You liked fastening my cuff links. I like fighting your simple battles over things like jeans versus white suits."

She searched his gaze. Ridiculous hope filled her chest to capacity. They really were getting to know each other and in knowing each other, they were beginning to genuinely like each other.

For once, having more than a surface relationship

didn't scare her. Maybe because she knew it had a time limit. She could get close, make love, get married, have a baby with Dom, knowing it was going to end. Secure in the fact that they would part amicably, she wouldn't suffer the pains of rejection. She would simply move on. And she would have had a chance she never thought she'd get: a chance to really be in love. To know what it felt like to share. To be part of something wonderful. All under the protection of the knowledge that it wouldn't last forever. She didn't have to be perfect forever. She didn't even have to be good forever. Or to suit Dom forever. She only had to make this work for a little over two years.

"And you don't think it's a good thing that we get along?"

"I have a job to do. I've told you that if you get in the way of that job, I will always pick the kingdom over you."

She swallowed and nodded, knowing exactly what he was saying, but her stomach fluttered. When they first decided to marry, he had been sure he'd always take the kingdom's side over hers. But this very argument proved that he was changing. And he clearly wasn't happy about that.

"Is this the part where I say I'm sorry?"

He sniffed and looked away. "Sorry again? Why this time?"

"Because I think I tempt you. I think that's why you're really mad. I think knowing me has made you feel that you'd like to be a real boy, Pinocchio."

"So I'm a puppet?"

"No. I think you'd like the freedom to make up your own mind, to make your own choices, but you're afraid of what will happen to your kingdom."

He caught her gaze. "You make it sound like an idiotic dilemma. But it isn't. We might be a small kingdom but we're an important one." He slid his hand across her shoulder and to her long ponytail. He ran the fat braid through his fingers as if it were spun gold. "One woman should not change that."

Even as he said the words, he stepped closer. He wrapped the braid around his knuckles and tugged her forward until they almost touched, but not quite. The air between them crackled, not with memories of how good they'd been together but with anticipation. If they kissed now, changed the terms of their deal now, the next two years would be very different.

And she wanted it. Not just for the sex. For the intimacy and the chance to be genuinely close to someone, even as she had the magical out of a two-year time limit.

He lowered his head slowly, giving her time, it seemed, to pull away if she wanted. But, mesmerized by the desperation in his black eyes, she stood perfectly still, barely breathing. He wanted this, too, and even though she knew he was going to kiss her, she also knew he fought a demon. He might want to be king, but he also wanted to be a man.

When his lips touched hers, she didn't think of that night two months ago, she thought of this moment, of how he needed her, even if he didn't see it.

She slid her arms around his neck as he released her braid, letting it swing across her back. With his hand now free, he brought her closer still. The press of her breasts to his chest knocked the air out of her lungs as his lips moved across hers roughly.

He was angry, she knew, because she was upsetting his well-laid plans. The irony of it was he'd been upsetting her plans, her life, from the second she'd met him. It only seemed fitting that finally she was doing the same to him.

Standing on tiptoe, she returned his kiss, as sure as he was. If he wanted to talk about unfair, she would show him unfair. The only way she could be intimate with someone was knowing she had an out. The inability to trust that her dad had instilled in her had crippled her for anything but a relationship that couldn't last. She wouldn't share the joy of raising children. She was lucky to get a child. She wouldn't grow old with someone. The best she would get would be memories of whatever love, intimacy, happiness they could cobble together in the next two years. And even as it gave her at least slight hope, it also angered her mightily.

They dueled for a few seconds, each fighting for supremacy, until suddenly his mouth softened over hers. His hands slid down her back to her bottom, while his mouth lured her away from her anger and to that place where the softness of their kisses spoke of their real feelings.

Like it or not, they were falling in love.

And it wasn't going to last.

But it was all Ginny Jones, high school guidance counselor from Texas with the alcoholic dad, was going to get in her lifetime.

So she wanted it. She wanted the intimacy, the friendship, the secrets and dreams.

The only problem was she had no idea how to go about getting any of it.

CHAPTER SEVEN

IT TOOK EVERY ounce of concentration Dom could muster to pull away from Ginny. He'd never before felt the things he felt with her, but that was the problem. He'd never experienced any of these things because he'd avoided them. Not because he'd never met anyone like Ginny, but because he'd always been strong.

So when he stepped away, it wasn't with regret. It was with self-recrimination. He did not want what she seemed to be offering. And if they didn't stop this idiotic game, just as he'd told her, he was going to hurt her.

"I'm going to bed. I'll see you in the morning." He turned and walked to his room, vowing to himself that something like that kiss would never happen again.

The next day, he left before breakfast and didn't come back to his quarters until long past time for supper. That worked so well he decided to keep up that schedule.

At first, she'd waited for him on the sofa in the sitting room. So he'd stride into the room, barely glancing at her, and walk right past the bar, saying, "It was a long day. I'm going to shower and go right to bed."

And pretty soon she stopped waiting up.

For two weeks, he managed to avoid her in their private times and keep his distance when they were in public, but he could see something going on in that crazy head of hers. Every time they got within two feet of each other, she'd smile so prettily she'd temporarily throw him off balance. But he'd always remind himself he was strong. And it worked, but he wasn't superhuman. If something didn't give, they'd end up talking again. Or kissing. Or just plain forming a team. And then she'd get all the wrong ideas.

A week before the wedding, her bridesmaids arrived and he breathed a sigh of relief. Jessica and Molly were two teachers from her school, both of whom had just finished their semester. Dom smiled politely when Ginny introduced them and he shook both of their hands, reminding them they had met when he visited their school.

Molly laughed. "Of course, we remember you. We didn't think you'd remember us."

He smiled briefly. "It's my job to care for a country full of people. Remembering names, really seeing people when I look at them, is part of that."

Jessica nodded sagely as if she totally understood and agreed, but his future bride tilted her head in a way that told him she was turning that over in her mind, putting that statement up against other things he'd said.

Good. He hoped she was. Because from here on out that was his main goal. If she wanted to be part of his life, and for the next two years or so she had to be, then she needed not just to hear that but to fully understand it. His country came first. She would be second. And then only for about two years. He did not intend to get personally involved with her. God knew he'd sleep with her in a New York minute if he could be sure nothing would come of it. But that ship had sailed. They were getting to know each other, getting to *like* each other. If they went any further, their breakup would be a disaster.

He turned and walked out of the apartment, on his way to his office, but Molly stopped him. "Aren't you going to kiss your bride goodbye?"

Dom slid a questioning glance to Ginny. Her eyebrows raised and her mouth formed the cute little wince she always gave when she had no defense. Obviously, she hadn't told her friends their marriage would be a fake. That was good news and bad news. The good news was if her friends believed this marriage would be real, there was no chance either of them would slip up and say the wrong thing. Unfortunately, that meant there was no rest from the charade for him and Ginny.

He walked over and put his hands on her shoulders. For two seconds, he debated kissing her cheek, but knew that would never work. So he pressed his lips to hers lightly and pulled back quickly, then he turned and walked out to the door.

"I'll be busy all day. You ladies enjoy yourselves."

Then he left. But the look on Ginny's face when he'd pulled away from their kiss followed him out the door. She hadn't minded the quick kiss. She was back to being on board with the charade. Back to fake kisses and no intimate conversations. They'd barely seen each other in two weeks. His doing. And she wasn't pouting. She didn't throw hissy fits the way he distantly remembered his mom doing to manipulate his dad.

He shook his head, wondering where that memory had come from. His mom hadn't been a manipulator. His dad had been brutally in love with her. So in love that the king had been putty in her hands. And so in love that when she got sick and died, the king's world had come to a crashing halt.

Not that he had to worry about that with Ginny. He was much stronger than his dad had been. He could always do what needed to be done. Always resist when he needed to.

With her guests in the palace and a charade to perpetuate, he phoned the kitchen staff and made arrangements for a formal dinner in their apartment, then had his assistant phone Ginny and tell her he was honoring her and her guests that evening with a formal dinner.

Hanging up the phone, Ginny pressed her hand to her stomach. After two weeks of him virtually ignoring her—except when they were in public—he was back to being nice again. She would have breathed a sigh of relief but Molly was two feet away and Jessica wasn't that much farther, standing with the fiftysomething female dressmaker who was measuring her for her bridesmaid's gown.

"So you chose a dress without even consulting us?" Molly groused good-naturedly.

"Yes." Ginny winced. "Sorry, but fabric had to be ordered."

Jessica said, "Oh! Special fabric!"

"It's just a nice silk."

"Listen to her," Molly teased, nudging her shoulder. "A week away from the wedding and she's already acting like a princess."

"I am not!"

Jessica stepped away from the woman who had measured her for her dress. "It's not a bad thing. I imagine that adjusting to being the most important woman in a country isn't easy."

"The most important woman in a country? Not hardly."

Molly fell to a club chair. "Well, Dom's mother is dead and he has no sisters. His dad doesn't date and his brother is some kind of jet-setter. You are the only girl permanently in the mix."

She hadn't thought of that, but when she did, her stomach fluttered oddly. It meant something that they'd brought her into the family. True, she was pregnant with the heir to the throne, but there were so many ways they could have handled this other than marriage. On some level, she'd passed enough tests that they'd brought her in.

"If that makes you queasy," Jessica said, "then you'd better toughen up."

"I'm not queasy."

Molly said, "Well, something's up. You let Dom believe we don't know about your situation. Almost as if you don't trust what he'd say if he knew you'd confided in your friends."

"That's true, Gin," Jessica agreed, slipping on her blue jeans and pretty peach T-shirt that showed off her Texas-girl tan. "If you don't grow a pair with this guy pretty soon, he's going to walk all over you."

"What if I think I have a better way to handle the next two years?"

Jessica cautiously said, "Better?"

"Yeah." She turned away, puttering around with picking up pins and tape measures, and putting them in the dressmaker's tote.

Taking the cue that Ginny wanted her to leave, the dressmaker grabbed her tote and said, "Thanks. I'll have dresses for you to try on tomorrow."

When she closed the suite door behind her, Molly gasped. "Tomorrow?"

She shrugged. "That's how it goes here in the palace." She walked to the table by the window and busied herself with straightening stationery and pens. "I say I want something, somebody comes up and measures, and the next day it's at my door."

Shrewd, Jessica narrowed her eyes. "You never told us your better plan for how to handle your situation."

Ginny looked up into the faces of her two trusted friends and decided it wasn't out of line to want a second opinion. "Okay. Here's the deal. You know how my dad sort of ruined my ability to trust?"

Molly nodded. Jessica crossed her arms on her chest.

"Well, I've been thinking that if Dom and I hadn't accidentally gotten pregnant, I probably never would have trusted anyone enough to have had a child."

Jessica said, "True. So I hope you're not about to tell us you want to make your marriage real with Prince Gorgeous. The very fact that you can't trust makes that just plain stupid."

"Not really. Because I don't want a permanent husband. But I do want this marriage."

Molly tilted her head. "What does that mean?"

"Well, we're stuck together for at least two years and he *is* gorgeous. Not only would I like the whole mother experience with my baby's father, but I just don't see why we can't sleep together and maybe be a real husband and wife for a while."

"How about because that's not what he wants."

"I'll still divorce him two years after the baby's born and gone through the initiation ceremony. That's the deal. But it's the very fact that I know we're getting divorced that makes me comfortable enough to, you know—"

"Want to have sex?"

"It's more than that. When he's comfortable with me,

we have fun. I think we could make very good parents. I think being a husband and wife for real for two years could pave the way for us to have a good relationship after we're divorced and I think all that is nothing but good for our child."

Molly mulled that over and suddenly said, "Actually, that makes sense."

Jessica turned on her. "How can you say that? She's going to get hurt."

Molly shrugged. "Or not. The situation is weird, Jessica. And not everybody's lucky enough to attract men like mosquitoes."

Jessica nodded at Ginny. "She could if she wanted to."

"That's the point. She doesn't want to. But she's going to marry this guy and have his baby. Why shouldn't she have two years of being a real princess before she has to let it all go?"

"That's like saying you should eat a whole cake before you start a diet."

Ginny laughed. "You mean, you don't?"

Jessica groaned.

"Look, I am never, ever, ever going to be married. The mistrust my dad instilled in me will never go away. But I am getting married. To Dominic. For a bit over two years. Not forever. So it'll be like playing house."

Jessica sighed. "Playing house?"

"Yes. Just another facet of the charade. Because I know it's fake, I'm not going to get hurt. But I also want to experience something I never would have if we hadn't gotten pregnant and decided to marry for the baby."

"I hope you know what you're doing."

Ginny sucked in a breath. "I think I do, but even if I don't, it's only two years. Once it's over, it's over. I will have no choice but to go back to normal. Especially with a baby to raise with him." Satisfied with her conclusion, she changed the subject. "Did you bring something to wear tonight, or do I need to call the clothier?"

"Clothier?"

"He's this guy, Joshua, who if you need something you call him, and he'll call a store or designer and have it in the room within hours."

Molly gaped at her. "So you can get us gowns for tonight?"

"If you need them. It's all about not embarrassing Dominic in front of his father."

Jessica shook her head. "I think you're enjoying this too much."

"Actually, this is the part I don't enjoy. The part I won't miss at all. There are lots of things about being a princess like the press and having a father-in-law who can have you deported that make this life hard. Not something I'd want to do forever."

Jessica drew a deep breath. "Okay. Now I think I get it. You know you don't want to be in this life forever, but you like Dom and you're going to make the best of it while you're here. So you'll have no regrets and be ready to move on."

Ginny sighed with relief. "Exactly."

"Okay. Then I'm on board, too. What do you want us to do?"

"Nothing. This is the part I need to handle myself. I just haven't figured out how yet." She couldn't exactly say, "Hey, let's sleep together." But she wasn't the queen of seductresses, either. She was going to have to wait for her moment and take it. Given that he'd managed to avoid her for the past two weeks, that wasn't going to be easy.

They called Joshua, who called his contact at a local boutique from Ginny's suite. Four gowns were delivered within two hours, and Molly and Jessica made their choices before they returned to their rooms to dress for the formal dinner.

Ginny took special care with her outfit that night, wearing a coral-colored gown. She fixed her hair in the long braid again, the way she'd had it the night he'd kissed her.

When she finally came out of her suite, everyone was already there, including her mom—and the king, who was his charming best, and anybody with eyes in their head could see the reason was Rose.

After cocktails, they passed the small dining room where Dom and Ginny ate breakfast and lunch, and entered a much bigger dining room, something almost as fancy as the king's. Dom let the king have the head of the table, taking the seat to his right and seating Ginny next to him.

The conversation ebbed and flowed around them as Ginny watched her mom, seated across from them at the king's right. They talked about everything from sports to politics, and the king took great delight in sparring with her.

"He's going to miss her when she's gone next week."

Ginny's gaze snapped around to meet Dom's. From the surprised expression that came to his face, she could tell he hadn't meant to say that out loud.

"It's okay. You can talk to me. We're a team, remember?" She motioned from herself to Dom. "In this together."

"Yes. But we don't want to go too far."

She turned on her seat, her taffeta gown ruffling and rustling, suddenly wondering if this was her moment.

Everybody at the table was deep in conversation. Her bridesmaids chatted up Dom's brother. The king and her mother were so engrossed, there might as well not have been anybody else at the table.

The best place for her most private conversation with him might just be in this crowded dining room.

She took a breath, caught his gaze. "Why not? We're in a mighty big charade. I think it's going to be impossible for us to set limits on how close it makes us."

"I told you that we don't want to get close because I don't want to hurt you."

"You think you're going to hurt me over a few shared comments? I'm not asking you to divulge state secrets. I'm just saying the charade works better when we're talking." She smiled slightly. "We haven't talked in weeks."

"And it's my fault?"

She shook her head. "Dom. Dom. Dom. You're so uptight. I'm not placing blame. That's the beauty of forming a team and maybe even the beauty of knowing this team doesn't have to last. We're only going to be together for two years or so. After that, we are the parents of your country's next heir who must get along."

Totally against the rules of etiquette, Dom picked up a fork and tapped it lightly against his plate. "So?"

She could think she made him nervous enough to do something out of line. Or she could see she made him comfortable enough to do something totally out of line.

She liked the second. She *believed* the second.

"So, I honestly, genuinely believe that if we would simply allow ourselves to be friendly—maybe even to get close—in these next few years, the rest of our lives would go a lot smoother."

He peeked over at her. "Really? *That's* what you think?"

"Look at it logically. How does it benefit us to never speak? It doesn't. It makes the charade more difficult and opens the doors for us to make mistakes."

"True."

"But if we talk at dinner and lunch, debrief about our days—"

This time when he peeked at her, he sort of smiled. "Debrief?"

"Sally and Joshua are rubbing off on me. I just mean we should talk about our days with each other."

"Ah."

"Then we won't make as many mistakes."

"It seems to me that just a few weeks ago, *you* were ignoring *me*."

"I was figuring everything out."

"And now you think you understand the whole situation?"

"I really do."

"And your answer is for us to debrief."

She met his gaze. "It's more than that."

His eyes darkened. "How much more?"

"I think we need to tell each other our reading interests, where we've been on vacation, a bit or two about our jobs. I think I need to fix your cuff links. You need to let me straighten your tie. I think we should be talking baby names and colors for the nursery."

He held her gaze. "That's going to take us into some dangerous territory."

She took a long breath and with all her strength, all her courage, she kept eye contact. "I'm a big girl. I'm also a smart girl. I sort of like knowing that this relationship will end."

His eyes searched hers. "So you've said."

"My dad was an alcoholic who made promises he never kept. He was his most charming when he wanted to manipulate me. If there's one thing I can't trust, it's people being nice to me. How am I ever going to create a relationship that leads to marriage if niceness scares me?"

He laughed unexpectedly. "You're saying you think a relationship with me will work because I'm not nice?"

"I'm saying this is my shot. Do you know I've never fantasized about getting married and having kids? I was always so afraid I'd end up like my mother that I wouldn't even let myself pretend I'd get married. So I've never had anything but surface relationships." She sucked in a breath. Held his gaze. "This baby we're having will probably be my only child. This marriage? It might be fake to you, but it's the only marriage I'll ever have. I'd love to have two years of happiness, knowing that I don't have to trust you completely, that you can't hurt me because we have a deadline."

"You really don't trust me?"

"I'll never trust anyone."

He glanced around the table at her bridesmaids, who were chatting up his brother, his dad and her mom, who clearly weren't paying any attention to them, and suddenly faced her again.

"No."

CHAPTER EIGHT

THE CATHEDRAL IN which Dom would marry Ginny was at least a thousand years old. It had been renovated six times and almost totally rebuilt once after a fire. The pews were cedar from Israel. The stained glass from a famous Italian artist. Two of the statues were said to have been created by Michelangelo, though no one could confirm it. And the art that hung in the vestibule? All of it was priceless.

But when Ginny stepped inside, her hand wrapped in her mom's, every piece of art, every piece of wood, every famous, distinguished and renowned person seated in the sea of guests, disappeared from Dom's vision.

She looked amazing.

She'd let her hair down. The yellow strands billowed around her beneath a puffy tulle veil. The top of her dress was a dignified lace with a high collar and snug lace sleeves that ran the whole way from her shoulders, down her arms, across the back of her hand to her knuckles. The skirt started at her waist, then flowed to the floor. Made of a soft, airy-looking material, it was scattered with the same shimmering flowers that were embroidered into the lace top, but these flowers stood alone, peeking out of the folds of the fabric and then hiding again as the skirt moved with every step Ginny took.

She'd managed to look both young and beautiful, while pleasing his father with a very dignified gown that took Dom's breath away.

His brother leaned forward and whispered, "I know you weren't happy about this marriage, so if you'd like to trade, you can have your princess back and I'll raise your love child."

Any other time, Dom would have said, "Shut up, you twit." Today, mesmerized by the woman who had already seduced him once, and if he'd read her correctly the night of the formal dinner with her bridesmaids, wanted to seduce him again, he very quietly said, "Not on your life."

Ginny and her mom reached the altar. Rose kissed his bride's cheek and then walked to her seat. Ginny held out her hand to Dom and he took it, staring at her as if he'd never seen her before. Because in a way he hadn't. He'd seen her silly and happy and playful the night of their date. He'd seen her dressed in jeans and T-shirts and even beautifully, ornately, for the night with the ambassador. But today, in this dress that was as beautiful as it was bridal, she was a woman offering herself to a man, as a bride.

Caught in the gaze of her pretty blue eyes, he was floored by the significance of it. Especially after their conversation about making their marriage real for their time together.

The minister cleared his throat. Their hands joined, Dom and Ginny turned to the altar and the service began. As the solemn words and decrees were spoken by his country's highest-ranking religious official, Dominic reminded himself that this wedding wasn't real. Even when they said their vows and exchanged jewel-encrusted rings, he told himself they were words he meant, truly meant, for a limited time.

But when the minister said, "You may kiss the bride," and she turned those big blue eyes up at him, his heart stuttered. She wasn't just a woman in a white dress, helping him to perpetuate a charade that would give legitimacy to Xaviera's next heir. She was an innocent woman, a bride...

She was his now.

She whispered, "You don't want to kiss me?"

His heart thundered in his chest and he realized he'd been standing there staring at her. In awe. In confusion. She wasn't just an innocent. She was someone who'd been hurt. Someone who couldn't trust. If he agreed to make this marriage real, no matter how much she protested that it wasn't true, he would hurt her. He *knew* he would hurt her. Because as much as he hated the comparison, it seemed being royal had made him very much like her dad. He was his most charming when he needed to get his own way, and selfish, self-centered, the rest of the time.

Still, he held her gaze as his head lowered and his lips met hers. He watched her lids flutter shut in complete surrender. Total honesty. His heart of stone chipped a bit. The soft part of his soul, the place he rarely let himself acknowledge, shamed him for being so strict with her.

They broke apart slowly. She smiled up at him.

He told himself she was playing a part. The smile, the expression meant nothing. If she was smart enough to realize she didn't trust anyone, she was also smart enough to play her role well. Smart enough to see he was doing what needed to be done not just for the next heir to the throne, but for *his child.*

The child in her stomach.

They turned to the congregation and began their recessional down the aisle to the vestibule, where they were spirited away to a private room while their guests left the church. They endured an hour of pictures before they walked out of the church, beneath the canopy of swords of his military's honor guard.

Dressed in black suits and white silk shirts and ties, his bodyguards whisked them into the back of his limo, to a professional photo studio for more pictures.

And the whole time Ginny smiled at him radiantly. Anyone who looked at her would assume—*believe*—this wedding was real. Because he was beginning to get the feeling himself. She wasn't such a good actress that she was fooling him. What she'd said haunted him. She wanted this to be real. At least for a little while. Because this, this sham, was as close as she'd ever get to a real marriage.

Her mother rode in the limo with his dad. Her bridesmaids rode with his brother and a distant cousin who served as his best man and groomsman.

Alone in their limo, he turned to her. Struggling to forget the bargain she'd tried to strike and come up with normal conversation, he said, "You look amazing."

She smiled, reached over and straightened his tie. "You do, too."

He shifted away, afraid of her. Not because he worried she was going to hurt him or cheat him. But because he knew she wasn't.

"Dominic, the straightening-the-tie thing is important. A piece of intimacy everyone expects to see. You need to be still and let me do it."

Because of her suggestion that they make this marriage real, and his desperate need not to hurt her, he was now the one who might ruin their ruse. "I suppose."

She shrugged, her pretty yellow hair shifted and swayed around her. "No matter what you decide, I intend to be a good wife for these two years."

His tongue stuck to the roof of his mouth. What did that mean? That he'd find her in his bed that night?

He remembered that yellow hair floating around them their one and only night together, remembered the softness of her skin, and wondered just how a man was supposed to resist that honesty or the sexual tug that lured him into a spell so sweet, another man would have happily allowed himself to be drawn in.

But he wasn't just any man. He was a prince, someday a king. Someone held to a higher standard. He did not deliberately hurt people.

They arrived at the palace. Bodyguards ushered them into the main foyer. They stopped in his father's quarters to have a toast with her mother and his dad and their wedding party. Then they took an elevator to the third floor of his dad's wing of the palace and stood on the balcony, waving to well-wishers.

A young woman edged her way through the crowd to the space just in front of security. She waved and called, "Toss your bouquet!"

Dom said, "That's odd."

Ginny laughed. "She's American. We have a tradition that whoever catches the bride's bouquet will be the next person to be married." She gave him a smile, then winked, before she turned and tossed the spray of fifty roses with strength that would have done any weight lifter proud.

The flowers bowed into a graceful arc before beginning their descent. The crowd gasped at Ginny's whimsy. The people closest to the woman who'd called realized they could intercept the bouquet and they scrambled forward, but it landed in the young girl's arms. As the crowd pressed forward to grab flowers from the bouquet, security surrounded her.

Ginny faced him. "Have her brought up for an audience."

He laughed. "Seriously?"

"Yes." She bowed slightly. "My lord," she said, her eyes downcast, her tone serious.

Those crazy feelings of wanting her rippled through him again. He raised her chin. "You don't have to bow to me."

"The etiquette books say I do." She smiled. "And I'm asking for the wedding favor the book also says I get. I'd like to meet the woman who wants so desperately to be married that she'd risk arrest."

Dom faced his bodyguard. He made a few hand gestures. The crowd called, "Kiss the bride," and he did. But he did so now with curiosity that nudged his fear of hurting her aside. He liked being able to do something for her.

When they returned to the king's receiving room, the young woman awaited them.

Ginny walked over and hugged her. "I hope the whole bouquet thing works out for you."

Their guest laughed nervously. Her big brown eyes stayed on Ginny's face. "I never thought you'd do it."

"I waited years for my prince. I know what you're feeling." She squeezed her hand and said, "Good luck."

Dominic nodded, the security detail motioned her to the door and she left with a quick wave. But the way Ginny had said, "I know what you're feeling," struck him oddly. She didn't say, "I've known what you feel." She said, "I know what you're feeling." He heard the sorrow there, maybe even a loneliness that almost opened that soft place in his soul again. But he hung on. He could not let sentiment destroy his plan. He could not become his dad.

Ginny said, "You know crazy people are going to try to steal that bouquet from her. You're going to have to have someone escort her to her hotel and maybe even out of the country."

"Yes. Security will take care of it."

But he couldn't stop staring at her. He might have closed the soft place in his soul, but his brain was working overtime to figure her out. What she had done had been a tad reckless, but it was very Ginny. Very sweet. Very warm. She'd used the wish her groom was to grant her for someone else.

And *that's* why he knew he couldn't sleep with her. No matter what she said or did or how she phrased things, she was innocent. Too nice for him.

But she was also hurting. She really believed she'd always be alone.

He couldn't think about that. He had to be fair.

They received dignitaries for hours. Even Dom was tired by the time his father, brother, cousin and Ginny's entourage escorted them to the palace ballroom.

They entered amid a trumpet blast and after toasts and a short speech by his father welcoming Ginny into the family, they finally ate.

Still, in between dances, he managed to find time to speak to his detail and arrange for their luggage to be taken to the yacht that night, instead of the next morning.

There was no way in hell he was taking her back to

his apartment, where they'd not only had privacy, they'd had friendly chats and a wonderful kiss.

Even he had his limits.

The staff on the *Crown Jewel* was too big to be in on the marriage ruse, but precautions were easier there. He and Ginny would be sleeping in the side-by-side bedrooms of the master suite, but the yacht was also so big that he could keep his distance. They'd sail so far out onto the ocean that even long lenses couldn't get pictures. And the staff would rotate so the same people wouldn't see them twice and wonder why they weren't kissing or holding hands.

Not only would this work, but it would be easy.

Piece of cake, as Ginny would say.

When they had to take a helicopter to the yacht, Ginny knew why Dom had chosen it as their honeymoon spot. The pilot put the helicopter down on the landing pad, and Dom helped her out, gathering the skirt of her gown so she didn't trip over it as she navigated the steps.

Walking across the deck, under the starlit sky, she glanced around in awe. "It's the friggin' Love Boat."

He turned to her with absolute horror in his eyes. "What?"

"You never saw the television show from the eighties? *The Love Boat?*"

Clearly relieved that she was referencing a television show, not referring to something about their relationship, he said, "You weren't even born in the eighties, so how did you see it?"

"My mom watched reruns all the time. It's a show about a cruise ship."

His eyes narrowed. "So you're saying our yacht is big?"

"Your yacht is huge."

"If that's a compliment, I accept it."

It wasn't a compliment. She was telling him she knew his plan. He intended to use this big ship to avoid her for the two weeks they were to be away. But he didn't seem to catch on to what she was saying.

It didn't matter. She was happy to have figured out his plan. She'd thought the night of the formal dinner for her friends had been her moment, and when it turned out that it wasn't, she'd hoped her honeymoon might give her another shot. And here she stood on a boat big enough to rival an aircraft carrier. It meant her options for finding another moment were seriously limited. But at least she knew what she was up against.

A security guard opened the door for them and Dom motioned for her to enter first. She stepped inside, expecting to see stairs with metal railings painted white, expecting to hear the hollow sound of a stairwell. Instead, she entered a small lobby. Sleek hardwood floors led to an elevator. Gold-framed paintings hung on the walls.

She spun around to face Dom. "Seriously? Is that a Picasso?"

Dom said, "Probably," as the elevator door opened. She hadn't even seen him press a button for it.

They rode down, only a few floors, before the door opened again onto a room so stunningly beautiful it could have been in a magazine. Huge windows in the back displayed the black sky with the faint dusting of stars. A taupe sofa flanked by two printed club chairs sat in front of a fireplace. The accent rug that held them all in a group was the same print as the club chairs. A long wooden bar gleamed in a far corner. Plants in elaborate pots converted empty space into focal points.

She wanted to say, "Wow," but her chest hurt. Her knees wobbled. This was her wedding night. But unlike a normal bride who knew what to expect, every step of her journey was a mystery. She wanted one thing. Dom wanted another. And only one of them could win.

Security guards entered behind Dom, rolling the cart carrying their luggage. She'd packed her four bags with care. Even though Dom had told her she'd need only a bikini and some sunblock, she'd brought clothes for romantic dinners—and undies. Pretty panties, bras and sleepwear that she and Joshua had chosen from catalogs so exclusive that prices weren't listed beneath the descriptions.

Joshua had said, "If you have to ask the price, you can't afford it."

And at that point she decided she didn't want to know. Dominic could afford to buy and sell small countries. She wasn't going to quibble over the price of the nighties she'd probably need to seduce him.

The bodyguards disappeared down the hall with the luggage cart carrying their bags.

"Nightcap?"

She pressed her hand to her tummy. "I probably could use some orange juice."

He walked to the bar. "Tired?"

Was he kidding? Even if she was exhausted, nerves would keep her awake tonight. The last time they'd been in this position, she hadn't had to seduce him. They'd seduced each other. Which meant, she shouldn't be nervous. She should be herself.

Pushing the empty luggage cart, the bodyguards left with a nod to Dom.

And suddenly they were alone.

Straightening her shoulders, she faced him with a smile. "You know what? I think I'll just go change."

She glanced down at her beautiful wedding dress. It would now be cleaned and pressed to be put on display in the part of the palace open to tourists.

"It seems a shame to take this off."

"It is pretty." He smiled. "You were a stunning bride."

Her spirits lifted. No matter how strong he was, he liked her. He'd always liked her. She could do this.

She walked back down the hall to the room she'd seen the guards take their bags and found herself in another sitting room. She shook her head. "These people must spend a fortune on furniture."

The tulle underskirt of her gown swishing, she turned to the right—the side of the suite her room was on in the palace—and headed to that bedroom. She opened the door on another sitting room, this one smaller, and walked into the bedroom, only to find it empty. She glanced in the walk-in closet, thinking they might have carried her bags the whole way in there, but that was empty, too.

She walked out of the bedroom, through the small sitting room, then the big sitting room and to the hall. "Dom?"

He ambled to the front of the hall where he could see her. "What?"

"My stuff's not in my room."

"It has to be. I saw the bodyguards carting it back."

"Well, it's not here."

He huffed out a sigh. "Let me see." He walked back along the hall and through the sitting room into the second bedroom of the master suite. Doing exactly as she had done, he frowned when he didn't see her bags in the bedroom, then checked the closet.

"That's weird."

"Yeah."

He slowly faced her. "They might have put your things in my room."

"Oh?"

"Don't get weird notions. My instruction was for your things to be put in your room." He went into the master bedroom.

On impulse, she followed him. Nothing ever really went as planned with the two of them, so maybe the thing to do would be let things happen.

His room didn't have a sitting room. The big double doors opened onto an enormous bed. Beige walls with a simple beige-and-white spread on the bed gave the room a soothing, peaceful feel. But Dom didn't even pause.

"No luggage here," he said, finding the bedroom empty. He turned to the walk-in closet. He opened the grand double doors and sighed. "And there's everything."

"They think we're sleeping together."

"I told them we're not."

"You actually told them?"

"I told them this marriage is a show for the heir."

"Oh."

"Don't be embarrassed. I'm the one who should be embarrassed. This is my mess we're cleaning up."

"Oh, yeah. Every woman loves it broadcast that her new husband doesn't want her."

"It wasn't broadcast. A few key servants know the secret. It's why we're on the yacht, not at the villa. There are many servants here, and they rotate. None of them is going to see us enough to put it all together."

Suddenly weary, she decided this was not a seduction night. It was a total bust. How on earth could she seduce a guy who had told his servants his marriage was a sham? She turned to leave but stopped and faced him again.

"You know how we did that thing with the cuff links?"

He cautiously said, "Yes."

"Well, there are a hundred buttons on the back of this dress, most of which I can't reach. Can I get some help?"

His relieved "Sure" did nothing to help her flagging spirit. If anything, it made her feel even worse.

Just wanting to get this over with so she could race out of his room, go to her room and be appropriately miserable, she presented her back to him.

His fingers bumped against the first button. She felt it slide through the loop. When it took a second for him to reach for the next button, she realized her hair was in the way and she scooped it to the side, totally revealing the long row of buttons to him.

"That's a lot of buttons."

Holding her hair to the side, she said, "Exactly why I need help."

He quickly undid three or four buttons, then she felt his fingers stall again.

"Getting tired, Your Majesty?"

"No. I'm fine."

But his voice was pinched, strained.

Another two buttons popped through the loops.

"You're not wearing a bra."

"Didn't want the straps to show through the lace."

He said, "Ump."

Another two buttons popped. Then two more. But when his fingers stalled again, she felt them skim along her skin. Not a lot, just a quick brush as if he couldn't resist temptation.

When he got to the last buttons, the three just above her butt, his hands slowed. When the last button popped, she almost turned around, but something told her to be still. His fingers trailed up her spine until he reached the place where he could lay his hands on the sides of her waist. He grazed them along the indent to her hips, then back up again. When they reached her rib cage, they kept going, under her dress to her naked breasts.

Her breath caught. She wanted to tell him she was his. That she'd been his from the moment she laid eyes on him. But she knew this wasn't as easy a decision for him as it was for her.

"You are temptation."

She turned, letting the top of her dress fall as she did so. "I don't intend to be."

"Liar."

She shrugged. "Maybe a little." She raised her gaze to his. "But would it be so, so terrible to pretend you like me?"

He shook his head, as he lowered it to kiss her. Their mouths met tentatively, then she rose to her tiptoes and pressed her lips against his strongly, surely.

She might not get forever. But she wanted this two years enough that she was willing to reach out and take it.

He cupped his hand on the back of her head and dipped her down far enough that her dress slithered around her hips. When he brought her back up again, the dress fell to the floor.

"No panties, either?"

She stood before him totally naked. No lies. No pretense. When she whispered, "It was actually a very heavy dress." He laughed.

Another woman might have worried, but Ginny

smiled. Part of what he liked about her was her ability to make him laugh. She wasn't surprised when he slid his arms around her back and knees, and carried her to the bed.

CHAPTER NINE

GINNY AWAKENED THE next morning with Dom's arms wrapped around her waist. She squeezed her eyes shut, enjoying the sensation, then told herself she had to get her priorities in line before he woke up.

They hadn't talked the night before. They'd had an amazing time, but they hadn't spoken one word. She hadn't been expecting words of love, but she knew making this marriage real hadn't been what he wanted. Though she hadn't actually seduced him, which had been her plan, he could still be upset that he hadn't been able to resist the temptation of their chemistry.

She opened her eyes to find him staring down at her. "Hey."

"Hey." He searched her eyes. "I hope you know what you're doing."

And pragmatic Dom was back.

So she smiled at him and stretched up to give him a kiss. "I do."

"I'm serious about not wanting this to last and about us not getting emotionally involved with each other."

"I hate to tell you, but I'm pretty sure raising a child together will more than get us emotionally involved."

"I'm not talking about being friendly. I'm talking about being ridiculously dependent."

Even as he spoke, he rose from the bed. With the fluidity and ease of a man comfortable with who he was, he stretched and reached for a robe.

She sat up, almost sorry he was covering all those wonderful muscles when he secured the belt around his waist.

He picked up the phone and, without dialing, said, "Bacon, eggs, bagels, croissants, and the usual fruit and juices."

He hung up the phone and walked into the bathroom.

Ginny stared after him. The man really was accustomed to getting everything he wanted. But constantly seeing the evidence of it was a good reminder that he wasn't going to be persuaded to do anything, be anything, other than what he wanted.

He came out of the bathroom, took off the robe and to her surprise climbed back into bed. He leaned against the headboard and reached down to catch her shoulders and bring her up beside him.

Bending to kiss her, he said, "We have about ten minutes before breakfast gets here. Any thoughts on what we should do?" The sexy, suggestive tone of his voice told her exactly what he wanted to do.

She laughed. "I think I need to eat and get my strength back."

He sobered suddenly. "You know, we rarely talk about your pregnancy. Are you okay? Really?"

"Millions of women have babies every day. I'm not special or in danger because I'm pregnant."

"You're pregnant with an heir to a throne." He looked away, then glanced down at her again. "And even if he wasn't heir to the throne, he's *my* baby."

He said it with such a proprietary air that her heart stuttered and she realized something unexpected. "So, like me, if we hadn't accidentally gotten pregnant, you wouldn't have had a child, either."

"No. A baby was part of the deal with the princess of Grennady. But this is different."

"I know." She ran her hand along her tummy, which was no longer flat. Though only slightly swollen, after a little over three months, it was beginning to show signs of cradling a child. "Do you think we're going to be good parents?"

"I don't know about you but I'm going to be an excellent father."

She laughed. "Conceited much?"

"I am going to be a good father," he insisted indignantly. "I know every mistake my father made with me and my brother—especially my brother—and I won't do those things." He shifted against the headboard. "What about you?"

"My mother was aces as a mom." She laughed. "Still is. My dad left a lot to be desired."

"So you're not going to drink?"

She shrugged. "I sometimes think it's smarter to demonstrate responsible behavior than to avoid something tricky like alcohol."

"Whew. For a while there I thought you were going to tell me I was going to have to give up drinking until our kid was in college or something."

Thinking of all the times she'd seen him come to the apartment and head directly to the bar, she turned slightly so she could look him in the eye. "It wouldn't hurt you to cut down. Maybe not drink in the afternoon."

"My job is stressful."

"Scotch isn't going to take that away."

"But it makes me feel better."

She peeked up at him again. "Really?"

He shrugged. "Some days. Others not so much. Those days it's better to keep a clear head."

"You deal with some real idiots?"

"Most of the people in our parliament come from old oil money. They care about two things. Keeping their families wealthy and keeping our waterways safe so that they can keep their families wealthy."

She laughed. "You're making fun, but it makes sense."

"Right after my mother died there was a problem with pirates."

"Pirates!" For that, she sat up and gave him her full attention. "I love pirates!"

He gave her a patient look. "These pirates aren't fun like Jack Sparrow. They're ruthless. Cutthroat. There was a particularly nasty band all but making it impossible for tankers to get through without paying a 'fee' for safe passage. The papers exploded with criticism of my dad for not taking a firm hand. Parliament called for his resignation. And he sat in his quarters, staring at pictures of my mom, having all his meals brought up, not changing out of sweats."

"Holy cow." Entranced now, she shimmied around to sit cross-legged on the bed so she could look directly at him as he spoke. "What happened?"

"On the last second of what seemed to be the last day before he would have been required to face down parliament, my dad sent the military to destroy the pirate ships. It was a war that lasted about forty-five minutes. He bombed the boats until there was nothing left but smoke and an oil slick."

"Wow."

"Then he sent the military to the country that was

aiding and abetting, and just about blew them off the map."

Two raps sounded on the door. Dominic pulled away. "That would be breakfast. You wait here."

"You're bringing me breakfast in bed?"

He tilted his head. "It looks like I am."

She saw it then. Not just his total confusion over his feelings for her, but the reason for it. He'd said before that his dad had made a mistake that he did not intend to repeat. This was it. Except she couldn't tell if the mistake was grieving his dead wife or being in love with his wife so much that he'd grieved her.

Dominic returned, rolling a cart covered with a white linen tablecloth into the room. He pulled a bed tray from beneath the cart and said, "I'm about to put bacon and eggs on this tray, so get yourself where you want to be sitting."

Still cross-legged in the middle of the bed, she patted a spot in front of her. "I like to be able to look at you when we talk."

"So you're going to want me to take off the robe while we eat?"

She pointed to herself. "I'm not dressed."

"You're certainly not dressed to receive company. But I like you that way."

The warmth of his feelings for her sent a shudder of happiness through her. He put the tray on the bed in front of her, lifted a lid from a plate of food and set that on the tray.

He motioned to the cart. "There's a variety of juices, pastries, toasts, fruit. What else would you like?"

"Just a bottle of water."

One of his eyebrows rose. "No fruit?"

"Oh, so suddenly you're not so unhappy with me eating fruit."

"I wasn't unhappy that you were eating fruit the day you fainted. I was unhappy that you seemed to be eating only fruit. You and the baby need a balanced diet."

Her spirits lifted again. She liked talking about the baby as a baby, not the next heir to Xaviera's throne. She patted her tummy. "I know exactly what to eat."

Though Dom took three calls after they ate and while Ginny showered, he couldn't shake the glorious feeling that he really didn't have to do anything for two whole weeks.

When she came out of the bathroom, dressed in a pretty sundress, he caught her shoulders and kissed her deeply before he pulled away and said, "I love the dress, but why don't you slip into a bikini and we'll sit on the deck and get some sun?"

She smiled cautiously. "Okay."

Unexpected fear skittered through him. "What's wrong?"

"Honestly, I have no idea what we're supposed to be doing."

"We can do anything we want, which is why I suggested sitting on the deck, getting some sun. I haven't had a vacation in a long time and just sitting in the sun for a few hours sounds really nice."

She bounced to her tiptoes and brushed a quick kiss across his mouth. "Bring a book."

He laughed. "I'm not *that* unaccustomed to taking a break."

"Good." She turned to go back into the bathroom/ dressing room, closet area.

Needing to get dressed himself, he followed her.

She stopped in front of a rack of clothes—her clothes—that now hung there. She frowned. "Did you unpack for me while I showered?"

"No. Servants must have done it. There's an entrance in the other side of the closet. Obviously, they came in, did what needed to be done and left."

She turned slightly and smiled at him. "So your privacy isn't really privacy at all."

"I have minions scurrying everywhere."

He meant it as a joke, but his comment caused her head to tilt. That assessing look came to her face again, but he took it as her trying to adjust to everything.

He was glad for that. Two years was a long time, and she'd need to be acclimated to everything around them—around him—in order to be casual in public.

Honesty compelled him to say, "You really won't get much in the way of privacy."

She smiled. "Do you think a guidance counselor in a school with two thousand kids ever gets privacy?"

He laughed. "At home." He winced. "At least I hope no one bothered you at home."

"It was never a bother to have someone contact me at home. If one of my kids thought enough to call me or come by, it was usually because they were so happy about something they wanted to share." She raised her gaze to meet his. "Or they were in trouble. And if they were, I wanted to help."

"That sounds a heck of a lot like my job. But multiply your two thousand by a thousand."

She nodded. "That's a lot of people."

He said, "All of them depending on me," then watched as she absorbed that.

"That's good for me to know."

"And understand. These people depend on me. I will not let them down."

As easy as breathing, she slid out of the sunny yellow dress and, naked, lifted a bikini out of one of the drawers.

He'd seen her naked, of course; they'd spent the night making love and the morning talking on his bed. What was odd was the strange sense of normalcy that rippled around him. He'd never pictured himself and the princess of Grennady sharing a dressing room. Even if they made love, she'd be dressing in the suite across from his, if only because she was as pampered as he was. Her wardrobe for a two-week cruise wouldn't have been four suitcases. It would have been closer to ten.

But Ginny was simple. Happy. And so was he. Not with sex. Not with the fact that living as a man and wife for real would make the ruse that much easier. He was happy with the little things. Breakfast in bed. The ability to be honest. Dressing together for a morning that would be spent reading fiction.

It was the very fact that these things were so foreign to him that grounded him to the reality that he shouldn't get used to them. In two years all this would be gone.

For the first time, he understood why Ginny had campaigned to make this marriage real. They'd never, ever have this again. He'd be a divorced prince, eventually king, who'd take mistresses while he ran a country and raised a son. And she'd be the king's ex-wife, mother of the heir to the throne.

"You know it's really going to be hard for you to get dates after we divorce."

She turned with a laugh. "Excuse me?"

"Nothing." He walked back to the section of the

dressing room that held his clothes and pulled out a pair of swimming trunks. He couldn't believe he'd thought of that. What she chose to do when they separated was her business. But he knew it might be a good thing for *her* to start thinking about that. Not just to remind her that this wasn't going to last but to get her realizing the next stage of her life wouldn't be easy.

They spent a fun, private two weeks on the yacht, with Dom called away only three or four times for phone calls from members of parliament. Otherwise, he'd been casual, restful and sexy.

When the royal helicopter touched down on the palace grounds, Dom and Ginny were greeted by the whir of cameras and a barrage of questions from reporters who stood behind the black iron fence surrounding the property.

Stepping out of the helicopter, helped by Dom, who took her hand to guide her to the steps, she smiled at the press.

"You look great! Very suntanned!"

She waved at them. "Don't worry. I used sunblock."

The reporters laughed.

Dom said, "We had a great time."

Ginny watched the reporters go slack jawed as if totally gob smacked by his answer. Then she realized they weren't accustomed to him talking to them outside of the press room or parliament.

As they walked to the palace behind bodyguards dressed casually in jeans and black T-shirts—with leather holsters and guns exposed—she turned to him. "That was kind of you to talk to them, Your Majesty."

He sniffed. "I'm rested enough that I threw them a bone."

She laughed. "You should rest more often."

They reached the palace. A bodyguard opened the door and they stepped into the cool air-conditioned space.

She took a long breath of the stale air. "I miss the ocean."

He dropped a quick kiss on her lips. "The yacht is at your disposal anytime you want."

"Are you trying to get rid of me?"

"No." He stopped walking and caught her hand. He kissed the knuckles. "No."

When their gazes met, she knew he thought the same thing he did. Two years would be over soon enough. But she couldn't be happy, be herself, make this relationship work, if it was permanent. And neither could he.

They'd been granted a very short window of time to be happy, but two years of perfection was a lot more than some people got.

So she raised herself to her tiptoes, kissed his cheek and said, "Go visit your dad. Get the rundown on what happened while we were away and I'll be waiting for you for supper tonight."

CHAPTER TEN

THEY SETTLED INTO a comfortable routine that was so easy, Dominic forgot this was supposed to be difficult. Dressing for the royal family's annual end-of-summer gala, he held out his arms to Ginny as naturally as breathing and she locked his cuff links.

"I heard your mother made it in this afternoon."

Ginny glanced up at him, then shook her head. "She didn't want to miss too much class time, so she only took two days off. Your father sent the jet and she got here about an hour ago. She almost got here too late to dress because she keeps forgetting that we're seven hours ahead of her."

He grunted. "She'll get used to it."

Her tummy peeped out a bit when her dress flattened against it as she turned to walk away. He caught her hand and spun her to face him again, his hand falling to the slight swelling. "What's this?"

She laughed. "I thought the flowing dress would hide the fact that I'm starting to show."

Emotion swelled in his chest, but he held it back, more afraid of it than he cared to admit. "You shouldn't hide it. Everybody's waiting to see it."

She groaned. "Everybody's waiting to see me get

fat? Thanks for the reminder that I'll be getting fat in front of the world."

He grabbed his jacket and motioned her out of their bedroom. "That's one way of looking at it. The other is to realize that since everybody's so eager to see you gain weight, you now have full permission to eat."

She stopped and pivoted to face him. "Oh, my gosh! I never thought of it that way. For the next five months I can eat on camera."

"Subjects will love seeing you eat on camera."

She rubbed her hands together with glee. "Bring on the steaks."

He opened the apartment door and led her into the echoing foyer. "Should I tell them to give you two from now on?"

She inclined her head. "Might not want to start big. I should work my way up to the second steak."

They entered the elevator. As it descended she slid her arm through his. The door opened and they made their way to his father's quarters, where her mother was holding court. He thought it odd for the real royal, his dad, to be letting Ginny's mom monopolize the conversation. Still, he walked into a room to the sound of his brother laughing and his dad trying to hide a laugh.

"Mother, please tell me you're not telling off-color jokes."

Rose gasped at the sound of her daughter's voice. When she turned and saw the same thing Dom had seen that evening—the slight evidence of a baby bump— her eyes misted. She raced over and put her hands on Ginny's tummy.

"Oh, my gosh."

As she had with him, Ginny groaned. "Great. Just great. Everybody's going to notice."

"Subjects are eagerly waiting for this," Dom's father said, sounding happier than Dom had ever heard him.

"That's what I told her." He nodded to the bartender to get him a Scotch but stopped midnod and shook his head. He didn't need a drink. Didn't want a drink. Not out of respect for her sensitivity because of her dad's alcoholism. But out of a sense of unity. This child was both of theirs, but technically she was doing all the work, all the sacrificing. He walked to the bar, got two orange juices in beautiful crystal and handed one to Ginny.

Alex laughed. "You're drinking orange juice?"

He glanced at his brother's double Scotch. "Maybe I'd like to have a clear head in case we go to war?"

"Bah. War!" The king batted a hand. "That miserable old sheikh who's been threatening had better watch his mouth."

Ginny spun to face him. "A sheikh's been threatening?"

"Rattling his saber." Dom took a sip of his orange juice.

She stepped back, tugging on his sleeve for him to join her out of the conversation circle. "Is that what the orange juice is about?"

He looked at the glass, then at her and decided to come clean. "No, as my dad said, the sheikh is just being an idiot. I realize you're doing all the heavy lifting with this pregnancy. I thought I'd show a little unity, if only in spirit."

"Oh." She kissed his cheek. "Now, there's something you should tell the press."

"Are you kidding?"

"No. If they like baby bumps, they'll love hearing that you're sacrificing your Scotch."

"This sacrifice isn't permanent. It's only for tonight."

"Still, it's charming."

"Oh, please. It took me decades to lose the Prince Charming title. I'd rather not go there again." He pointed at his brother. "Alex lives with it now."

"Still…" She sucked in a breath and caught his gaze. "Thank you."

He displayed the glass. "It's a little thing. Not much really." Yet he could see it meant a lot to her, and knowing that gave him a funny feeling inside. Add that to his ability to see her baby bump every time she shifted or moved and he couldn't seem to take his eyes off her.

His father led them to the ballroom, where they entered to a trumpet blast. After an hour in a receiving line, he noticed Ginny looked a little tired and was glad when they walked to the dais. His father made a toast. As minister of finance, he gave a longer toast.

The press was escorted out as dinner was served and, relieved, Dom sat back. Watching Ginny dig into her pork chops with raspberry sauce served with mashed potatoes and julienned steamed carrots, he laughed.

"You're going to be finished before I get three bites into mine."

"Everyone said pregnancy would make me hungry all the time. They should have said ravenous."

He chuckled.

She eyed his dish. "You got a bigger serving than I did."

"Wanna switch plates?"

She sighed. "No."

"Seriously. I'll save some. If you're still hungry you can have it."

"I'm gonna get big as a house."

"In front of the whole world," he agreed good-naturedly. But when she was done eating, he slid a piece of his pork to her plate. "I don't want you to faint from hunger while we're dancing."

But as he said the words, he got a funny sensation. A prickling that tiptoed up his spine to the roots of his hair. He glanced to the left and right, not sure what he was looking for. He saw only dinner servers in white jackets and gloves. People milling about the formal dining room.

Calling himself crazy, he went back to the entertainment that was watching his wife eat and didn't think of the prickling until he and Ginny were on the dance floor an hour later. With everyone's attention on his father and Ginny's mother, who were doing their own version of a samba, he felt comfortable enough to enjoy holding Ginny, dancing with her. He'd spun her around twice, then dipped her enough to make her laugh, and there it was again. A tingling that raced up his back and settled in his neck.

Still, he didn't mention it to Ginny. They danced and mingled with the dignitaries invited to their annual gala, including the sheikh currently giving them trouble.

She curtsied graciously when introduced. "I was hoping you could settle your differences tonight."

The sheikh's gaze bounced to Dominic's. Dominic only shrugged. She hadn't really said anything *too* bad.

The sheikh caught Ginny's hand and kissed it. "We don't talk business at the gala."

She bowed apologetically. "I'm so sorry. But since I was hoping that settling this agreement might get me two weeks on the yacht with my husband I guess I didn't see it as business."

The sheikh laughed. "I like a woman who doesn't mind asking for what she wants."

Ginny smiled. Dominic took the cue and said, "Perhaps we could meet first thing Monday morning."

"If your father's schedule is free."

"I'm sure it will be for you."

An hour later, seeing that Ginny was tired, Dominic excused himself to his father who—along with Ginny's mother—thought it was a good idea for her to leave.

He took her hand and led her down a few halls to their elevator. When they were securely behind the door of their apartment, he tugged on her hand and brought her to him for a long happy kiss.

"You do realize you just accomplished what diplomacy hasn't been able to get done in three weeks."

"Does this mean I get my three weeks on the yacht?"

"I thought it was two."

"I want three."

"You're getting greedy."

She curtsied. "I just like my time with you, Your Majesty. And your undivided attention."

He scooped her off her feet and carried her to their bedroom. "I'm about to give you all the undivided attention you can handle."

The next morning Ginny awakened as she had every day since their marriage, wrapped in his arms. At six, Dom rolled out of bed and used the bathroom. He slid into a robe and, from seeing his daily routine, Ginny knew he'd gone to their everyday dining room. Sliding into a pretty pink robe, Ginny followed him.

"Not sleepy this morning?"

Rather than take her chair, she slid to his lap. "I feel extraordinarily good."

"So maybe we should do what we did last night every night."

"Maybe we should."

The sound of the servant's door being opened brought Ginny to her feet. As she walked to her side of the table, a young girl wheeled in a cart containing his breakfast of bacon and eggs, plus bowls of fruit, carafes of fruit juices, and plates of pastries and breads.

She smiled at Ginny expectantly. Knowing she was waiting for her breakfast order, Ginny said, "I'll just eat what we have here."

Dom glanced over. "No bacon? No eggs?"

"Wait until you see now many bagels I eat."

He laughed as the serving girl left.

As always, their meal was accompanied by fourteen newspapers. She grabbed *USA TODAY* as he took London's the *Times.* Their table grew quiet until Dom flipped a page and suddenly said, "What?"

Busy putting cream cheese on a bagel, Ginny didn't even look over. "What's the *what* for?"

He slammed the paper to the table and reached for the house phone behind him. "Sally, get up here."

Ginny set down her bagel. "What's going on?"

He shoved the paper across the table. She glanced down and saw a picture of her and Dom with their heads together as their dinners were served, a picture of her and Dom dancing, a picture of Dom leading her out the back door of the ballroom. All beneath the headline: The Affectionate Prince.

"At least they didn't call you Prince Charming."

He glared at her.

"Dom, I'm sorry. Your picture gets in the paper almost every day here in Xaviera. I'm missing the significance of this."

"First, no press is allowed in that ballroom once dinner starts. So one of our employees got these pictures."

As the ramifications of that sank in, she said, "Oh."

"Second, look at that headline."

"'The Affectionate Prince'?" She caught his gaze. "When you want to be, you are affectionate."

"No ruler wants to be thought of as weak."

"Weak? It's not weak to love someone." Instantly realizing her mistake in saying the *L* word, Ginny shot her gaze to his. For a few seconds they just stared at each other, then he bounced from his seat, almost sending it across the room.

"This was exactly what I didn't want to happen!"

Ginny said, "What?" not quite sure if the unexpected anger coursing through her made her bold or if she was just plain tired of skirting the truth. "Are you mad that your happiness shows? Or are you really that surprised or that angry that we fell in love?"

"I can't love you."

"Oh, really? Because I think you already do."

There. She'd said it.

Their gazes met again, but this time his softened. He took his seat again. "Ginny. I can't love you."

Since she'd already made her position clear, she said nothing, only held his gaze.

"My dad loved my mother."

"Oh, damn him for his cruelty."

"Don't make fun. When my mother got sick, my dad slipped away, let our country flounder because he was searching the globe for someone, *something* that could save his wife."

"And you think that was weakness?"

"Call it what you want. Weakness. Distraction. Whatever."

"How about normal human behavior?"

"Or a lack of planning."

"You think your dad should have had a contingency plan in case his wife got sick?"

"I think he let pirates get a foothold because he put my mother first."

"Oh, Dominic, of course he put his sick wife first."

He shook his head as if he couldn't believe what she'd just said. "A king cannot put anyone ahead of his country. At the first sign of those pirates he should have involved the military."

"Even though his wife, the woman he obviously adored, was dying? How could he have avoided scrambling to save her?"

His gaze rose until it met hers. "By not falling in love in the first place."

Something fluttered oddly in her stomach. The conversation was making her sick and sad and scared. But the feeling went away as quickly as it came. "I see."

"The stakes of this game, my life, are very high, Ginny. We don't govern or rule our people as much as we protect them. I can't afford a slip, a lapse." He combed his fingers through his hair. "When I'm king I won't get two private weeks on a yacht. I'll get vacations that include video conferencing and daily briefings. I'll get two hours, at most, in the sun. A twenty-minute swim." He sucked in a breath. "And this is why I warned you. Even if I wanted to love you. Even if I fell head over heels for you…coming in second to a country isn't like being second to a hobby. You would get very little of my time. It wouldn't be worth loving me."

Stunned, Ginny watched him toss his napkin to the table. "Where is Sally?"

Then he stormed out of the dining room because he didn't have anything to give her.

And that was the truth he'd been trying to tell her all along.

CHAPTER ELEVEN

GINNY SAT STARING at her bagel when there was a knock on the apartment door. She expected it to be Sally, so when her mom walked into the dining room and said, "I thought we were going to swim this morning," Ginny dropped her bagel to a plate.

"I'm not much in the mood."

Her mom took a seat, grabbed a Danish pastry and popped a bite into her mouth. "First fight?"

"You know this isn't a real relationship."

"Oh, sweetie, of course it is. Get any man and woman involved in a plot or plan of any type and what results is a relationship."

"Yeah, well. It's short-term."

"Why is this bothering you suddenly?" Her eyes narrowed. "You want to change the rules."

Ginny rose from her seat. "I'm in my robe. I need to get some clothes on. Sally's supposed to be coming up."

"Dom was on his way out when he let me in."

"He must have called Sally and told her he would come down to her." She headed toward the bedroom. "I need to get dressed anyway."

She wasn't surprised when her mom followed her out of the dining room and into Dom's bedroom.

Seeing the entire bed was happily rumpled, she faced Ginny. "Well, this is a change of plans."

"You don't really think we were going to be married and not sleep together, Mom." She put her hand on her stomach and the strange flutter happened again.

"Honey, I knew you'd be sleeping together. I just didn't think you realized it would happen." She walked over. "What's up with your tummy? You're not sick, are you?"

"I don't know. I don't think so. But every couple of minutes this morning I've been getting this strange flutter in my stomach."

"Oh, my gosh! The baby's moving!"

"He is?"

"Or she is!" She plopped her palm on Ginny's stomach. "Let me feel." Her eyes filled with tears. "Oh, my gosh. Oh, Ginny. I'm going to be a grandma."

Ginny fell to the bed. "That fluttering is my baby?"

Rose sat beside her on the unmade bed. "Yep." She nudged Ginny's shoulder. "Mama."

She pressed her lips together. "Mama. I'm going to be somebody's mom."

Rose slid her hand across her shoulders. "Yes, you are. And whatever nonsense is going on between you and Dom, you have to straighten it out."

"There is nothing to straighten out. The deal is made. I leave two years after the baby's born."

Rose studied her face. "But you don't want to go now. You love him."

"And I think he loves me, too, but he doesn't want to."

"Oh, what man willingly falls in love?"

Ginny laughed.

Rose said, "Give him time."

"Time won't heal the fact that he thinks love makes a ruler weak."

"Really?"

"You know his mom died, right?"

Rose winced. "Kind of hard not to see that Ronaldo's wife isn't around."

"She was apparently sick for years with cancer." Ginny sighed. "He tried everything to save her and in that time the country fell apart."

"So?"

"So, parliament called for his resignation. Had he not snapped out of it he would have lost his crown."

"Oh."

Ginny rose from the bed and paced to the dresser. "I never realized how difficult their job was."

Her mom leaned back, balancing herself with her hands behind her. "How so?"

"Their location forces them into a position of needing to protect the waterways. While Dom's dad was scrambling to save his wife, pirates began attacking ships, demanding money to pass."

"That's not good."

"The press crucified the king. Parliament called for removal of his crown."

"So you said." She sat up. "But I still don't get how this means he can't have a wife."

"He doesn't want to be weak."

"You know the marriages I've seen that work the best are the ones where a husband and wife form a team."

"If you're suggesting that I should help him rule, you are out of your mind. Not only would he *never* let that happen, but I can't rule. I could make a suggestion or two, but I couldn't rule."

Rose batted a hand. "You're good with people,

sweetie, but not that good." She stood up and walked over to Ginny. "You love this guy."

Ginny didn't even try to deny it.

"So how in the hell could you possibly be willing to let him live this demanding, difficult life alone?"

Ginny blinked.

"You're looking at this from your side of the street, but what about his? Ronaldo told me that his wife was the treasure he came home to at night. That when the world was rocky, her silliness was his salvation. She was beautiful, elegant and could charm the birds out of the trees. But he didn't care about any of that. He liked that she played gin rummy with him until the sun came up on nights he couldn't sleep. He liked that he could talk about anything with her, knowing she'd never abuse the power of his confidences and that no one would ever know she'd heard things that were supposed to be secret."

Rose took a breath and patted Ginny's shoulder. "Do you really think Dom will live much past sixty if he doesn't have a friend, a buddy, a confidante, a lover who's willing to be whatever he wants without making demands?"

"No."

"And can you see the lonely life he'll have unless you try to work this out?"

She sucked in a breath. "Yes."

"Ginny, you always believed that being a guidance counselor was a calling. But what if this is your calling? Not just being Dom's true partner, but also raising your child so that he or she isn't buried under the stress of ruling?"

"Maybe I have been looking at this selfishly."

"Not selfishly, but ill informed. Now that you know

how difficult all this is, you've got to do whatever you can to make Dom's life easier."

Dom and Sally easily found the serving boy who had taken the pictures, but that didn't change the fact that the damage was done. Dom looked at photos of himself on the dais, on the dance floor and leading Ginny to the rear entrance to return to their apartment, and even he saw it—the weakness. The ease with which he stepped out of his role as leader and into the role of what? A smitten lover?

He could not have that. He would not be his dad. If anything, now was the time to prove that he was stronger than his father.

He didn't have lunch with Ginny, didn't return to the apartment until after eight that night. When he opened the door and entered the sitting room, he found her on the sofa, reading a magazine. Dressed in a soft red robe with a floral nightgown beneath it, she rose when she saw him.

"Did you catch the creep who took those pictures?"

He headed for the bar. "Yes."

"Want to talk about it?"

"No."

She returned to her seat. "Okay."

Silence descended on the room. He looked at the Scotch with disgust, remembering the orange juice he'd been drinking for "unity." What was wrong with him that he'd been such a schmuck? All he'd been doing since their honeymoon was giving her the wrong idea.

He set the glass on the bar and didn't even tell her he was going to get his shower. He let the water sluice over him, reminding himself that he was a ruler, royalty, someone set aside to do the noble task of keeping his people safe. He stood in the shower until he began to feel like his old self.

He put on a pair of pajamas and crawled into bed with the latest popular thriller. He might not be a television guy or a movie buff, but he liked a good story, a good book. He read until ten when his eyelids grew heavy. He set the book on the bedside table at the same time that Ginny entered the room.

He wanted to suggest that she go back to her old room, but couldn't quite bring himself to be that mean. Eventually she'd grow weary of him ignoring her and she'd come to the decision on her own.

Soundlessly, she slipped out of her red robe, exposing the pretty flowered nightie. His gaze fell to her stomach, which peeped out every time she moved in such a way that the gown flattened against it. She said nothing. Just crawled into bed.

But she rolled over to him. She put her head on his shoulder and her hand on his stomach.

He resisted the urge to lower his arm and cuddle her to him. This was, after all, part of how he'd get her to see the truth of their situation and go back to her own room. But when her breathing grew even and soft and he knew she was asleep, he let his arm fall enough that he could support her.

Then he laid his hand on her stomach.

He closed his eyes, savoring the sensations of holding her, and fell asleep telling himself that it wouldn't hurt to hold her every once in a while.

Dom's life became a series of long days and empty meals. With Ginny's mom deciding to retire to help Ginny care for the baby, he didn't have to worry if she had company or if she was being cared for or entertained. In fact, the way she slept in in the morning and had lunches and most dinners with her mom made him feel they were establishing a great system for being together without being together.

The thing of it was, though, she was in his bed every night. She never said a word. Didn't try to seduce him. She just rolled against him, put her head on his shoulder and her hand on his chest and fell asleep.

He didn't resist it. Not because he took comfort from the small gesture, but because she was pregnant with his child, and he was hurting her. It almost seemed that this little ritual was her way of easing away from him. And if this was what she needed to do to get through the next months, he would let her have it.

But one night, she rolled against him and something bounced against his side. He peered down. The stomach beneath her thin yellow nightgown looked much bigger when she was on her side.

The bounce hit him again. He stiffened but she laughed.

"That's your baby."

He sprang up. "What?"

"Your baby." She took his hand and set it on her stomach. "He's moving."

The rounded stomach beneath his hand rippled. His jaw dropped. He smoothed his fingers along the silken nightie.

She sat up. "Here." She wiggled out of the nightie and tossed it. Sitting naked in the dark with him, she took both his hands and positioned them on either side of her belly.

The baby moved. A soft shift that almost felt like a wave.

He laughed, but his throat closed. "Oh, my God."

She whispered, "I know."

The desire to take her into his arms overwhelmed him and he pulled her close, squeezing his eyes shut. "Thank you."

She leaned back so she could catch his gaze. "For showing you the best way to feel the baby or for actually having the baby?"

Her eyes warmed with humor. The tension that had seized his back and shoulders for the past six weeks eased and he laughed. "It's a big deal to have a baby."

"Millions of women do it every day."

He sobered. "But not under such ridiculous conditions."

She took his hand, pressed it to her stomach again. "The conditions aren't that bad."

"You're not going to have a life."

She shrugged. "I know. I already figured out it'll take some hellaciously special guy to ask out a woman who's divorced from a king and mother to a child who's about to become king." She met his gaze. "Very few guys will want to get on the bad side of a man who can answer the question 'you and what army?'"

With the baby wiggling under his fingers, he said, "I'm so sorry."

She waited until he looked at her again, then she whispered, "I'm not."

"Then you haven't fully absorbed the ramifications of this mess yet."

"First, I don't think it's a mess. I told you. I didn't think I'd ever become a mom. This baby is a great gift to me." She shrugged. "So I have to give up dating permanently?" She put her hands on top of his. "This is worth it."

"It is."

He didn't mean to say the words out loud. He now hated doing *anything* that gave her false hope. But she smiled and lay down.

"I'm sorry. Are you tired? Do you want to go to sleep?"

"Sleep?" She laughed and pointed at her stomach, which still rippled with movement. "You think I'm going to sleep with the Blue Man Group rolling around?"

He laughed, too, and settled on his pillow again. "Have you thought of names?"

"I pretty much figured your country would name her."

He sat up again and looked down into her eyes. "The country?"

She shrugged. "Parliament." She shrugged again. "Maybe your dad. Maybe tradition."

"Tradition plays a role but essentially we get to name the baby."

Her eyes lit. "Really? So if I want to call her Regina Rose, I can?"

He winced. "Sure."

"You don't like Regina?"

"I'd rather she just be Rose. It's a good solid name."

"It is." She paused a second before she said, "And if it's a boy?"

"I've always been fond of James Tiberius Kirk."

"*Star Trek!* You'd name our baby after someone in *Star Trek*?"

"Not just any old someone. The captain. Plus Tiberius is an honorable name." He met her gaze. "So is James."

"I might not mind it if we dropped the Kirk."

"I think that goes without saying."

He lay down again. She snuggled into his side.

"You know the sheikh still asks about you."

She laughed.

"He wanted to know if you got your three weeks on the yacht."

"Did you tell him I didn't?"

"No."

"Did you explain that we had a fight?"

He sat up again. "This isn't a fight. It's the way things have to be."

She said, "Yes, Your Majesty." Not smartly. No hint of sarcasm and he knew she understood.

It should have made him feel better. It didn't.

He lay back down again. "Have you thought about what you're going to do in two years?" He couldn't bring himself to say *after we divorce*. He knew that would hurt her too much.

"I'm still debating something Sally said about using my notoriety to bring attention to my causes."

"Education?"

He felt her nod.

"You know, you can still live in the palace."

"I know."

That would be hard for her, but having just felt his baby move for the first time, strange emotions coursed through him. He couldn't imagine Ginny gone. Couldn't quite figure out how two people raised a child when they lived in separate houses. He'd been so cool about this in the beginning. So detached. But now that he'd felt his child, was getting to know Ginny, he saw all those decisions that were made so glibly had sad, lonely consequences.

"I just think it would be easier if I lived on the other side of the island. I'd be close, but not too close."

He swallowed, grateful she wasn't taking his baby

halfway around the world. Still, an empty, hollow feeling sat in his stomach. "Makes sense."

She said, "Yeah," but he heard the wobble in her voice. She fell asleep a few minutes later, but Dom stayed awake most of the night. Sometimes angry with himself for hurting her. Other times angry with life. An ordinary man would take her and run with the life they could have together.

But he was a king—or would be someday. He didn't get those choices.

CHAPTER TWELVE

THE FIRST DAY of every month, Dom and Ginny made a public appearance that always included questions from the press. With her eight-months-pregnant stomach protruding, Ginny struggled to find something that wouldn't make her look like a house while Dom attended to some matters in his office.

She finally settled on straight-leg trousers and a loose-fitting blue sweater—knowing it would make her eye color pop and hopefully get everybody's attention on the baby. After stepping into flat sandals, she walked into the living room just as there was a knock at the door. Her mom entered without her having to answer the door.

"You're not glowing today."

"Nope. Why didn't anybody tell me that pregnant women didn't get any sleep when they got close to their due date?"

"Nobody wants to scare women off," her mother said with a laugh as she entered the sitting room. She bent and kissed Ginny's forehead, then sat beside her on the sofa.

"Dom not coming around?"

"Nope. And I'm out of tricks. We talked baby names. I've shown him how to feel the baby move. We eat breakfast and dinner together every day, and nothing. I'm out of ideas, short of seduction." She pointed at her stomach. "And we both know seduction would be a little awkward now."

"I'm so sorry, sweetie."

"It's fine. But I've gotta run. I get to play loving princess now, while he ignores me."

They left through the front of the palace so long-range lenses could pick up photos of Dom opening the door for Ginny.

Every inch of Dom now hated the charade he'd created. It was working, but it was also a strain on Ginny. When she was just a normal woman, a one-night stand, he didn't see the strain as being as much of a big deal, though he knew it was a sacrifice.

But now that he could see the effects of her sacrifice, her swollen stomach, the sadness that came to her eyes every time she realized how empty, how hollow their relationship was, it burned through him like a guilty verdict pronounced by the gods. She had been the sweetest woman in the world, and in spite of the way he was using her, she was still sweet, still genuine, still helping him.

If he didn't go to hell for this, it would be a miracle. Because he certainly believed he deserved the highest punishment.

She slid into the limo and blew her breath out in a long, labored sigh.

His gaze darted to hers. "Are you okay?"

She placed her hands on her basketball stomach. "I'm not accustomed to carrying twenty-five extra pounds." She laughed good-naturedly. "Sometimes I get winded."

The funny part of it was she didn't look bad. Wearing slim slacks that tapered to the top of her ankle and a loose blue sweater that didn't hide her baby bump but didn't hug it, either, she just looked pregnant. Her arms hadn't gained. Her legs hadn't gained. She simply had a belly.

A belly that held his child.

"If the trip is too much, we can go back to the palace."

"Only to have to reschedule it for tomorrow?" She shook her head. "Let's just get this over with."

The guilt pressed down again. He glanced at her feet, pretty in her pink-toned sandals. Her whimsy in the choice of color made him smile.

"You have an interesting fashion sense."

She gaped at him. "I have a wonderful fashion sense, Mr. White-Shirt-and-Tie-Everywhere-You-Go. You need to read *Vogue* every once in a while."

The very thought made him laugh.

Her head tilted as she smiled at him. "It's been a long time since I heard you laugh."

"Yeah, well, our saber-rattling sheikh is back and he isn't the country's only problem. It's hard for me to laugh when I have business to attend to."

Her pretty blue eyes sought his in the back of the limo. "Is it really that difficult?"

He turned his head to the right and then the left to loosen the tension. "Yes and no." Oddly, he felt better. He could twist his neck a million times, sitting in the halls of parliament, and nothing. But two feet away from her and the tension began to ebb.

"Ruling is mostly about paying attention. Not just to who wants what but also to negotiating styles and nonverbal cues. There are parliamentarians who get quiet right before they walk out of a session and spill their guts to the press. There are others who explode in session." He caught her gaze again. "I'd rather deal with them."

She smiled and nodded, and the conversation died. But when he helped her out of the limo at Marco's seaside coffee shop, she was all smiles.

A reporter shouted, "Coming back to the scene of the crime?"

She laughed. "If fainting was a crime, tons of pregnant women would be in jail." She smiled prettily as she slid on the sunglasses that made her look like a rock star. "Just hungry for a cookie."

With his bodyguards clearing a path, they made their way into the coffee shop. Standing behind the counter, Marco beamed with pleasure.

He bowed. "It is an honor that you love my cookies."

She laughed. "The pleasure is all mine. Not only do I want a cookie and a glass of milk for now, but I'm taking a half-dozen cookies back to the palace."

Marco scurried to get her order. Dominic frowned. "Don't you want to hear what I want?"

"Hazelnut coffee," Marco said, clearly disinterested in Dominic as he carefully placed cookies in a box for Ginny. Antonella brought Dominic's coffee to the counter.

He pulled a card out to pay, but Marco stopped him with a gasp. "It is my honor to serve our princess today."

Dominic said, "Right."

Because Ginny didn't faint this time, Dom could actually lead her out to the long deck that became a dock. He set her milk on the table in front of her, along with her single cookie. He handed the box of six cookies to a bodyguard.

Ginny said, "There better be six cookies in that box when we get back to the palace."

Dominic's typically staid and stoic bodyguard laughed.

After a sip of coffee, he said, "They love you, you know?"

She unwrapped her big sugar cookie as if it were a treasure. "Everybody loves me. But there's a reason for that. It's not magic. I'm a child of an alcoholic. I *know* everybody has something difficult in their life so I treat everyone well."

"I treat everyone well."

She lifted her cookie. "Yeah. Sort of."

"Sort of? I never yell at anyone. And if I reprimand, it's with kindness."

"You're still a prince."

"Dominic?"

Dom glanced up to see his boarding school friend, Pietro Fonichelli. The son of an Italian billionaire and a billionaire several times over in his own right, thanks to his computer software skills, Pietro was probably better known around the globe than Dominic was. He was also on Dominic's list of friends, the people his bodyguards were told to allow access to him.

Dominic rose. "What are you doing here?"

As he said the words, Dom noticed Pietro wore shorts and a big T-shirt.

"Vacationing." He faced Ginny. "And this is your lovely bride."

It was the first time Dominic was uncomfortable with the ruse. Engaging in a charade to help his subjects enjoy the birth of the country's next heir? That was a good thing. Fooling someone he considered a friend? It didn't sit well. Pietro had been at the wedding, but there had been so many people that at the time it hadn't registered that he was tricking a friend.

He politely said, "Yes, this is Ginny Jones."

Pietro laughed. "Ginny Jones? Is she so American that she didn't take your last name?"

Ginny rose, extending her hand to Pietro. "No. Dom sometimes forgets we're married."

Laughing, Pietro took the hand she extended. Instead of shaking it, he kissed the knuckles.

Something hot and fuzzy whipped through Dom. The custom in Xaviera was that a man had a choice. A handshake or a kiss. He should not be upset that his friend chose a kiss. It was nothing more than a sign of affection for the wife of a friend.

Holding Dom's wife's gaze, Pietro said, "I'm not entirely sure how a man forgets he's married to such a beautiful woman."

Ginny smiled as if she thought Pietro's words were baloney, but Dom had never seen his friend so smitten before. Just as Dom had been tongue-tied and eager the day he'd met Ginny, Pietro all but drooled.

Ginny said, "Dom's a great husband."

"Yeah, well, if he ever isn't—" he let go of Ginny's hand and pulled out a business card "—this card has my direct line on it."

Ginny laughed, but Dom said, "What? Are you flirting with my wife?"

"Teasing," Pietro said. He pulled Dom into a bear hug, released him and said, "It was great to run into you." He glanced at Ginny, then back at Dom. "We should do dinner sometime."

The air came back to Dom's lungs and he felt incredibly stupid. He knew Pietro was a jokester. He knew his friend loved getting a rise out of Dom. It was part of what made them click. They could joke. Tease. "Yes. We should."

With his coffee gone and Ginny's cookie demolished, they walked back to the limo, one bodyguard conspicuously holding a box of a half-dozen brightly painted sugar cookies.

He helped Ginny into the limo, then sat beside her, realizing Pietro was the kind of man who wouldn't care if her ex was a king. He would pursue Ginny. With the money to buy and sell loyalty, her connection to a king would mean nothing to him. Once Ginny was free of Dom, it wouldn't even cross Pietro's mind to care that she'd been his wife. He'd pursue her.

His nerves endings stood on edge like the fur of a hissing cat. *Not out of jealousy*, he told himself. Out of fear for her. Pietro might be a great friend, but he wouldn't be a good husband. Like Dom, he took what he wanted. Discarded it when he was done.

His nerves popped, and he suddenly knew another consequence of this fake relationship. In two years, he was going to have to watch his wife with another man.

That night in bed, the tension that vibrated from Dom rolled through Ginny. She considered shifting away, going to her own side of the bed, but she couldn't. Her baby would be born in thirty-two days, give or take a week for the unpredictability of first babies, and in two short years she would be gone. She wouldn't give up one second of her time with him. Even if it meant she wouldn't sleep tonight because the muscles of Dom's arm beneath her head had stiffened to concrete.

Finally, unable to take the tension anymore, she said, "What's wrong?"

"Nothing."

"Right." Knowing they weren't going to get any sleep anyway, she ran her fingers along the thick dark hair on his chest and said, "So I'll bet it was nice seeing your friend today."

He laughed. "Yeah. Nice."

"You know he was only teasing."

"Yes. He's a jokester and if he'd do something stupid at a bar, the press would love it and it could take the heat off of us."

"I don't mind the heat."

He didn't say anything for a second, then his arm tightened around her shoulders. "I know you don't."

"So we don't need for your friend to get punched out at a bar."

"Especially since I would like to have dinner with him. Actually, he's somebody I'd like to have in the baby's life. He started off wealthy, could have bummed around the world forever on his dad's money, but he knew the importance of being strong, being smart. I might just make him the baby's godfather so he's here for more than the big events."

She nodded but tears came to her eyes as an awful scenario ran through her brain. In two years, she and Dom would be divorced, but Dom and the baby's lives would go on—without her. She would come and go for those big events in the baby's life. She'd even be a part of things, but not really. After her two years were up, she'd be an outsider looking in.

"Are you crying?"

Dom's soft voice trickled down to her.

She swallowed. "It's just a pregnancy thing."

He sat up slightly and shifted her to her pillow so he could look down at her. "Is there anything I can do?"

You could love me, she thought and wished with

all her heart she could say the words. But she'd seduced this guy twice. She'd agreed to his plan to have their child born amid celebration. She was good to his family, good to his employees, good to the press and his subjects. She didn't spend a lot of money, but she did spend enough that she looked like the princess he wanted her to be.

And what did she get for her troubles? The knowledge that in two years she'd be nothing to him.

She sniffed.

Dominic's eyes widened with horror. "Please. Silent tears are one thing. Actually crying will make us both nuts."

"Really? I'm fat. I'm hungry. I'm *always* hungry. I'm always *on.* I've been good to you, good to your family, good to your subjects and you can't love me."

He squeezed his eyes shut. "It isn't that I can't love you."

"Oh, it's just that you *don't want to love me.* That makes it so much better."

He popped his eyes open. "It isn't that, either."

"Then explain this to me because I'm tired but can't sleep. And I'm hungry even though I eat all the time. And I just feel so freaking alone."

"We could call your friends."

"I want my husband."

"The Affectionate Prince."

"I don't give a flying fig what the press calls you. This is our baby. Half yours. You should be here when I need you."

"I am here when you need me."

"Yeah. Right. You're here physically, but emotionally you're a million miles away."

"I rule a country."

She shook her head. "Your dad rules the country. You work for him. Technically you're just the minister of finance."

"I need to be prepared for when I take over."

"Really? Your dad is around fifty-five. He's nowhere near retirement age. You and I could have three kids and a great life before your dad retires."

He laughed. "Seriously?" But she could tell from his tone of voice that the thought wasn't an unpleasant one.

She sat up. Holding his gaze, she said, "Would it be so wrong to ease off for the next ten years?"

He shook his head with a laugh. "First you wanted two years…now you want ten?"

"Yes." A sense of destiny filled her. The this-is-your-moment tug on her heart. There was something different in his voice. He wasn't hard, inflexible, as he usually was. In some ways, his eyes looked as tired as hers.

Could he be tired of fighting?

"I'm asking for ten years, Your Majesty, if your dad retires at sixty-five."

Dom frowned.

She plowed on, so determined that her heart beat like a hummingbird's wings. "What if he works until he's seventy? What if he's like Queen Elizabeth, keeping the throne until he's ninety? We could have a long, happy life."

Dom shook his head. "My dad won't rule until he's ninety." He caught her gaze. "But he could—will—rule another ten years."

"Doesn't ten years even tempt you?"

"You tempt me."

"So keep me. See if we can't figure this whole thing out together? See if we can't learn to have a family—be a family—in ten years."

* * *

It sounded like such a good plan when his heart beat slow and heavy in his chest from the ache of knowing he was about to lose her. He lowered his head and kissed her. Her arms came up to wrap around his shoulders and everything suddenly made sense in Dominic's world.

The buzz of the phone on his bedside table interrupted his thoughts. He didn't want to stop kissing Ginny. Didn't want this moment filled with possibilities to end. So he let the phone go, knowing it would switch to voice mail after five rings, only to have it immediately start ringing again.

The call of duty was stronger than his simple human needs. He pulled away from Ginny with a sigh, but didn't release her. Stretching, he retrieved the receiver for the phone and said, "Yes?"

"One of our ports has been taken by the sheikh. We are at war."

CHAPTER THIRTEEN

DOMINIC DIDN'T JUMP out of bed; he flew. "I don't know how much of this is going to hit the press or how soon, but the sheikh has taken one of our ports. He's telling people we're too weak to protect our waterways, so he's taking over. Which means that port is the first step to all-out war."

Ginny sucked in a breath. On top of all the other odd things she was feeling tonight, having her husband go to war made her chest hurt. She grabbed his arm as he turned to find clothes and get dressed.

"Where will you be? You don't actually have to lead troops into battle, do you?"

"No. There's a war room. My father and I will direct the military from there." He pursed his lips for a second as if debating, then sat on the edge of the bed. "I'll be fine. It's our military who will suffer casualties. Because we don't want to attack our own facility, we have to try diplomacy first. Worst-case scenario happens if he tries to move farther inland or take another port. Then there will be battles, casualties." He caught her gaze. "And then you might not see me until it's over."

She nodded, but the tears were back. No matter how strange or odd she felt, she didn't want to stop him from doing his duty. In fact, there was a part of her that was proud of him.

She leaned forward and kissed him. "Go stop that guy."

He nodded, dressed and raced out of the room.

Ginny lay in bed, breathing hard. Her stomach felt like a rock. Everything around her seemed out of control. So she did some of the breathing she'd been taught in the childbirth classes Sally had arranged for her. Even though Dom was supposed to be in the delivery room, he hadn't attended the classes. But since most of it was about breathing and remaining calm, he really hadn't needed to. Nobody could remain calm and detached the way Dom could.

She breathed again, in and out, and her stomach relaxed. Knowing she wouldn't sleep, she got out of bed and grabbed her book. Sitting on the sofa—with all her lights on because she was just a little afraid, and stupid as it sounded, the light made her feel better—she read until three o'clock in the morning. Her stomach tensed often enough that a horrible realization sliced through her. Still, with weeks until her due date, she didn't want to think she was in labor. So she let herself believe these contractions would pass.

But at seven, she couldn't lie to herself anymore. She picked up the house phone and dialed her mom's extension. "I think I'm in labor."

"Oh, no! Ginny, sweetie...this is too early."

Her stomach contracted again and she doubled over with pain. "All right. I no longer *think* I'm in labor. I know I am."

"Did they tell you what to do?"

"I have to call the doctor, but—" She doubled over again. "Oh, my God, this hurts."

"That'd be labor. Okay. I'm coming over. I'll call Sally who will tell Dom."

"He's in the war room. We're at war."

Her mom was quiet for a few seconds, then she said, "Didn't know if you'd been told, but, yes. I saw the news this morning. We're at war."

"I don't even know if Dom can come out for this."

"Oh, dear Lord, of course, he can. You just go get some clothes on so security can get you to the hospital. I will take care of calling Sally who will get Dom to the hospital."

Ginny did as she was told. The week before she'd been advised by her birthing coach to pack a bag for the hospital "just in case." So after sliding into maternity jeans and a sweater, she lugged the bag from Dom's room to the sitting area.

Then pain roared through her stomach and she fell to the sofa. She tried to breathe, but the fear that gripped her kept her from being able to focus. Her new country was at war and she was in labor. Four weeks too early. She didn't even want to contemplate that her baby might not be ready, but how could she not?

When she was almost at the point of hyperventilation, her door swung open and her mom raced in. "I talked to Sally, who said she will talk to the king. She said not to worry. She'll take care of everything."

She rose from the sofa, the pain so intense, tears speared her eyes again. "Good."

The doors opened again and Dom's top security team ran in.

"Ma'am? Can you walk?"

She caught her mother's hand. "Oh, jeez. Now I'm ma'am."

Her mother led her to the door. "That's right, sweetie. Keep your sense of humor."

Her labor lasted twelve long hours. Every twenty minutes she asked where Dom was. Every twenty-one minutes her mother would say, "He's been told you're in labor. He'll be here any minute."

She gave birth to a healthy, albeit tiny, baby boy. The happy, smiling doctor, a man who'd clearly gotten sufficient sleep the night before, joyfully said, "Can you tell me his name?"

She blinked tiredly. "For the birth certificate?"

He laughed. "No, just because I'm curious."

She swallowed. "We didn't really pick a name yet." But she remembered James Tiberius Kirk. There were some times Dom could be so much fun, so loving, that she *knew* this war had to be god-awful to keep him away from his son's birth.

The doctor placed her little boy, her little king, in her arms, and the tears that fell this time were happy tears. "Look at him, Mom." But she wished she was saying that to Dom. She should be saying, "Look at your son."

But they were at war. And he was needed.

Still, the sting of giving birth to their child alone caused tears to prick her eyelids.

"He's beautiful." Her mom kissed her cheek. "But you're tired."

"Have you heard from Sally?"

"Not a peep."

"Okay."

The doctor walked to the head of her bed. "The nurses need to take your son to be cleaned up and examined. You can have him back in an hour or so."

"You're taking him?" She hadn't been told this protocol, but it just didn't seem right to hand over the future king to people who were essentially strangers.

The doctor laughed and pointed outside the delivery room doors where her security detail stood guard. "Don't worry. He's already been assigned security. He might be leaving your sight but he won't be leaving the royal family's sight."

Her mom took the future king from her arms. "Why don't you go to sleep, honey?"

She said, "Okay," and felt herself drifting off as her mom handed her little boy to the doctor.

When she woke forty minutes later, she took off the ugly hospital gown they'd insisted she give birth in, and with her mom's help put on a pretty nightgown. She prayed Xaviera's war didn't last long, and also knew that when he could Dom would slip out and see his son. She wanted him to see she'd done okay. That she was fine. She was being the stiff-upper-lip princess she needed to be in this difficult time.

Nurses brought her baby back almost exactly an hour after he'd been taken away. The royal pediatrician came in and told her that her son was in good health, but he was small, so a few precautions would be taken.

The pediatrician returned the next morning and gave her the same report. She squeezed her hands together nervously. With her mom there, security outside her door and very attentive nurses, she shouldn't feel alone, but she did. They wouldn't let her see a newspaper so she knew whatever was going on had to be terrible.

She wondered how safe the war room was—how safe the palace was? The sheikh had barrels of money, and money bought weapons and soldiers. She knew very little about Xaviera's army and worried that Dom would have to bomb his own ports.

The next day she noticed security outside her room had been doubled. That's when it dawned on her that she hadn't seen any press. When she got out of bed and looked out her window, the world looked calm. Peaceful. Knowing that everybody in the kingdom was waiting for this baby, it seemed odd that the press wasn't climbing the walls, trying to get pictures.

She asked her mom about it when she arrived for a visit and her mom said the baby's birth hadn't been announced.

She gave Ginny a weak smile. "If anyone knew he'd already been born, he would be a target. The king told Sally he believes it's for the best that this news not yet hit the press."

She swallowed, but her fears mounted. "So things are bad?"

"Actually, things aren't bad at all. The way I understand it, the whole mess involves one port and some hostages. Which is why Sally thinks the king believes it's so important that we protect the baby. He would be the kind of leverage the sheikh needs to get himself out of this mess."

"So it's a standoff?"

"According to Sally, it's hours of drinking coffee and waiting."

Incredulous, Ginny gaped at her mom. "They're waiting, but Dom hasn't been able to get away to see me...to see *his son*?"

"Honey, I wasn't supposed to tell you any of this, but I could tell you were worried and it's not right for you to worry."

She fell back on her bed. "No. It's better for me to feel like a complete idiot."

Her mom fluffed her pillow. "You're not an idiot. Anybody would have worried."

"That's not the part that makes me feel like an idiot. I've been sitting here for three days, waiting for my husband, who apparently doesn't care to show up."

"He's dedicated."

"So is the king, but he's talked to Sally, who's gotten messages to you."

"Have you checked your cell phone? Maybe he's tried to call?"

She gasped. "I never thought to take it. I was in so much pain I just left the apartment."

Her mom pulled out her phone. "I'll call security and have someone bring it over."

That brightened her spirits for about an hour. But when the cell phone arrived and there were no calls, they sank like a rock.

"How could he not care?"

Rose busily, nervously, tucked the covers around her. "I'm sure he cares."

"No, Mom. He doesn't." And it took something this extreme to finally, finally get that through Ginny's head. Her husband did not love her. He probably didn't really love their child. He most certainly wasn't curious about their child, who had been born early and who could have had complications.

But a war came first—

Didn't it?

Not when the war wasn't really a war. When there were stretches of time and waiting. When her husband wasn't even king yet. When there was a king who should be doing the decision making but he had time to call one of his staff—not even a family member.

She got out of bed. "Help me pack my bag."

"Ginny, you can't go home yet! You just had a baby."

"My friend, Ellen, had a difficult birth and was home in forty-eight hours."

"But the baby—"

"Is fine. You heard the pediatrician this morning. He's gained the two ounces he needed to put him over five pounds." She grabbed her suitcase and tossed it to the bed. "If he'd been full-term he probably would have weighed eight pounds."

Her mom put her hand over Ginny's to stop her from opening her suitcase. "You cannot leave."

"The hell I can't. And let them try to stop me from taking my own child." She motioned around the room. "As long as I take the thirty bodyguards, I'm fine."

Rose grabbed her cell phone and hit a speed-dial number.

Ginny snatched her phone out of her mother's hands and disconnected it. "What are you doing? Tattling on me to Sally?"

"Ginny, you can't just leave."

"Mom, this isn't about Xaviera or my baby someday being a king. This is about me knowing that if I don't get out of this country with my baby, I'm going to be stuck here forever with a guy who doesn't love me and a king who thinks he's God." She tossed her mom's cell phone to the bed and took her hands. "I have a baby to protect. I'll be damned if my child will grow up to be a man so stuck to his duties that he can't even see his own babies born or love his wife."

She took a long breath and stared at her suitcase. "To hell with this junk! I didn't want these clothes in the first place."

She poked her head out the door and motioned for the two bodyguards to come inside. "I want a helicopter on the roof of this hospital in five minutes. Then I want flown to the nearest safe airport and one of the royal jets waiting for me there." She sucked in a breath. "I'm going home."

The buzz of the king's cell phone had all heads in the war room turning in his direction. Cell phones had been banned. Too many opportunities for picture taking, voice recordings and just plain dissemination of their plans. In fact, no one but the king had left these quarters.

They slept on cots in a barracks-like room, ate food that was made in the attached kitchen and hadn't had contact with the outside world except through the video feed they stared at.

He missed Ginny. More to the point, he *worried* about Ginny. Something had been wrong the night they came here and he just wanted to fix it. But he knew he couldn't, so maybe it was better that he spend three days cut off from her so he didn't make promises he couldn't keep.

His father walked over to where Dom sat in front of a computer, staring at the feed of the port, feed that hadn't changed in twenty-four hours.

His father sat. "What do you think they're doing?"

"Undoubtedly, trying to figure out how to distance themselves from the sheikh since he seems to have deserted them."

"Should we give them a chance to surrender?"

He caught his father's gaze. There was a look in his eye that told Dom this was a test. A real-life hostage crisis for sure, but a chance for his father to test him.

"I'd say we offer them generously reduced prison

terms for surrender and testimony against the sheikh, and go after the sheikh with both barrels."

"You want to kill him?"

"I'd rather arrest him and try him for this. I think making him look like a common criminal rather than a leader who'd started a war he couldn't finish sends a stronger message to the world."

His dad laughed unexpectedly. "I agree." He bowed, shocking Dominic. "Now what are you going to use to negotiate terms?"

He pointed at his father's cell phone. "This might be appropriate. Except I think we should get hostage negotiators from our police to do that. Once again making it look more like a criminal act that a military one."

"Agree again."

Dom called Xaviera's police commissioner and within the hour the rebels had surrendered, all hostages safe. The sheikh was in hiding, but he was too accustomed to luxury to stay underground for long. Dominic had every confidence they would find him, and when they did, he would stand trial.

The fifty military and security personnel in the war room cheered for joy when they received the call that all rebels were safely in jail.

But Dominic didn't want to stay around for the party. He might not be able to love Ginny, but she was pregnant with his child and not feeling well. He needed to get back to her.

He tapped his dad's shoulder. "I'm going to get going."

"Tired?"

"And I need a shower but I need to see Ginny."

As Dom turned to walk away, his dad stopped him. "Dom, there are a few things you need to know."

Expecting more details or facts about their problem, he faced his dad again.

"Ginny has gone home."

"What? Of course, she's home. She's in the apartment."

"No. She's gone back to Texas." He shrugged. "Some women can't handle war. She got a helicopter to take her to a safe airport this morning and took a jet back to her old hometown."

He gaped at his dad. "She's never mentioned wanting to leave before. She was committed—"

"Like I said, some women can't handle war. We've never been at war when she was with us."

"This is absurd. This was hardly a war. It was an ill-conceived attempt to take over our country by a guy who we clearly gave too much credit to."

"She didn't know that."

"How could she not know that! It's been all over the papers!"

"We weren't letting her see the papers."

"What! Why?"

"Because she had the baby the first day we were in here."

This time, Dom fell to a chair in disbelief. Absolutely positive he had not heard right, he looked up at his dad. *"She had the baby?"*

"Yes."

His kept his voice deceptively calm as he said, "And you didn't think to tell me."

"Duty comes before family."

Anger coursed through him. "But I notice you had your phone."

"I did."

"You talked to staff."

"Quite often. I had to keep track of the baby. Because he was born too soon, he was small. They monitored him. I made decisions."

The anger in Dom's blood went from blue to white hot. *"You made decisions."*

"You were at war. And duty comes before family."

Dominic bounced from his chair and punched his father in the mouth so hard the king flew into the wall behind him.

Fifty military men and ten bodyguards drew their weapons.

His dad burst out laughing. He waved his hands at the military and bodyguards. "Stand down."

But nobody dropped his weapon.

Not giving a damn about the sixty-plus guns trained on him Domini roared, "You think this is funny!"

"No. I think it's about time."

He grabbed his father's collar and yanked him off the floor.

"Dominic, you're the one who's always said duty comes before family."

"So you kept my baby from me!"

"I was showing you that what you were doing with your life was wrong. What you thought you wanted didn't work." He calmly held Dom's gaze even as Dom tightened his hold on his collar. "I'd tried hundreds of things over the years to get you to see that you couldn't live the life you all planned out. I thought Ginny would break you. When she couldn't and the sheikh took our port and then Ginny went into labor, I saw a golden opportunity."

Dominic cursed and squeezed his eyes shut.

"I loved my wife, your mother. And I was neglect- ful of my duties but I never dropped them the way you were so sure I had. All those months, we were in private negotiations, trying to avoid a confrontation with the pirates, trying to keep from going to war. Because of your mother's death, they did get a few extra weeks. But in the end, I didn't attack until I knew it was the right thing to do. Loving somebody didn't make me weak. Your mother's love made me strong. And you're a fool if you think can do this alone."

"So you took my baby from me, made Ginny go through labor and childbirth alone."

"For years I'd been talking to you and for years you've ignored me, treating me like somebody who only deserved respect because I had a title. I had to do something drastic or know you would ruin your life."

He released his dad as if he were poison he didn't want to touch.

"Maybe the lesson I learned, Father—*Your Majesty*—is that I no longer want to be connected to you."

His dad very calmly said, "Go after, Ginny. Bring the baby home."

"And then what? Let you torture him the way you tortured me and Alex?"

"When you see the lesson in this, you're going to apologize. Not just for hitting me but for not trusting me."

Dom sincerely doubted it.

CHAPTER FOURTEEN

GINNY'S CONDO HAD long ago been sold. And because her mom had decided to move to Xaviera for the two years Ginny would live there, her mom's house had also been sold. But the new owners hadn't taken possession yet, so that was the sanctuary Ginny targeted. Unfortunately, when her bodyguard unlocked the front door, they found two women and a man, packing her living room lamps.

"Excuse me, this house has sold."

Ginny patted her baby's back. "I know. It was my mom's. It doesn't close for a few weeks. Until then I can use it."

"Your mom hired us to sell the furniture."

"Well, I'm sure by next week I'll have my own house and you can do that. Until then, the house is mine."

The tall woman looked ready to argue, but when she looked at Ginny with her twelve bodyguards and very tiny baby, she sighed.

"Fine." Disgruntled, the two women and one angry man headed for the back door, clipboards in hand.

Ginny turned to Artemus, the leader of her detail. "I don't even know if there's food in the house."

"I have credit cards. I'm authorized to get you anything you want."

"Really? I ran away with the next heir to the throne and they're feeding me?"

"Yes, ma'am."

She glanced around at the small house that wouldn't sleep herself and twelve bodyguards. Plus, she didn't have a crib. And she was beginning to feel bad about taking the baby from Xaviera before Dom even saw him.

Worse, she missed Dom.

She wondered if her rash decision hadn't been caused by postpartum depression, but reminded herself that her husband hadn't wanted to see his child. He'd never loved her, didn't want to. And he planned on bringing their child up to be just like him. She couldn't let that happen.

Still, that didn't mean this was going to be easy.

"This is a mess."

Artemus agreed. "Yes, ma'am."

Just as her mother said, she hadn't really thought this through. But she had to forget about everything except setting up a household. She'd worry about Dom, what she would say to him, how she'd keep her baby safe from his ridiculous rule, when she had the house set up with beds and food.

"I guess I should feed the baby and get on the phone to find a crib."

Artemus nodded. "And I'll send two guys out for groceries."

She took the baby into her mother's small bedroom, breast-fed him and then made a bed for him out of a drawer from her mother's dresser. With the baby secure, she went online and ordered a crib to be express delivered the next day, along with linens, baby clothes, diapers and some sweatpants and T-shirts for herself. Then she started exploring the real estate sites, looking for a house. The baby woke up twice and she fed him once, changed him the other time. Artemus came in and offered her food, but she refused it. She couldn't eat until she got at least something in her life settled.

Dom showered on his father's private jet. Taking the plane had been another way he'd vented his anger, but though he was bone tired he couldn't sleep in the luxurious bed.

Even after a few hours for his dad's duplicity to sink in, Dom still wanted to punch him. He couldn't believe his father had treated Ginny so cruelly, but unexpectedly realized *he'd* been treating Ginny cruelly all along.

And what would he have done while she was in labor? Coached her? Helped her? Or held himself back because he didn't want to give her false hope? He'd have ruined that moment for Ginny every bit as much as his father had ruined it. Maybe more because she'd see him there, but feel the distance between them, the tangible reminder that he didn't want her in his life.

Which was a lie.

He did want her in his life. The feeling of fury that thundered through him when he realized what his father had done hadn't just shocked him. It had been so pure, so total that Dominic hadn't had a chance to mitigate it. In that moment of blazing-hot anger that resulted from white-hot pain, he knew what it was like to miss out on something so important he couldn't even describe it.

His father was right. Dom never would have felt this if his dad hadn't orchestrated it. He'd have covered, hidden, pretended, postured—whatever it took to fool himself into believing he was fine.

But faced with the raw truth of having those moments snatched away from him—he felt it all. The pain. The loss.

And he knew that pain, that loss, that horrible empty feeling truly was the result of the life he'd built.

He also knew that if he wanted Ginny back, all he had to say was that his bastard father had kept him from seeing the baby's birth, from being with her, and he'd be free in her eyes. She loved him. She'd believe him. She'd take him back with open arms.

He fell to the corner of the big, big bed in the outrageous jet that he could use because he would someday be a king.

The only problem was his dad was right. Even if he'd known his baby was being born, he wouldn't have rushed to Ginny's side. He might have seen the final few minutes of the baby's birth. But even then he would have raced back to the war room.

But what his father had done hadn't just opened his eyes. It had changed him. And he didn't want Ginny to take him back on something that wasn't quite a lie, but was a way to get out of being honest.

He had to be honest with her. He wouldn't even hint that she should come home—that he intended to love her—if he didn't know for sure he wouldn't hurt her again.

And that he couldn't promise.

After hours of combing through real estate sites, Ginny heard Artemus enter her room again. Staring at the computer screen, she said, "How big of a house should I get? I mean, should there be rooms for all of you or does the crown pay for separate quarters for you?"

"We pay for separate quarters."

Hearing Dom's voice, she spun around on her seat.

His chin and cheeks bore dark shadows, evidence that he hadn't shaved in days. His eyes looked pale and hollow from lack of sleep—even though he'd just had a ten-hour flight, which was perfect for catching up on sleep. But the killer was that he wore jeans and a T-shirt.

The desire to tease him almost outweighed the desire to jump into his arms and weep. Except this was the man who didn't love her. Who hadn't thought enough of her to come out of a bunker when apparently he could have. Who hadn't been with her for the birth of their child.

This was also the man she'd have to fight for their child. If he thought he'd just fought a war, he was in for a rude awakening because she was about to show him what real war was.

"Get out."

He peered beyond her to the bed, where their son lay in the bottom drawer of her mom's dresser. "Is that my son?"

His voice was soft, reverent.

She tensed her face to stop the muscles from weakening or tears from forming in her eyes. She would not be weak in this fight. Her child would not grow up afraid to love.

Still, they might ultimately get into a battle over this child, but Dom also had a right to see his son.

"Yes. That's our baby."

He caught her gaze. "You didn't name him."

"I didn't think James Tiberius Kirk was your final answer."

He laughed. She didn't.

He took a few steps closer to the bed. "Oh, my God. He's so little."

She had to fight the tremor of emotion that ripped through her at the awe in his voice.

"You would know that if you'd been there for his birth."

He took another step toward the bed. "My father didn't tell me you were in labor."

That sucked the air out of her lungs. "What?"

He paused and faced her, preparing to answer her, but her heart ached for him. His ridiculously pompous dad had kept his baby from him? She saw the anguish on his face. Knew there might be bigger reasons he hadn't shaved, hadn't slept and suddenly wore blue jeans and a T-shirt.

She rose from her chair, took the baby out of the drawer and watched his little face scrunch as he woke. "Hey, little guy, here's your daddy."

She presented the child to Dom and he stared at him. "Wow."

"Yeah, wow." She smiled. "Hold him."

"He's just barely bigger than my hand." He caught her gaze. "Won't I break him?"

She laughed. "I'm going to trust you to be careful." She nudged the blanket-wrapped baby to him. "Put your one hand under his bum and the other under his head."

Dom did as he was told and took the baby. He bent and pressed a kiss to his forehead. Ginny stepped back, unable to handle the sweetness of the meeting anymore. Or Dom's confusion. He was so new to the baby business that it would have been fun to watch him learn and grow with the baby—their baby. But even though his dad had kept the news that she was in labor from him, he'd always said the kingdom would come first. And they'd just lived the reality of what that meant.

She deserved better than that. Her baby deserved better than that.

He caught her gaze. "My dad said something about complications."

"He was just small, so they monitored him."

"You know his birth hasn't even been announced."

"No. Not at first. Eventually my mom told me."

"It seems my dad was teaching me a lesson."

The pompous old windbag.

"I'd always said the kingdom came first. I'd said I'd never love anybody." He glanced over at her. "I said I wouldn't do what he did when my mom died. Apparently that insulted him. So when the war and you going into labor just sort of happened, he saw it as a chance to show me what my attitude really meant."

"Oh." So maybe the king wasn't so much pompous as interfering. Not good, but at least not god-awful. She wanted to ask Dom if he'd learned anything. But he looked so sad and so broken. And she didn't want to soften to him.

"I missed the birth of my son."

"If you'd known I was in labor, would you have come out of that bunker? In those first hours before you knew the threat wasn't as bad as you and your dad had believed…could you have come out?"

"I'd have pushed it." He unexpectedly hugged the baby to him. "I'd have given instructions for the hospital to let me know when you were close—"

"So you might have missed it anyway?"

"Maybe."

His honestly hit her like the swell of an ocean wave. The king might have kept the news from him, but he probably would have stayed away anyway. "Well, that certainly shines a light on that."

"That's why my dad's lesson was such a good one. I had to see what it felt like to have all my choices taken away from me. When I thought…knew…he was behind my not seeing the baby's birth, I felt the unfairness of it and ridiculous anger. But flying over on the plane, I realized what I just told you. That I might have pushed it back and put it off until I missed it by my own doing. I would have been disappointed but I would have made those crazy royalty excuses about duty, and I'd have forgiven myself. I had to experience it this way to feel the real loss."

He met her gaze again. "It gave me a totally new perspective."

Her heart jumped a bit. "So you're going to be a good dad?"

He laughed. "Yes."

And suddenly her war with him lost some of its oomph, too. Even as his changing attitude made her glad for their baby's sake, it also made her very sad. Very tired. Technically, she and Dom were back to where they were when they made this silly deal.

She said, "That's good," but her heart absolutely shattered. She'd have loved to have raised her baby with this Dom.

"Can you forgive me?"

"For missing the baby's birth? Since it means you're going to be a better dad? Yes." She tried to smile but just couldn't quite do it.

"What about for the other stuff?"

"Like…" The man had been sweet and kind. Attentive in a way that might not have been romantic, but he'd been good to her the whole time they were together. He'd always told her he didn't want to fall in love. She was the one who'd pushed. "…what?"

"You wanted me to love you."

Oh, great. Just what she wanted to talk about again. How he didn't love her.

"It's okay."

"Not for me. If you decided you don't want me to love you anymore, I'm in real trouble, because I realized flying over that ocean that I've probably always loved you."

Tears stung her eyes. "Really? Because I've told you that."

He chuckled. "I know you did. But just like the lesson my dad gave me, I sort of needed to lose you—lose everything—before I could realize what I had."

He laid the baby in the makeshift bed. "We're putting a future king in a dresser drawer."

She tried to laugh but a sob came out. He walked over and enfolded her in his arms. "I am so sorry."

She wanted to say, "That's okay," but she couldn't stop sobbing. She'd been alone for days, making decisions she didn't want to make, trying to get food in a house that was way too small. And she'd missed him. And felt betrayed. Alone.

He let her cry until her sobs became hiccups. Then he whispered, "Shouldn't you be in bed, too?"

"I'm fine."

"Right. Just like you were fine right before you fainted in front of poor Marco." He shifted the baby drawer to one side of the bed and pulled down the covers. "Come here."

She did. He helped her lie down, took off her shoes, pulled the covers to her chin and she fell into her first sound sleep in days.

When she woke, it was to the sounds of her son crying.

Dom lay beside her on the bed, watching her. "I think our son wants to be fed."

"Sounds like."

"We are going to have to name him sometime."

"I'm starting to think of him as Jimmy."

"He'll be King James…like in the Bible."

"Better than captain of the starship *Enterprise*."

She slid out of the bed, got James from his drawer, opened her shirt and began to nurse.

Some of the strain appeared to be gone from Dom's face. "You napped?"

He stretched and said, "A bit."

"Do we have to go home right away?"

His eyes leaped to hers. "You're coming with me?"

"We are raising a king together."

"Yes, we are."

"And your dad is nuts with his rules and his tests."

"I think he's going to let us alone with the tests."

"Yeah, wait until you see the dress I'm going to have made for his next formal dinner. He's not the only one who can push people's buttons. Except this time I owe him."

He laughed and for the first time in days, Ginny felt normal. She nudged her head, indicating he should join her and the baby. "Come watch."

"Really?"

"Sure. He's cute. It's fun to watch him eat like a little horse."

Dom scooted down the bed and looked at their baby suckling. He waited a few seconds, then his gaze rose to meet hers. "There is one thing we haven't sorted out."

She smiled. "What?"

"I love you."

She closed her eyes, savoring the words, then she laughed. "You already said that."

"Yes, but I wanted to say it by itself. You know…so you get the real meaning."

She laughed again. And the quiet, two-o'clock-in-the-morning world of Terra Mas, Texas, righted itself.

EPILOGUE

THE DAY GINNY and Dominic returned from Texas, the baby's birth was announced in the papers. It was reported that he'd been born in the time of crisis for the country, and to keep him safe, his birth had been concealed. Most of their subjects had agreed that keeping his birth a secret had made sense. Others yammered on and on about it on talk radio.

Ginny didn't care. Her life was perfect. She just wanted one more promise from her husband.

Rolling Jimmy into a tiny onesie, she said, "This is our last lie."

Dom pulled his sweater over his head before he said, "It isn't a lie. Technically, Jimmy *was* born in an insecure time for the country. Technically, my dad *had* been working to keep him safe. Technically, I *had been* too involved to leave to witness his birth."

"Now you're stretching things." She picked up the baby and he cooed with delight. "I think he likes these pj's."

Dominic put a quick kiss on her lips. "Or he likes his mom."

"He'd better. It'll take me decades to get my figure back."

"I like you a little rounded."

She sniffed. "Right."

Carrying the baby, she walked to the sitting room, Dom on her heels.

"Sally says it will look better if I hold the baby while we're standing on the balcony, waving."

"Drat. I was hoping to do a Princess Kate and strategically place the blanket so no one can see I still have a baby bump."

Diaper bag over his shoulder, Dom held the apartment door open for her. "You're paranoid."

"Isabelle doesn't think so," she said, referring to the nanny who had just been hired by Sally. "She perfectly understands wanting to look my best in public."

They entered the elevator. Dom pressed the button for the second floor. When the doors opened, the king and Ginny's mom stood waiting for them.

Rose said, "I get to hold him first."

The king nudged her aside. "You held him first yesterday."

Bodyguards silently, expressionlessly stood by doors, glanced out windows.

Rose sighed. "Fine."

Ronaldo said, "Maybe I should be the one to hold him on the balcony."

Dom and Ginny simultaneously said, "No!"

"I need him and a long blanket to cover my baby weight."

"And Sally says my holding Jimmy will go a long way toward repairing my image for not being around for the baby's birth."

The king laughed as he led the three adults to his quarters. "You're a war hero."

Dom blew out his breath disgustedly. "Some war hero."

"Hey, you made the choice to call in the local police rather than send in the military. Technically, that was the big decision of the conflict."

Jimmy squirmed and began to whimper. Rose immediately took him from Ronaldo's arms. "Come to your Grammy Pajammy, sweet boy," she crooned, patting his back.

Dom said, "Grammy Pajammy?"

His father sighed. "It's a long story."

Ginny rolled her eyes. "I called her Mama Pajama until I was about ten."

Dom laughed. "Really?" Then he frowned and glanced at his dad. "And how do you know this?"

The king slid his arm around Rose's shoulders. "I suppose this is as good of a time as any to come clean about our relationship."

Ginny laughed but Dom's mouth fell open. "What?"

Rose grinned. "Second chance at love, honey." She leaned over the baby to put a kiss on the king's cheek. "There's nothing like it."

Dom stood shell-shocked, and Ginny held her breath. She'd suspected a little something was going on with her mom and the king, but buried in their own problems, neither she nor Dom had actually seen it.

Finally, Dom's lips lifted into a smile. His simple heartfelt "Welcome to the family" warmed Ginny all over. So did the realization that her mom would be staying. Forever.

She had a family.

They walked through two sitting rooms and a den to get to the balcony. Ginny put a blanket over her arm in such a way it draped in front of her stomach, and Rose placed the baby in her arms.

But right before they would have stepped out onto the balcony, she stopped and smiled at Dom. "Here."

"You're letting me hold him?"

"He's yours as well as mine." She sighed. "Besides, the bigger I look today the easier it will be for people to notice I'm losing weight."

He laughed and stepped out onto the balcony, but he stopped, too.

He caught his dad's gaze. "You and Rose come with us."

His dad waved a hand. "No. No. You and Ginny and Jimmy are the stars here. Have your moment in the sun."

"I'd rather we looked like a family."

Rose said, "Mmm-hmm."

Ginny pressed a finger to her lips to keep her still-humming hormones from making her cry. They hadn't had a big discussion about the king keeping Ginny's labor from Dom. When they'd returned the day before, Dom had simply said, "You were right," and King Ronaldo had nodded. Dom wanting them to be a family spoke volumes.

The king said, "I think that would be nice."

They stepped out onto the balcony to present their son to the kingdom and in the last second, Alex came racing through the door. "I heard this is a family moment."

Dom said, "It is."

Alex straightened to his full height, grinning like an idiot.

Ginny leaned over to Dom and whispered, "What's up with him?"

"Our father and Princess Eva's father are having a phone call tomorrow to talk about the wedding. He's trying to get on Dad's good side, hoping he'll give him another year of freedom."

Ginny winced. "Do you think your dad will do it?"

Dom glanced at his father, who beamed at little Jimmy and laughed. "Nope. I think my dad likes being a grandfather." He cuddled Jimmy to him, then waved to the crowd below.

Ginny nestled against him. "We'll give him another one soon."

Dom glanced down at her. "Really?"

Ginny laughed and snuggled more tightly against him. "Sure, we'll have two kids, and then I'll get my figure back, and then it's Alex and Eva's turn."

Cameras whirred and flashed, but Ginny didn't care. For twenty-five years she'd longed for a family and she'd finally gotten one.

* * * * *

CROWNED FOR THE PRINCE'S HEIR

SHARON KENDRICK

With special thanks to a dear friend – the wildly talented and inspirational Stewart Parvin – who designs amazing clothes and wedding dresses for discerning royals and women everywhere!

CHAPTER ONE

THE NAME LOOMED up in front of him and on the back seat of the limousine, Luc's powerful body tensed. He knew what he ought to do. Ignore it. Drive on without a backward glance. Forget the past and accept the future which was waiting for him. But the dark voice of his conscience was forgotten as he leaned forward to speak to his driver, because sometimes curiosity was just too damned strong to resist.

'Stop the car,' he ordered harshly.

The car slid to a halt in the quiet street of London's Belgravia, a street full of unusual restaurants and tasteful shops. But only one of these caught his eye—which was surprising, since Luciano wasn't the kind of man who had ever featured shopping as a hobby. He didn't need to. Even the expensive baubles discreetly bought as compensatory keepsakes for departing lovers were purchased on his behalf by one of his many staff.

But there had been no purchase of baubles for quite a while now and no heartbroken lovers to pacify. He had recently undertaken two long years of celibacy—not exactly happily, but because he'd recognised it was something he needed to do. And he had risen to the challenge. His mouth hardened at the unintended pun. He had channelled his considerable energies into his work. He had worn out his hard body with exercise. His mind had been clear, strong and focussed—yet he wondered where that focus was now as he read the two words scrolled in fancy letters above the shop across the street.

Lisa Bailey.

He could feel the sudden throbbing of his groin as her name whispered into his memory just as her soft voice had once whispered urgent little entreaties into his ear as he drove deep inside her. Lisa Bailey. The hottest lover he'd ever known. The talented designer with the unblinking gaze. The tumble-haired temptress with the delicious curves.

And the only woman to kick him out of her bed.

Luc shifted in his seat, locked in an uncharacteristic moment of indecision because ex-lovers had the potential to be complicated—and complications he didn't need right now. He should tap on the glass and tell his chauffeur to drive on. Continue the journey to his embassy and deal with any last-minute queries before he returned to his island home after the wedding. He thought about what awaited him in Mardovia, and a sudden stillness settled over him. He had a duty to fulfil, or a burden to carry. It all depended which way you looked at it, and if he preferred to look for the positive rather than the negative—who could blame him?

His gaze returned to the shop front, and it was then that he saw her walking across the showroom and the pounding in his heart increased as he glimpsed the tumble of her curls. She turned slightly—showcasing the swell of her magnificent breasts. Lust arrowed sharply down into his groin, and stayed there.

Lisa Bailey.

His eyes narrowed. It was strange to see her here in this expensive part of town—far away from the edgier area of London where their paths had first crossed, in the tiny studio where she had designed her dresses.

He told himself it didn't matter why she was here because he didn't care. *Yet he was the one who had directed his driver to take this route, wasn't he?* And all because he'd heard some woman mention her name and had discovered that Lisa Bailey had come up in the world. His tongue snaked out over suddenly dry lips. What harm could it do to drop in and say hello, for old times' sake? Wasn't that what ex-lovers did? And wouldn't it convince him—as if he needed any convincing—that he was over her?

'Wait down the road a little,' he told the driver, opening the door himself and stepping onto the pavement. A few discreet yards away, a second car containing his bodyguards had also stopped, but Luc gave an almost imperceptible signal to tell them to keep their distance.

The August sun was hot on his head and there wasn't a whisper of wind in the leaves of the trees in the nearby square, despite the fact that it was getting on for five o'clock. The city had been caught up in a heatwave so fierce that news bulletins had been featuring clips of people frying eggs on the pavement and lying sprawled in the city's parks in various states of undress. Luc was looking forward to getting back to the air-conditioned cool of his palace in Mardovia. There white doves cooed in the famous gardens and the scent of the roses was far sweeter than the clogging traffic fumes which surrounded him here in the city. If it hadn't been for Conall Devlin's wedding party this weekend then he might have taken an earlier flight. Back to begin the process of embracing his new future—which he intended to do with whole-hearted dedication.

He pushed open the shop door and there she was, crouched down beside a rail of dresses with a needle in her hand and a tape measure around her neck—worn in the same way as a doctor might wear a stethoscope.

'Hello, Lisa,' he said, his tongue curling around the words as once it had curled around the soft swell of her breasts.

Lisa glanced up and narrowed her eyes against the light and at first she didn't recognise him. Maybe because he was the last person she was expecting to see, or maybe because she was tired and it was the end of a long day. A hot day at the end of August, with most people away on holiday and the city overrun by tourists who weren't really interested in buying the kind of clothes she was selling.

She felt the clench of rising hope as the doorbell gave its silvery little tinkle and a tall figure momentarily blotted out the blaze of the summer sun as the man stepped inside. She was due to close soon—but what did that matter? If this was a customer then he could stay until midnight for all she cared! She would switch on her best smile and persuade him to buy an armful of silk dresses for his wife. As he moved towards her she got an overwhelming impression of power and sensuality, and she tried to keep the cynicism from her smile as it crossed her mind that a man like this was more likely to be buying for his mistress than his wife.

But then he said her name and she stiffened because nobody else had an accent quite like his. She could feel the painful squeeze of her heart and the sudden rush of heat to her breasts. The needle she was holding fell to the carpet and vaguely she found herself thinking that she *never* dropped a needle. But then the thought was gone and the only one left dominating her mind was the fact that Luc was standing in her shop. His full name was Prince Luciano Gabriel Leonidas—head of the ancient royal House of Sorrenzo and ruler of the island principality of Mardovia.

But Lisa hadn't cared that he'd been a prince. She had known him simply as Luc. The man who had—unbelievably—become her lover. Who had introduced her to physical bliss and shown her that it had no limits. He'd made her feel things she'd never believed herself capable of feeling. Things she hadn't *wanted* to feel if the truth was known—because with desire came fear. Fear of being hurt. Fear of being let down and betrayed as women so often were—and that had scared the life out of her. He'd told her he wasn't looking for love or commitment and that had suited her just fine until she'd started to care for him.

She'd done her best to hide her growing feelings and had succeeded, until the day she'd realised she was fighting a losing battle with her heart. And that was when common sense had intervened and she had shrunk away from him—like someone picking up a pan to discover that the handle was burning hot. Telling him it was over hadn't been easy—and neither had the sleepless nights which followed. But it was easier than getting her heart broken and she hadn't once regretted her decision. Because men like Luc were dangerous—it was written into their DNA.

Her gaze flickered over him and immediately she became aware of the powerful sex appeal which surrounded him like an aura. His black hair was shorter than she remembered, but his eyes were just as blue. That brilliant sapphire blue—as inviting as a swimming pool on a hot day. Eyes you just wanted to dive straight into.

As always he looked immaculate. His handmade Italian suit was creaseless and his silk shirt was unbuttoned at the neck, revealing a tantalising triangle of silken skin. Lisa wished she didn't feel so warm and uncomfortable. That she'd had a chance to brush her wayward curls or slick a little lipstick over lips which suddenly felt like parchment.

'Luc,' she said, and the name sounded so right—even though it was two years since she'd spoken it. Two long years since she'd gasped it out in delight as he'd filled her and her body had splintered into yet another helpless orgasm around his powerful thrust. 'You're...' She swallowed. 'You're the last person I expected to see.'

He closed the shop door behind him and Lisa glanced over his shoulder, wondering where his body-guards were. Lurking out of sight, probably. Trying to blend in to the upmarket location by peering into win-dows, or melting into the dark shadows of a shop door-way as they controlled access to their royal boss. And then she saw two low black cars with tinted windows parked further down the road and she was reminded of all the protocol which surrounded this charismatic man.

'Am I?' he questioned softly.

His voice was velvet and steel and Lisa felt a rush of desire which made her feel momentarily breathless. Against her lace brassiere her nipples hardened and her skin grew tight. She could feel the instant rush of heat to her sex. And it wasn't fair. How did he manage to provoke that kind of reaction with just one look?

So stay calm. Act like he's a customer. Maybe he *was* a customer—eager to commission one of her trademark silk dresses for one of his countless girl-friends. After all, wasn't that how she'd met him, when he'd walked into her workroom near Borough Market and she hadn't had a clue who he was? Her designs had just been taking off—mainly through word of mouth and thanks to a model who had worn one of her dresses to a film premiere. All sorts of people had started com-ing to see her, so it hadn't been that surprising to see the imposing, raven-haired man with a beautiful blonde model on his arm.

She remembered the blonde trying to draw his atten-tion to one of the embroidered cream gowns Lisa had been making at the time and which women sometimes

wore as wedding dresses. And Lisa remembered looking up and witnessing the faint grimace on Luc's face.
Somehow she had understood that he was no stranger
to the matrimonial intentions of women, and their eyes
had met in a shared moment of unwilling complic-
ity until she had looked away, feeling awkward and
slightly flustered.

But something had happened in that split second
of silent communication. Something she could never
entirely understand. He had dumped the blonde soon
afterwards and laid siege to Lisa—in a whirlwind of
extravagant gestures and sheer determination to get
her into his bed. He had turned all that blazing power
on her and at first she'd thought she had been dreaming—especially when she'd discovered that he was a
prince. But she hadn't been dreaming. The amazing
flowers which had started arriving daily at her workshop had borne testament to his wealth and his intentions. Lisa had tried to resist him—knowing she had
no place at the side of someone like him. But it had
turned out he hadn't really wanted her by his *side*—
he'd just wanted her writhing underneath him, or on
top of him, or pushed up against a wall by him, and in
the end she'd given in. Of course she had. She would
have defied any woman to have held out against the
potent attraction of the Mediterranean Prince.

They had dated—if you could call it that—for six
weeks. Weeks which had whizzed by in a blur of sensuality. He'd never taken her to any of the glitzy functions featured on the stiff cards which had been stacked
on the marble fireplace of his fancy house, which she

had visited only once, under the cloak of darkness. He had been reluctant to be anywhere which didn't have a nearby bed, but Lisa hadn't cared. Because during those weeks he had taught her everything he knew about sex, which was considerable. She had never experienced anything like it—not before, and certainly not since.

The memory cleared as she realised that he was standing in her shop, still exuding that beguiling masculinity which made her want to go right over there and kiss him. And she couldn't afford to think that way.

'So you were just passing?' she questioned politely as she bent and picked up her fallen needle.

'Well, not exactly,' he said. 'I heard in a roundabout way that you'd moved premises and was interested to see how far up in the world you've come. And it seems like you've come a long way.' His eyes glittered as he looked around. 'This is quite some change of circumstance, Lisa.'

She smiled. 'I know.'

'So what prompted the transformation from edgy designer to becoming part of the establishment?'

Lisa kept her expression neutral as she met his curious gaze and even though she owed him no explanation, she found herself giving him one anyway. He probably wouldn't leave until she told him and she wanted him to leave, because he was making her feel uncomfortable standing there, dominating her little shop. 'I was selling stuff online and from my workshop—but it was too far out of the city centre to appeal to the kind of women who were buying my clothes.'

'And?'

She shrugged. 'And then when the opportunity came up to lease a shop in this area, I leapt at the chance.' It had been a bad decision of course, although it had taken her a while to see that. She hadn't realised that you should never take out an expensive lease unless you were confident you could meet the charges, and she'd chosen a backer who didn't know a lot about the fashion industry. But she had been buoyed up and swept away on a wave of acclaim for her dresses—and had needed a new project to fill the void left in her heart after Luc had gone. And then when her sister had announced she was going to have a baby, Lisa's desire to increase her income had become less of an ego-boosting career move and more of a necessity...

He was looking around the shop. 'You've done well,' he observed.

'Yes. Very well.' The lie slipped with practised ease from her tongue, but she justified it by telling herself that all she was doing was protecting herself, though she wasn't quite sure from what. And everyone knew that if you talked yourself up, then people might start to believe in you. 'So what can I do for you?' She fixed him with her most dazzling smile. 'You want to buy a dress?'

'No, I don't want to buy a dress.'

'Oh?' She felt the unsteady beat of her heart. 'So?'

He glittered her a smile. 'Why am I here?'

'Well, yes.'

Why indeed? Luc studied her. To prove she meant nothing? That she was just some tousle-haired temptress who had made him unbelievably hot and horny—before she'd shown him the door.

But wasn't that what rankled, even now? That she had walked away without a second glance—despite his expectation that she'd come crawling back to tell him she'd made the biggest mistake of her life. His pride had been wounded in a way it had never been wounded before, because no woman had ever rejected him—and his disbelief had quickly given way to frustration. With Lisa, he felt like a man who'd had his ice cream taken away from him with still half the cone left to lick.

As his gaze roved over her, the sheer individuality of her appearance hit him on a purely visceral level. He had dated some of the world's most desirable women—beautiful women whose endlessly long legs gave him the height he preferred in his sexual partners. But Lisa was not tall. She was small, with deliciously full breasts which drew a man's eyes to them no matter what she was wearing, or however much she tried to disguise them. She was none of the things he usually liked and yet there was something about her which he'd found irresistible, and he still couldn't work out what that something was.

Today she was wearing a simple silk dress of her own design. The leafy colour emphasised the unusual green-gold of her eyes and fell to just above her bare knees. Her long, curly hair was caught in tortoiseshell clips at the sides, presumably in an attempt to tame the corkscrew curls. Yet no amount of taming could disguise the colour of her crowning glory—a rich, shiny caramel which always reminded him of hazelnut shells.

A glossy tendril of it had escaped and was lying against her smooth skin.

But then he noticed something else. The dark shadows which were smudged beneath her eyes and the faint pinching of her lips. She looked like a woman who was short on sleep and long on worry.

Why?

He met question in her eyes. 'I'm often in this part of town and it seemed crazy not to come in and say hello.'

'So now you have.'

'Now I have,' he agreed as his mind took him off on a more dangerous tangent. He found himself remembering the silken texture of her thighs and the way he had trailed slow kisses over them. The rosy flush which used to flower above her breasts as she shuddered out her orgasm. And he wondered why he was torturing himself with memories which had kick-started his libido so that he could barely think straight.

His mouth hardened. Soon his life would follow a predictable pattern which was inevitable if you were born with royal blood. Yet some trace of the man he would never be called out to him now with a siren voice—and that siren's name was Lisa Bailey. For this was the woman who had fulfilled him on almost every level. Who had never imposed her will on him or made demands on him as so many women tried to. Was that why the sex had been so incredible—because she had made him feel so *free*?

And suddenly the self-imposed hunger of his two celibate years gnawed at his senses. An appetite so long denied now threatened to overwhelm him and he didn't feel inclined to stop it. What harm could there be in one final sweet encounter before he embraced his new life and all the responsibilities which came with it? Wouldn't that rid him of this woman's lingering memory once and for all?

'I've just flown in from the States and I'm here for a party this weekend,' he said. 'And on Monday I leave for Mardovia.'

'This is all very fascinating, Luc,' she observed drily. 'But I fail to see what any of this has to do with me.'

Luc gave a short laugh, for nobody had ever spoken to him as candidly as Lisa—nor regarded him quite so unflinchingly. And wasn't that one of the things which had always intrigued him about her—that she was so damned *enigmatic*? No dramatic stream of emotion ever crossed *her* pale face. Her features were as cool as if they had been carved from marble. The only time that serene look had ever slipped was when he'd been making love to her and it was then that her defences had melted. He'd liked making her scream and call out his name. He'd liked the way she gasped as he drove deep inside her.

He smiled now, enjoying the familiar lick of sexual *frisson* between them. 'And I thought I might ask you a favour,' he said.

'*Me?*'

'Well, we're old friends, aren't we?' He saw her pupils dilate in surprise and wondered how she would respond if he came right out and told her what was playing in his head.

I want to have sex with you one last time so that I can forget you. I want to bend my lips to those magnificent nipples and lick them until you are squirming. I want to guide myself into your tight heat and ride you until all my passion is spent.

His pulse pounded loudly in his ears. 'And isn't that what old friends do—ask each other favours?' he murmured.

'I guess so,' she said, her voice uncertain, as if she was having trouble associating their relationship with the word *friendship.*

'I need a date,' he explained. 'Someone to take to a fancy wedding with me. Not the ceremony itself—for those I avoid whenever possible—but the evening reception afterwards.'

Now he had a reaction.

'Oh, come on, Luc,' she said quietly. '*You* need a date? You of all people? I can't believe you're revisiting an old lover when there must be so many new ones out there. There must be women lining up around the block to go out with you—unless something is radically different and you've had a complete personality change.'

He gave an answering smile and wondered what she would say if she knew the truth. 'I cannot deny that there are any number of women who would happily accompany me,' he said. 'But none of them entice me sufficiently enough to take them.'

'So why not go on your own?'

'Unfortunately, it is not quite that simple.' He glanced out of the window, where he could see the shadowy shapes of his bodyguards standing beside one of the waiting limousines. 'If I turn up without a woman, that will leave me in a somewhat vulnerable position.'

'You? *Vulnerable?*' She gave a little snort of a laugh. 'You're about as vulnerable as a Siberian tiger!'

'An interesting metaphor,' he mused. 'Since, in my experience, weddings are a prime hunting ground for women.'

'Hunting ground?' she repeated, as if she'd mis-heard him.

'I'm afraid so.' He gave an unapologetic shrug. 'Some women see the bride and want to be her and so they look around to find the most suitable candidate for themselves.'

Her eyebrows arched. 'You being the most suitable candidate, I suppose?'

Luc looked at the tendril of hair still lying against her pale cheek and wanted to curl it around his finger. He wanted to use it like a rope and pull her towards him until their lips were mere inches apart. And then he wanted to kiss her. He shifted his weight a little. 'I'm afraid that being a prince does rather put me in that category—certainly amongst some women.'

'But you think you'd be safe with me?'

'Of course I would.' He paused. 'Our relationship was over a long time ago, and even when it was in full swing neither of us was under any illusion that there was any kind of future in it. You were probably the only woman who truly understood that. You can pro-tect me from the inevitable predators.' He smiled. 'And it might be fun to spend the evening together. Because we know each other well enough to be comfortable around each other, don't we, Lisa?'

Lisa looked at him. *Comfortable?* Was he insane? Didn't he realise that her pulse had been hammering like a piston ever since he'd stepped inside the shop? That her breasts were so swollen that it felt as if she'd suddenly gone up a bra size? Slowly, she drew in a deep breath. 'I think it's a bad idea,' she said flatly. 'A very bad idea. And now if you don't mind—I'm about to shut up shop.'

She walked over to the door and turned the sign to *Closed* and it was only afterwards that she wondered if it was that gesture of finality which suddenly prompted him to try a different approach, because Luc was nothing if not persistent. Because suddenly, he began to prowl around the shop like a caged tiger. Walking over to one of the rails, he slowly ran his fingertips along the line of silk dresses, a thoughtful expression on his face as he turned around to look at her.

'Your shop seems remarkably quiet for what should be a busy weekday afternoon,' he observed.

She tried not to look defensive. To replicate the same cool expression he was directing at her. 'And your point is?'

'My point is that a society wedding would provide an excellent opportunity for you to showcase your talent.' His blue eyes glittered. 'There will be plenty of influential people there. You could wear one of your own designs and dazzle the other guests—isn't that how it works? Play your cards right and I'm sure you could pick up a whole lot of new customers.'

And now Lisa really *was* tempted, because business hadn't been great. Actually, that was a bit of an understatement. Business had taken a serious dive, and she wasn't sure if it was down to the dodgy state of the economy or the more frightening possibility that her clothes had simply gone out of fashion. She'd found herself looking gloomily at magazines which featured dresses which looked a lot like hers—only for a quarter of the price. True, most of the cheaper outfits were made from viscose rather than silk, but lately she'd started wondering if women really cared about that sort of thing any more.

She kept telling herself that the dip in her profits was seasonal—a summer slump which would soon pick up with the new autumn collection, and she prayed it would. Because she had responsibilities now—big ones—which were eating into her bank account like a swarm of locusts rampaging through a field of maize. She thought about Brittany, her beloved little sister. Brittany, who'd flunked college and become a mother to the adorable Tamsin. Brittany, who was under the dominating rule of Jason, Tamsin's father. Lisa helped out where she could, but she didn't have a bottomless purse and the indisputable fact was that Jason wasn't over-keen on earning money if it involved setting the alarm clock every day. Just as he seemed to have a roving eye whenever any female strayed into his line of vision. But Brittany trusted him, or so she kept saying.

A bitter taste came into Lisa's mouth. Trust. Was there a man alive who could be trusted—and why on earth would any woman ever want to take the risk?

'So pleased you're giving my proposal some serious consideration,' Luc said, his sardonic observation breaking into her thoughts. 'Though I must say that women don't usually take *quite* so long to respond to an invitation to go out with me.'

'I'm sure they don't.'

'Though maybe they would if they realised how much a man enjoys being kept guessing,' he added softly. 'If they knew just how irresistible the unpredictable can be.'

Lisa looked at him. Instinct was telling her to refuse but the voice of common sense was suddenly stronger. It was urging her to stop acting as if millions of offers like this came her way. She thought about the kind of wedding someone like Luc would be attending and all the upmarket guests who would be there. Women with the kind of money who could afford her dresses. Women who wouldn't *dream* of wearing viscose. Surely she'd be crazy to pass up such an opportunity—even if it meant spending the evening with a man who symbolised nothing but danger. She swallowed. And excitement, of course. She mustn't forget that. *But she could resist him. She had resisted him once and she could do it again.*

'Who's getting married?' she questioned carelessly.

He failed to hide his triumphant smile. 'A man named Conall Devlin.'

'The Irish property tycoon?'

'You've heard of him?'

'Hasn't everyone? I read the papers like everyone else.'

'He's marrying a woman named Amber Carter.'

Lisa nodded. Yes. She'd seen pictures of Amber Carter, too—a stunning brunette and the daughter of some industrial magnate. Someone like that would be unbelievably well connected, with friends who might be interested in buying a Lisa Bailey dress. And mightn't this wedding serve another purpose at the same time? Mightn't it get Luc out of her system once and for all if she spent some time with him? Banish some of her dreamy recollections and reinforce some of the other reasons why she'd finished with him. It would do her good to remember his fundamental arrogance and in-built need to control. And while she had shared his bed for a while, she realised she didn't really *know* him.

Because Luc hadn't wanted anything deeper—she'd understood that right from the start. He'd made it clear that the personal was taboo and the reason for that was simple. He was a royal prince who could never get close to a foreigner. So there had been no secrets shared. No access to his innermost thoughts just because they'd been sleeping together. He'd said it would be a waste of their time and make their parting all the more difficult if they became more intimate than they needed to be. She had understood and she had agreed, because her own agenda had been the same—if for different reasons—and she had also been determined not to get too close. Not to him. Not to anyone. And so they had just lived in the present—a glorious present which had been all about pleasure and little else.

She returned his questioning look. 'Where is this wedding happening?'

'At Conall's country house at Crewhurst, this Saturday. It's only just over an hour out of London.'

She looked directly into his eyes. 'So it would be possible to get there and back in an evening?'

He held her gaze and she wondered if she'd imagined another flicker of triumph in his smile. 'Of course it would,' he said.

CHAPTER TWO

WHY THE HELL was she *here*? Lisa's fingers tightened around her clutch bag. Alone in a car with the handsome Prince as they approached a stately mansion which was lit up like a Christmas tree.

Had she been crazy to accompany Luc to the A-list wedding of two complete strangers? Especially when she wasn't even sure about his motives for asking her. And meanwhile her own motives were becoming increasingly muddled. She was *supposed* to be concentrating on drumming up new business, yet during a journey which had been short on words but high on tension, all she'd been able to think about was how gorgeous Luc looked in a dark suit which hugged his powerful body and emphasised the deep olive glow of his skin.

The summer sky was not yet dark but already the flaming torches lining the driveway had been lit— sending golden flames sparking into the air and giving the wedding party a carnival feel. On an adjacent field Lisa could see a carousel and nearby a striped hut was dispensing sticks of candyfloss and boxes of popcorn. A smooth lawn lay before them—a darkening sweep of emerald, edged with flowers whose pale colours could still be seen in the fading light.

It looked like a fairy tale, Lisa thought. Like every woman's vision of how the perfect wedding should be. *And you're not going to buy into that.* Because she knew the reality of marriage. She'd witnessed her stepfather crushing her mother's spirit, like a snail being crushed beneath a heavy boot. And even though they weren't even married, she'd seen Brittany being influenced by Jason's smooth banter, which had changed into a steely control once Britt had given birth to Tamsin. Lisa's lips compressed into a determined line. *And that was never going to happen to her. She was never going to be some man's tame pet.*

A valet opened the car door and out she got. One of her high-heeled sandals wobbled as she stepped onto the gravel path, and as Luc put out his hand to steady her Lisa felt an instant rush of desire. Why was it *still* like this? she wondered despairingly as her nipples began to harden beneath her silky dress. Why could no other man ever make her feel a fraction of what she felt for the Prince? She looked into his eyes and caught what looked like a gleam of comprehension and she wondered if he could guess at the thoughts which were racing through her head. Did he realise she was achingly aware of her body through the delicate fabric as she wondered whether he was still turned on by a woman with curves…?

'Look. Here comes the bride,' he said softly.

Lisa turned to see a woman running towards them,

the skirt of her white dress brushing against the grass, a garland of fresh flowers on top of her long, dark hair.

'Your Royal Highness!' she exclaimed, dropping a graceful curtsey. 'I'm so happy you were able to make it.'

'I wouldn't have missed it for the world,' answered Luc. 'Amber, do you know Lisa Bailey—the designer? Lisa, this is the brand-new Mrs Devlin.'

'No.' The bride shook her head and smiled. 'I don't believe we've met. I've heard of you, of course—and your dress is gorgeous.'

Lisa smiled back. 'So is yours.'

She was introduced to Amber's new husband Conall—a tall and striking Irishman, who could barely tear his eyes away from his wife.

'We're not having a formal dinner,' Amber was saying, her fingers lacing with those of her groom as they shot each other a look which suggested they couldn't wait to be alone. 'We thought it much better if people could just please themselves. Have fun and mingle. Ride on the carousel, or dance and eat hot dogs. You must let me get you and Lisa a drink, Your Highness.'

But Luc gave a careless wave of his hand. 'No, please. No formality. Not tonight,' he said. 'Tonight I am simply Luc. I shall fetch the drinks myself, which we will enjoy in this beautiful garden of yours, and then I think we might dance.' His eyes glittered as he turned his head. 'Does that idea appeal to you, *chérie*?'

Lisa's heart smashed against her ribcage as his sapphire gaze burnt over her skin and the unexpected French endearment reminded her of things she would prefer to forget. Like the way he used to slide her panties down until she would almost be pleading with him to rip them off—and his arrogant smile just before he did exactly that. But those kinds of thoughts were dangerous. Much. Too. Dangerous.

'I like the sound of looking round the garden,' she said. 'Not having any outside space is one of the drawbacks of living in London, and this is exquisite.'

'Thanks,' said Amber happily. 'And, Luc, you must look out for my brother Rafe, who's over from Australia and prowling around somewhere. I thought you might like to talk diamonds and gold with him.'

'Of course,' said Luc, removing two glasses of champagne from the tray of a passing waitress and handing one to Lisa. But he barely noticed the newlyweds walk away because all he could focus on was the woman beside him. She looked... He took a mouthful of the fizzy wine, which did nothing to ease the dryness in his throat. She looked *sensational*, in a silvery dress that made her resemble a gleaming fish—the kind which always slipped away, just when you thought you might have captured it. Her shoulders were tense and she was sipping her champagne, determinedly looking everywhere except in his direction.

With a hot rush of hunger he found himself wanting to reacquaint himself with that magnificent body. To press himself up against her. To jerk his hips—hard—and to lose himself inside her as he had done so many times before. He swallowed. Would it be so wrong to sow the last of his wild oats in one glorious finale, before taking up the mantle of duty and marriage which awaited him?

They moved before he had time to answer his own question, making their way across a lawn washed deep crimson by the setting sun where many of the other guests stood talking in small groups. Some of these Luc recognised instantly, for Conall moved in similarly powerful circles. There were the Irish Ambassador and several politicians, including an Englishman rumoured to be the next-but-one Prime Minister. There was a Russian oil baron and a Greek hotel magnate, and Conall's assistant, Serena, came over with Rafe Carter, the bride's brother—and somehow, in the midst of all the introductions, Lisa slipped away from him.

Yet even though she wasn't next to him, Luc knew exactly where she was as he went through the mechanics of being a dutiful guest. He accepted a bite-sized canapé from a passing waitress and popped it into his mouth, the salty caviar exploding against his tongue. It was an unusual situation—for *him* to be doing the watching, rather than for a woman's eyes to be fixed jealously on him. But she seemed completely oblivious to his presence as she chatted to a clutch of trust-fund babes.

He watched her long curls shimmering down over her tiny frame as she laughed at something one of the women said. He saw a man wander up to the group and say something to her, and Luc's body grew rigid with an unexpected sense of possessiveness.

And suddenly he wanted to be alone with her. He

didn't want small talk—or, even worse, to get stuck with someone who was hell-bent on having a serious conversation about his island principality. He didn't want to discuss Mardovia's recent elevation to join the ranks of the world's ten most wealthy islands, or to answer any questions about his new trade agreement with the United States. And he certainly didn't want one of Hollywood's hottest actresses asking quite blatantly whether he wanted her telephone number. Actually, she didn't really put him in a position to refuse—she just fished an embellished little card from her handbag and handed it over, with a husky entreaty that he call her...*soon*. Not wanting to appear rude and intending to dispose of it at the earliest opportunity, Luc slipped the card into his jacket pocket before excusing himself and walking over to where Lisa stood.

There was a ripple of interest as he approached, but he pre-empted the inevitable introductions by injecting an imperious note into his voice. 'Let's go and explore,' he said, taking her half-drunk champagne from her and depositing their glasses on a nearby table. 'I can hear music playing and I want to dance with you.'

Lisa felt a flicker of frustration as he took her drink away, wondering why his suggestions always sounded like *commands*. Because he was a prince, that was why, and he had spent his entire life telling people what to do. Not only was he interrupting her subtle sales pitch, he also wanted to dance with her—an idea which filled her with both excitement and dread. She knew she should refuse, but what could she say? *Sorry, Luc. I'm terrified you're going to hit on me and I'm not sure I'll be able to resist.*

The trouble was that everyone was looking at her and the other women weren't even bothering to hide their envy. Or maybe it was disbelief that such an eligible man wanted to dance with a too-small brunette with an overdeveloped pair of breasts. She wanted to make a break for it, to run towards that copse of trees at the end of the lawn and to lose herself in their darkness. But she hid her insecurity behind the serene mask she'd perfected when her mother had married her stepfather and overnight their world had changed. When she'd learnt never to let people know what you were thinking. It was the first lesson in survival. Act weak and people treated you like a weakling. Act strong and they didn't.

'Okay,' she said carelessly. 'Why not?'

'Not the most enthusiastic response I've ever received,' he murmured as they moved out of earshot. 'Do you get some kind of kick from making me wait?'

Her eyes widened. 'Why? Is it mandatory to answer immediately when spoken to by the Prince?' she mocked.

He smiled. 'Something like that.'

'So why don't you just enjoy the novelty of such an experience?'

'I'm trying.'

'Try harder, Luc.'

He laughed as they walked across the grass to the terrace and up a flight of marble steps leading into the ballroom, from where the sultry sound of jazz filtered out into the warm night air. Lisa's chest was tight as Luc led her onto a quiet section of the dance floor, and as he drew her into his arms she was conscious of the power in his muscular body and the subtle scent of bergamot which clung to his warm skin.

It was hard not to be overwhelmed by his proximity and impossible to prevent the inevitable assault on her senses. This close he was all too real and her body began to stir in response to him. That pins-and-needles feeling spiking over her nipples. That melting tug of heat between her thighs. What chance did she have when he was holding her like this? I haven't danced with a man in a long time, she realised—and the irony was that she'd never actually danced with Luc before. He'd never taken her to a party and held her in his arms like this because their affair had been conducted beneath the radar. And suddenly she could understand why. The hard thrust of his pelvis was achingly evocative as it brushed against her. Dancing was dangerous, she thought. It allowed their bodies to be indecently close in a public place and she guessed that Conall's tight security was the only reason Luc was okay with that. Anywhere else and people would have been fishing out their cell phones to capture the moment on camera.

Yet somehow, despite her misgivings, she couldn't help but enjoy the dance—at least up to the point where her throat suddenly constricted and her breathing began to grow shallow and unsteady. Had he pulled her closer? Was that why the tips of her breasts were suddenly pushing so insistently against his chest?

And if *she* could feel her nipples hardening, maybe so could *he*.

'You seem tense,' he observed.

She moved her shoulders awkwardly. 'Are you surprised?'

'You don't like dancing? Or is being this close to me again unsettling you?'

Lisa drew her head back to meet the indefinable expression in his eyes. 'A little,' she admitted.

'Me, too.'

She pursed her lips together, wishing she could control the thundering of her heart. 'But you must get to dance with hundreds of women.'

'Not at all. I'm not known for my love of dancing.' His finger stroked distractingly at her waist. 'And no woman I've ever danced with makes me feel the way you do.'

'That's a good line, Luc.' She laughed. 'Smooth, yet convincing—and with just the right note of disbelief. I bet you hit the jackpot with it every time.'

'It's not a line.' His brow furrowed. 'And why so cynical?'

'I'd prefer to describe it as having taken a healthy dose of realism and I've always been that way. You never used to object before.'

Reflectively, his finger stroked her bare arm. 'Maybe I was too busy taking off your clothes.'

'Luc—'

'I'm only stating the truth. And please don't give me that breathless little gasp and look at me like that, unless you want me to drag you off to the nearest dark corner.'

'Carry on in that vein and I'll walk off all by myself.'

'Okay.' He sucked in a deep breath before moving his hands to her waist—the slender indentation of her flesh through the delicate silk feeling almost as intimate as if he were touching her bare skin itself. 'Let's keep things formal. Tell me what's been happening in your life.'

'You mean the shop?'

A faint frown arrowed his dark eyebrows together, as if he hadn't meant the shop at all. 'Sure,' he said. 'Tell me about the shop.'

Lisa fixed her gaze on the tiny buttons of his dress shirt. Did she tell him about how empty she'd felt when they'd split, which had made her throw herself headlong into her work—not realising that her ambition was outpacing her and that by aiming so high, she'd made the potential crash back to earth all the harder? 'People kept telling me I ought to expand and so I found myself a backer,' she said. 'Someone who believed in me and was willing to finance a move to a more prestigious part of the city.'

'Who?'

His voice had suddenly roughened and she looked up into his face. 'Is that really relevant?'

'That depends.' There was a pause before he spoke again. 'Is he your lover?'

She screwed up her nose. 'You're implying that I started a relationship with my new backer?'

'Or maybe it was the other way round? Your change

in fortune seems a little…dramatic,' he observed. 'It would make sense.'

Her feet slowed on the polished floor and Lisa felt a powerful spear of indignation. Was Luc really coming over as *jealous*—when he'd told her from the get-go that there was never going to be any future in their relationship? Was that what powerful princes did—played at being dog in the manger, not wanting you themselves, but then getting all jealous if they imagined someone else *did*? But she wasn't going to invent a closeness with her backer which did not extend outside the boardroom door. She and Martin were business buddies and nothing more.

She gave a laugh. 'Everyone knows you should never mix business and pleasure, and I'm afraid there hasn't been time for much in the way of recreation.'

'Why not?'

Again, she moved her shoulders restlessly. 'The stakes are much higher now that I've got the shop and then there's Brittany…'

Her words trailed off but he picked up on her hesitation.

'Your sister?'

Amazed he'd remembered the little sister he'd never even met, Lisa nodded. 'Yes,' she said. 'She had a baby.'

He frowned. 'But she's very young herself, right?'

'Yes, she is and…' Her voice faded because Luc wouldn't be interested in hearing about Brittany's choice of partner. And even though part of her despised Jason and the way he lived, wasn't there still some kind of stubborn loyalty towards him because he was Tamsin's father? 'I've been pretty tied up with that,' she finished.

'So you're an aunt now?' he questioned.

She looked up at him and Luc watched her face dissolve with soppy affection—her green-gold eyes softening and her mouth curving into a wistful smile. He felt a beat of something unfamiliar because he'd never seen her look that way before and a whisper of something he didn't understand crept over his skin.

'Yes, I'm an aunt. I have a little niece called Tamsin and she's beautiful. Just beautiful. So that's my news.' She raised her eyebrows. 'What about you?'

Luc's throat thickened with frustration, because ironically he felt so at ease in her company that Lisa would be the perfect person to confide in. To reveal that soon he would be marrying another woman—the Princess from a neighbouring island who had been earmarked as his bride since birth. A long-anticipated union between two wealthy islands, which he couldn't continue to delay.

And Lisa was a realist, wasn't she? She'd told him that herself. She might even agree that arranged marriages were far more sensible than those founded on the rocky ground of romance, with their notoriously high failure rate. If he hadn't wanted her quite so much he *might* have confided in her, but the truth was that he *did* want her. He wanted her so badly that he could barely move without being acutely aware of his aching groin, and he was glad she was standing in front of him, concealing his erection from any prying eyes.

But something stopped him from starting the inevitable seduction process—something which felt uncomfortably like the fierce stab of his conscience. For a moment he fought it, resenting its intrusion on what should have been a straightforward conclusion to the evening. He knew how much she still wanted him. It was obvious from the way she looked at him—even if he hadn't felt her nipples hardening against his chest or heard the faltering quality of her words, as if she was having difficulty breathing. Just as he knew that his desire for her was greater than anything he'd felt for any other woman. The words he'd spoken while they'd been dancing were true.

But his duty lay elsewhere and he had no right to lose himself in her soft and curvy body. No right to taste her sweetness one last time, because what good would it do—other than trigger a frustration which might take weeks to settle? It wasn't fair to the woman who was intended as his wife, even though it had been twelve months since he'd even seen her. And it wasn't fair to Lisa either.

He remembered that yearning look on her face when she'd spoken about her sister's child—a look which indicated a certain broodiness, as women of her age were programmed to be broody. He needed to let her go to find her own destiny, one which was certainly not linked to his.

Reluctantly, he drew away from her and it was as though he had flicked a switch inside himself. Self-discipline swamped desire as it had done for the past two years, and, now that sex was off the agenda, he noticed again the pallor of her complexion and faint shadows beneath her eyes. Suddenly, Luc was appalled at his thoughtlessness and ruthlessness. Had he really been planning to satisfy himself with her and then simply walk away and marry another woman?

Yes, he had.

His mouth twisted. *What kind of a man was he?*

'Let's go,' he said abruptly.

'Go?' She looked up at him in bewilderment. 'But it's still early.'

'You're tired,' he said tightly. 'Aren't you?'

She shrugged her shoulders. 'I guess so.'

'And you've probably done all the sales pitching you can for tonight. The party will really get going in a minute and I doubt whether anyone will be asking you how long your turnaround times are or whether you can make them a dress in time for their birthday party. So let's just slip away without a big fuss.'

Aware that she was in no position to object, Lisa nodded but her mood was strangely deflated as they walked towards Luc's waiting car and the sounds of music and laughter grew fainter. For a while back then it had felt so magical and so *familiar* being in his arms again. She'd felt warm and sexy as he'd held her close and his hard body had tensed against hers in silent acknowledgement of the powerful attraction which still pulsed between them. She hadn't thought beyond the dance but had thought they might stay like that for most of the evening. But now, with the moon barely beginning to rise and a trip back to her grotty home in London on the horizon—she felt strangely *cheated*. And embarrassed. As if she had been somehow presumptuous. Because hadn't she wondered if they might end up in bed together? Hadn't that been the one thought which had *really* been on her mind?

Once in the car, she accelerated her Cinderella mood by kicking off the high-heeled shoes and folding herself into one corner of the wide back seat, as if she could simply disappear if she made herself small enough. But Luc didn't react. He simply took out his cell phone and began to read from the screen. It was as if he had retreated from her. As if she were just part of the fixtures and fittings—as inconsequential as the soft leather seat on which they sat.

So don't show him you care, she told herself— even though she could feel the unfamiliar pricking of tears behind her eyes. Had she arrogantly thought he wouldn't be able to keep his hands off her? That he still found her as irresistible as she found him? She closed her eyes and leaned back against the soft leather, wondering if she had misread the whole situation.

Luc stared unseeingly at the screen of his phone until the regular sound of Lisa's breathing told him she was sleeping. It was torture to sit beside her without touching her—when all he wanted to do was to slip his hand beneath her dress and make her wet for him.

He was silent throughout the journey and it was only as they began to edge towards London that he glanced out of the window and began to notice his surroundings. The city was still buzzy as he leaned forward and quietly told the driver to go to Lisa's address.

'You want me to drop you off on the way, boss?' asked the driver.

Luc glanced at his watch. Tempting to call it a night and get away from the enticement she presented, but he owed her more than waking up alone in an empty car. She didn't deserve that. The frown at his brow deepened. She'd never given him any trouble. She hadn't tried to sell her story to the press or to capitalise on her royal connections, had she?

'No,' he said. 'Let's take her home first.'

But he was surprised when the car changed direction and entered the badly lit streets of an unfamiliar neighbourhood, where rubbish fluttered on the pavement and a group of surly-looking youths stood sucking on cigarettes beneath a lamp post. Luc frowned as he remembered the ordinary but very respectable apartment she'd had before. What the hell was she doing living somewhere like this?

As the car slid to a smooth halt, he reached out and gently shook her awake.

'Wake up, Lisa,' he said. 'You're home.'

Lisa didn't want to leave the dream—the one where she was still locked in Luc's arms and he was about to kiss her. But the voice in her ear was too insistent to ignore and her eyes fluttered open to see the Prince leaning over her, his face shadowed.

Feeling disorientated, she sat up and looked around. She was home—and she didn't want to be. Still befuddled, she bent to cram her feet back into her shoes and picked up her silver clutch bag. 'Thanks,' she said.

'This is where you live?'

She heard the puzzled note in his voice and understood it instantly. She bet he'd never been somewhere
like this in his privileged life. For a split second she
was tempted to tell him that she was just staying here
while her own home was being redecorated, but she
quickly swallowed the lie. Why be ashamed of what
she was and who she'd become?

'Yes,' she said, her voice still muzzy from sleep.
'This is where I live.'

'You've moved?' he demanded. 'Why?'

'I told you that Brittany had a baby and the three of
them were cramped in a too-small apartment. So…'
She shrugged. 'We just did a swap. It made sense. I'm
planning to get myself something better when—'

'When business picks up?' he questioned astutely.

'When I get around to it,' she said quickly. Too
quickly. 'Anyway, thanks for taking me to the party.
Hopefully, I'll have drummed up some new business
and it…well, it was good to catch up.'

'Yeah.' Their eyes met. 'I'll see you to the door.'

'Honestly, there's no need.' She flashed him a smile.
'I'm a big girl now, Luc.'

'The subject isn't up for debate,' he said coolly. 'I'll
see you to your door.'

The night air was still warm on her bare arms yet
Lisa shivered as Luc fell into step beside her. But it
wasn't shame about him seeing her home which was
bothering her—it was the sudden sense of inevitability
which was washing over her. The realisation that this
really was goodbye. Fishing the key from her bag, she
fumbled with the lock before turning back to face him,

unprepared for the painful clench of her heart and an aching sense of loss. She would never see him again, she realised. Never know that great rush of adrenaline whenever he was close, or the pleasurable ache of her body whenever he touched her. For a split second she found herself wondering why she'd been stupid enough to finish with him, instead of eking out every available second until her royal lover had ended the relationship himself. She'd done it to protect herself from potential heartache, but what price was that protection now?

Sliding her arms around his neck, she reached up on tiptoe and brushed her lips over his. 'Be happy,' she whispered. 'Goodnight, Luc.'

Luc froze as the touch of her lips ignited all his re-pressed fantasies. He felt it ripple over his skin like the tide lapping over dry sand as he tried to hold back. He told himself that kissing a man was predatory and he didn't like predatory women. He was the master—in charge of every aspect of his life—and he'd already decided that no good could come from a brief sexual encounter.

Yet his throat dried and his groin hardened as the warmth of her body drew him in, because this was different. This was Lisa and her kiss was all the things it shouldn't be. Soft yet evocative—and full of passionate promise. It reminded him of just how hot she'd been in his bed and yet how cool the next morning.

And it was over.

It had to be over.

So why wasn't he disentangling her arms and walking back towards his purring limousine? Why was he pushing her through her door and slamming it shut behind them? A low moan of hunger erupted from somewhere deep inside him as he pushed her up against the wall and drove his mouth down on hers.

CHAPTER THREE

Luc was aware of little other than a fierce sexual need pumping through his veins as he crushed his lips down on Lisa's. He barely noticed the cramped hallway as he levered her up against the peeling wallpaper, or the faint chill of damp in the air as her arms closed around him. He was aware of nothing other than her soft flesh and the hard jerk of the erection which throbbed insistently at his groin.

He kissed her until she cried out his name. Until she circled her hips over his with a familiar restlessness which made him slide his hand underneath the hem of her silver dress. His heart pounded. Her legs were bare and her thighs were cool and he could hear the silent scream of his conscience as his fingertips began their inevitable ascent. He thought about all the reasons why this shouldn't happen, but he was too hot to heed caution and this was too easy. As easy as breathing. He swallowed. With her it always had been that way.

She gave a shuddering little moan as he reached her panties and the sound only fuelled his own hunger.

'Luc,' she gasped.

But he didn't answer. He was too busy sliding the panties aside to provide access for his finger. Too busy reacquainting himself with her moist and eager flesh. He teased her clitoris until she bucked with pleasure and he could smell the earthy scent of sex in the air.

'Hell, you're responsive,' he ground out.

'Are you surprised when you touch me like...*that*?'

Her hands were reaching blindly for his zip and Luc held his breath as she eased it down. His trousers concertinaed to the ground like those of a schoolboy in an alley, and her dextrous hands were now dealing with his boxer shorts—peeling them down until his buttocks were bare. She was cupping his balls and scraping her fingernails gently over their soft swell and in response he reached down and tore her panties apart with a savage rip of the delicate material. Her low laugh reminded him of how much she liked to be dominated in the bedroom and, although his conscience made one last attempt to tell him this was wrong, ruthlessly, he erased it from his mind. Halting her just long enough to remove a condom from his pocket, he tore open the foil with unsteady fingers before sheathing himself.

And then it was happening and there didn't seem to be a damned thing he could do about it. It was as if he were on a speeding train with no idea how to stop. He cupped her bottom so that she could wrap her legs around his hips. Her lips were parted against his cheek and her breasts were flattened against his chest.

'Are you sure you want this?' he whispered, his tip grazing provocatively against her slick flesh.

Her words came out as gasps. 'Are you?'

'I'll give you three guesses,' he murmured and drove deep into her.

His thrusts were urgent and her cries so loud that he had to kiss them silent. It was mindless and passionate and it was over very quickly. She came almost instantly and so did he, hot seed spurting into the rubber and making his body convulse helplessly. He pressed his head against her neck and, as one of her curls attached itself to his lips, he wished it hadn't been so brief. Why the hell hadn't he taken his time? Undressed her slowly and tantalised them both, while demonstrating his legendary control?

He cupped his hand over her pulsating mound, feeling the damp curls tangling in his fingers and enjoying the last few spasms as they died away. Already he could feel himself growing hard and knew from experience that Lisa would like nothing better than to do it all over again. But he couldn't stay for a repeat performance. No way. He needed to get out of there, and fast. To forget this had ever happened and put it to the back of his mind. To get on with his future instead of stupidly allowing himself to be dragged back into the past. He bent down and tugged his trousers back up, struggling to slide the zip over his growing erection, before glancing around the cramped hallway.

'Bedroom?' he questioned succinctly.

She swallowed. 'Third door along.'

It wasn't difficult to find in such a small apartment, and he thought the room was unremarkable except for the rich fabric which covered a sagging armchair and a small vase of fragrant purple flowers on the windowsill. Luc drew the curtains and snapped on a small lamp, intending just to see her safely in bed. To kiss her goodbye and tell her she was lovely—maybe even cover her up with a duvet and suggest she get some sleep. But somehow it didn't quite work out that way. Because once inside her bedroom it seemed a crime not to pull the quicksilver dress over her head and feast his eyes on her body. And an even bigger crime not to enjoy the visual fantasy of her lying on top of the duvet, wearing nothing but an emerald-green bra and a pair of sexy high-heeled shoes.

'Lisa,' he said, thinking how hollow his voice sounded.

In the soft lamplight he could see the bright gleam of her eyes.

She wriggled a little, her thighs parting fractionally in invitation. 'Mmm…?'

Luc knew she was teasing him and that this was even more dangerous. He told himself he didn't want to get back into that special shorthand of lovers or remind himself how good this part of their relationship had always been. Yet somehow his body was refusing to heed the voice of reason as he took her hand and guided her fingers to the rocky hardness at his groin.

'Seems like I want you again,' he drawled.

She laughed as her fingers dipped beneath the waistband and circled his aroused flesh. 'No kidding?'

'What do you think we ought to do about it?' he questioned silkily.

Her voice grew husky as she mimicked his voice. 'I'll give you three guesses.'

His mouth was dry as he undressed them both, impatiently pushing their discarded clothing onto the floor as he reacquainted himself with her curves. He groaned as she caressed the tense muscles of his thighs with those beautiful long fingers. Her curls tickled him as she bent to slide her tongue down over the hollow of his belly. But when she reached the tip of his aching shaft, he grabbed a thick rope of curls.

'No,' he said unsteadily.

'But you like—'

'I like everything you do to me, Lisa, I always did. But this time I want to take it a bit more slowly.' He groaned as he pushed her back against the mattress and leaned over her, his eyes suddenly narrowing. 'But you do realise that this changes nothing? I'm still not in a position to offer you any kind of future.'

Her smile was brittle. 'Don't make this all about you, Luc,' she said. 'It's supposed to be about mutual pleasure.'

A spear of jealousy ran through him. 'And have you had many other lovers?' he questioned. 'A stream of men lying just like this on your bed?''

'You have no right to ask me something like that.'

'Is that a yes?'

She shook her head but now her voice was shaking with indignation.

'If you must know, there's been nobody since you,' she declared. 'And before you start reading anything into that—don't bother. There hasn't been time for sex, that's all. I've been juggling too many balls and trying to keep my business afloat.'

But Lisa knew she wasn't being completely honest as she heard his low laugh of triumph. Of *course* there hadn't been anybody else—because who could compare to the arrogant Prince? Who else could make her feel all the stuff that Luc did? But he didn't want feelings—he wasn't in the market for that and he never had been. Hadn't he just emphasised that very fact? So pretend you don't care. Show him you're independent and liberated and not building stupid fantasies which are never going to happen.

'And just to put your mind at rest, yes—I do realise you're not in the market for a wedding ring,' she added drily.

For a moment she felt him grow tense—as if he was going to say something—and she looked up at him expectantly. But the moment passed and instead he bent his head to kiss her—a kiss that was long and slow and achingly provocative. It made her remember with painful clarity just what she'd been missing. The intimate slide of his fingertips over her skin. The way he could play her body as if he were playing a violin. He grazed his mouth over her swollen breasts, teasing each nipple with his teeth as her hands clutched at the bedclothes beneath her.

She realised she was still wearing her shoes and that the high heels were in danger of ripping through the cotton duvet. She bent one knee to unfasten the buckle but he forestalled her with an emphatic shake of his head.

'No,' he growled as he straddled her, his finger

reaching down to caress the leather as if it were an extension of her own skin. 'The shoes stay.'

She could feel the weight of his body and his erection pressing against her belly. He put his hand between her thighs and started to stroke her and Lisa wondered how she could have lived without this for so long.

'Luc,' she breathed as a thousand delicious sensations began to ripple over her.

His thumb stilled. 'You want more?'

She wanted him to hold her tightly and tell her how much he'd missed her, but she was never going to get that. So concentrate on what he can give you.

'Much more,' she said, coiling her arms around his neck. 'I want to feel you inside me again.'

He made her wait, eking out each delicious touch until she was almost weeping with frustration. She could feel the wetness between her thighs as he pushed them apart at last and heard his soft words of French as he entered her.

There was triumph as well as pleasure in his smile as he started to thrust his pelvis and suddenly Lisa wanted to snatch some of the control back. With insistent hands she pushed at his chest and, their bodies still locked, rolled him onto his back so that she was now on top. She saw the light of pleasure which danced in his eyes as she cupped her breasts and began to play with them, tipping her head backwards so that her curls bounced all the way down her back.

'Lisa!' Now it was his turn to gasp as he clamped his hands over her hips, anchoring her to him as their movements became more urgent. He pulled her head down so that he could kiss her, the movement of his tongue mimicking the more intimate thrusts he was making deep inside her.

Lisa shuddered because it felt so real. So *primitive*. This was the most alive she'd felt in a long time. Maybe ever.

She found herself wanting to rake her fingernails over his flesh—even though he'd always been so insistent she shouldn't mark him. But suddenly the desire to do just that was too strong to resist. Caught in a moment made bittersweet by the knowledge that it would never be repeated, she felt the first waves of her orgasm as she touched her lips to his shoulder. The first ripple of pleasure hit her and just before it took her under, she bit him. Bit him and sucked at his flesh like some rookie vampire, and the salty taste of his sweat and his blood on her lips only seemed to intensify her pleasure. His too, judging by the ragged cry he gave as he bucked inside her.

Afterwards she lay there, slumped against his damp body—not wanting to move or speak or to do anything which might destroy the delicious sense of *completeness* which enveloped her.

Go to sleep, she urged him silently as she listened to the muffled pounding of his heart. Go to sleep and let's pretend we're two normal people one last time. I can make you toast and coffee in the morning, and we can sit on stools in my tiny kitchen and forget that you're a prince and I'm a commoner before you walk out of my life for good.

But he was wide awake. She could tell from the tension in his body and the way he suddenly eased himself out of her body. Without a word, he pushed back the sheet and got out of bed.

'Luc?' she questioned, but he had switched on the main light and was walking over to the oval mirror which hung on the wall.

The harsh light emphasised just how cheap the room must look to a man used to palaces—throwing into relief the threadbare rug and the chipped paintwork which she hadn't yet got around to restoring. Tipping his head back, he narrowed his eyes as he studied the bite on his neck, which was already turning a deep magenta colour.

'Bathroom?' he snapped.

'J-just along the corridor,' she stumbled.

He was back some minutes later, having obviously splashed his face with water and raked his fingers through his ruffled black hair in an attempt to tame it. And then her heart clenched with disbelief as he bent down to pick up his clothes and began pulling them on. Surely he wasn't planning on leaving straight away? She'd known it was only ever going to be a one-off but she'd hoped he'd at least sleep with her.

'Is something wrong?' she asked.

'You mean, apart from the fact that you've bitten my neck, like some teenage girl on a first date?' He paused in the act of buttoning up his shirt, his lips tight with anger as he turned to look at her. 'What was the point of that, Lisa? Did you want to make sure you left a trophy mark behind?'

'I know. I know. I shouldn't have done it.' She gave

a helpless shrug. 'But you were just too delicious to resist.'

But he didn't smile back. In the glaring light she could see how stony his sapphire eyes looked. He finished dressing and slipped on his shoes. 'I have to go,' he said, giving a quick glance at his watch. 'I shouldn't even be here.'

'Oh?' Her voice was very quiet as she looked at him. 'Have you suddenly decided that my new downmarket accommodation is a little too basic for His Royal Highness? Can't wait to get away now you've had what you came for?'

'Please don't, Lisa,' he said. 'Don't make this any more difficult than it already is. This should never have happened. We both know that.'

She sat up in bed then, her hair falling over her shoulders as she grabbed at the rumpled sheet to cover her breasts, shielding them from the automatic darkening of his eyes as they jiggled free. 'But you were the one who came into my shop!' she protested furiously. 'The one who practically bribed me into going to that wedding party with you—'

'And you were the one who came onto me on your doorstep when I had already decided to resist you.'

'I didn't hear you objecting at the time!'

'No, you're right. I didn't.' He gave a bitter laugh. 'Maybe I was just too damned weak.'

'Okay. So we were both weak. We wanted each other.' She stared at him. 'But what's the big deal? Why start regretting it now? I mean, it's not as if we're hurting anyone, is it?'

Luc let out a low hiss of air. He didn't want to tell her, but maybe telling her was the only option. The only way she might get the message that this really was the last time and it could never happen again. Yet he wouldn't have been human if he hadn't experienced a sense of regret. His heart clenched in his chest as he looked at her—at the golden-brown curls tumbling down over her milky skin. He stared into the spiky-lashed green-gold of her eyes and felt another unwanted jerk of lust. Another deep desire to go over there and kiss her until there was no breath left in her lungs—until she was parting her thighs and pulling him deep inside her again. And judging from the hunger in her eyes, she was feeling exactly the same.

He wondered if she was aware of just how irresistible he still found her. Perhaps she thought there might be more episodes like this in the future. Maybe she was labouring under the illusion that he would start making regular trips to see her, which would all end up with this seemingly inevitable conclusion. And didn't part of him long for such a delicious scenario?

Yet his sexual hunger was tempered by a deep sense of guilt at what had just happened, because hadn't he just betrayed the woman who had been waiting so patiently for him on the island of Isolaverde? Hadn't he broken his self-imposed celibacy—big time—and with the very last woman he should have chosen?

'I'm afraid it is a big deal,' he said slowly.

She looked at him and grew completely still, as if sensing from the sudden harshening of his voice that she was about to hear something she would prefer not to.

'I don't understand.'

'There's someone else.'

The words hung in the air between them and for a moment they were met with nothing other than a disbelieving silence before her shoulders stiffened in shock.

'Someone else?' she repeated blankly.

'Yes.'

'You mean...?' she managed at last, her green-gold eyes icing over. 'You mean you're sleeping with two women at the same time? Or is that a little conservative of me? Maybe there are more than two—are you operating some sort of outdated harem?'

'Of course I'm not!' he gritted back. 'And it isn't that simple. Or that easy.'

'Oh, Luc. Your tortured face is a picture. You poor thing! My heart bleeds for you.'

'I have been betrothed to a princess since she was a child,' he said heavily.

'Betrothed?' Lisa gave a brittle little laugh, as if sarcasm could protect her from the pain which was lancing through her heart. As if it would blind her to the fact that she had misjudged him. Worse, she had trusted him. She hadn't asked him for the stars but she had expected him to behave with some sort of integrity towards her. *But why should she expect integrity when she knew how ruthless men could be?* 'This is the twenty-first century, Luc. We don't use words like *betrothed* any more.'

'Where I come from, we do. It's the way things work in my country.' He picked up one of his gold cufflinks

which were lying next to the vase of purple flowers.
'The way they've always worked, ever since—'

'Please! I don't want a damned lesson in Mardovian
history!' she hissed. 'I want you to tell me how you've
just had sex with me if there's…someone else.'

He clipped first one cufflink and then the other, before lifting his eyes to hers. 'I'm sorry.'

'You *bastard*.'

'I made it very clear from the beginning that there
could never be any future between us. I always knew
that my destiny was to marry Sophie.'

Sophie. Somehow knowing her name made it even
worse and Lisa started to tremble.

'But you didn't think to tell me that at the time.'

'At the time there was no reason to tell you, for
she and I had an agreement that we should both lead
independent lives until the time of the wedding approached.'

'And now it has.'

'Now it has,' he agreed, and his voice was almost
gentle. Like a doctor trying to find the kindliest way of
delivering a deadly diagnosis. 'This was my last foreign
trip before setting the matrimonial plans in motion.'

'And you thought you'd have one final fling—with
the woman who would probably ask the least questions?'

'It wasn't like that!' he said hotly.

'No? What, you just *happened* to come into my shop
last week?'

'I wanted to tie off some of the loose ends in my
life.'

There was a pause. Lisa had never imagined herself being described as a *loose end* and something told herself to kick him out. To get his cheating face out of her line of vision and then start trying to forget him. But she didn't. Some masochistic instinct made her go right ahead and ask the question. 'What's she like? *Sophie.*'

He winced, as if she had committed some sort of crime by saying the Princess's name out loud while she sat amid sheets still redolent with the scent of sex.

'You don't want to know,' he said roughly.

'Oh, but that's where you're wrong, Luc. I do. Indulge me that, at least. I'm curious.'

There was a brief pause before he answered. 'She is young,' he said. 'Younger even than you. And she is a princess.'

Lisa closed her eyes as suddenly she wished this night had never happened. Because if he hadn't come back she would never have known about Sophie. Luc would have existed in her imagination as the perfect lover she'd had the strength to walk away from and not as the duplicitous cheat he really was. 'And how does she feel, knowing just what her precious fiancé is up to the moment her back is turned?' she questioned in a shaking voice. 'Or doesn't she mind sharing you with another woman?'

'I have never been intimate with Sophie!' he bit out. 'Since tradition dictates she will come to me as a virgin on our wedding night.' He paused as he surveyed her from between his lashes, his expression suddenly sombre. 'Because that is my destiny and the duty which has been laid down for me since the moment of my birth. And a prince must always put duty, Lisa, above all else. That has always been my guiding principle.'

She shook her head, terrified she was going to do something stupid, like picking up the vase of purple flowers and hurling it at him. Or bursting into useless tears. 'You wouldn't know the meaning of the word *principle* if it was staring out of a dictionary at you!'

His voice tensed, but he forged on—sounding as if someone had written him a script and he was reading from it. 'And once my ring is on her finger, I will stray no more.'

Lisa closed her eyes. So that was all she was to him. Someone to 'stray' with. Like a stray cat—lost and hungry and taken in by the first person to offer it a decent meal. What a stupid mistake she'd made. She'd let herself down. She'd tarnished the past and muddied the present. And all because of one little kiss. Because she'd reached up and brushed her lips over his and the whole damned thing had got out of hand.

So show some dignity. Don't scream and rage. Don't let his last memory of you be of some woman on the rampage because he's passing you over for someone else. Because she had never given him access to her emotions and she wasn't about to start now. Bitterness and vitriol were luxuries she couldn't afford, because she might not have much—but she still had her pride. She opened her eyes and met the sapphire glint of his, only now she barely noticed their soft blaze—just as she no longer saw the beauty in his olive-skinned features. All she saw was duplicity and deceit.

'Just go, Luc,' she said.

He hesitated and for a moment she thought he might be about to come over to the bed and kiss her good-bye, and she tried to tell herself that she would slap his cheating face if he attempted *that*—because how was it possible to want something and to fear it, all at the same time? But he didn't. He just turned and walked out of the bedroom and Lisa slumped back on the pillows and lay there, listening to the sounds of his leaving. The front door clicked shut and she heard the thud of his footsteps on the pavement before a door slammed and his powerful car pulled away.

She lay there until she needed to go to the bathroom and then padded across the room to where her discarded green panties lay and beside them a small, cream-coloured card, which must have fallen from his trouser pocket.

She picked it up and stared at it and a feeling of self-disgust rippled over her shivering skin. She'd thought it wasn't possible to feel any worse than she already did but she was wrong. Oh, Luc, she thought. How *could* you? He had taken her to a party and had sex with her afterwards—but had still managed to bag himself a calling card from the beautiful Hollywood actress she'd seen at the wedding.

Compressing her lips together to stop them from trembling, Lisa crushed the card between her fingers and dropped it into the bin.

CHAPTER FOUR

'JASON THINKS YOU'RE PREGNANT.'

Lisa almost dropped the toddler-sized dress she had been in the process of folding and slowly turned her head to stare at her sister. They were sitting side by side on the carpet as they sorted out Tamsin's clothes, deciding which ones would still fit her for the cold winter months ahead. But now the tiny dress dangled forgotten from her fingers as she looked into green-gold eyes so like her own. 'What...did you say?'

Brittany appeared to be choosing her words with care. 'Jason says you've got the same look I had when I was carrying Tamsin. And I've noticed that you've stopped wearing your own dresses, which struck me as kind of strange.' Brittany gave a little wriggle of her shoulders. 'Since you've always told me that wearing your own dresses was your best advertisement. And you've never been the kind of woman to slop around in jeans and a loose shirt before.'

Lisa didn't answer as she put the dress down and picked up a tiny pair of dungarees, knowing she was playing for time but not caring. She didn't owe Brittany an explanation. Or Jason, for that matter. Especially not Jason—who was so fond of judging other people but who never seemed to take the time to look at his own grasping behaviour.

But Jason's scrounging was irrelevant right now, because somehow he had unwittingly hit on the truth and passed it on to her sister—and the hard fact remained that she *was* starting to show. At just over sixteen weeks Lisa guessed that was inevitable. Unless she was still in that horrified state of denial which had settled over her at the beginning, when the countless pregnancy tests she'd taken had all yielded the same terrifying results—but at least they'd explained why she'd felt so peculiar. Why her breasts had started aching in a way which was really uncomfortable. Eventually, she had taken herself off to the doctor, who had pronounced her fit and healthy and then smilingly congratulated her on first-time motherhood. And if Lisa's response had been fabricated rather than genuine, surely that wasn't surprising. Because how could she feel happy about carrying the child of a man who no longer wanted her? A man who was about to marry another woman?

'So who's the father?' questioned Brittany.

'Nobody you know,' said Lisa quickly.

There was a pause. 'Not that bloke you used to go out with?'

Lisa stiffened. 'Which bloke?'

'The one you were so cagey about. The one you never wanted anyone to meet.' Brittany sniffed. 'Almost as if you felt we weren't good enough for him.'

Lisa bit her lip. It was true she'd never introduced

Brittany or Jason to the Prince—and not just that she had been worried that Jason might attempt to 'borrow' money from the wealthy royal without any intention of ever paying it back. She'd known there was no future in the relationship and therefore no point of merging their two very different lives.

And she didn't want to bring Luc into the conversation now. If she told her sister that she was expecting the child of a wealthy prince, Brittany would inevitably tell Jason and she wouldn't put it past him to go hawking the story to the highest bidder. 'I'd rather not discuss the father,' she said.

'Right.' Brittany paused. 'So what are you going to do?'

'Do?' Lisa sat back on her heels and looked at her sister blankly. 'What do you mean, *do*?'

'About the *baby*, of course! Does he know?'

No, he didn't know—though she'd done her best to try to contact him. Lisa chewed on her lip. Even that had been another stark lesson in humiliation. She had tried to ring him on the precious number she still had stored in her phone—but the number was no longer in service. Of course it wasn't. So she'd summoned up all her courage to telephone the palace in Mardovia, somehow managing to get through to one of his aides— a formidable-sounding woman called Eleonora. But Eleonora had stonewalled all her attempts to speak to the Prince and, short of blurting out her momentous news on the phone, Lisa had eventually given up—because how could she possibly disclose something like that to a member of Luc's staff?

And if she was being totally honest, she had been slightly relieved, thinking perhaps it was better this way. He was due to marry another woman. Someone called Princess Sophie—a woman who had never done *her* any harm. How could she ruin her life by announcing that an impulsive one-night stand had resulted in another woman carrying his baby? Damn Luc Leonidas, Lisa thought viciously. Damn him for not bothering to tell her about his impending marriage *before* he'd jumped into bed with her.

'No,' Lisa said, steeling herself against the curiosity in her sister's eyes. 'He doesn't know and he isn't going to. He doesn't want to see me again and he certainly doesn't want to be a father to my child. So I'm going to bring this baby up on my own and it's going to be a happy and well-cared-for baby.'

'But, Lisa—'

'No, please. Don't.' Lisa shook her head, feeling little beads of sweat at the back of her neck and so she scooped up the great curtain of curls and waved it around to let the air refresh her skin. She looked pointedly at her sister, her gaze intended to remind her of the harsh truth known to both of them. That a child brought up in a home with a resentful man was not a happy home. 'I'm not asking your opinion on this, Brittany,' she said quietly. 'I'm just telling you how it's going to be.'

There was a pause. 'Is he married?'

Not yet.

'No comment. Like I said, the discussion is over.'

Lisa gave a grimace of a smile as she rose to her feet. 'But you've given me an idea.'

'*I* have?' Brittany looked momentarily puzzled.

'Yes. I keep saying that you're much cleverer than you give yourself credit for.' Lisa narrowed her eyes, her mind suddenly going into overdrive. 'And if I'm going to spend the next few months getting even bigger, I might as well do it in style.'

Brittany's green-gold eyes narrowed. 'What's that supposed to mean?'

'It means that although I've had a few extra orders since I went to that fancy wedding back in August, it hasn't been enough to take the business forward as I'd hoped. What I need is a completely new direction— and I think I've just found one.' Lisa sucked in a deep breath as she patted her expanding stomach. 'Think about it. There aren't many really fashionable maternity dresses on the market right now—especially ones in natural fabrics, which "breathe". I can work in more fabrics than just my trademark silk. Cotton and linen and wool. There's an opportunity here staring me right in the face, and it seems I'm the perfect person to model my new collection.'

'But…won't that get publicity?'

Lisa smiled and it felt like the first genuine smile she'd given in a long time. 'I sincerely hope so.'

'You aren't afraid that the father will hear about it and come to find you?'

Lisa shook her head. No. That was one thing she *wasn't* worried about. Luc certainly wouldn't be trawling the pages of fashion magazines now that he'd turned his back on his playboy life and locked himself away on his Mediterranean principality. Luc had made his position very clear.

'No,' she said quietly. 'He won't find out.'

She sat back on her heels and as a rush of something like hope flooded through her, so did a new resolve. She needed to be strong for her baby and that wasn't going to happen if she sat around wailing at the unfairness of it all. She was young, fit and hard-working and she had more than enough love to give this innocent new life which was growing inside her.

Her baby *would* be happy and well cared for, she vowed fiercely. No matter what it took.

Luc sat at his desk feeling as if he had just opened Pandora's box. The blood pounded inside his head and his skin grew clammy. There must be some kind of mistake. There *must* be. He had been bored. Why else would he have tapped Lisa's name into the search engine of his computer? Yet wasn't the truth something a little more unpalatable? That he couldn't get her out of his head, no matter how hard he tried.

Nearly six months had passed since he'd seen her and he had been eaten up with guilt about what had happened just before he'd left London. He had broken his self-imposed celibacy with his ex-lover, instead of the woman he was due to marry. But he was over that now and the date for his wedding to Sophie was due to be announced next week. It was the end of an era and the beginning of a new one, and he intended to embrace it wholeheartedly. And that was why he had typed Lisa's name into the search engine—as a kind of careless test to see whether he could now look on her with indifference.

A muscle at his temple flickered as once again he stared with disbelief at the screen. He was no stranger to shock. He had lost his mother in the most shocking of circumstances—and in some ways he had lost his father at the same time. He had thought nothing would ever rock him like that again, but a faint echo of that disbelief reverberated through him now. He stared at the image in front of him and his mouth dried. A picture of Lisa at a fashion show. Her lustrous caramel curls were pulled away from her face and her eyes and skin seemed to glow with a new vitality—but it hadn't been that which had made his blood run cold.

He stared at her swollen belly. At the hand which lay across her curving shape in that gently protective way which pregnant women always seemed to adopt. Features hardening into a frown, he read the accompanying text.

DESIGNER LAUNCHES SWELL NEW LINE!
Lisa Bailey, famous for the understated dresses which captivated a generation of 'Ladies Who Lunch', last night launched her new range of maternity wear. And stunning Lisa just happened to be modelling one of her own designs!

Coyly refusing to name the baby's father, the six-months-pregnant St Martin's graduate would say only that, 'Women have successfully been

bringing up children on their own for centuries.
It's hardly ground-breaking stuff.'
   Ms Bailey's collection is available to buy from
her Belgravia shop.

Luc sat back in his chair.

Lisa, *pregnant*? He felt the ice move from his veins to his heart. It couldn't be his. Definitely not his. He shook his head as if his denial would make it true, but memories had started to crowd into his mind which would not be silenced. Her heated claim that there had been no other lover than him since they'd been apart—and he had *believed* her, because he knew Lisa well enough to realise she wouldn't lie about something like that. Six months pregnant. He sat back in his chair, his heart pounding as he raked a strand of hair away from his heated face. Of *course* it was his.

Lisa Bailey was carrying his baby.

His baby.

Disbelief gave way to anger as he shut down the computer. Why the hell hadn't she told him? Why had she left him to find out in such a way—and, just as importantly, who else knew?

He reached out for the phone, but withdrew his hand again. He needed to think carefully and not act on impulse, for this was as delicate a negotiation as any he had ever handled. Using the phone would be unsatisfactory and there was no guarantee the call wouldn't be overheard by someone at her end. Or his. It occurred to him that she might refuse to speak to him—in fact, the more he thought about it, the more likely a scenario that seemed, for she could be as stubborn as hell.

Leaning forward, he pressed the buzzer on his desk and Eleonora appeared almost immediately.

'Come in and close the door.' Luc paused for a moment before he spoke. 'I want you to cancel everything in my diary for the next few days.'

Her darkly beautiful face remained impassive. 'That might present some difficulties, Your Royal Highness.'

Luc regarded her sternly. 'And? Is that not what I pay you for—to handle the tricky stuff and smooth over any difficulties?'

'Indeed.' Eleonora inclined her dark head. 'And does Your Royal Highness wish me to make any alternative arrangements to fill the unexpected spaces in your diary?'

Luc's mouth flattened as he nodded. 'I need to fly to Isolaverde and afterwards I want the plane on standby, ready to take me to London.'

'And am I allowed to ask why, Your Royal Highness?'

'Not yet, you're not.'

Eleonora bit her lip but said nothing more and Luc waited until she had left the office before slowly turning to stare out of the window at the palace gardens. Already the days hinted at the warm weather ahead, yet his heart felt as wintry as if it had been covered with layers of ice. He couldn't bear to sit here and think about the unthinkable. He wanted to go to England now. To go to Lisa Bailey and…and…

And what? His default mechanism had always been

one of action, but it was vital he did nothing impulsive. He must think this through carefully and consider every possibility which lay open to him.

The following morning he flew to Isolaverde for the meeting he was dreading and from there his jet took him straight to London—but by the time he was sitting in his limousine outside Lisa's shop, his feelings of disbelief and anger had turned into a clear focus of determination.

The evening was cold and a persistent drizzle had left the pavements shining wet, with a sickly orange hue which glowed down from the streetlights. In the window of Lisa's shop was a pregnant mannequin wearing a silk dress, her hand on her belly and a prettily arranged heap of wooden toys at her feet. Luc had sat and watched a procession of well-heeled women being dropped off by car or by taxi, sheltered from the rain by their chauffeurs' umbrellas as they walked into the shop. Business must be booming, he thought grimly.

He forced himself to wait until the shop closed and a couple of women who were clearly staff had left the building. As Luc waited, a passing police officer tapped on the window of the limousine, discreetly overlooking the fact that it was parked on double yellow lines once he was made aware of the owner's identity.

He waited until the lights in the shop had been dimmed and he could see only the gleaming curls of the woman sitting behind a small desk—and then he walked across the street and opened the door to the sound of a tinkly bell.

Lisa glanced up as the bell rang, wondering if a

customer had left their phone behind or changed their mind about an order—but it was nothing as simple as that. It felt like a case of history repeating itself as Luc walked into her shop, only this time there wasn't a look of curiosity on his face which failed to conceal the spark of hunger in his eyes. This time she saw nothing but fury in their sapphire depths—though when she stopped to think about it, could she really blame him?

Yet she had stupidly convinced herself that this scenario would never happen—as if some unknown guardian angel were protecting her from the wrath of the man who stood in front of her, his features dark with rage. She was glad to be sitting down, because she thought her knees might have buckled from the shock of seeing him standing there—trying to control his ragged breathing. He didn't have to say a word for her to know why he was here; it was as obvious as the swell of her belly, which he was staring at like a man who had just seen a ghost.

Don't be rash, she reasoned, telling herself this was much too important to indulge her own feelings. She had to think about the baby and only the baby.

'Luc,' she said. 'I wasn't expecting you.'

He lifted his gaze from her stomach to her face as their eyes met in a silent clash. 'Weren't you?' he said grimly. 'What's the matter, Lisa? Surely you must have known I would turn up sooner or later?'

She licked her suddenly dry lips. 'I tried not to think about it.'

'You tried not to think about it?' he repeated. 'Is

that why I was left to discover via social media that you're pregnant?'

'I didn't mean—'

'I don't care what you did or didn't mean because you're going to have a baby.' Ruthlessly, he cut across her words. But for the first and only time since she'd known him, he seemed to be struggling with the rest of the sentence, because when finally he spoke, he sounded choked. '*My* baby.'

Lisa could feel the blood draining from her face and thought how wrong this all seemed. A miracle of life which should—and did—fill her with joy and yet the air around them throbbed with accusation and tension. Her hands were unsteady and she felt almost dizzy, and all she could think was that this kind of emotion couldn't be good for the baby. 'Yes,' she breathed at last, staring down at the tight curve of her belly as if to remind herself. 'Yes, I'm having your baby.'

There was an ominous silence before he spoke again. A moment when he followed the direction of her gaze, staring again at her new shape as if he couldn't believe it.

'Yet you didn't tell me,' he accused. 'You kept it secret. As if it was your news alone and nobody else's. As if I had no right to know.'

'I did try to tell you!' she protested. 'I tried phoning you but your number had changed.'

'I change my number every six months,' he informed her coldly. 'It's a security thing.'

Lisa pushed a handful of hair away from her hot

face. 'And then I phoned the palace and got through to one of your aides. Eleonora, I think her name was.'

Luc's head jerked back. 'You spoke to Eleonora?'

'Yes. And she told me that you weren't available. Actually, it went further than that. She said I wasn't on your list of telephone contacts. If you must know she made me feel like some pestering little groupie who needed to be kept away from the precious Prince at all costs.'

Luc let out a long sigh. Of course she had. Eleonora was one of his most fiercely loyal subjects, and part of her role had always been to act as his gatekeeper, and never more so than when he'd returned to Mardovia following his illicit night with Lisa. When he'd been full of remorse for what he'd done but unable to shake off the erotic memories which had clung to his skin like the soft touch of her fingers. He had thrown himself into his work, undertaking a punishing schedule which had taken him to every town and city on the island. And he had instructed his fiercely loyal aide not to bother him unless absolutely necessary.

'You could have written,' he said.

'What, sent you a postcard, or a letter which was bound to be opened by a member of your staff? Saying what? *Dear Prince Luciano, I'm having your baby*?' Her gaze was very steady. 'You told me you were going to marry another woman. You made it very clear you never wished to see me again. And after you'd gone, I found a card on my bedroom floor—a card from some Hollywood actress you must have met at the wedding. My lowly place in the pecking order was confirmed there and then.'

'I could tell you that I took the card simply as a politeness with no intention of contacting her again, but that is irrelevant,' he gritted out. 'Because the bottom line is that you're pregnant, and we're going to have to deal with that.'

She shook her head. 'But there's nothing to deal with. You don't have to worry. I have no wish to upset your fiancée or your plans for the future. And lots of women have children without the support of men!' she finished brightly.

'So you said in your recent interview,' he agreed witheringly.

'And it doesn't matter what you say.' She looked at him defiantly, because defiance made her feel strong. It stopped her from crumpling to the ground and just opening her mouth and *howling*. It stopped her from wishing he would cradle her in his arms, like any normal father-to-be—his face full of wonder and tenderness. She licked her lips. 'Because when it boils down to it, this is just a baby like any other.'

'But that's where you're wrong, Lisa,' he negated softly. 'It *is* different. This is not *just a baby*. The child you carry has royal blood running through its veins. Royal Mardovian blood. Do you have any idea of the significance of that?' His face hardened. 'Unless that was the calculated risk you took all along?'

She stared at him in confusion. 'I'm not sure I understand.'

'No?' The words began to bubble up inside him, demanding to be spoken and, although years of professional diplomacy urged Luc to use caution, the shock

of this unexpected discovery was making him want
to throw that caution to the wind. 'Maybe this is what
you hoped for all along,' he accused. 'I saw your face
at the wedding when you started talking about your
niece. That dreamy look which suggested you longed
to become a mother yourself. I believe women often become broody when they're around other people's children. When their body clock is ticking away as yours
so obviously is. Is that what happened to you, Lisa?
Only instead of saddling yourself with a troublesome
partner as your sister seems to have done—maybe you
decided to go it alone.'

'You're *insane*,' she breathed. 'Completely insane.'

'Am I? Don't they say that children are the new ac-
cessories for the modern career woman? Was that why
you threw yourself at me that night, when I was trying
to do the honourable thing of resisting you?' He gave
a bitter laugh. 'Was that why you made love to me so
energetically—riding me like some rodeo rider on a
bucking bronco? Perhaps hoping to test the strength
of the condom we used—because you wanted my seed
inside you. It is not unknown.'

She stared at him in disbelief as his words flooded
over her in a bitter stream. 'Or maybe I went even further?' she declared. 'Perhaps you think I was so desperate to have your child that I went into the bathroom
after you'd gone and performed some sort of amateur
DIY insemination? That's not beyond the realms of
possibility either!'

'Don't be so disgusting!' he snapped.

'Me?' She stared at him. 'That's rich. You're the

one who came in here making all kinds of bizarre suggestions when all I wanted was to try to do the decent thing—for everyone concerned. You're going to marry Sophie and...' She stood up then, needing to move around, needing to bring back some blood to her cramped limbs. Leaving behind the clutter of her desk, she walked over to a rail of the new maternity dresses which she'd worked so hard on—pretty dresses which discreetly factored in the extra material needed at the front. She'd been feeling so proud of her new collection. She'd taken lots of new orders after the show and had allowed herself the tentative hope that she could carry on supporting Brittany and Tamsin and still make a good life for herself and her own baby. Yet now, in the face of Luc's angry remarks—her will was beginning to waver.

She straightened a shimmery turquoise dress before forcing herself to meet his gaze. 'Don't you understand that I'm letting you off the hook? I don't want to mess up your plans by lumbering you with a baby you never intended to have. A commoner's baby. You're going to be married to someone else. A princess.' The hurt she'd managed so successfully to hide started to creep up, but she forced herself to push it away. To ask the question she needed to ask and to try to do it without her voice trembling, which suddenly seemed like one of the hardest things she'd ever had to do. 'Because how the hell do you think Princess Sophie is going to feel when you tell her you're going to be a father?'

CHAPTER FIVE

'SHE KNOWS,' SAID LUC, the words leaving his mouth as if they were poison. 'Princess Sophie knows about the baby and it's over between us.'

He watched Lisa grow still, like an animal walking through the darkened undergrowth suddenly scenting danger. Her green-gold eyes narrowed as she looked at him and her voice was an uncertain tremble.

'B-but you said—'

'I know what I said,' he agreed. 'But that was then. This is now. Or did you really think I was going to take another woman as my wife when you are pregnant with my child? This changes everything, Lisa.' There was a heartbeat of a pause. 'Which is why I went to see the Princess before I came to England.'

She winced, closing her eyes briefly—as if she was experiencing her own, private pain. 'And what...what did she say?'

Luc picked his words carefully, still trying to come to terms with the capriciousness of women. He didn't understand them and sometimes he thought he never would. And when he stopped to think about it—why should he, when the only role models he'd known had all been paid for out of the palace purse?

He had been expecting a show of hurt and contempt from his young fiancée. He had steeled himself against her expected insults as he had been summoned into the glorious throne room of her palace on Isolaverde, where shortly afterwards she had appeared—an elegant figure in a gown of palest blue which had floated around her. But the vitriol he deserved hadn't been forthcoming.

'She told me she was relieved.'

'Relieved?'

'She said that a wedding planned when the bride-to-be was still in infancy was completely outdated and my news had allowed her to look at her life with renewed clarity. She told me that she didn't actually *want* to get married—and certainly not to a man she didn't really know, for the sake of our nations.' He didn't mention the way she had turned on him and told him that she didn't approve of his reputation. That the things she'd heard and read in the past—exploits which some of his ex-lovers had managed to slip to the press—had appalled her. She had looked at him very proudly and announced that maybe fate was doing her a favour by freeing her from her commitment to such a man. And what could he do but agree with her, when he was in no position to deny her accusations? 'So I am now a free man,' he finished heavily.

Lisa's response to this was total silence. He watched her walk over to the desk and pour herself a glass of water and drink it down very quickly before turning back to face him. 'How very convenient for you,' she said.

'And for you, of course.'

Abruptly, she put the glass down. 'Me?' The wariness in her green-gold eyes had been replaced by a glint of anger. 'I'm sorry—you've lost me. What does the breaking off of your engagement have to do with me? We had a one-night stand with unwanted consequences, that's all. Two people who planned never to see one another again. Nothing has changed.'

Luc studied her defensive posture, knowing there were better methods of conveying what he needed to say and certainly more suitable environments in which to do so than the shop in which she worked. But he didn't have the luxury of time on his side—for all kinds of reasons. His people would be delighted by news that his royal bloodline would be continued, but he doubted they'd be overjoyed to hear that the royal mother was an unknown commoner and not their beloved Princess Sophie. He would have to ask the Princess to issue a dignified announcement before introducing Lisa as his bride, for that would surely lessen the impact. And he would get his office to start working on image control—on how best to minimise the potential for negative repercussions for him and for Mardovia.

'Everything has changed,' he said. 'For I am now free to marry you.'

Lisa's heart missed a beat, but even in the midst of her shock she reflected what cruel tricks life could play. Because once Luc's words would have affected her very differently. When she'd been starting to care for him…really care. When she'd been standing on the edge of that terrifying precipice called love. Just before she'd pulled back and walked away from him— she would have given everything she possessed to hear Luc ask her to marry him.

And now?

Now she accepted that the words were as empty as a politician's sound bites. The mists had cleared and she saw him for who he really was. A powerful man who shifted women around in his life like pawns in a game of chess. Why, even his brides were interchangeable! Princess Sophie had been heading for the altar, only to be cast aside with barely a second thought because a pregnant commoner counted for more than a virgin princess. And now *she* was expected to step in and take her place as his bride. Poor Sophie. And poor *her*, if she didn't grow a backbone.

She drew in a deep breath. 'You really think I'd *marry* you, Luc?'

The arrogant smile which curved his mouth made it clear he thought her protest a token one.

'I agree it isn't the most conventional of unions,' he said. 'But given the circumstances, you'd be crazy not to.'

Lisa could feel herself growing angry. Almost as angry as when she'd looked down at her dead mother's face and thought how wasted her life had been. She remembered walking away from the funeral parlour hoping that she had found peace at last.

She'd been angry too when Brittany had dropped out of her hard-fought-for place at one of England's top universities because Jason had wanted her to have his baby, and nothing Lisa had said could talk her sister out of it, or make her wait. Another woman who had allowed herself to be manipulated by a man.

But maybe she no longer had a right to play judge and jury when now she found herself in a situation which was wrong from just about every angle. She stared into Luc's face but saw no affection on his rugged features—nothing but a grim determination to have things on *his* terms, the way he always did. And she couldn't afford to let him—because if she gave him the slightest leeway, he would swamp her with the sheer force of his royal power.

'I think we'll have to disagree on the level of my craziness,' she said quietly. 'Because you must realise I can't possibly marry you, Luc, no matter what you say—or how many inducements you make.'

His sudden stillness indicated that her reply had surprised him.

'I don't really think you have a choice, Lisa,' he said.

'Oh, but that's where you're wrong. There is always a choice. And mine was to have this child alone and to love it with all my heart. It still is.'

'But I am the father.'

'I know you are. And now that it's all out in the open you must realise that I shan't deny you access to your child.' She smiled up at him. 'We'll keep emotion out of it and try to come to some satisfactory arrangement for all of us.'

He didn't smile back.

'You seem to forget that you carry a prince or princess,' he said softly. 'And it is vital they should grow up on the island they will one day inherit.'

She met his gaze. 'I didn't realise illegitimate offspring were entitled to inherit.'

A muscle began to flicker at Luc's temple because this conversation wasn't going according to plan. His marriage proposal had been intended to pacify her and possibly to thrill her. To have her eating out of his hand—because women had been trying to push him towards the altar most of his adult life and deep down he had imagined Lisa would be no different. He'd thought she would be picturing herself walking down the wide aisle of Mardovia's famous cathedral—a glittering tiara in her curly hair. Yet all she was doing was surveying him with a proud look and he felt the slow burn of indignation. Who the *hell* did she think she was—turning down his offer of marriage without even a moment's consideration?

For a split second he felt powerless—an unwelcome sensation to someone whose power had always been his lifeblood. He wanted to tell her that she *would* do exactly as he demanded and she might as well resign herself to that fact right now. But the belligerent expression on her face told him he had better proceed with caution.

His gaze drifted over her, but for once the riot of curls and green-gold eyes were not the focus of his attention. He noted how much fuller her breasts were and how the swell of her belly completely dwarfed her tiny frame. *And inside that belly was his child.* His throat thickened.

She looked like a tiny boat in full sail, yet she was no less enticing for all that. He still wanted her and if circumstances had been different he might have pulled her in his arms and started to kiss her. He could have lulled her into compliance and taken her into one of those changing rooms. Drawn the velvet curtains away from prying eyes and had her gasping her approval to whatever it was he asked of her.

But she was heavy with child. Glowing like a pomegranate in the thin winter sun—and because of that he couldn't use sex as a bargaining tool.

'Get your coat,' he said. 'And I'll take you home.'

'I haven't finished what I was doing.'

'I'll wait.'

'There's no need. Honestly, I can get a cab.'

'I said, I'll wait. Don't fight me on this, Lisa—because I'm not going anywhere.' And with this he positioned himself on one of the velvet and gilt chairs, stretching his long legs in front of him.

Lisa wanted to protest, but what was the point? She couldn't deny they needed to talk, but not now and not like this—when she was still flustered by his sudden appearance and the announcement that he'd called off his wedding. She needed to have her wits about her but her brain currently felt as if it were clouded in mist, leaving her unable to think properly. And that was dangerous.

He had taken out his cell phone and was flicking through his emails and giving them his full attention, and she found herself almost envying him. If only she were capable of such detachment of thought! The figures in front of her were a jumble and in the end she gave up trying to make sense of them. How could she possibly concentrate on her work with Luc distracting her like this?

She shut down her computer and gave him a cool look. 'Okay. I'm ready,' she said.

She sensed he was exerting considerable restraint to remain patient as she carried the jug and water glass out into the kitchen, set the burglar alarm, turned off the lights and locked the door. Outside, the drizzle was coming down a little heavier now and his driver leapt from the car to run over and position a huge umbrella over her head. She wanted to push the monstrous black thing away—uncaring that the soft rain would turn her hair into a mass of frizz—but she stopped just in time. She needed to be calm and *reasonable* because she suspected that she and Luc were coming at this pregnancy from completely different angles. And if she allowed her fluctuating hormones to make her all volatile, he would probably get some awful Mardovian judge to pronounce her unfit to be a mother!

She sat in frozen silence on the way to her apartment and a feeling of frustration built up inside her when he made no attempt to talk to her. Was he playing mind games? Trying to see which of them would buckle first? Well, he had better realise that this wasn't a game—not for her. She was strong and resolute and knew exactly what she wanted.

But when they drew up outside her humble block, he surprised her with his words.

'Have dinner with me tomorrow night.'

'Dinner?'

'Why not?' he said. 'We need to discuss what we're going to do and there's nothing in the rulebook which says we can't do it in a civilised manner.'

In the dim light Lisa blinked. She thought about the two of them making an entrance in the kind of fancy restaurant he would no doubt frequent—the handsome Prince and the heavily pregnant woman.

'But if we're seen out together,' she said slowly, 'that would be making a fairly unequivocal statement, wouldn't it? A prince would never appear alone in public with a woman in my condition unless he was willing to be compromised. Is that what you want, Luc?'

His eyes glittered as he leaned towards her. 'Yes,' he said. 'That's exactly what I want. I *want* the world to know that I am the father. You have my child in your belly, Lisa. Do you really think I intend to relinquish my claim on my own flesh and blood?'

The words sounded almost *primitive* and they were filled with a sense of possession. They reminded Lisa of the full force of his power and the fact that he had grown up with very different values from her. 'Of course I don't!' she said. 'We can meet with a lawyer and have a legal agreement drawn up. You can see your child any time you like—within reason. Surely you can have no objection to that?'

His eyes were cold and so was his voice. 'I think you are missing the point, *chérie*. I intend to marry you.'

'I'm sorry, Luc.' She gave a slight shake of her head as she reached for the door handle. 'I'm afraid that's just not going to happen.'

But he leaned across the seat and placed his hand over her forearm, and Lisa hated the instant ripple of recognition which whispered over her skin the moment he touched her. Did he feel it, too—was that why he slid his thumb down to her wrist as if to count the beats of the rocketing pulse beneath?

'Let me see you to your door,' he said.

The set of his jaw told her that objection would be a waste of time and so she shrugged. 'Suit yourself. But you're not coming in.'

Luc made no comment as he accompanied her to her front door as he'd done what now seemed a lifetime ago. But this time there was no warmth and light gilding the summer evening into a golden blur which matched their shared desire. This time there was only the cold bite of a rainy night and a barely restrained sense of hostility. But she was pregnant, he reminded himself. *Inside her beat the tiny heart of his own flesh and blood. And that changed everything.*

Luc was not a sentimental man and emotion had been schooled out of him from an early age, but now he became aware of something much bigger than himself. He stared at her swollen frame with the realisation that here lay something more precious than all the riches in his entire principality. And he was shaken by just how badly he wanted it.

'I don't want to have to fight you to get what I want, Lisa,' he said softly as they reached her door. 'But if you force my hand then I'm afraid that's what's going to happen. Perhaps I should warn you now that it is better not to defy me.'

Her eyes narrowed like those of a cornered cat. 'If only you could hear yourself!' she retorted, unlocking her front door and pushing it open. 'I can defy you all I like! I'm a free spirit—not your possession or your subject. This is the twenty-first century, Luc, and you can't make me do something I don't want to—so why don't we resume this discussion in the cold light of day when you're ready to see sense?'

His powerful body grew still and for one hopeful moment Lisa thought he was about to take her advice. But she was wrong. He lifted his hand to rake his fingers back through his rain-spangled hair and she hated the sudden erotic recall which that simple gesture provoked.

'Your backer is a man called Martin Lawrence,' he said slowly.

She didn't ask how he knew. She didn't show her surprise or foreboding as she raised her eyebrows. 'And?'

'And yesterday afternoon he sold all his interest in your business to me.'

It took her a few seconds to process this and once the significance hit her, she shook her head. 'I don't believe you,' she said. 'Martin wouldn't do that. He wouldn't. Not without telling me.'

'I'm afraid he did.' A cynical smile tugged at the corners of his mouth. 'The lure of money is usually enough to eclipse even the most worthy of principles and I offered him a price he couldn't refuse.'

'You...bastard,' she said, walking like a robot into her hallway, too dazed to object when he followed her and snapped on the harsh overhead light. But this time there were no frantic kisses. No barely controlled hunger as they tore at each other's clothes. There was nothing but a simmering mistrust as Lisa stared into his unyielding blue eyes. 'So what are you planning to do?' she questioned. 'Dramatically cut my funds? Or slowly bleed me dry so that you can force me into closure?'

'I'm hoping it won't come to that,' he said. 'My acquisition of your business was simply a back-up. An insurance policy, if you like, in case you proved to be stubborn as I anticipated, which is exactly what has happened. But I have no desire to be ruthless unless you make me, Lisa. I won't interfere with your business if you return to Mardovia with me as my wife.'

She shook her head. 'I can't do that, Luc,' she breathed. 'You know I can't.'

'Why not?' His gazed bored into her. 'Is it because I'm the wrong man? Are you holding out for Mr Right? Is that what this is all about?'

She gave a short laugh. 'Mr Right is a fictional character created by women who still believe in fairy tales. And I don't.'

'Well, isn't that just perfect, because neither do I. Which means that neither of us have any illusions which can be shattered.'

But his declaration gave Lisa little comfort. Her back was aching and her feet felt swollen. She walked into the tiny sitting room and slumped into one of the overstuffed armchairs without even bothering to put the light on. But Luc took control of this, too, following her and snapping on a lamp before drawing the curtains against the darkness outside. She found herself thinking that his servants must usually do this kind of thing for him and wondered what it must be like, to live his privileged life.

'We don't have to go through with a sham marriage,' she said wearily. 'I told you. We can do this the modern way and share custody. Lots of people do. And given all the wealth at your disposal, it will be easier for us to achieve than for most people.' From somewhere she conjured up a hopeful smile. 'I mean, it's not like we're going to be worried about whether we can afford to run two households, is it?'

But he didn't respond to her feeble attempt at humour.

'You're missing the point,' he said. 'I have a duty to my people and the land I was born to rule. Mardovia's stability has been threatened in the past and the principality was almost destroyed as a result. It cannot be allowed to happen again and I will not let it. This child is the future of my country—'

'What? Even if it's a girl?'

He went very still. 'Do you *know* the sex of the baby?' he questioned.

Lisa thought about lying. Of saying she was going to have a girl in the hope that the macho rules which seemed to define him would make him reconsider his demand that she marry him. But she couldn't do that. It would be a cheap move to use their baby as a pawn in their battle, and she sensed it wouldn't make any difference.

She shook her head. 'No. I told the sonographer

I didn't want to know. I didn't like the idea of going through a long labour without even the promise of a surprise at the end. A bit like getting your Christmas presents and discovering that nobody had bothered to wrap them.'

He smiled at this and, inexplicably, Lisa felt herself softening. As if nature had programmed her to melt whenever the father of her child dished out some scrap of affection. *And she couldn't afford to melt.*

'Whatever the sex of the baby, there's no reason why the act of succession cannot be re-examined some time in the future,' he said and walked across the room towards her, towering over her, his muscular body completely dominating her line of vision. 'I am doing my very best to be reasonable here and I will do everything in my power to accommodate your desires, Lisa. And before you start glowering at me like that, I wasn't referring just to physical desires, though I'm more than happy to take those into account.'

Lisa could feel her face growing hot and her breasts beginning to prickle. And the most infuriating thing of all was that right then she wanted him to touch them again. To cup and fondle them and flicker his tongue over them. She wanted him to put his hand between her legs and to ease the aching there. Was it *normal* for a pregnant woman to feel such a powerful sense of desire?

'I can't do that,' she said in a low voice. 'My life is here. I can't leave my little niece, or my sister.'

'Why not?'

'Because I…help them.'

'What do you mean, you help them?'

She shrugged. 'They have no regular income.'

'Your sister is a single parent?'

'Sort of. She's with Jason, only they're not married and he's rather work-shy.'

'Then it's about time he changed his attitude,' he said. 'Your sister and child will receive all the support they require because I will be able to help with that, too. And soon you will have a family of your own to think about.'

'And my business?' she demanded, levering herself into a sitting-up position and trying to summon the energy to glare at him. 'What about that? I've worked for years to establish myself and yet now I'm expected to drop everything—as if my work was nothing but some disposable little hobby.'

'I am willing to compromise on that and I don't intend to deprive you of your career,' he said softly. 'You have people who work for you. Let them run the shop in your absence while you design from the palace.'

And Lisa knew that whatever objection she raised Luc would override her. Because he could. He didn't care that she was close to her little niece and terrified that everything she'd worked for would simply slip away if she wasn't there to oversee it. He didn't care about her—he never had. All he cared about was what *he* wanted. And he wanted this baby.

'You don't understand.' She raised her hands in a gesture of appeal, but the answering look in his eyes was stony.

'I understand more than you might think,' he said.

'I shall accommodate your wishes as much as possible. I don't intend to be a cruel husband. But be very clear about one thing, Lisa—that this topic is not open for debate. That if it comes to it, I will drag you screaming and kicking to the altar, because you *will* be my wife and my child *will* be born on Mardovian soil.'

There was a pause as she bit her lip before looking up at the grim determination which made his blue eyes look so cold. 'If…if I agree to this forced marriage, I want some form of compensation.'

'Compensation?' he echoed incredulously, as if she was insulting him—which in a way she guessed she was. Unless you counted what she wanted as some old-fashioned kind of dowry.

'Yes,' she said quietly. 'I want you to buy my sister a house of her own and provide her with a regular income which will free her from the clutches of her sponging partner.'

His mouth twisted. 'And that is the price for your consent?'

Lisa nodded. 'That is my price,' she said heavily.

CHAPTER SIX

Luc looked around the room—a relatively small room but the one where his wedding to Lisa Tiffany Bailey was about to take place. It was decked out with garlands of flowers, their heavy fragrance perfuming the air, and over the marble fireplace was the crimson and gold of the Mardovian flag. Everything around him was as exquisitely presented as you would expect in the embassy of a country which had a reputation for excellence—and the staff had pulled out all the stops for the unexpected wedding of their ruler to his English bride. But when it boiled down to it, it was just a room.

His face tightening with tension, he thought about the many generations of his family who had married in the august surroundings of the famous cathedral in Mardovia's capital. Grand weddings attended by other royals, by world leaders, politicians and aristocracy. Huge, glittering affairs which had been months in the planning and talked about for years afterwards.

But there would be no such wedding for him.

Because how could he marry in front of his traditionally conservative people with such a visibly pregnant bride in tow? Wouldn't it flaunt his own questionable behaviour, as well as risking offending Princess Sophie—a woman adored by his subjects? This was to be a small and discreet ceremony, with a woman who did not want to take part in it.

He allowed himself a quick glance at the chairs on which her small family sat. The sister who looked so like her, and her boyfriend Jason, who Lisa clearly didn't trust. *Just as she didn't trust him.* Luc watched the casually dressed man with the slightly too long hair glance around the ornate room, unable to hide his covetous expression as he eyed up the lavish fixtures and fittings. He sensed Lisa was disappointed that the new house and income which had been given to her sister had failed to remove Jason from the equation. It seemed that her sister's love for him ran deep...

But her dysfunctional family wasn't the reason he was here today and Luc tensed as the Mardovian national anthem began to play. Slowly, he turned his head to watch as Lisa made her entrance, his heart pounding as she started to walk towards him and he was unprepared—and surprised—by the powerful surge of feeling which ran through him as she approached.

His mouth dried to dust as he stared at his bride, thinking how *beautiful* she looked, and he felt the inexplicable twist of his heart. More beautiful than he could ever have imagined.

She had left her hair spilling free—a glossy cascade broken only by the addition of white flowers which had been carefully woven into the honeyed locks. To some extent, the glorious spectacle of her curls drew the eye

away from her rounded stomach, but her dressmaker's
eye for detail had also played a part in that—for her
gown was cleverly designed to minimise the appearance of her pregnancy. Heavy cream satin fell to her
knee and the matching shoes showcased shapely legs
which, again, distracted attention from her full figure.
And, of course, the gleaming tiara of diamonds and
pearls worn by all Mardovian brides drew and dazzled
the eye. Beside her, with one chubby little hand clinging on tightly, walked the toddling shape of her little
niece—her only bridesmaid.

And then Luc looked into Lisa's face. At the unsmiling lips and shuttered eyes, and a sense of disappointment whispered over him. She certainly wasn't
feigning a joy she clearly didn't feel! Her expression
was more suited to someone about to attend their own
execution rather than their wedding.

Yet could he blame her? She had never sought
closeness—other than the purely physical variety.
This must be the last thing in the world she wanted.
His jaw tightened. And what about him? He had never
intended for this to happen either. Yet it *had* happened.
Fate had presented him with a very different kind of
destiny from the one mapped out for him, and there
wasn't a damned thing he could do about it. He stared
at her as a powerful sense of certainty washed over
him. Except vow to be the best father and husband he
could possibly be.

Could he do that?

'Are you okay?' he questioned as she reached
his side.

Okay? Chewing on her lip, Lisa bent to direct her little niece over to the ornate golden chair to sit beside her mother. No, she was *not* okay. She felt like a puppet. Like a *thing*. She was being dragged into matrimony like some medieval bride who had just been bought by her powerful master.

But if she was being forced to go through with this marriage, maybe she ought to do it with at least the *appearance* of acceptance. Wouldn't it be better not to feed the prejudices of his staff when she sensed they already resented his commoner bride? So she forced a smile as she stepped up beside Luc's towering figure.

'Ecstatic,' she murmured and met the answering glint in his eyes.

The ceremony passed in a blur and afterwards there was a small reception. But an overexcited Tamsin started running around and ground some wedding cake into an antique rug, and Lisa didn't like the way Jason seemed to be hovering over a collection of precious golden artefacts sitting on top of a beautiful inlaid table.

It was Luc who smoothly but firmly brought the proceedings to an end—and Lisa had to swallow down the sudden tears which sprang to her eyes as she hugged her little niece goodbye, before clinging tightly to her sister.

'I'm going to miss you, Britt,' she said fiercely.

And Brittany's voice wobbled as she hugged her back. 'But you'll be back, won't you, Lisa? My lovely new house is certainly big enough to accommodate my princess sister,' she whispered. 'Or we can come

out and stay with you in Mardovia. We'll still see each
other, won't we?'

Lisa met her sister's eyes. How did you tell your
closest relative you were terrified of being swallowed
up by an alien new life which would shut out the old
one for good? With a deep breath, she composed herself. You didn't. You just got on with things and made
the best of them, the way she'd done all her life. 'Of
course we will,' she said.

'Are you ready, Lisa?' came Luc's voice from behind
her and she nodded, glad that confetti was banned on
the surrounding fancy London streets—because she
honestly didn't think she could smile like some happy
hypocrite as she walked through a floating cloud of
rose petals.

A car whisked them to the airfield, where they were
surrounded by officials. Someone from the Aviation
Authority insisted on presenting Lisa with a bouquet,
which only added to her feelings of confusion because
she wasn't used to people curtseying to her. It wasn't
until they were high in the sky over France that she
found herself alone with Luc at last, and instantly she
was subjected to a very different kind of confusion—
a sensual tug-of-war which had become apparent the
moment the aircraft doors had closed and they were
alone together.

He had changed from his Mardovian naval uniform and was wearing a dark suit which hugged his
powerful frame, and his olive skin looked golden and
glowing. His long legs were spread out in front of him
and, distractingly, she couldn't stop remembering their

muscular power and the way he had shuddered with pleasure as she had coiled her fingertips around them. Her mouth dried and she wondered if he knew how uncomfortable she was feeling as his sapphire gaze rested thoughtfully on her.

'Now, as weddings go...' he elevated his black brows in a laconic question '...was that really so bad?'

She shrugged. 'That depends what you're comparing it with. Better than being adrift at sea for three days with no water, I suppose—though probably on a par with being locked up for life and having the key thrown away.'

'Oh, Lisa.' The brief glint of amusement which had entered his eyes was suddenly replaced with a distinct sense of purpose. 'Your independent attitude is something I've always enjoyed but this marriage isn't going to work if you're going to spend the whole time being obstructive.'

'And what did you think I was going to do?' she questioned, her voice low because she was aware that although the officials were out of sight, they were still very much present. 'Fall ecstatically into your arms the moment you slid the ring on my finger?'

'Why not? You wouldn't hear any objection from me and it's pretty obvious that the attraction between us is as powerful as it ever was—something which was demonstrated on the night our baby was conceived. And now we're man and wife,' he said, sliding his hand over her thigh and leaving it to rest there, 'isn't that what's supposed to happen? Isn't it a pity to let all this frustrated desire go to waste?'

Lisa stared down at the fingers which were outlined against the grey silk jersey of her 'going away' dress and thought how right they felt. As if they had every right to be there—ready to creep beneath the hem of her dress. Ready to slip inside her panties, which were already growing damp with excitement. She thought about the pleasure he was capable of giving her. Instant pleasure which could be hers any time she liked.

But something told her that she shouldn't slip into intimacy with him—no matter how tempting the prospect—because to do so would be to lose sight of his essential ruthlessness. He had brought her here like some kind of *possession*. An old-fashioned chattel who carried his child. He had married her despite all her protestations, and there hadn't been a thing she could do about it. She was trapped. The deal had been sealed. She had made her bed and now she must lie in it.

She just didn't intend sharing it with him.

That was the only thing she was certain of—that she wasn't going to complicate things by having sex with a man who had blackmailed her to the altar. Her resistance would be the key to her freedom, because a man with Luc's legendary libido would never endure a sexless marriage. Inevitably, he would be driven into the arms of other women and she would be able to divorce him on grounds of infidelity. She pushed his hand away, telling herself it was better this way. Better never to start something which could only end in heartache. But that didn't stop her body from missing that brief caress of his fingers, from wishing that she could close her eyes and pretend not to care when they slipped beneath her dress and began to pleasure her...

'We may be married,' she said. 'But it's going to be in name only.'

'Do I take that to mean you're imposing a sex ban?' he questioned gravely.

She smoothed down the ruffled silk jersey, which still bore the imprint of his hand, and waited until her heart had stopped racing quite so much. 'A ban would imply that something was ongoing, which is definitely not the case. We had one night together—and not even a whole night because you couldn't wait to get away from me, could you, Luc? So please don't try suggesting that I'm withdrawing something which never really got off the ground.'

Luc frowned, unused to having his advances rejected, or for a woman to look at him with such determination in her eyes. His power and status had always worked in his favour—but it was his natural *charisma* which had always guaranteed him a hundred per cent success rate with the opposite sex. Yet he could sense that this time was different. Because *Lisa* was different. She always had been. He remembered the silent vow he had taken as she'd walked towards him in all her wedding finery. A vow to be the best husband he could. She was a newly crowned princess and she was *pregnant*—so shouldn't he cut her a little slack?

'I hear what you say,' he said. 'But the past is done, Lisa. All we have is the present. And the future, of course.'

'And I need you to hear this,' she answered, in a

low and fervent voice. 'Which is that I will perform my role as your princess, at least until after the birth. But I will be your wife in name only. I meant what I said and I will not share a bed with you, Luc. I don't intend to have sex with you. Be very clear about that.'

'And is there any particular reason why?' His eyes mocked her, his gaze lingering with a certain insolence on the swell of her breasts. 'Because you want me, Lisa. You want me very badly. We both know that.'

There was silence for a moment as Lisa willed her nipples to stop tingling in response to his lazy scrutiny. She swallowed. 'Because sex can weaken women. It can blind them to the truth, so that they end up making stupid mistakes.'

'And you have experience of this, do you?'

She shrugged. 'Indirectly.'

His voice was cool. 'Are you going to tell me about it? We need something to do if we aren't going to celebrate our union in the more conventional manner.'

Lisa hesitated. As usual, his words sounded more like an order than a question and her instinct was to keep things bottled up inside her, just as she'd always done. He'd never been interested in this kind of thing in the past, but she guessed things were different now. And maybe Luc needed to know why she meant what she said. To realise that the stuff she'd experienced went bone deep and she wasn't about to change. She didn't *dare* change. She needed to stay exactly as she was—in control. So that nobody could get near to her and nobody could ever hurt her. 'Oh, it's a knock-on effect from my scarred childhood,' she said flippantly.

Pillowing his hands behind his dark head, he leaned back in the aircraft seat and studied her. 'What happened in your childhood?'

It took a tense few moments before the words came out and that was when she realised she'd never talked about it before. Not even with Britt. She'd buried it all away. She'd shut it all out and put that mask on. But suddenly she was tired of wearing a mask all the time—and she certainly had no need to impress Luc. Why, if she gave him a glimpse into her dysfunctional background, maybe he might do them both a favour and finish the marriage before it really started.

'My father died when my sister and I were little,' she said. 'I was too young to remember much about him and Britt was just a baby. He was much older than my mother and he was rich. Very rich.' She met his sapphire gaze and said it before he could. 'I think that was the reason she married him.'

'Some women crave security,' he observed with a shrug.

She had expected condemnation, not understanding, and slowly she let out the breath she hadn't even realised she'd been holding. 'She was brought up in poverty,' she said slowly. 'Not the being-broke-before-payday kind, but the genuine never knowing where your next meal is coming from. She once told me that if you'd ever experienced hunger—*real* hunger—then you never forgot it. And marrying my father ensured that hunger became a thing of the past. When he died she became a very wealthy woman…'

'And?' he prompted as her voice trailed off, his eyes blue and luminous.

'And…' Lisa hesitated. She had tried to understand her mother's behaviour and some of it she could. But not all. She compressed her lips to stop them wobbling. 'She found herself in the grip of lust for the first time in her life and decided to reverse her earlier trend by marrying a man much younger than herself. A toy boy,' she finished defiantly. 'Although I don't believe the word was even invented then.'

'A man more interested in her money than in a widow with two young children to care for?'

She gazed at him suspiciously. 'How did you know that?'

'Something in your tone told me that might be the case, but I am a pragmatist, not a romantic, Lisa,' he said drily. 'And all relationships usually involve some sort of barter.'

'Like ours, you mean?' she said.

'I think you know the answer to that question,' he answered lightly.

She stared down at the silk-covered bump of her belly before lifting her gaze to his again. 'He wasn't a good choice of partner. My stepfather was an extremely good-looking man who didn't know the meaning of the word fidelity. He used to screw around with girls his own age—and every time he was unfaithful, it broke my mother just a little bit more.'

'And that affected you?'

'Of course it affected me!' she hit back. 'It affected me *and* my sister. There was always so much *tension* in the house! One never-ending drama. I used to get home from school and my mother would just be sitting there gazing out of the window, her face all red and blotchy from crying. I used to tidy up and cook tea for me and Britt, but all Mum cared about was whether or not *he* would come home that night. Only by then he'd also discovered the lure of gambling and the fact that she was weak enough to bankroll it for him, so it doesn't take much imagination to work out what happened next.'

His dark lashes shuttered his eyes. 'He worked his way through her money?'

Lisa stared at him, trying not to be affected by the understanding gleam in his eyes and the way they were burning into her. But she *was* affected.

'Lisa? What happened? Did he leave you broke?'

She thought she could detect compassion in his voice, but she didn't want it. Because what if she grew to like it and started relying on it? She might start wanting all those things which women longed for. Things like love and fidelity. Things which eluded them and ended up breaking their hearts. She forced herself to remember Luc's own behaviour. The way he'd coldly left her in bed on the night their child had been conceived. The way he'd focussed only on the mark she'd left on his neck instead of the fact that he had *used* her. And that there was some poor princess waiting patiently in her palace for him to return to marry her. Kind Princess Sophie who had been generous enough to send them a wedding gift, despite everything which had happened.

So don't let on that it was a stark lesson in how a man could ruin the life of the women around him. Let him think it was all about the money. He would understand that because he was a rich man and rich men were arrogant about their wealth. Lisa swallowed. He'd shown no scruples about buying out her business and exerting such powerful control over her life, had he? So tell him what he expects to hear. Make him think you're a heartless bitch who only cares about the money.

'Yeah,' she said flippantly. 'The ballet lessons had to stop and so did the winter holidays. I tell you, it was hell.'

She saw the answering tightening of his lips and knew her remark had hit home. And even though she told herself she didn't *care* about his good opinion, it hurt to see the sudden distaste on his face. Quickly, she turned her head towards the window and looked out at the bright blue sea as they began their descent into Mardovia.

CHAPTER SEVEN

'AND THIS,' SAID LUC, 'is Eleonora.'

Lisa nodded, trying to take it all in. The beautiful green island. The white and golden palace. The child kicking frantically beneath her heart. And now this beautiful woman who was staring at her with an expression of disbelief—as if she couldn't quite believe who Luc had married.

'Eleonora has been my aide for a number of years,' Luc continued. 'But I have now assigned her to look after you. Anything you want or need to know—just ask Eleonora. She's the expert. She knows pretty much everything about Mardovia.'

Lisa tried to portray a calm she was far from feeling as she extended her hand in greeting. She felt alone and displaced. She was tired after the flight and her face felt sticky. She wanted to turn to her new husband and howl out her fears in a messy display of emotion which was not her usual style. She wanted to feel his strong arms wrapped protectively around her back, which would be the biggest mistake of all. So instead she just fixed a smile to her lips as she returned Eleonora's cool gaze.

She wondered if she was imagining the unfriendly glint in the eyes of the beautiful aide. Did Eleonora realise that Lisa had been feeling completely out of her depth from the moment she'd arrived on the island and her attitude wasn't helping? The aide was so terrifying elegant—with not a sleek black hair out of place and looking a picture of sophistication in a slim-fitting cream dress, which made Lisa feel like a barrel in comparison. Was she looking at her and wondering how such a pale-faced intruder had managed to become Princess of Mardovia? She glanced down at her bulky tum. It was pretty obvious how.

Lisa sucked in a deep breath. Maybe she was just being paranoid. After all, she couldn't keep blaming Eleonora for not putting her in touch with Luc that time she'd telephoned. She hadn't known Lisa was newly pregnant because Lisa hadn't told her, had she? She'd only been doing her job, which was presumably to protect the Prince from disgruntled ex-lovers like her.

So she smiled as widely as she could. 'It's lovely to meet you, Eleonora,' she said.

'Likewise, Your Royal Highness,' said Eleonora, her coral lips curving.

Luc glanced from one woman to the other. 'Then I shall leave you both to become better acquainted.' He turned towards Lisa. 'I have a lot of catching up to do so I'll see you at dinner. But for now I will leave you in Eleonora's capable hands.'

Lisa nodded, because what could she say? *Please don't go. Stay with me and protect me from this woman with the unsmiling eyes.* She and Luc didn't have that kind of relationship, she reminded herself, and she was supposed to be an independent woman. So why this sudden paralysing fear which was making her feel positively *clingy*? Was it the see-sawing of her wretched hormones playing up again?

In silence Lisa watched him go, the sunlight glinting off his raven hair and the powerful set of his shoulders emphasising his proud bearing. Suddenly the room felt empty without him and the reality of her situation finally hit home. She was no longer ordinary Lisa Bailey, with a failing shop, a mortgage and a little sister who was being dominated by a feckless man. She was now a princess, married to a prince adored by all his people—and all the curtseying and bowing was something she was going to have to get used to.

And despite all her misgivings, she couldn't help but be entranced by the sun-drenched island. During the drive to Luc's palace, she had seen rainbows of wild flowers growing along the banks of the roads and beautiful trees she hadn't recognised. They had passed through unspoiled villages where old men sat on benches and watched the world go by in scenes which had seemed as old as time itself. Yet as they had rounded a curve in one of the mountain roads she had looked down into a sparkling bay, where state-of-the-art white yachts had dazzled like toys in an oversized bathtub. It had been at that point that Lisa had realised that she was now wife to one of the most eligible men in the world.

'You would like me to show you around the palace?' questioned Eleonora in her faultless English.

Lisa nodded. What she would have liked most would have been for Luc to give her a guided tour around his palatial home, but maybe that was asking too much. She could hardly tell him she had no intention of behaving like a *real* wife and then expect him to play the role of devoted husband. And mightn't it be a good idea to make an ally out of his devoted aide? To show a bit of genuine sisterhood? She smiled. 'I should like that very much.'

'You will find it confusing at first,' said Eleonora, her patent court shoes clipping loudly on the marble floors as they set off down a long corridor. 'People are always taken aback by the dimensions of the royal household.'

'Were you?' questioned Lisa as she peeped into a formal banqueting room where a vast table was adorned with golden plates and glittering crystal goblets. 'A bit shell-shocked when you first came here?'

'Me?' Eleonora's pace slowed and that coral-lipped smile appeared again. 'Oh, no. Not at all. My father was an aide to Luc's father and I grew up in one of the staff apartments on the other side of the complex. Why, the palace is the only home I've ever really known! I know every single nook and cranny of the place.'

Lisa absorbed this piece of information in silence, wondering if she was supposed to feel intimidated by it. But she wasn't going to *let* herself be intimidated. She had been upfront with Luc and maybe she should be just as upfront with his aide—and confront the enormous elephant which was currently dominating the palatial corridor.

'I know that Luc was supposed to marry Princess Sophie,' she said quietly. 'And I'm guessing that a lot of people are disappointed she isn't going to be Luc's bride.'

It was a moment before Eleonora answered and when she did, her voice was fierce. 'Very disappointed,' she said bluntly. 'For it was his father's greatest wish that the Princess should marry Luc. And the Princess is as loved by the people of Mardovia as she is by her own subjects on Isolaverde.'

'I'm sure she is,' said Lisa. 'And...' Her voice tailed off. How could she possibly apologise for having ruined the plans for joining the two royal dynasties? She couldn't even say she would do her best to make up for it by being the best wife she possibly could. Not when she had every intention of withholding sex and ending the marriage just as soon as their baby was born.

So she said very little as she followed Eleonora from room to room, trying to take in the sheer scale of the place. She was shown the throne room and several reception rooms of varying degrees of splendour. There was a billiards room and a huge sports complex, with its fully equipped gym and Olympic-sized swimming pool. She peered through the arched entrance to the palace gardens and the closed door to Luc's study. *'He doesn't like anyone to disturb him in there. Only I am permitted access.'* Last of all they came to a long gallery lined with beautiful paintings, and Lisa was filled with a reluctant awe as she looked around, because this could rival some of the smaller art galleries she sometimes visited in London.

There were portraits of princes who were clearly Luc's ancestors, for they bore the same startling sapphire eyes and raven tumble of hair. There were a couple of early French Impressionists and a sombre picture of tiny matchstick men, which Lisa recognised as a Lowry. But the paintings which captured her attention were a pair hanging together in their own small section of the gallery. Luminously beautiful, both pictures depicted the same person—a woman with bobbed blonde hair. In one, she was wearing a nineteen-twenties flapper outfit with a silver headband gleaming in her pale hair, and Lisa couldn't work out if she was in fancy-dress costume or not. In the other she was flushed and smiling in a riding jacket—the tip of her crop just visible.

'Who is this?' Lisa questioned suddenly.

Eleonora's voice was cool. 'This is the Englishwoman who married one of your husband's ancestors.'

It was a curious reply to make but the coral lips were now clamped firmly closed and Lisa realised that the aide had no intention of saying any more. She sensed the guided tour was over, yet it had thrown up more questions than answers. Suddenly, the enormity of her situation hit her—the realisation of how *alien* this new world was—and for the first time since their private jet had touched down, a wave of exhaustion washed over her.

'I think I'd like to go to my room now,' she said.

'Of course. If you would like to follow me, I will show you a shortcut.'

Alone at last in the vast marital apartment, Lisa

pulled off her clothes and stood beneath the luxury shower in one of the two dazzling bathrooms. Bundling her thick curls into the plastic cap she took with her everywhere, she let the powerful jets of water splash over her sticky skin and wash away some of the day's tension. Afterwards she wrapped herself in a fluffy white robe which was hanging on the bathroom door and began to explore the suite of rooms. She found an airy study, a small dining room—and floor-to-ceiling windows in the main reception room, which overlooked a garden of breathtaking beauty.

For a moment Lisa stared out at the emerald lawns and the sparkling surface of a distant lake—reflecting that it was worlds away from her home in England. Inside this vaulted room, the scent of freshly cut flowers wafted through the air and antique furniture stood on faded and exquisite silken rugs. Peeping into one of the dressing rooms, she saw that all her clothes had been neatly hung up in one of the wardrobes.

The bedroom was her last port of call and she hovered uncertainly on the threshold before going in, complicated feelings of dread and hunger washing over her as she stared at the vast bed covered with a richly embroidered throw. She didn't hear the door open or close, only realising she was no longer alone when she heard a soft sound behind her—like someone drawing in an unsteady breath—and when she turned round she saw Luc standing there.

Instantly, her mouth dried with lust and there wasn't a thing she could do about it. His hair was so black and his eyes so blue. How was it possible to want a man who had essentially trapped her here, like a prisoner? He looked so strong and powerful as he came into the bedroom that her heart began to pound in a way she wished it wouldn't, and as her breasts began to ache distractingly she said the first thing which came into her head.

'I told you I wasn't going to share a bed with you.'

He shrugged as he pulled off his jacket and draped it over the back of a gilt chair. 'It's a big bed.'

She swallowed, acutely aware of the ripple of muscle beneath his fine silk shirt. 'That's not the point.'

'No?' He tugged off his tie and tossed it on top of the jacket. 'What's the problem? You think I won't be able to refrain from touching you—or is it the other way round? Worried that you won't be able to keep your hands off me, *chérie*? Mmm…? Is that it? From the hungry look in your eyes, I'm guessing you'd like me to come right over there and get you naked.'

'In your dreams!' she spat back. 'Because even if you force me to share your bed, I shan't have sex with you, Luc, so you'd better get…get…' Her words died away as he began to undo his shirt and his glorious golden torso was laid bare, button by button. 'What… what do you think you're doing?'

'I'm undressing. What does it look like? I want to take a shower before dinner, just like you.'

'But you can't—'

'Can't what, Lisa?' The shirt had fluttered to the ground and his blue eyes gleamed as he kicked off his shoes and socks. She was rendered completely speechless by the sight of all that honed and bronzed torso before his fingers strayed suggestively to his belt. 'Does the sight of my naked body bother you?'

She told herself to look away. To look somewhere—anywhere—except at the magnificent physique which was slowly being revealed. But the trouble was that she couldn't. She was like a starving dog confronted by a large, meaty bone, which was actually the worst kind of comparison to make in the circumstances. She couldn't seem to tear her eyes away from him. He was *magnificent*, she thought as he stepped out of his trousers and she was confronted with the rock-hard reality of his powerful, hair-roughened thighs. His hips were narrow and there was an unmistakably hard ridge pushing insistently against his navy blue silk boxers—and, oh, how she longed to see the complete reveal. But she didn't dare. With a flush of embarrassment mixed with a potent sense of desire, she somehow found the courage to turn her back on him before walking over to the bed.

Heaving herself down onto the soft mattress—her progress made slightly laborious by her swollen belly—she shut her eyes tightly but she was unable to block out the sound of Luc's mocking laughter as he headed towards the bathroom.

'Don't worry, you're quite safe from me, *chérie*,' he said softly. 'I've never found shower caps a particular turn-on.'

To Lisa's horror she realised that her curls were still squashed beneath the unflattering plastic cap, and as she heard the bathroom door close behind him she wrenched it free, shaking out her hair and lying back down on the bed again. For a while she stared up at the ceiling—at the lavish chandelier which dripped like diamonds—wishing it could be different.

But how?

Luc had married her out of duty and brought her to a place where the woman she'd usurped was infinitely more loved. How could she possibly make that right?

She must have slept, because she awoke to the smell of mint and, disorientated, opened her eyes to see Luc putting a steaming cup of tea on the table beside the bed. He had brought her *tea*?

'Feeling better?' he said.

His kindness disarmed her and she struggled to sit up, trying to ignore the ache of her breasts and the fact that he was fully dressed while she was still wearing the bathrobe which had become looser while she slept. She pulled the belt a tiny bit tighter but that only emphasised the ballooning shape of her baby bump and she silently cursed herself for caring what she looked like. At least the sight of her was unlikely to fill him with an uncontrollable lust, she reflected. It wasn't just the shower cap which wasn't a turn-on, it was everything about her…

She cleared her throat. 'Much better, thanks,' she lied. 'What time is dinner?'

Luc walked over to the window and watched as she began to sip at her tea. With her face all flushed and her hair mussed, she looked strangely vulnerable—as if she was too sleepy to have remembered to wear her familiar mask of defiance. Right then it would have been so easy to take her into his arms and kiss away some of the unmistakable tension which made her body look so brittle. But she'd made her desires clear—or, rather, the lack of them. She didn't want intimacy and, although right now he sensed she might be open to *persuasion*, it wouldn't work in his favour if he put her in a position which afterwards she regretted. And she was *pregnant*, he reminded himself. She was carrying his baby and therefore she deserved his consideration and protection.

'Dinner is whenever you want it to be.'

She put the cup back down on the saucer, looking a little uncomfortable. 'Will it be served in that huge room with all the golden plates?'

'You mean the formal banqueting room which we use for state functions? I don't tend to eat most meals in there,' he added drily. 'There are smaller and less intimidating rooms we can use.' He paused. 'Or I could always have them bring you something here, on a tray.'

'Seriously? You mean like a TV dinner?' Her green-gold eyes widened. 'Won't people think it odd if we don't go down?'

'I am the Prince and you are my wife and we can do whatever we damned well like,' he said arrogantly. 'What would you like to eat?'

'I know it probably sounds stupid, but I'd love... well, what I'd like more than anything is an egg sandwich.' She looked up at him from between her lashes. 'Do you think that's possible?'

He gave a short laugh. When she looked at him like that, he felt as if anything were possible. But how ironic that the only woman in a position to ask for anything

should have demanded something so fundamentally
humble. 'I think that can be arranged.'

A uniformed servant answered his summons, soon
reappearing with the sandwich she'd wanted—most
of which she devoured with an uninhibited hunger
which Luc found curiously sensual. Or maybe it was
the fact that she was ignoring him which had stirred
his senses—because he wasn't used to *that* either.

After she'd finished and put her napkin down, she
looked up at him, her face suddenly serious.

'Eleonora showed me the gallery today,' she said.

'Good. I wanted you to see as much of the palace
as possible.'

She traced a figure of eight on the linen tablecloth
with the tip of her finger before looking up.

'I noticed two paintings of the same woman. Beautiful paintings—in a specially lit section of the gallery.'

He nodded. 'Yes. Two of Kristjan Wheeler's finest
works. Conall Devlin acquired one of them for me.'

'Yes, I knew he was an art dealer as well as a property tycoon,' she said. 'But what I was wondering
was…'

He set down his glass of red wine as her voice tailed
off. 'What?' he questioned coolly.

She wriggled her shoulders and her hazelnut curls
shimmered. 'Why Eleonora seemed so *cagey* when I
asked about the paintings.'

He shrugged. 'Eleonora has always been the most
loyal of all my aides.'

'How lovely for you,' she said politely. 'But surely
as your wife I am expected to know—'

'Who she is? The woman in the paintings?' he finished as he picked up his glass and swirled the burgundy liquid around the bowl-like shape of the glass. 'She was an Englishwoman called Louisa De Lacy, who holidayed here during the early part of the last century. She was an unconventional woman—an adventuress was how she liked to style herself. A crack shot who smoked cheroots and wore dresses designed to shock.'

'And is that relevant? She sounds fun.'

'Very relevant. Mardovia was under the rule of one of my ancestors and he fell madly in love with her. The trouble was that Miss De Lacy wasn't deemed suitable on any grounds, even if she'd wanted to be a princess, which she didn't. Despite increasing opposition, he refused to give her up and eventually he was forced to renounce the throne and was exiled from Mardovia. After his abdication his younger brother took the crown—my great-great-grandfather—and that is how it came to be passed down to me.'

'And was that a problem?' she questioned curiously.

He shrugged. 'Not for me. Not even for my father— because we were born knowing we must rule—but for my great-great-grandfather, yes. He had never wanted to govern and was married to a woman who was painfully shy. The burden of the crown contributed to his early death, for which his wife never forgave Louisa De Lacy, and in the meantime…'

'In the meantime, what?' she whispered as his voice trailed off.

'Unfortunately the exiled Prince was killed in a riding accident before he could marry Louisa, who by then had given birth to his child.'

Her head jerked up. 'You mean...'

Luc's temper suddenly shortened. Maybe it was because he was tired and frustrated. Because she was sitting there with that cascade of curls flowing down over her engorged breasts and he wanted to make love to her. He wanted to explore her luscious body with fingers which were on the verge of trembling with frustration, not to have to sit here recounting his family history. Because this was not the wedding night he had anticipated.

'I mean that somewhere out there a child was born out of wedlock—a child of royal Mardovian blood who was never seen again—and they say that there is none so dangerous as a dispossessed prince.' His voice grew hard. 'And I was not prepared for history to repeat itself. Because I have no brothers, Lisa. No one else to pass on the reins to, should I fail to produce an heir. Succession is vital to me, and to my land.'

'So that's why you forced me to marry you,' she breathed.

He nodded. It was not the whole truth, but it was part of it—because he was slowly coming to realise that there were worse fates than having a woman like Lisa by his side. Duty, yes—he would not shirk from that—but couldn't duty be clothed in pleasure?

Wasn't she aware that now he had her here, he had no intention of letting her or the child go? If she accepted that with a good grace then so much the better, but accept it she would. His will was stronger than hers and he would win because he *always* won.

And then something else occurred to him—a fact which he had pushed to the back of his mind because the sheer logistics of getting her here had consumed all his thoughts. But it was something he needed to address sooner rather than later. He tensed as he realised that until they consummated the marriage, their union was not legal. His heart missed a beat. He realised that, but did she?

He remembered her defiant words on the plane—a variation on what she'd said just now, when she'd announced she had no intention of sharing a bed with him. He didn't doubt her resolve, not for a moment, for Lisa was a strong and proud woman. Yet women were capricious creatures who could have their minds changed for them. But only if you played them carefully. He had learnt his first lessons in female manipulation from the governesses who'd been employed to look after him after his mother's death. Run after a woman and it gave her power. Act like you didn't care and she would be yours for the taking.

Duty clothed in pleasure.

He had vowed to be a good husband as well as a good father, so surely one of his responsibilities was making sure his wife received an adequate share of sexual satisfaction? He looked at her green-gold eyes and as he detected the glint of sexual hunger she could not disguise, he smiled.

His for the taking.

CHAPTER EIGHT

THE NEXT FEW weeks were so full with being a new wife, a new princess *and* mother-to-be that Lisa had barely any time to get homesick. Eleonora introduced her to most of the palace staff, to her own personal driver and the two protection officers who would accompany her whenever she left the palace. She was given her own special servant—Almeera—a quiet, dark-eyed beauty who chattered excitedly about how much she loved babies. She met the royal dressmaker who said she'd happily make up Lisa's own designs for the duration of her pregnancy, or they could send to Paris or London for any couture requirements the Princess might have.

She also had her first appointment with the palace obstetrician, Dr Gautier, who came to examine her in her royal apartments, accompanied by a midwife. At least Eleonora made herself scarce for that particular appointment, although Lisa was surprised when Luc made a sudden appearance just before the consultation began.

Her heart began to pound as he walked into the room, nodding to the doctor and midwife who had stood up to bow, before coming to sit beside her and giving her hand a reassuring squeeze. And even though she knew the gesture was mainly for the benefit of the watching medics, she stupidly *felt* reassured. Could he feel the thunder of her pulse? Was he aware that her breasts started to ache whenever he was close? She wondered if they looked like any other newly-wed couple from the outside and what the doctor would say if he realised they hadn't had sex since the night their child was conceived. And she wondered what Luc would say if he knew how at night she lay there, wide-eyed in the dark—unable to sleep because her body was craving his expert touch…

Dr Gautier flicked through the file which lay on the desk before him before fixing his eyes firmly on Luc.

'I am assuming that Your Royal Highness already knows the sex of the baby?' he questioned.

Did Luc hear Lisa's intake of breath? All he had to do was to ask the doctor what he wanted to know and it would be done. The fact would be out there. Lisa swallowed. Some people might think she was being awkward in not wanting this particular piece of information, but it was important to her. It felt like her last remnant of independence and the only control she had left over her life.

'My wife doesn't wish to know,' said Luc, meeting her eyes with a faintly mocking expression. 'She wants it to be a surprise on the day.'

'Very sensible,' said the doctor, turning to ask Lisa if there was anything she wanted to know.

The questions she wanted to ask were not for the

obstetrician's ears. Nor for the ears of the husband sitting beside her.

How soon can I return to England after the birth?

When will Luc let me leave him?

Or the most troubling of all.

Will I ever stop wanting a man who sees me only as the vessel which carries his child?

But some of Lisa's fears left her that day and she wasn't sure why. Was it Luc's simple courtesy in not demanding to know the sex of their baby? Or that meaningless little squeeze of her hand which had made her relax her defences a little? Afterwards, when they were back in their suite, she turned to him to thank him and the baby chose that moment to deliver a hefty kick just beneath her ribs. Automatically, she winced before smiling as she clutched her stomach and when she looked into Luc's face, she was surprised by the sudden *longing* she read in his eyes.

She asked the question because she knew she had to, pushing aside the thought that it was a somehow dangerous thing to do—to invite him to touch her. 'Would you like to…to feel the baby kick?'

'May I?'

She nodded, holding her breath as he laid his hand over her belly and they waited for the inevitable propulsion of one tiny foot. She heard him laugh in disbelief as a tiny heel connected with his palm and, once the movement had subsided, she wondered if he would now do what her body was longing for him to do— and continue touching her in a very different way. She thought how easy it would be. He could move his hand upwards to cup a painfully engorged breast and slowly caress her nipple with the pad of his thumb. Or downwards, to slide his fingers between her legs and find how hot and hungry she was for him.

But he didn't.

He removed his hand from her belly and although she silently cursed and wanted to draw him back to her, she was in no position to do so. She wondered if she had been too hasty in rejecting him, particularly when she hadn't realised he could be so *kind*. And she was fast discovering that kindness could be as seductive as any kiss.

Maybe that was the turning point for Lisa. The discovery that as the days passed the palace stopped feeling like a prison. Or maybe it was a direct result of Luc's sudden announcement that he had a surprise for her. One morning after breakfast, he led her through the endless maze of corridors to a part of the palace she hadn't seen before, where he opened a set of double doors, before beckoning her inside.

'Come and take a look at this,' he said. 'And tell me what you think.'

Lisa was momentarily lost for words as she walked into an airy studio overlooking the palace gardens. She glanced around, trying to take it all in—because in it was everything a dress designer could ever desire. On a big desk were pencils and paints and big pads of sketch paper. There was a computer, a sophisticated music system, a tiny kitchen and even a TV.

'For when you get bored,' Luc drawled. 'I wasn't sure if artwork on the walls would inspire you or distract you—but if you'd like some paintings, then speak to Eleonora and she'll arrange for you to have something from the palace collection.' He searched her face with quizzical eyes. 'I hope this meets with your satisfaction?'

It was a long time since anyone had done something so thoughtful. Something just for *her* and Lisa felt overwhelmed—a feeling compounded by the way Luc was looking at her. His skin was glowing and his black hair was still ruffled from the horse ride he liked to take before breakfast each morning. Which she guessed explained why he was never there when she woke up. Why on more than one occasion she'd found herself rolling over to encounter nothing but a cool space where his warm body should have been.

Because he had spoken the truth. It *was* a big bed. Big enough for two people to share it without touching. For them to lie side by side like two strangers. For her to be acutely aware of his nakedness, even though she couldn't actually see it. Yet as the dark minutes of the night ticked by—punctuated only by the rhythmical sounds of Luc's steady breathing—Lisa was furious with herself for *wanting* him to make love to her. Wondering why hadn't he even *tried* to change her mind? Was her swollen belly putting him off? More than once she had wondered what he would do if she silently moved to his side of the bed. She could put her hand between his legs and start to caress him in that way he liked. She swallowed. Actually, she had a pretty good idea what he'd do...

'I love it,' she said softly, cheeks flushing with embarrassment at her erotic thoughts as she lifted her gaze from the pencils lined up with military precision. 'Thank you.'

There was a pause as their eyes met. An infinitesimal pause when Lisa thought she saw his mouth relax. A moment when his eyes hinted at that flinty look they used to get just before he kissed her. She held her breath. Hoping. No, praying. Thinking—to hell with all her supposedly noble intentions. He was her husband, wasn't he? He was her husband and right then she wanted him with a hunger which was tearing through her body like wildfire. He could make love to her right now—she was sure he would be gentle with her. She felt the molten ache of frustration as she imagined him touching her where she was crying out to be touched.

But just like always, he moved away from her. Only by a fraction, but it might as well have been a mile. She found her cheeks growing even pinker; she walked over to one of the pristine drawing pads in an effort to distract herself. 'I'll start work on my next collection right away,' she said.

He turned to leave but at the door, he paused. 'Has Eleonora told you about the May Ball?'

Lisa shook her head. No. That was something Eleonora must have missed during daily conversations, which usually managed to convey how matey Princess Sophie's father had been with Luc's father, and about the blissful holidays the two families used to enjoy on the island of Isolaverde.

'No,' she said slowly. 'I don't believe she did. Anyway, shouldn't it have been you who told me?'

He raised his eyebrows. 'I'm telling you now,' he said, with a trace of his customary arrogance. 'It's something of a palace tradition. The weather is always fine and the gardens are at their loveliest. It will be the perfect opportunity for you to meet the great and the good. Oh, and you might want to wear some jewels from the royal collection. Speak to Eleonora and she'll show you.'

Lisa forced a smile. She seemed to do nothing but *speak to Eleonora*, but she nodded her head in agreement. And after Luc had gone, she emailed her sister and asked for some new photos of Tamsin, before taking herself off into the palace grounds for a walk.

The gardens were exquisite. Not just the rose section or the intricate maze which led onto the biggest herb garden she'd ever seen, but there were also high-hedged walkways where you could suddenly turn a corner and find some gorgeous marble statue hidden away. Yet today Lisa had to work hard to focus on the beauty of her surroundings because all she could think about was Luc's attitude towards her. He could do something immensely kind and thoughtful like surprising her with a new studio or bring her tea in bed, but he seemed content to keep her at arm's length and push her in the direction of his ever-loyal Eleonora.

But that was what she had wanted.

Only now she was beginning to realise she didn't want it any more. She didn't want to lie chastely by his side while he slept and her body hungered for him. She wanted him to take her in his arms and kiss her. If not to love her—then at least to *make* love to her.

Suddenly, withholding sex as a kind of bargaining tool seemed not only stupid, but self-sacrificing. Maybe she had misjudged the whole situation. She wanted the freedom to be able to return to England but she recognised that she needed Luc's blessing in order to do so. Wouldn't he be more amenable to reason if he was physically satisfied?

And wouldn't she?

He had told her about the ball and he wanted her to wear some of the royal jewels. Couldn't she embrace her new role as his princess and appear comfortable in it? Wouldn't he be pleasantly pleased—maybe even proud of her—giving her the perfect opportunity to seduce him? And since Luc showed no sign of coming on to *her*, she was going to have to be proactive. If she wanted him, then she must show him how much...

She felt the baby stirring inside her, almost as if it were giving her the proverbial thumbs-up, and Lisa felt a sudden warmth creep through her veins. Fired up by a new resolve, she made her way back towards the palace, sunlight streaming onto her bare head. Going straight to her studio, she rang for Eleonora and the aide arrived almost immediately, a questioning look on her smooth face.

Lisa drew a deep breath. 'Luc told me about the ball. He suggested I might wear some of the crown jewels for the occasion.'

Eleonora gave a bland smile. 'Indeed. He has already mentioned it to me.'

Lisa didn't miss a beat, squashing down her indignation. Didn't matter that he confided in Eleonora, because soon he would be in *her* arms and confiding in *her*. 'Could we go and take a look at them, please? Now? Because I think I'd like to design my outfit around the jewels.'

'Of course.'

The collection was housed in a section of the palace not far from the art gallery, and Lisa was momentarily startled when she walked into the spotlighted room, where priceless gems sparkled against inky backdrops of black velvet. Her eyes widened at the sheer opulence of the pieces on display. There were glittering waterfalls of diamonds—white ones and pink ones and even citrusy yellow ones, some with matching drop earrings and bracelets. There were sapphires as blue as Luc's eyes and mysterious milky opals, shot through with rainbows. Lisa was just about to choose a choker of square-cut emeralds when Eleonora indicated a set of drawers at the far end of the room.

'How about these?' Eleonora suggested softly, pulling open one of the drawers and beckoning for Lisa to take a closer look.

Lisa blinked. Inside was a flamboyant ruby necklace with glittering stones as big as gulls' eggs—their claret colour highlighted by the white fire of surrounding diamonds.

'Oh, my word,' she breathed. 'That is the most exquisite thing I've ever seen.'

'Isn't it just?' agreed Eleonora softly as she carefully removed the necklace. 'It hasn't been worn for a long time and is probably the most valuable piece in our entire collection. Why not surprise your husband with it?'

The jewels spilled like rich wine over Lisa's fingers as she took them from the aide, and she could picture exactly the kind of dress to wear with them.

It became a labour of love. Something to work towards. Making her dress for the ball became her secret and she decided it would be her gift to Luc. An olive branch handed to him to make him realise she was prepared to do things differently from now on. That the current situation was far from satisfactory and she'd like to change it. She wanted to be his lover as well as his wife.

'You are looking very pleased with yourself of late,' he observed one evening as they walked down the wide marble corridor towards the dining room.

'Am I?'

'Mmm.' His gaze roved over her as a servant opened the doors for them. 'Actually, you look...*blooming*.'

'Thank you.' She smiled at him. 'I think that's how pregnant women are supposed to look.'

Luc inclined his head in agreement, waiting until she'd sat down before taking his seat opposite and observing her remarkable transformation. When she'd first arrived she had looked strung out and her expression had been pinched—something which had not been improved by their unsatisfactory sleeping arrangements. He had briefly considered moving into his old bachelor rooms to give her the peace she so obviously needed. To make her realise that the only thing worse than sharing a bed with him was *not* sharing a bed with him.

But then some miraculous thaw had occurred. Suddenly, she seemed almost…contented. He heard her humming as she brushed her teeth before bed. He noticed that she'd started reading the Mardovian history book he had given her on the plane. Hungrily, he had watched the luscious thrust of her breasts as she walked into the bedroom with a silken nightdress clinging to every ripe curve of her body, and realised he had nobody but himself to blame for his frustration. He could feel himself growing hard beneath the sheets and had to quickly lie on his belly, willing his huge erection to go away, and he wondered if now was the time to make a move on her. Because his experience with women told him that she would welcome him with open arms…

'You are excited about the ball?' he questioned one evening when they were finishing dinner.

'I'm…looking forward to it.'

His eyes flicked over her. 'You have something to wear?'

'You mean…' on the opposite side of the table she smoothed her hand down over the curve of her belly '…something which will fit over my ever-expanding girth? It's not very attractive, is it?'

'If you really want to know, I find it very attractive,' he said huskily.

She stilled, her hand remaining exactly where it was. 'You don't have to say that just to make me feel better.'

'I never say anything I don't mean.' He touched the tip of his tongue to his lips to help ease their aching dryness and wished it were as simple to relieve the aching in his groin. 'So why don't you go and put on your dress? Show me what you'll be wearing.'

She hesitated. 'It's a secret.'

For some reason her words jarred, or maybe it was his apparent misreading of the situation. The idea that she was softening towards him a little—only to be met with that same old brick wall of resistance.

'So many secrets,' he mocked.

At this her smile died.

'That's a bit rich, coming from the master of secrecy,' she said. 'There's so much about yourself that you keep locked away, Luc. And, of course, there's the biggest concealment of all. If you hadn't kept your fiancée such a big *secret*, we wouldn't have found ourselves in this situation, would we?'

'And doubtless you would have preferred that?'

'Wouldn't you?'

Her challenge fell between them like a stone dropped into a well but Luc told himself he would not allow himself to be trapped into answering hypothetical questions. Instead, he deflected her anger with a careless question. 'What is it about the hidden me you would like revealed, my princess?'

She put down the pearl-handled knife with which she had been peeling an apple and he wondered how deeply she would pry. Whether she would want him to divulge the dark night of his soul to her—and if he did, would that make her understand why he could never really be the man she needed?

'What was it like for you, growing up here?'

It was an innocent enough query but Luc realised too late that all questions were a form of entrapment. That if you gave someone an answer, it paved the way for more questions and more exposure. He gave a bland smile, the type he had used countless times in diplomatic debate. He would not lie to her. No. He would be... What was it that accountants sometimes said? Ah, yes. He would be economical with the truth.

'I imagine it was the same for me as for many other princes born into palaces and surrounded by unimaginable riches,' he said. 'There is always someone to do your bidding and I never wanted for anything.'

Except love, of course.

'Whatever I asked for, I was given.'

But never real companionship.

'I was schooled with other Mardovian aristocrats until the age of eighteen, when I went to school in Paris.'

Where he had tasted freedom for the first time in his life and found it irresistible. But the truth was that nothing had ever been able to fill the emptiness at the very core of him.

'And what about your mum and dad?'

Luc flinched. He had never heard his royal parents described quite so informally, and his first instinct was to correct her and ask her to refer to them by their titles. But he slapped his instinct down, because a lesson in palace protocol would not serve him well at this moment. Not when she was looking at him with that unblinking gaze which was making his heart clench with something he didn't recognise.

'Like you, my mother died when I was very young.'

'I'm sorry for your loss,' she said instantly and there was a pause. 'Did your father remarry?'

He shook his head. 'No.' His father had been locked in his own private world of grief—oblivious to the fact that a small boy was hurting and desperately missing his mother. Unable to look at the child who so resembled his dead wife, he had channelled that grief into duty—pouring all his broken-hearted passion into serving his country. And leaving the care of his son to the stream of governesses employed to look after him.

'I don't think he considered anyone could ever take the place of my mother,' he continued slowly and he felt a twist of pain. Because hadn't he witnessed his father's emotional dependence on the woman who had died—and hadn't it scared him to see such a powerful person diminished by the bitterness of heartbreak?

'How old were you?'

'Four,' he said flatly.

'So who looked after you?'

'Governesses.' Even the sound of the word sent shivers down his spine as he thought of those fierce women, so devoted to his father—who had put duty to the throne above everything else. They had taught him never to cry. Never to show weakness, or fear. They had taught him that a prince must sublimate his own desires in order to best serve his country.

'What were they like?'

He considered Lisa's question—about how many countless variations there were on the word *cold*. 'Efficient,' he said eventually.

She smiled a little. 'That doesn't tell me very much.'

'Maybe it wasn't supposed to.'

But still she persisted. 'And did they show you lots of affection?'

And this, he realised, was an impossible question to answer except with the baldness of truth. 'None whatsoever,' he said slowly. 'There were several of them on some sort of rotation and I think it must have been agreed that they should treat me politely and carefully. I don't think it was intended for any of them to become a mother substitute, or for me to attach myself to anyone in particular. I suspect there was a certain amount of competitiveness between them and they were unwilling to tolerate me having a favourite.'

'Oh, Luc.' Did she notice his faint frown, intended to discourage further questioning? Was that why she deliberately brightened her tone?

'You were lucky,' she added. 'At least you didn't have the proverbial wicked stepmother to deal with.'

He looked into her eyes. Was he? Was anyone ever really 'lucky'? You worked with what you had and fashioned fate to suit you.

He sensed she was softening towards him and that filled him with satisfaction. He had played his part with his restraint—now let her play hers. Let her admit that she wanted him. He gave a grim smile.

Because you made your own luck in life.

CHAPTER NINE

THE MAY BALL was the biggest event in the palace calendar, and Lisa planned her first formal introduction to the people of Mardovia with the precision of a military campaign. She ordered a bolt of crimson silk satin and made a gown specially designed to showcase the ruby and diamond necklace from the royal collection.

For hours she worked to the familiar and comforting sound of the sewing machine, painstakingly finishing off the gown with some careful hand stitching. She would surprise Luc with her dress, yes. Her pulse began to race. And not just at the ball. Her self-imposed sex ban had gone on for long enough and now she wanted him in her arms again. He had heeded her words and treated her with respect. Night after night he had lain beside her without attempting to touch her—even though there had been times when she'd wished he would. When that slow heat would build low in her belly, making her want to squirm with frustration as he slept beside her.

She finished the dress to her satisfaction but as she got ready for the ball she felt shot with nerves—because what if Luc had decided he no longer wanted her? What if their stand-off had killed his desire for her? Smoothing down the full-length skirt, she stared at her reflected image in the mirror. He *had* to want her.

She thought back to how she'd felt when she had first arrived here, when she'd married him under duress and had been apprehensive about what lay ahead. But he had respected her wishes and not touched her. And as he had gradually opened up to her, so had her fears about the future diminished. For fear had no place in the heart of a mother-to-be and neither did selfishness. The life she had been prepared to embrace now seemed all wrong. She'd thought a lot about Luc's lonely childhood and the repercussions of that. And she knew she couldn't subject this baby to single parenthood without first giving her husband the chance to be a full-time father. *And a full-time husband.*

Her heart began thundering with an emotion she could no longer deny. Because when tonight's ball was ended, she was going to take her husband in her arms and tell him she wanted them to start over. Tell him she was willing to try to create the kind of family unit which neither of them had ever had before. And then she was going to seduce him…

The woman in the mirror looked back at her with hope shining from her eyes and Lisa allowed herself a small smile. Years of working in the fashion industry had taught her to be impartial—especially about her own appearance. She knew that her already curvy body was swollen with child but she was also aware that never had she looked quite so radiant as she did tonight. Her hair was glossy and her skin was glowing. Her handmade dress was fitted tightly on the bodice and cleverly pleated at the front, so that it fell to the ground in a flattering silhouette. And the stark, square neckline provided the perfect setting for the real star of the show—the royal rubies which blazed like fire against her pale skin.

'Lisa!'

She heard Luc calling and, picking up the full-length black velvet cloak lined with matching crimson satin, she slipped it around her shoulders. Luc would see her at the same time as all his subjects and friends, she thought happily. Tonight she was going to *do him proud*.

'Nervous?' he questioned as she walked alongside him through the flame-lit corridors in a rustle of velvet and silk.

'A little,' she admitted.

He glanced down at the dramatic fall of black velvet which covered her entire body. 'Aren't you going to show me this dress you've been working on so furiously?'

'I will when we get there.'

'Are you hiding your bump until the last minute? Is that it?'

'Partly.' Lisa felt the heavy necklace brushing against her throat and shivered a little as she pulled the cloak closer. 'And I'm a little cold.'

But it wasn't just nerves which were making her skin prickle with little goosebumps, because the fine weather which traditionally characterised the May Ball hadn't materialised. As soon as Lisa had opened her eyes that morning, she'd realised something was different. For the first time since she'd been on the island, the sun wasn't shining and the air was laced with an unseasonable chill. According to the servant who had served her breakfast, the temperamental wind they called Il Serpente was threatening to wreak havoc on the Mediterranean island.

But although the predinner drinks had now been moved inside, the palace looked more magnificent than Lisa had ever seen it. Dark roses threaded into ivy were woven around the tall ballroom pillars, giving the place a distinctly gothic feel, and more crimson roses decorated the long table where the meal would be served. The string section of the Mardovian orchestra was playing softly, but as soon as the trumpets announced her and Luc's arrival they burst into the national anthem. As the stirring tune drew to a close, Lisa slipped the velvet cloak from her shoulders.

She was not expecting such an OTT reaction as the collective gasps from the guests who had assembled to greet the royal guests of honour. Nor for her to glance up into Luc's face to find herself startled by the dark look stamped onto his features which seemed to echo the growing storm outside. Was her dress a mistake? Did the vibrant colour draw attention to the swell of her body, reminding the Prince and all his subjects of the real reason she was here?

'Is something…wrong?'

Luc's cold gaze was fixed on the blaze of jewels at her throat, but he must have been aware that everyone around them was listening because he curved his lips into a smile which did not meet his eyes. 'Wrong?' he questioned smoothly. 'Why should there be anything wrong? You look exquisite. Utterly exquisite, *ma chérie.*'

But Lisa didn't feel exquisite as she sat down to dinner, in front of all that shiny golden cutlery. She felt *tawdry.* As if she'd broken a fundamental rule which nobody had bothered to tell her about. What on earth was the matter? And then she glanced down the table and met Eleonora's eyes and wondered if she was imagining the brief look of triumph which passed over the aide's face.

Somehow she managed to get through the lavish meal, perversely relieved that protocol meant she wasn't sitting next to her husband, because no way could she have eaten a thing if she'd been forced to endure another second of his inexplicable rage. She had lost her appetite anyway and merely picked at her food as she tried to respond to the Sultan of Qurhah's amusing observations, when all she could think about was Luc's forbidding posture. But it wasn't until the dancing started and he came over to lead her imperiously onto the ballroom floor for the first dance that she found herself alone with him at last.

'Something *is* wrong,' she hissed as he slid his arms around her waist, but instead of it being a warm embrace, it felt as if she were locked inside a powerful vice. 'Isn't it? You've been glaring at me all evening. Luc, what's the matter? What am I supposed to have *done*?'

'Not here,' he bit out. 'I'm not having this discussion here.'

'Then why are you bothering to dance with me?'

'Because you are my wife and I must be *seen* to dance with you.' His words were like ice. 'To paint the illusion of marital bliss for my idealistic subjects. That is why.'

Distress welled up inside her and Lisa wanted to push him away from her. To flounce from the ballroom with her head held high so that nobody could see the glimmer of tears which were pricking at the backs of her eyes. But pride wouldn't let her. She mustn't give anyone the opportunity to brand her as some kind of hysteric. That would be a convenient category for a woman like her, wouldn't it?

So she closed her eyes to avoid having to look at her husband and as she danced woodenly in his arms, she wondered how she could have been so stupid. Had she really thought that some silent truce had been declared between them? That they had reached a cautious kind of harmony?

Stupid Lisa, she thought bitterly. She had let it happen all over again. Despite everything she knew to be true, she had allowed herself to trust him. She had started to imagine a marriage they might be able to work at. A marriage which might just succeed.

Behind her tightly shut eyelids she willed away her tears and finished her dance with Luc, and afterwards she danced with the Sultan and then the cousin of the Sheikh of Jazratan. Somehow she managed to play the part expected of her, even though her smile felt as if it had been plastered to her lips like concrete.

But at least her late pregnancy gave her a solid reason to excuse herself early. She slipped away from the ballroom and had one of the servants bring her cloak, which she wrapped tightly around herself as she made her way back along the deserted corridors to their apartments.

Once inside the suite, she didn't bother putting the lights on. She stood at the window and watched as the storm split open the skies. Forked lightning streaked like an angry silver weapon against the menacing clouds and the sound of thunder was almost deafening. But after a while she didn't even see the elemental raging outside because the tears which were streaming down her face made her vision blurry. She dashed them away with an impatient hand, unsure of what to do next. Should she get ready for bed? Yet wouldn't lying on that monstrous mattress in her nightgown make her even more vulnerable than she already felt?

So she rang for some camomile tea and had just finished drinking it when the doors were flung open and the silhouetted form of her husband stood on the threshold. He was breathing heavily and his body was hard and tense as he stared inside the room. She could tell that he was trying to adjust his vision to the dim light, but when he reached out to put on one of the lamps, she snapped out a single word.

'Don't.'

'You like sitting in the dark?'

'There's nothing I particularly *like* right now, Luc.

But somewhere near the top of my dislikes is having you try to control the situation yet again. If anyone's going to put the light on, it's going to be me. Understand?' She snapped on the nearest lamp, steeling herself against the sight of his powerful body in the immaculate dress suit as he shut the door behind him with a shaking hand. And even though she felt the betraying stir of her senses, her anger was far more powerful than her desire. 'Do you want to tell me what I've done wrong?' she demanded. 'What heinous crime I'm supposed to have committed?'

She could see the tension in his body increase and when he spoke, his words sounded as if they had been chipped from a block of ice. 'Why the hell did you wear that necklace without running it past me first?'

For a moment she blinked in surprise. Because he'd told her to choose some jewels from the royal collection. Because Eleonora had drawn her attention to the undoubted star of the collection and quietly suggested that she 'surprise' her husband. Lisa opened her mouth to tell him that, but suddenly her curiosity was piqued. 'I didn't realise I had to *run it past* you first. You made no mention of any kind of *vetting* procedure. What was wrong with me wearing it?'

There was a pause as his face became shuttered and still his words were icy-cold. 'That necklace was given to my mother by Princess Sophie's mother. My mother wore it on her wedding day. It was—'

'It was supposed to be worn by Sophie on the day of her marriage to you,' finished Lisa dully, her heart clenching. 'Only you never married her, like you were supposed to do. You married a stranger. A commoner. A woman heavy with your child who appeared at the ball tonight looking like some spectre at the feast. The wrong woman wearing the jewels.'

Her remarks were greeted by silence, but what could he possibly say? He could hardly deny the truth. Lisa ran her tongue over her lips. She supposed she could tell him it had been Eleonora's subtle lead which had made her choose the rubies, but what good would that do? She would be like a child in the classroom, telling tales to the teacher. And it wouldn't change the facts, would it? That she was like a cuckoo in the nest with no real place here. An outsider who would always be just that. The human incubator who carried the royal heir. Reaching up, she unclipped the necklace and pulled it from her neck, dropping it down onto a bureau so that it fell there in a spooling clatter of gems.

But as her anger bubbled up, so did something else—a powerful wave of frustration, fuelled by the sudden violent see-sawing of her hormones. For weeks now she'd been trying her best to fit in with this strange new life of hers. Night after night she had lain by his side, staring up at the ceiling while he had fallen into a deep sleep. She had been polite to the servants and tried to learn everything she could about Mardovia—only now he was treating her with all the contempt he might have reserved for some passing tramp who had stumbled uninvited into his royal apartment. How dared he? How *dared* he?

'Well, damn you, Luc Leonidas!' she cried, and she launched herself across the room and began to batter her fists hard against his chest. 'Damn you to high heaven!''

At first he tried to halt her by imprisoning her wrists, but that only made her kick even harder at his shins and he uttered something soft and eloquent in French—before swooping his mouth down on hers.

His kiss was hard—and *angry*—but his probing tongue met no resistance from her. On the contrary, it made her give a shuddering little moan of something like recognition—because she could do anger, too. So she kissed him back just as hard, even though he was now trying to pull away from her, something impossible to achieve when he was still holding her wrists. And then his grip on her loosened and she took that opportunity to stroke her fingertip down his cheek and then over the rasp of his chin. And although he shook his head when she continued down over his chest, he didn't stop her—not until her hand reached his groin, where he was so hard for her that her body stiffened in anticipation.

'Lisa, no,' he warned unsteadily as she slid her palm over the rocky ridge beneath his trousers.

'Luc, *yes*,' she mimicked as she began to slide down the protesting zip.

After that there was no turning back. Nothing but urgent and hungry kissing as she freed his erection and gazed down at it with wide-eyed pleasure. But when she began to slide her finger and thumb up and down over the silken shaft, he batted her hand away then picked her up and carried her over to the bed. He set her down beside it, his eyes flicking over the long line of hooks which went all the way down the back of her dress, and his hands were shaking as he reached for the first.

'No,' she said, wriggling away from him as she pushed him down onto the bed. 'It will take too long and I'm done with waiting. I'm not going to wait a second longer for this.' With an air of determination, she began to tug off his trousers and boxer shorts, before slithering out of her panties and climbing on top of him, uncaring of her bulkiness. Not caring that this was wrong—because the powerful hunger which was pulsing through her body was blotting out everything but desire.

'Lisa…' His words sounded slurred and husky as her bare flesh brushed against his. He swallowed. 'We can't…we can't do this.'

'Oh, but we can. There are many things we can't do, but this isn't one of them.' The red silk dress ballooned around her as she positioned herself over him, and she saw his eyes grow smoky as the tip of him began to push insistently against her wet heat.

'But you're…pregnant,' he breathed.

'You think I don't know that?' She gave a hollow laugh. 'You think pregnant women don't have sex? Then I put it to you that you, Luc Leonidas, with all your supposed experience of the female body, are very wrong.' Slowly she lowered herself down onto his steely shaft, biting out a gasp as that first rush of pleasure hit her.

He lay there perfectly still as she began to rock forward and back and she could see the almost helpless look of desire on his face as her bulky body accustomed itself to the movements. And she *liked* seeing him like that. Powerful Prince Luc at *her* mercy. But her sense of victory only lasted until the first shimmerings of pleasure began to ripple over her body and then, of course, he took over. His hands anchored to her hips, he angled his own to increase the level of penetration while leaning forward to whisper soft little kisses over her satin-covered belly. And it was that which was her undoing. That which made her heart melt. His stupid show of tenderness which *didn't mean a thing.*

Not a thing.

All it did was make her long for the impossible. For Luc to love her and want her and need her. And that was never going to happen.

But she could do nothing to stop the orgasm which caught her up and dragged her under, and as her body began to convulse around him she heard his own ragged groan. His arms tightened as he held her against him, his lips buried in the hard swell of her stomach as he kissed it, over and over again. For a while there was nothing but contentment as Lisa clung to him, listening to the muffled pounding of her heart.

But not for long. Once the pleasure began to ebb away, she forced herself to pull away from him, collapsing back against the pile of pillows and deliberately turning her face to the wall as a deep sense of shame washed over her. How could she? How *could* she have done that? Climbed on top of him with that out-of-control and wanton desire?

'Lisa?'

She felt the warmth of his hand as he placed it over one tense shoulder and some illogical part of her wanted to sink back into his embrace and stay there. Because when he touched her it felt as if all the things she didn't believe in had come true. It felt like love. *And she couldn't afford to think that way because love was nothing but an illusion.* Especially with Luc.

She closed her eyes as she pushed his hand away, because she was through with illusions. With going back on everything she knew to be true and allowing herself to get sucked into fantasy. He was a man, wasn't he? And no man could really be trusted. Did she need someone to carve it on a metal disc for her, so she could wear it around her neck? She needed to be strong enough to resist him and, for that, she needed him to go.

'Lisa?' Luc said again and his ragged sigh ruffled the curls at the back of her neck. 'Look, I know I over-reacted about the necklace and I'm sorry.'

She pulled away. 'It doesn't matter.'

'It *does* matter.'

But she wasn't in the mood to listen. She made herself yawn as she curled up into a ball—well, as much of a ball as her heavily pregnant state would allow. 'I just want to go to sleep,' she mumbled. 'And I'd prefer to do it alone.'

CHAPTER TEN

'LISA, WE HAVE to talk about this. We can't keep pretending nothing has happened.'

Lisa closed her eyes as Luc's voice washed over her skin, its rich tone setting her senses tingling the way it always did. It made her think of things she was trying to forget. Things she *needed* to forget. She swallowed. Like the night of the ball when she'd let her raging hormones get the better of her and had ended up on the bed with him. When passion and anger had fused in an explosive sexual cocktail and, for a short and surreal period, she had found herself yearning for the impossible.

And now?

She turned away from the window, where the palace gardens looked like a blurred kaleidoscope before her unseeing eyes.

Now she felt nothing but a deep sense of sadness as she met his piercing sapphire gaze.

'What is there left to say?' she questioned tiredly. 'I thought we'd said it all on the night of the ball. Considering what happened, I thought we'd adapted to a bad situation rather well.'

'You think so?' His eyebrows arched. 'With me occupying my former bachelor apartments while you sleep alone in the marital suite?'

'What's the matter, Luc? It can't be the sex you're missing. I mean, it isn't as if we were at it like rabbits before all this blew up, is it?'

'There's no need to be crude,' he snapped.

If they'd been a normal couple Lisa might have made a wry joke about that remark, but they weren't. They were about as far from normal as you could get—two strangers living in a huge palace which somehow felt as claustrophobic as if they were stuck in some tenement apartment.

'Are you worried what people are saying?' she demanded. 'Is that it? Afraid the servants will gossip about the Prince and Princess leading separate lives?' She pushed a handful of curls away from her hot face and fixed him with a steady look. 'Don't you think that's something they should get used to?'

Luc clenched the fists which were stuffed deep in the pockets of his trousers and tried very hard not to react to his wife's angry taunts. If he'd been worried about gossip he would never have brought her back here. He would never have... He closed his eyes in a moment of frustration. How far back did he have to go to think about all the things he *wouldn't* do with her—and why couldn't he shake off the feeling that somehow all his good intentions were meaningless, because he felt *powerless* when it came to Lisa?

He shook his head. 'No. I'm not worried about what people are saying.'

'Maybe you're still regretting the other night?' she said softly. 'Wishing you hadn't had sex with me?'

Luc swallowed as her words conjured up a series of mental images he'd tried to keep off limits but now they hurtled into his mind in vivid and disturbing technicolour. Lisa pushing him back onto the bed. Lisa on top of him in the billowing crimson dress, her face flushed with passion as she rode him. His mouth dried. He *wanted* to regret what had happened, but how could he when it had been one of the most erotic encounters of his life? He had felt like her puppet. Her slave. And hadn't that turned him on even more? Dazed and confused, he had left their suite afterwards and stumbled to the library to discover that what she'd said had been true—that pregnant women *did* have sex. It seemed his wife had been right and there were some things he *didn't* know about women.

Especially about her.

'No, I'm not regretting that.'

'What, then?'

His gaze bored into her. 'Why didn't you tell me that Eleonora persuaded you to wear the necklace?'

'Why bother shooting the messenger?' she answered. 'Eleonora might have had her own agenda but she wasn't the one who made you react like that. You did that all by yourself.' She glanced at him from between her lashes. 'Did she tell you?'

'No,' he said grimly. 'I overheard her saying something about it to one of the other aides and asked to see her.'

'Gosh. That must have been a fun discussion,' she

said flippantly. 'Did she persuade you that it had been a perfectly innocent gesture on her part? Flutter those big eyes at you and tell you that you'd be better off with her beloved Princess Sophie?'

'I wasn't in the mood for any kind of *explanation*,' he bit out angrily. 'And neither was I in the mood for her hysterical response when I sacked her.'

Lisa blinked. 'You...*sacked* her?'

'Of course I did.' He fixed her with a cool stare. 'Do you really think I would tolerate that kind of subversive attitude in my palace? Or have an aide actively trying to make trouble for my wife?'

Lisa didn't know what to think. She'd been stupid and gullible in agreeing to Eleonora's suggestion that she 'surprise' Luc, but she shouldn't allow herself to forget why she had embraced the idea so eagerly in the first place. She had wanted to impress him. To show him she was willing to be a good wife and a good princess. And if she was being brutally honest—hadn't she been secretly longing for some kind of answering epiphany in him? Hoping that the emotional tide might be about to turn with her first public presentation?

But it hadn't and it never would. If anything, the situation was a million times worse. The sex had awoken her sleeping senses but highlighted the great gulf which lay between them. And wouldn't she be the world's biggest fool if she started demanding something from a man who was incapable of delivering it?

She stared at him. 'So what do you want to talk about?'

Repressing another frustrated sigh, Luc met her

gaze, knowing there was no such thing as an easy solution. But had he expected any different? She was
the most complicated and frustrating woman he'd ever
met. He gave a bitter smile. And never had he wanted
anyone more.

When she had walked towards him at the Mardovian Embassy in her subdued wedding finery, he had
made a silent vow to be the best husband and father
he possibly could be, and he had meant it. Yet now he
could see that it might have been a challenge too far.
Because he didn't know how to be those things. And
for a woman who was naturally suspicious of men—
He suspected that he and Lisa were the worst possible
combination.

So did he have the strength to do what he needed to
do? To set her free from her palace prison? To release
her from a relationship which had been doomed from
the start? It wasn't a question of choice, he realised—
but one of necessity. He had to do it. A lump rose in
his throat. He could do it for her.

'Do you want to go back to England?' he questioned
quietly. 'Not straight away, of course. But once the
baby is born.'

Lisa jerked back her head and looked at him with
suspicious eyes. 'You mean you'll let me go?'

'Yes, Lisa.' He gave a mocking smile. 'I'll release
you from your prison.'

'And you're prepared to discuss shared custody?'
Now she was blinking her eyes very hard. 'That's
very…civilised of you, Luc.'

His mouth twisted. 'None of this sounds remotely

civilised to me—but it's clearly what you want. And I am not so much of a tyrant to keep you here against your will.'

She lifted her clear gaze to him. 'Thank you,' she said.

He walked away from her, increasing the distance between them, removing himself from the tantalising danger of her proximity. But once he had reached the imposing marble fireplace, he halted, his face grave. 'I guess we should look on the bright side. At least now we've had sex, it means that our marriage has been legitimised and our child will be born as the true heir to Mardovia.'

She stiffened, her lips parting as she stared at him. '*What* did you say?'

'I was just stating facts,' he answered coolly. 'Up until the other night our marriage wasn't legal because we hadn't consummated it.'

'Was that why you did it? Why you let me make love to you?' she whispered, her face blanching. 'Just to make our marriage *legal*?'

'Please don't insult me, Lisa. We both know why I had sex with you that night and it had nothing to do with legality.' He met her gaze for a long moment before turning away from her. 'And now, if you'll excuse me—I have a meeting with my ministers, which I really can't delay any longer.'

Lisa watched him go but it wasn't until he had closed the door behind him that she collapsed on the nearest chair as the significance of his words began to sink in. He was letting her go. After the baby was born, he was going to let her leave the island. She would no longer be forced to stay in this farce of a marriage with a cold man who could only ever express himself in bed. He would probably give her a house, just as he had given one to her sister, and she would be free to live her life on *her* terms.

So why did she feel as if someone had twisted her up in tight knots?

She forced herself to be logical. To think with her head instead of her heart. As Luc's estranged wife, she would never again have financial worries. And she would work hard at forging an amicable relationship with Luc. That would be a priority. They wouldn't become one of those bitter divorced couples who made their child's life a misery by their constant warring.

But Lisa couldn't shake off her sudden sense of emptiness as she went to her studio and looked at her sketches she'd been making for her next collection. Maybe she should make some more. Because what else was she going to do during the days leading up to the birth? Prowl around the palace like a bulky shadow, staring at all the beauty and storing it away in her memory to pull out on lonely days back in England—as if to remind herself that this hadn't all been some surreal dream.

For the next few days she immersed herself completely in her work. She began drawing with a sudden intensity—her designs taking on clean new lines as she liaised with her workshop back in London about an overall vision for the new collection. She worked long sessions from dawn to dusk—punctuated only by brisk walks in the gardens, where sometimes she would sit on a stone bench and watch the sunlight cast glittering patterns on the sapphire sea far below—and tried not to wonder what her husband was doing.

Mostly he left her alone, but one evening he came to her studio, walking in after a brief knock, to find her bent over a swatch of fabrics.

'Don't you think you're overdoing the work ethic a little?' he observed, with a frown. 'One of the servants told me you've been here since sunrise.'

'I couldn't sleep. And I'm nearly finished. I just want to get this last bit done.'

'You're looking tired,' he said critically. 'You need to rest.'

But this single concerned intervention had been the exception, because mostly she only saw him at mealtimes. Perhaps he was already withdrawing from her and preparing for the reality of their separation. And in truth, it was better this way. She spent a lot of time convincing herself of that. It was how it was going to be and she had better get used to it.

Dr Gautier visited daily, pronouncing himself quietly satisfied at her progress—and if he wondered why Luc no longer attended any of the appointments, he made no mention of it. That was yet another of the advantages of being royal, Lisa realised. People just accepted what you did and never dared challenge you—and that couldn't be a good thing. It would make you grow up thinking that you could fashion the world according to whim. Wasn't that what Luc had done by bringing her here and forcing her to marry him?

She was over a week away from her due date when the first pain came in the middle of the night, waking her up with a start. A ring of steel clamped itself around her suddenly rock-hard belly and Lisa clutched her arms around it in the darkness, trying to remember the midwife's instructions. It was the early hours of the morning and the contractions were very irregular—she had plenty of time before she needed to let anyone know.

But as they got stronger and more painful, she rang for Almeera, whose eyes widened when she saw her mistress sitting on the edge of the bed, rocking forward and back.

'Fetch the Prince,' said Lisa, closing her eyes as she felt the onset of another fierce contraction. 'Tell him I'm in labour.'

Luc arrived almost immediately, looking as if he'd just thrown his clothes on and not bothered to tidy his hair. His cell phone was pressed to his ear as he walked into the room, his gaze raking over her.

'Dr Gautier wants to know how often the contractions are coming,' he said.

'Every...' She gasped as she glanced at the golden clock on the mantelpiece. 'Every five minutes.'

He relayed this information, slipping naturally into French before cutting the connection. 'The ambulance is on its way and so is Dr Gautier.'

She gazed up at him. 'My...my waters have broken,' she stumbled.

He smiled. 'Well, that is normal, isn't it, *chérie*?'

His soft tone disarmed her and so did his confidence.

It made her forget about the distance between them. And suddenly Lisa wanted more than his support—she needed some of his strength. And comfort. 'Luc?' she said brokenly as another contraction came—surely far sooner than it was supposed to.

He was by her side in an instant, taking her hand and not flinching when her fingernails bit into his flesh as another contraction powered over her. 'I'm here,' he said.

'I'm supposed to have the baby in the hospital,' she whispered.

'It doesn't matter where you have the baby,' he said. 'We have everything here you need. You're going to be fine.'

And somehow she believed him, even when Dr Gautier arrived with another doctor and two midwives and said there was no time to go anywhere. All the things she'd read about were starting to happen, only now they were happening to *her*. At first she was scared and then it all became too intense to be anything but focussed. She tried to concentrate on her breathing, aware of the immense pressure building up inside her and Luc smoothing back her sweat-tangled curls. The medical staff were speaking to each other very quickly—sometimes in French—but Luc was murmuring to her in English. Telling her that she was brave and strong. Telling her that she could do this. She could do anything.

And then it was happening. The urge to push and being told she couldn't push, and then being unable to do anything *but* push. Still gripping Luc's hand,

Lisa gritted her teeth and tried to pant the way she'd been taught—and just as she thought the contractions couldn't get any more intense, her baby was delivered into the hands of the waiting doctor and a loud and penetrating wail filled the air.

'C'est une fille!' exclaimed Dr Gautier.

'A girl?' said Lisa, looking up into Luc's eyes.

He nodded. 'A beautiful baby girl,' he said unsteadily, his eyes suddenly very bright.

Lisa slumped back against the pillows as a sense of quiet and purposeful activity took over. The intensity of the birth had morphed into an air of serenity as the doctor finished his examinations, and, now cocooned in soft white cashmere, the baby was handed to her.

She felt so light, thought Lisa as a shaft of something fierce and protective shot through her. So light and yet so strong. With unfamiliar fingers, she guided her daughter to her breast, where she immediately began to suckle. Dimly, she became aware that Luc had left the room and, once the baby had finished feeding, the midwives helped her wash and gave her a clean silk nightgown. And when she next looked up, Luc was back and it was just the three of them.

She felt strangely shy as he dragged up a gilt chair and sat beside her, his elbows on his knees, his palms cupping his chin as he watched her intently. Their eyes met over the baby's head and Lisa suddenly felt a powerful sense of longing, wishing he would reach out and touch her. But they didn't have that kind of relationship, she reminded herself. They'd gone too far in the wrong direction and there was no turning back.

'We need to discuss names,' she said.

'Names?' he echoed blankly.

'We can't keep calling her "the baby". Are you still happy with Rose and then both our mothers' names?'

'Rose Maria Elizabeth,' he said, his slow gaze taking in every centimetre of the baby's face. 'They are perfect. Just like her.'

'Rose,' Lisa echoed softly, before holding out the snowy bundle towards him. 'Would you like to hold her?'

Luc's hesitation was brief as he reached out but his heart maintained its powerful pounding as he held his baby for the first time. He had never known real fear before, but he knew it now. Fear that he would prove inadequate to care for this tiny bundle of humanity. Fear that he might say the wrong thing to the woman who had just blown him away by giving birth to her.

As he cradled his sleeping daughter and marvelled at her sheer tininess, he felt the thick layer of ice around his heart begin to fracture. He could feel the welling up of unknown emotion—a whole great storm of it— packed down so deeply inside him that he hadn't even realised it was there. It felt raw and it felt painful, but it felt *real*—this sudden rush of devotion and a determination to protect his child for as long as he lived.

'Thank you,' he said softly, glancing up to meet Lisa's eyes.

'You're welcome.'

He saw the cloud which crossed like a shadow over her beautiful face but there was no need to ask what had caused it. For although their child had been born safely and mother and daughter were healthy, none of their other problems had gone away. They were still estranged. Still leading separate lives, with Lisa no doubt counting down the days until she could return to England. Concentrating only on her shadowed eyes, he stood up, carrying Rose over to her crib and laying her gently down before looking at Lisa's pinched face.

'You're exhausted,' he said. 'Shall I phone your sister and tell her the news and you can speak to her yourself later?'

She folded her lips together as if she didn't trust herself to speak, and nodded.

Resisting the desire to go over and drop a grateful kiss onto her beautiful lips, he took one last look at her before walking over to the door. 'Go to sleep now, Lisa,' he said unevenly. 'Just go to sleep.'

CHAPTER ELEVEN

IT WAS LIKE living in a bubble.

A shining golden bubble.

Lisa woke up every morning feeling as if she weren't part of the outside world any more. As if her experience was nothing like that of other women in her situation—and she supposed that much was true. Most new mothers didn't live in a beautiful palace with servants falling over themselves to make her life easier. And most new mothers didn't have a husband who was barely able to look at them without a dark and sombre expression on his face.

She told herself to be grateful that Luc clearly adored their daughter, and she was. It made a lump stick in her throat to see how gentle he was with their baby. It was humbling to see such a powerful man being reduced to putty by the starfish hands of his daughter, which would curl themselves tightly around his fingers as she gazed up at him with blue eyes so like his own.

Lisa would sit watching him play with Rose, but the calm expression she wore didn't reflect the turmoil she was feeling inside. Did Luc feel just as conflicted? she wondered. She didn't know because they didn't talk about it. They discussed the fact that their daughter had the bluest eyes in the world and the sweetest nature, but *they didn't talk about anything which mattered.*

Before the birth he'd promised Lisa she could return to England, and she knew she had to broach the subject some time. But something was stopping her and that something was the voice of her conscience. She had started to wonder how she could possibly take Rose away from here, denying Luc the daily parenting he so clearly enjoyed.

Because Lisa had never had that kind of hands-on fathering. When her own father had died she'd been too young to remember if he cuddled her or read her stories at night. And she'd never really had the chance to ask her mother because she had remarried so quickly. All evidence of the man who had died had been ruthlessly eradicated from the house. Her new stepfather had been so intolerant of her and Brittany that the two little girls had walked around on eggshells, terrified of stirring up a rage which had never been far from the surface. They'd learnt never to speak unless spoken to and they'd learnt never to demand any of their mother's time. Lisa had watched helplessly as he had whittled away at their fortune—and she wondered if it had been that which had made her so fiercely independent. Was the lack of love in their childhood the reason why Brittany had jettisoned her university course and fallen straight into the arms of the first man to show her some affection?

All Lisa knew was that she couldn't contemplate bringing Rose up without love. At the moment things were tolerable because it was all so new. She was getting used to motherhood and Luc was getting used to fatherhood. But the atmosphere between the two of them was at best polite. They were like two people stuck together in a broken-down lift, saying only as much as they needed to—but it wouldn't stay like that, would it? Once they were out of the baby-shock phase, things would return to 'normal'. But she and Luc had no 'normal'. Sooner or later they were going to start wanting different things.

She decided to speak to him about it after dinner one evening—a meal they still took together, mainly, she suspected, to maintain some sort of charade in front of the staff.

Leaving Almeera with Rose, Lisa washed her hair before slipping into a long, silk tunic which disguised the extra heaviness of her breasts and tummy. She even put on a little make-up, wondering why she was going to so much trouble. *Because I want to look in control. I want to show him that I mean business.*

But when she popped her head in to check on Rose before going down for dinner, it was to find Luc standing by the crib, his fingers touching the baby's soft black hair as he murmured to her softly.

'Oh,' she said. 'You're here.'

He glanced over at Almeera, who was fiddling with the intricate mobile which hung over the crib. 'I wonder if you'd mind leaving us for a moment, Almeera,' he said.

The servant nodded and slipped away and Lisa looked at Luc, feeling suddenly disorientated.

'I thought we were having dinner,' she said.

He raised his eyebrows. 'I think we're able to apply a little flexibility about the time we eat, don't you?' he said drily. 'Unless you're especially hungry.'

Lisa shrugged, wondering why tonight he was looking at her more intently than he had done for weeks. Automatically, she skated a palm down over the curve of one hip without considering the wisdom of such an action. 'I ought to be cutting back on food,' she said.

'Don't be ridiculous,' he said, his voice growing a little impatient before it gentled. 'You look beautiful, if you really want to know. Luscious and ripe and womanly.'

Actually, she didn't want to know and she didn't want his voice dipping into a sensual caress like that, making her long for something which definitely *wasn't* on the menu. She took an unsteady breath. 'We have to discuss the future,' she said.

There was a pause. 'I know we do.'

Luc looked into the questioning face of his wife and wondered afterwards if it was the sense of a looming ultimatum and dread which made him drop his guard so completely. He stared at her shiny hazelnut curls and the fleshy curves of her body and he felt his throat dry to dust as he forced himself to confront the truth.

Because in a sudden flash of insight he realised that the feelings he had were not just for their child, but for the woman who had given birth to her. A woman he'd brought here as a hostage, but who had tried to reach out to him all the same. He could recognise it now but he'd been too blind to see at the time. Because once her initial opposition to being his wife had faded, he realised that she'd tried to make the best of her life here. She had studied the history of his country and quietly gone about her own career without making undue demands on his time.

But despite the silent vow he'd made on their wedding day, he had continued to keep her at arm's length, hadn't he? He had kept himself at a physical distance even though he'd sensed that she'd wanted him. He had deliberately not laid a finger on her, knowing that such a move was calculated to make her desire for him grow. To *frustrate* her. And deep down, his disapproval had never been far from the surface. If he was being honest, hadn't he experienced a certain *relief* that he'd been able to chastise her over the damned necklace? As if he had needed something to justify why he could never allow himself to get close to her. The truth was that he had treated Lisa as an object rather than a person. *Because he hadn't known how to do it any other way.*

But suddenly he did—or at least, he thought he did. Was Rose responsible for opening the floodgates? Emotion flooded over him like a warm tide as he looked down at his daughter. Tentatively, she opened her eyes, and as he gazed into a sapphire hue so like his own he felt his heart clench. He lifted his head to meet Lisa's watchful gaze, the dryness in his throat making the thought of speech seem impossible, but that was no excuse. Because this was something he could not turn away from. Something he could no longer deny.

'I love her, Lisa,' he said simply.

For a moment there was silence before she nodded. 'I know. Me, too. It's funny, isn't it?' She gave a little laugh, as if she was embarrassed to hear him say the words out loud. 'How you can feel it so instantly and completely.'

Luc drew in a deep breath as he met her eyes. He thought about the first time he'd met her and that rare glint of shared understanding which had passed between them. The way he hadn't been able to get her out of his head in all the months which had followed. When he'd seen her again, the chemistry between them was as explosive as it had ever been—but what he felt now was about more than sex. Much more. Because somehow he'd come to realise that his spunky designer with the clear green-gold gaze treated him as nobody else had ever done.

She treated him like a man and not a prince.

So tell her. Take courage and tell her the words you never imagined you'd say.

'And I love you, too, Lisa,' he said. 'More than I'd ever realised.'

At first Lisa thought she must be dreaming, because surely Luc hadn't just told her that he loved her? She blinked. But he had. Even if the words hadn't still been resonating on the air, she knew she hadn't misheard them from the look on his face, which seemed to be savage yet silky, all at the same time. She felt a shiver whispering its way over her skin as she tried to ignore the sensual softening of his lips and to concentrate on facts, not dreams. Be careful what you wish for—that was what people said, wasn't it? And suddenly she understood why.

Luc had let his cold mask slip for a moment. Or rather, it hadn't *slipped*—he had just replaced it with a different mask. A loving mask which was far more suitable for ensuring he got what he wanted.

His baby.

Yet she wouldn't have been human if her first response hadn't been a fierce burst of hope. If she hadn't pictured the tumultuous scene which could follow, if she let it. Of her nodding her head and letting all the tears which were gathering force spill from her eyes before telling him shakily that yes, she loved him, too.

And, oh, the exquisite irony of that—even if it happened to be true. Admitting she loved a man who was cold-bloodedly trying to manipulate her emotions by saying something he didn't mean. What about all the lessons she was supposed to have learnt?

He was looking at her from between narrowed lashes and she knew she had to strike now. Before she had the chance to change her mind and cling to him and beg him to never let her go.

'Do you think I'm stupid?' she questioned quietly, her voice low and unsteady. 'Because I would have to be pretty stupid not to realise why you just told me you loved me. You don't *love* me, Luc. You've fallen in love with your daughter, yes—and I'm over the moon about that. But this isn't like going to the supermarket— which you've probably never done. We don't come as a two-for-one deal! And you can't smooth-talk me into staying on Mardovia just because you've trotted out the conditional emotional clause which most women are brainless enough to fall for!'

He went very still, his powerful body seeming to become the whole dark focus of the room. 'You think I told you I loved you because I have an ulterior motive?' he questioned slowly.

'I don't think it—I *know* it!'

He flinched and nodded his head. 'I had no idea you thought quite so badly of me, Lisa.'

Something in the quiet dignity of his words made Lisa's heart contract with pain, but she couldn't retract her accusation now—and why should she? He was trying to manipulate her in every which way and she wouldn't let him. She couldn't *afford* to let him. Because she'd crumble if he hurt her, and she never crumbled.

'I don't think badly of you,' she said. 'I think you're a great dad and that's what's making you say all this stuff. But you don't have to pretend in order to make things work. I want things to be...amicable between us, Luc.'

'Amicable?' he bit out before slowly nodding his head, and in that moment Lisa saw a cold acceptance settle over his features. 'Very well. If that's what you want, then that's what you'll get.' There was a pause. 'When *exactly* do you want to leave?'

Lisa and Rose's journey was scheduled for the end of the week. She was to fly back to London with Rose and Almeera and two protection officers, who would move into a section of Luc's large London house, which would now be her home. The idea of two of Luc's henchmen spying on her filled her with dread and Lisa tried to assert her independence.

'I don't need two protection officers,' she told Luc.

'You may not, but my daughter does.'

Lisa licked her lips. 'So I'm trapped any which way?'

He shrugged. 'Trapped or protected—it all depends how you look at it. And now, if you've quite finished, there are things I'd like to do while Rose is still in residence, and today I'd like to take her into Vallemar to meet some friends.'

Lisa told herself she didn't want to be parted from her baby and that was why she asked the question. 'Can't I come?'

'Why?' he questioned coolly. 'These are people you are unlikely to see in the future—so why bother getting to know them? No point in complicating an already complicated situation.'

So Lisa was forced to watch as Luc, Rose and Almeera were driven away in one of the palace limousines while she stayed put. She paced the gardens, unable to settle until they returned—with an exquisite selection of tiny Parisian couture dresses for Rose, from someone called Michele—and Lisa could do nothing about the sudden jealous pounding of her heart. But she didn't dare ask Luc who Michele was. Even she could recognise that she didn't have the right to do that.

At last, after a final sleepless night, it was time to leave. Lisa stood awkwardly in the main entrance of the palace, feeling small and very isolated as she pre-

pared to say goodbye to Luc. Already in the car with
Almeera, Rose was buckled into her baby seat—but
now there was nothing but a terrible sense of impending doom as Lisa looked up into the stony features of
her royal husband.

'Well,' she said, her bright voice sounding cracked.
'I guess this is it. And you'll…you'll be over to London next week?'

'I'll be over whenever I damned well please and I
shall come and go as I please,' he said, his blue eyes
glittering out a warning. 'So don't think you can move
some freeloader into my house while I'm away, because
I will not tolerate it.'

Don't rise to it, thought Lisa. Don't leave with the
memory of angry words between you. She nodded instead. 'I have no intention of doing that, which I suspect you already know. So…goodbye, Luc. I'll… I'll
be seeing you.'

And suddenly his cold mask seemed to dissolve to
reveal the etching of anger and pain which lay behind.
Did he realise she had witnessed it? Was that why he
reached out and gripped her arms, his fingers pressing
into the soft flesh, as if wanting to reassert the control
he had momentarily lost?

'Better have something other than a tame goodbye
to remember me by, dear wife,' he said. 'Don't you
agree?'

And before she could raise any objection, his lips
were pressing down on hers in a punishing kiss which
was all about possession and nothing whatsoever to
do with affection. But it worked. Oh, how quickly it

worked. It had her opening her lips beneath the seeking pressure of his and gasping softly as she felt the tip of his tongue sliding over hers. She swayed slightly and as his big hands steadied her she could feel the clamour of her suddenly hungry body as it demanded more. Touch me, she thought silently, wishing that they were somewhere less public, though pretty sure none of the servants were around. Just *touch* me.

But just as suddenly he terminated the kiss—stepping away from her, the triumph darkening his eyes not quite managing to hide his contempt, so that she could hardly bear to look at him. As she stumbled out of the door towards the car she could feel his gaze burning into her back.

Rose was sleeping and Almeera was sitting in the front beside the driver as the car headed towards the airfield, and all Lisa could think about was Luc. Raw pain ripped through her. She found herself wishing that it could all have been different. Wishing he'd meant it when he told her that he loved her.

They were almost at the airfield when her thoughts jarred and then jammed—the way CDs used to get stuck if there was a fault on the disc and started repeating the same piece of music over and over again. She creased her brow as she tried to work out what it was which was bothering her.

She found herself remembering what he'd told her about his upbringing and the women paid to look after him after his mother's death. His words had moved her, despite the flat and matter-of-fact way in which he'd delivered them—as if he were reading from the minutes of a boring meeting. But you would have needed a heart of stone not to be affected by the thought of the lonely little boy growing up alone in a palace, with nobody but a grieving father and a series of strict governesses for company.

Had those governesses ever told him they loved him? Held him tightly in their arms and hugged him and kissed his little head? She bit her lip. Of course not—because that hadn't been in their job description. They had been there to serve. To drum in his duty to his country. A duty he must be reminded of whenever he saw the Wheeler portraits of Louisa De Lacy, whose love affair with his ancestor had almost destroyed the Mardovian dynasty. But it had not. The principality had survived and today it was strong—and powerful.

Yet despite all his wealth and power, Luc had not fought her for his daughter's custody, had he? With his access to the world's finest lawyers she sensed he had the ability to do that—and to win—so why hadn't he?

What did that say about him as a man? That he could be understanding, yes. Magnanimous, compassionate and kind. Or even that he cared more about her happiness and Rose's than about his own.

That he *loved* her?

She stared out of the car window and thought about how closed up he could seem. About the courage it must have taken for him to come out and say something like that. The way his voice had cracked with emotion as he'd spoken—and she knew then that he would never have said it if he didn't mean it. He had even told her that, once. Yet she had just batted his words back to him as if they'd been of no consequence, hadn't she? She had turned away from him, too frightened and so entrenched in her own prejudices to believe him.

For how could either of them know about the giving and receiving of love if neither of them had ever witnessed it?

'Stop the car!' she yelled, before recovering herself slightly and leaning forward to speak to the driver. 'Please. Can you take us back to the palace?'

Lisa's heart was racing during a drive back which seemed to take much longer than the outward journey, and she couldn't stop thinking that maybe it was already too late. What if he'd gone out, or refused to see her, or...?

But there were a million variations on 'what if' and she tried to push them from her mind as they drove up the mountain road with the beautiful blue bay glittering far below.

Leaving Almeera to bring Rose inside, Lisa went rushing into the palace, knowing that she should be walking calmly in a manner befitting a princess—even if she was an estranged one—but she couldn't seem to stop herself. She was about to ask one of the footmen where she could find the Prince when she saw Luc's rather terrifying new aide, Serge, coming from the direction of one of the smaller anterooms.

'I need to see the Prince,' she blurted out.

Serge's face remained impassive. 'The Prince has left strict instructions that under no circumstances is he to be disturbed.'

Had her departure already robbed her of any small

vestige of power her royal status might once have given her? Stubbornly, Lisa shook her head and sped noise-lessly in the direction she'd seen Serge walking from.

With shaking fingers she opened doors. The first room was empty, as was the second, but in the third Luc stood alone by the window, his body tense and his shoulders hunched as he stared out.

Behind her Lisa could hear rapid footsteps and she turned round to see that the Russian had almost caught her up.

'Your Highness...' Serge began.

'Leave us, Serge,' said Luc, without turning round.

Lisa's heart was pounding but she waited until the aide had retreated and closed the door behind him be-fore she risked saying anything.

'Luc,' she said breathlessly, but all the things she'd been meaning to say just died in her throat as nerves overcame her.

He turned around then, very slowly, and she was shocked by the ravaged expression on his face—at the deep sense of sorrow which seemed to envelop him, like a dark cloud. His sapphire eyes were icy-cold and she'd never seen someone look quite so unwelcoming.

'Where's Rose?' he demanded.

'Almeera's just bringing her in. I needed...' she swallowed '...to speak to you.'

'Haven't we said everything which needs to be said, Lisa? Haven't we completely exhausted the subject?'

'No,' she said, knowing that she needed the courage to reach into her frightened heart, despite the forbid-ding look on his face. 'We haven't.'

But clearly he wasn't about to help her. 'What do you want?' he questioned impatiently, as if she were a servant who had neglected to remove one of the plates.

'I want to tell you,' she whispered, before drawing in a deep breath, 'how very stupid I've been. And to try to tell you why.'

'I'm not interested in your explanations,' he snapped.

'I want to explain,' she continued, with a sudden feeling of calm and certainty, which she sensed was her only lifeline, 'that I was scared when you told me you loved me. Scared you didn't mean it. Scared I'd get hurt—'

'And you've spent your whole life avoiding getting hurt, haven't you, Lisa?' he finished slowly, as if he had just worked it out for himself. 'You learnt a bitter lesson at your mother's knee that love could destroy you.'

'Yes. *Yes!* Those feelings aren't always logical, but that doesn't make them any less valid. That's why I finished with you the first time.' She stared down at her shiny gold wedding band, before lifting her gaze to his. 'Oh, I knew there was no future in it—you told me that right from the start—but that wasn't why. Because who wouldn't have wanted to prolong every wonderful second of what we had? It was because I had started to fall in love with you and I knew that was a mistake. You didn't want love. Not from me. You told me you didn't want anything from me. I tried to forget you—I tried so very hard—and then when you walked into the shop that day, I realised nothing had changed.' She shrugged. 'Not a single thing. I still wanted you.'

'And I still wanted you,' he said. 'Even though everything about it was wrong and even though I tried to resist you, in the end I couldn't.'

'Maybe you just can't resist sex when it's offered to you on a plate.'

'Oh, but I can,' he assured her softly. 'I hadn't—haven't—had sex with anyone else since my relationship with you first ended.'

She stared at him in disbelief. 'Nobody?'

'Nobody.'

'But why? I mean, why not? There must have been plenty of opportunities to bed all kinds of women.'

Luc rubbed his thumb over his lips, realising that you could say words of love and mean them, but that was only the beginning. Because you needed to go deeper than that. To be prepared to show another person every part of you—to draw aside the curtain of mystique and admit that inside even *he* could be vulnerable.

'Initially I convinced myself that I needed a time of celibacy before settling down with Sophie, but that wasn't the real reason.' He shook his head and shrugged. 'Because the truth was that I just didn't want anyone else but you, Lisa. I don't know how and I don't know why—but you're the woman who has made me feel stuff I didn't even realise existed. The only one. And I want—'

'No,' she rushed in, as if eager to show him her own vulnerability. 'Let me tell you what I want, Luc. I want to be a real wife to you, in every sense of the word. I want to live here or anywhere, just so long as it's with you and Rose. I'd like to have more children, if you would. And I'd like to be the best princess I can possibly be. I want time to love you and to show you all the stuff I've never dared show you before. So what have you got to say to that, Luciano Gabriel Leonidas? Will you take me on?'

He could feel the powerful beat of his heart as he pulled her into his arms, but for the first time in his adult life he realised that his cheeks were wet with tears. And so were hers. He dried them with his lips and then bent his head so his mouth met hers. 'I'll take you on any time you like,' he said unsteadily, just before he kissed her. 'Because I love you.'

EPILOGUE

'Is she asleep?'

'Flat out.' Lisa walked into their bedroom, pulling the elastic band from her hair and letting her curls tumble free. Luc was lying on top of the bed, reading. His eyes slitted as he watched her and he put the book down and smiled.

Lisa smiled back as her heart gave an unsteady thunder as she looked at her beloved husband. The light from the sunset was bathing everything in rose gold as it flooded in through the open windows—turning his naked body into a gilded statue. He really was magnificent, she thought hungrily, enjoying the way that the glowing light highlighted the hard muscle and silken flesh of his physique. She looked into his eyes, thinking how very quickly time passed and how important it was to treasure every single moment.

Sometimes it was hard to believe that their daughter was already two years old and probably the most sophisticated little jet-setter of all her peers. But everyone said that Princess Rose had the sweetest and sunniest nature in the world and her besotted parents tended to agree with them.

She wiped her still-damp hands down over her dress. 'Your daughter seems to think that bath time was made for fun,' she observed, with a smile.

'Just like her mother.' Luc's eyes gleamed. 'I think you and I might share a shower in a little while, but I have other plans for you first.'

'Oh? What plans?'

'Well, you are looking a little overdressed compared to me.' A lazy gesture of his hand lingered fractionally over his hardening body and he slanted her a complicit smile. 'So why don't you take off your dress and come over here?'

'That sounds like a very sensible idea to me,' she murmured, shivering a little with anticipation as she pulled the dress over her head and joined him on the bed.

He unclipped the rose-black lace of her bra and bent his mouth to the puckered point of her nipple, giving it a luxurious lick, before raising his eyes to hers. 'Looking forward to tomorrow?'

'I can't wait.'

He smiled. 'Then I guess we'd better do something to help pass the time as satisfactorily as possible. Don't you?'

Lisa stroked her toes against his foot as he slithered her panties down. Tomorrow the three of them were joining Brittany, Jason and Tamsin for a week-long break on the quieter southwestern shores of Mardovia—a sprawling idyll of a royal retreat, well away from all the servants and protocol of the main palace. It was one of the few places where they could be totally free, but Lisa accepted that the occasional loss of freedom was the price to be paid for the honour of ruling this ancient island alongside her husband. And she was happy to pay it, because she had worked hard to ensure her smooth transition into palace life and all its expectations.

Early on she'd recognised that maintaining a business in England while trying to settle into her new role was probably not sustainable in the long term—though Luc had told her that if she wanted to continue, then somehow they would make it happen. But being a full-time designer did not fit in with being a full-time princess and mother—and a part-time designer was never going to make waves. So she sold the label and the few pangs of regret she experienced soon passed.

Luc had invested in and commandeered the building of a new Art and Fashion School, which was named after her, and she had been taken aback and humbled by this gesture of his love. She was proud and honoured to be the patron of the state-of-the-art institution and planned to give monthly lectures on design, as well as making sure Mardovia became a hub for fashion innovation. There was a lot of young talent on this island, she realised—and she was going to make sure that every Mardovian child's talent would be fulfilled.

She had tried very hard to understand Eleonora's behaviour towards her. Lisa soon recognised that it had been an overdeveloped sense of patriotism and rather warped sense of devotion towards Luc which had made the aide resent the new commoner princess so much. But, as Lisa whispered to Luc one evening, she didn't want to start out her royal life with enemies, and forgiveness was good for the soul. So she had given Eleonora a key administrative role in the new Art School, and Eleonora had rewarded her with genuine loyalty ever since.

She and Luc had done everything in the wrong order, Lisa reflected ruefully as her panties fluttered to the floor. Her pregnancy had come before the wedding and there hadn't been a honeymoon for many months—not until Rose had been settled enough to leave with Almeera.

The other big change was with Jason. Brittany's new-found independence had given her the strength to tell Jason that there was no future for them until he got himself a job. And she'd meant it. Jason had found himself a job in a warehouse and had put in the hours and the backbone. It wasn't the most glamorous job in the world, but it proved something to them all—that Tamsin's father did have grit and commitment somewhere inside him. Six months later he and Britt were married and Luc offered him a role with his security facility at the Mardovian Embassy in London.

'What are you smiling to yourself for?' Luc's deep voice interrupted her reverie—as did the finger drifting over her ribcage—and Lisa looked into the sapphire gleam of her husband's eyes.

'I'm just thinking how perfect my life is.'

'I'm pleased to hear it. Perhaps I can think of a way to make it even more perfect.'

She batted her eyelashes. 'Really?'

'Really.' A smoky look entered his eyes as he

brushed his lips over hers. 'I intend making love to you until the moon is high in the sky, *chérie*—but first there is something I need to do.'

She lifted her hand to his face, resting it tenderly against the angled contours of his cheek. 'Which is?' she whispered, though she knew what was coming for it was something of a daily ritual for them—a glorious reaffirming of the vows they had once made under duress. At times they had each felt this particular emotion, but neither of them had dared say it, but now the words could be spoken freely and spoken from the heart. And they said them just as often as they could, as if to remind themselves of their good fortune.

'I love you,' he said softly.

Was it crazy that tears had begun to prick at the backs of her eyes? Lisa didn't care because she no longer shied away from showing emotion. And when something felt this good, you just had to let it all come rushing out.

'I love you, too, my darling Luc,' she whispered back. 'Now and for ever.'

And she drew his dark head towards her so that she could kiss him, in a room gilded rose gold by the glorious Mardovian sunset.

* * * * *

HEIRESS'S ROYAL BABY BOMBSHELL

JENNIFER FAYE

PROLOGUE

Mid-August, Milan, Italy

A CASUAL PARTY full of joy and hope for the future was just what she needed.

It was her chance to forget that her opinions were unwanted and disregarded. That acknowledgment sliced deep into her heart. But she refused to become a silent shadow in her own family.

Noemi Cattaneo, heiress to the Cattaneo Jewels dynasty, welcomed the loud music and the sound of laughter. After yet another argument with her older brother, Sebastian, she needed space. She took a drink from her second glass of pink champagne. When was he ever going to treat her like an adult instead of his kid sister and realize that her opinions had merit?

She took another sip of bubbly, hoping to cool off her rising temper. Every time she recalled her brother saying that being a *silent partner* suited her, frustration bubbled within her. How dare he tell her to stick to modeling! There was more to her than her looks—a lot more. And she refused to spend the evening worrying about her brother.

Someone bumped into her. The champagne sloshed over the edge of the glass and onto Noemi's new white dress. She glanced down at the pink stain starting at her chest and streaking down to her midsection.

She might need to cool off, but this wasn't how she'd intended to do it. Noemi's gaze lifted as she looked around for the klutz who'd bumped into her, but she couldn't pinpoint the culprit. They hadn't hung around to express their regret. Maybe coming to this engagement party hadn't been such a good idea.

She searched the crowd for Stephania, her friend who'd convinced her to come to the party. As Noemi's gaze scanned the room, it strayed across a man with mysterious hazel eyes. He was standing across the room surrounded by a half dozen eager, smiling women. Even though each woman appeared to be vying for his attention, he was staring at Noemi. Her pulse quickened. This wasn't the first time that she'd noticed him staring her way.

"Hey, Noemi," Stephania said. "What are you doing standing over here all alone?"

"Apparently getting champagne spilled on me."

Stephania gasped when she saw the stain. "I'm sure they have some club soda around here."

Noemi shook her head. "I'll just go home."

"But you can't leave yet. We just got here. Besides, if you go home, you'll just mope around."

And think about how her brother refused to give her any respect. Noemi hated to admit it but Stephania was right. Her gaze strayed to the tall sexy stranger. His eyes caught and held hers. Her pulse quickened. Perhaps there was a reason to stay.

Twenty or so minutes later, with the help of club soda, paper towels and a hair dryer, Noemi's dress was once again presentable. By then, she'd talked some sense into herself about the attractive man whose gaze seemed to follow her around the room. He was probably the type who enjoyed the chase—not the capture.

However, there was something slightly familiar about him. Not one to keep up with gossip or who to know, Noemi couldn't place him. But if he was at this exclusive gathering, he must be someone important.

She glanced around the room but didn't see any sign of

him. Disappointment assailed her. This wasn't like her. She could take guys or leave them. She thought of asking Stephania if she knew the man's name but shrugged off the idea. Her life had enough complications. She didn't need more.

But just the same, her mood had dimmed. Her problems once again started to crowd in around the edges of her mind. Needing some fresh air, she stepped out onto the terrace. There was just enough of the evening sun for her to admire the distant mountain range as a gentle breeze caressed her skin.

"Beautiful."

The deep rich voice had her turning her head. And there stood the intriguing stranger with the mesmerizing eyes. His voice held a slight accent. She couldn't place it, but it was extremely sexy—just like the rest of him.

"I'm sorry. Am I disturbing you?" She glanced around for his harem of women, but he appeared to at last be alone—with her.

"Not at all. Please join me." He motioned for her to join him at the edge of the terrace.

She stepped closer but not quite the whole way. "You were admiring the mountains, too?"

He sent her a puzzled look.

"When I stepped out here, you said beautiful. I assumed you were referring to the view."

He smiled and shook his head. "No. I was talking about you. You are beautiful."

She'd been complimented many times over the years. Being the face of Cattaneo Jewels, compliments came with the job. But the man looked at her as though he wanted to take her in his very capable arms and devour her with hungry kisses. The heat of a blush engulfed her cheeks.

"Thank you."

The warm August evening was no help in cooling her down. She knew it was polite to make small conversation, but for once, her mind was a blank. This man didn't seem to know who she was, and for the moment, she found that to be a welcome relief. She didn't want him to treat her differently. For tonight, she wanted to be just a face in the crowd.

But when she turned her head and gazed into this man's eyes, her heart began to race. For a moment, she glanced at his mouth. If she were someone else tonight, would it be wrong to give in to her desires—to live in the moment?

But then she realized if she wanted people to take her seriously, she couldn't give in to her whims. No matter how delicious they may be.

"We should probably get back inside before people start to wonder where we've gone," she said, though there wasn't any part of her that wanted to return to the party. She was quite content to stay right here with him.

He leaned in close. "Let them wonder. I like it much better out here, especially now that you are here."

She cocked her head to the side and looked at him. "I'm starting to understand."

His brows drew together. "Understand?"

"Yes. I understand why all the women surround you. If you flatter them like this, they simply can't help themselves."

The worry lines on his face smoothed and a devastatingly sexy smile lifted his lips. "Trust me. I have done nothing to encourage those women. But when it comes to you, it's different. What brings you to such an exclusive party alone?"

She wanted to believe him when he said she was different. His words were like a soothing balm on her bruised ego. Her parents and her brother might think she should remain nothing more than a silent partner, but this man wanted to hear what she had to say. A smile lifted her lips.

"I'm not alone." The smile immediately slipped from his face. Then realizing how her response must have sounded, she was quick to supply, "I came here with a friend."

"And your friend doesn't mind that you're out here instead of inside with them celebrating the engagement?"

Noemi couldn't help but notice his strange wording. "Do you even know the engaged couple?"

"As a matter of fact, I don't."

Noemi's mouth gaped. Only the very famous or the very rich who knew the couple had been invited. The newly engaged couple didn't want the paparazzi to know the details. They wanted a chance to celebrate and enjoy the moment. And he was a party crasher.

She tilted her chin upward, taking in the man's handsome face. He didn't strike her as the type to intrude upon a stranger's good time. His chiseled jawline gave his face a distinctive look. But it was his mesmerizing eyes that held her gaze captive. The breath caught in her throat.

And then the urge once again came over her to kiss this stranger. But she didn't even know him. She glanced away. She was letting his good looks and sexy smile get to her.

Maybe if she got to know him a little better. There was something about him that made her curious to know more about him. "So if you don't know the engaged couple, why are you here?"

He shrugged. "The host of the party invited me."

She took in the man's straight nose and fresh-shaven jaw. "Do you live in Milan?"

He shook his head. "I'm just passing through."

"On your way to where?"

He shrugged. "I haven't decided yet."

The fact he didn't live in Milan—that he was moving on—appealed to her. The last thing she wanted at this juncture in her life was a relationship. She had her modeling career to focus on—even though it was rapidly losing its appeal.

But an evening of fun—an evening with no strings—what would be the harm? Tomorrow she could decide if she wanted to continue to fight for a more significant place in the family business or look elsewhere. Just then, the French doors burst open and a couple wrapped in each other's arms stumbled onto the veranda. When they bumped into Mr. Tall and Sexy, they straightened up.

"Sorry about that," Matteo DeLuca, an award-winning actor, said. "We didn't know anyone was out here."

The young woman in his arms burst out in a giggle. Her eyes were glazed and as Matteo led her away, she tripped over her own feet. Upon their exit, they forgot to close the doors. The loud music and cacophony of voices came spilling forth.

Noemi's companion closed the doors and then turned back to her. "How would you feel about going someplace quieter?"

"But I don't even know your name."

His brows rose ever so briefly. She couldn't help wondering if his reaction was due to the fact that he expected her to know him. Or whether he was surprised that she'd resisted jumping at his offer. Because right at that moment, she couldn't think of anything she'd like better than spending the evening with this intriguing man.

She took a moment to study him. His dark designer suit definitely didn't come off a rack. As he took a drink of what appeared to be bourbon, she noticed his watch. A Rolex no less. This man looked right at home at this party.

He smiled and his eyes lit up. This man, he was… Well, he was confident. It was in the way he stood with his broad shoulders pulled back and his chin held high. But he wasn't unapproachable either. He seemed to have a sense of humor. But most of all, he came across as the type to go after what he wanted. And right now, he appeared to want her.

"My name is Max."

"Max, huh?" She tried the name on for size. It wasn't as imposing as Zeus or Hercules but it'd do—it'd do just fine.

"You don't like my name?"

"It's not that." It's that it was such a simple name for such a complicated man. And yes, she sensed there were many facets to this man in the ten or so minutes that they'd been talking.

"Then what is it?"

She shrugged. "I just wasn't expecting such a common name."

He smiled and it made her stomach shiver with nerves. "I won't tell my mother you said that."

"Please don't." They were acting like one day soon she would meet the woman. That was never going to happen. But it was fun to play along with him.

"And what's yours?" His voice interrupted her troubled thoughts.

"My what?"

Amusement twinkled in his eyes. "Your name?"

"Oh." Heat rushed up from her chest and settled in her cheeks. "It's Noemi."

"Noemi. That's a beautiful name for a very beautiful woman." He took a step closer to her, leaving little distance between them. She searched his face for any sign of recognition of who she was. There was nothing in his expression to suggest that he recognized her as an heiress to the infamous Cattaneo Jewels worn by the rich and famous worldwide. But there was something else reflected in his eyes.

Desire.

Their gazes locked. This gorgeous hunk of a man, who could have his pick of the eligible women and some not quite so eligible at this party, desired her. Her heart raced. It'd been such a long time since a man had turned her head. But there was something special about Max.

The *thump thump* of her heart was so loud that she could barely hear her own thoughts. And then he reached out to her. His thumb ever so gently traced down her jaw before his finger brushed over her bottom lip. It was such a simple gesture but it sent a bolt of heat ricocheting from her mouth down to her very core.

Before she could figure out how to react to these unexpected sensations, his gaze lowered to her lips. He was going to kiss her?

Her heart lodged in her throat. She should… She should do something. But her body betrayed her. Her feet refused to move and her chin lifted ever so slightly.

As though that was all the invitation he needed, Max lowered his head. Her eyes fluttered closed. She shouldn't want this—want him. But she did, more than she thought possible.

His lips were smooth and warm. And a kiss had never felt so good. She didn't make a habit of going around kissing strangers, but in the short time she'd spent with Max, she had this uncanny feeling that she could trust him.

She slipped her arms up over his muscled shoulders. As the kiss deepened, her hands wrapped around the back of his neck. She'd never been kissed quite so intently and with such unrestrained passion. She wasn't even sure her feet were still on the ground.

Suddenly Max pulled back. It happened so quickly she had to wonder if she'd imagined it. But her lips still tingled where his mouth had touched hers. And he sent her a dazzling smile that promised more of the same.

If she were wise, she would end things right here, but her body hummed with unquenched desire. For once, she wanted to throw caution to the wind and enjoy herself. After all, her brother accused her of being impulsive. Why not live up to the accusation…just this once?

Max pulled his cell phone from his jacket pocket.

"What are you doing?" The words slipped from her lips.

"I'm calling my driver." And then he spoke into his phone. Seconds later, the conversation ended. He turned back to her. "The car will be waiting for us downstairs in a couple of minutes. Shall we?"

But she'd never said she would go anywhere with him. Was it that obvious in the way she looked at him? More than likely he was taking his cues from that kiss they'd shared. That short but arousing kiss.

"What are you thinking?" His eyes searched hers.

"I was thinking…um…that it would be nice to go somewhere a little quieter."

He smiled again. "My thoughts exactly."

He held his arm out to her. It took her a moment to figure out what he was doing. Did men even do that anymore? Wasn't it just something she saw in the old black-and-white movies that her mother collected?

But Noemi found the gentlemanly gesture endearing, even

if it was a little dated. There was something about this man that was so different from anyone she'd ever known and that appealed to her. She had a feeling this evening was going to be totally unforgettable.

CHAPTER ONE

Three months later
Mont Coeur ski resort, the Swiss Alps

WHAT WAS SHE going to do?

Noemi paced back and forth in her luxurious bedroom in her family's palatial chalet. A gentle fire flickered in the fireplace, keeping her suite cozy. She couldn't sit still.

So much had happened in the last few months that it made her head spin. First, the pregnancy test had turned up positive. As she'd struggled to come to terms with what this meant to her future, she'd stumbled across the fact that she had a long-lost brother. The realization had jarred her entire world. How could her parents have kept Leo a secret all her life?

An ensuing row between her and her parents had her shouting out hurtful words—words she didn't mean. And yet now she couldn't take them back. She couldn't tell her parents she was sorry and that she loved them.

They were dead.

The reading of their will had succeeded in driving home the fact that her parents wouldn't be here at the chalet as was their Christmas tradition. But the three siblings intended to spend the holiday together.

It had been strange to meet her brother Leo for the first time, even stranger to hear the contents of her parents' will. She never would have imagined that the terms of the will would be the way they were. Clearly Sebastian hadn't either, because when he'd discovered that his parents had given Leo controlling shares in Cattaneo Jewels for six months, he'd been furious. And although Leo had been clearly reluctant, the terms stated that should Leo refuse, Cattaneo Jewels would cease trading and be liquidated. And none of them had wanted that.

But tempers and emotions had risen, and it was all Noemi had been able to do to convince her brothers to think on it and to return here to the chalet in Mont Coeur just before Christmas for the final decision.

Even now, she could only guess at what her parents had been thinking when they'd written the will and its unusual terms. She missed them dearly—most especially her mother. She needed her now more than ever.

Noemi swiped at her eyes as she thought of her mother. And though their last conversation had been heated and hurtful, Noemi didn't doubt her parents had loved her—even if she had made mistakes along the way. But all the wishing in the world wasn't going to erase the last angry words that they'd exchanged, nor would it bring them back to her.

Noemi moved to the French doors in her room and stared out at the cloudy afternoon sky as big lazy snowflakes drifted ever so slowly to the ground. It was a light snow. The kind that melted as soon as it touched the roads. And any other time she'd be caught up in the peaceful relaxing view. But not today.

She was running out of time to keep her secret to herself. Her hand pressed to her slightly rounded abdomen. No amount of baggy clothes was going to hide her pregnancy much longer.

And what was she supposed to say to people when they asked who the father was? *His name is Max? He has the dreamiest eyes that appear to change colors to suit his mood? And his body is like a sculpture of defined muscles? Or when he laughs it is deep and rich?* Even now, his memory brought a smile to her face.

After the most magical night, he'd insisted that it would be best not to exchange full names or phone numbers. She'd hesitantly agreed. Neither of them had been looking for a lasting relationship. And now that she really needed to speak to him, she didn't know how to reach him. She'd even asked Stephania about him, but she didn't know him—

Noemi's cell phone buzzed. She moved to the bed and picked it up. She wasn't in the mood to speak to anyone, but when she saw that it was Maria, her sister-in-law and close friend, she answered.

"How are you doing?" Maria asked.

"Okay. I guess." Noemi sighed.

"Really? I'd hate to hear you if something was wrong."

"What's that supposed to mean?"

"You're usually bubbly but lately you've been really down. Is it your parents?"

"No. I mean, I miss them a lot."

"So something else is bothering you?"

Maria had always been good at reading her. And she was the closest thing Noemi had to a big sister. If she didn't talk to someone soon, she was going to burst.

Noemi worried her bottom lip. "Can I tell you something?"

"Sure. You know you can always talk to me. Is it about the reading of your parents' will?"

Noemi shook her head and then realized Maria couldn't see her. "It's not that. But if I tell you this, you have to promise not to say a word to Sebastian."

There was a slight pause on the other end of the phone.

"Never mind," Noemi said. "I never should have asked you to keep anything from my brother."

"It's okay. You need someone to confide in and I promise your brother won't hear a thing from me. Sometimes he can be a bit overprotective where you're concerned."

"And when he hears about this, he's going to hit the roof. He'll be just like Papa—" She stopped, recalling how poorly her parents had taken the news of her pregnancy.

Even though her parents had had a child in their teens and had given him up for adoption, they'd still been disappointed with her unplanned pregnancy. What was up with that? It wasn't like she'd set out to wreck her life. She'd thought that out of all the people in the world, they would have been the ones to understand. They hadn't. And it had hurt Noemi deeply. Worse yet, they'd died before she could ever put things to right.

"Relax." Maria's voice drew Noemi out of her thoughts. "We'll figure out how to deal with him."

"Thanks. But I'll deal with him."

"Whatever you want. But you still haven't told me your problem. Maybe I can help. Perhaps it isn't as big as you're imagining."

"No. It's bigger." Noemi's insides quivered with nerves. By saying the words out loud, it was going to make this pregnancy real. Just like the reading of the will had made her parents' deaths startling real. Once she told Maria about the baby, there would be no more pretending. In less than six months, she was going to give birth.

"Noemi…"

"I'm pregnant."

Silence. Utter and complete silence.

Noemi's heart raced. Her hands grew clammy. And her stomach churned. What was Maria thinking? Was she disappointed in her, too, just like her parents had been?

"Are you sure?"

Noemi nodded. "I took three home pregnancy tests and then I went to see the doctor. It's official."

"I don't know what to say." There was a pause as though Maria was searching for the right words. "How do you feel about it?"

"I knew I wanted kids someday, but not yet—not now. I'm only twenty-six."

"And the father, how does he feel?"

"I… I don't know."

"Noemi, you've told him, haven't you?"

She inhaled a deep breath, trying to calm her nauseous stomach. And then she launched into how she'd met Max and how stupid she'd been that night. She'd been hurting and not thinking straight. And she thought it would be a good time without any strings.

"Don't worry. Everything will be all right," Maria said, though her voice said otherwise.

"Even you don't believe it. What am I going to do? I'm not going to be able to hide my condition much longer. Most of my clothes don't fit."

"I know." Maria's voice rose as though she'd just discovered the answer to all Noemi's problems.

"What?" She was desperate for some good advice.

"You need some retail therapy."

Noemi's shoulders drooped. That was the very last thing she wanted to do. "Are you serious?"

"Yes. I'm very serious. What are you doing right now?"

"Maria..."

"Tell me what you're doing?"

"Pacing in my room."

"And that is helping you how?"

"I'm thinking."

"And so far it hasn't gotten you any answers. You need to get out of that chalet. The fresh air will do you good. Shopping is just what you need."

"Is that what you did when you and Sebastian separated?" And then realizing that she was touching on a very painful subject, she said, "Forget I said that. I'm just not myself today."

"Actually, it is what I did."

"Did it help?"

"Temporarily." Her voice filled with emotion. "Enough about me. I hope you know that if I could manage it, I'd be there with you, but trust me, after you buy some Christmas presents and new clothes for yourself that are comfortable, you'll feel much better. There's nothing worse than squeezing into clothes that don't fit."

Maria had given birth to Noemi's nephew, Frankie, nearly two years ago. She knew a lot more about pregnancy than Noemi. Maybe she was right. She glanced over at her discarded jeans on the bed. She'd barely gotten them buttoned, but she hadn't been able to pull up the zipper. And no matter how much she enjoyed her leggings, she couldn't stay in them forever.

"You'll do it, won't you?" Maria prompted.

"Yes, I'll go."

"Good. Call me later and let me know how it goes."

After the conversation ended, Noemi still wasn't certain that shopping was the right thing to do, but what else did she have to do considering she was at the chalet alone? Her gaze moved to the discarded jeans on her king-size bed. No way was she going to put those on again. Her black leggings would have to do.

She moved to the walk-in closet, hoping she could find something to wear besides her T-shirt. She sifted through the hangers until she strayed across a white long-sleeve V-neck knit tunic. It was loose but not too baggy and it'd go great with her leggings as well as her knee-high black boots.

With her wardrobe sorted, she was ready to head into the village. She would search for some roomier clothes and see what she could find for Christmas, which was only a few weeks away.

He didn't want to be here.

Not really.

Crown Prince Maximilian Steiner-Wolf, known to his friends as Max, sat in the back seat of his sports utility vehicle as one of his three bodyguards maneuvered it along the windy road in the Swiss Alps. His bodyguard and friend, Roc, sat in the passenger seat while Shaun, a bodyguard of similar stature and looks, sat next to him. He couldn't go anywhere without at least a small security detail.

Being the crown prince came with certain nonnegotiable restrictions. One of them was his safety. He may insist on traveling but the king demanded that his safety always be taken into consideration. It was a hassle but the guards were very good at becoming invisible unless their presence was required.

Max turned his head to the window and stared out at the snowy landscape of the mountainous region with some of the best slopes in all Europe. He was planning to spend a week or two skiing at Mont Coeur before returning to the palace in the European principality of Ostania.

He hadn't been home in months, but the approaching holidays were a big thing, not only at the palace but also throughout Ostania. And his mother had called, insisting he spend Christmas with them. After all, he was still the crown prince, even though he would never be king. However, the royal family was still keeping up appearances with the public.

Though Max was the firstborn and had been groomed from birth to take the throne of the small European country, no one had foreseen that he would be diagnosed with cancer in his teens. Although his treatment had been successful, doctors informed him that the cure had very likely rendered him sterile. Royal decree stated that the ruler of Ostania must produce an heir verified by a paternity test. From then on, Max knew it was impossible for him to take the throne.

So as not to cause the nation to panic over the future of Ostania, the palace had kept Max's infertility quiet while attentions turned to preparing his younger brother, Tobias, to become the future ruler of Ostania. No one outside of the court circle knew, and meanwhile, to the world, Max was still the crown prince.

While all of his parents' attention was showered on his little brother, Max roamed the world. He wasn't as much of a party animal as the press claimed him to be, but he did know how to have a good time. However, that was all about to change.

The truth was he was tiring of his partying ways. Moving from city to city, beach to beach and resort to resort was growing old or maybe he was getting old. In the beginning, it had been fun. The freedom had been intoxicating, but now he was starting to get a hangover from too much partying. He needed to do more with his life and to do that he had to go home—he had to officially step down from his position as crown prince in order to find his future.

That acknowledgment stabbed deep into his heart. He'd always been competitive. His parents had raised him that way. And stepping aside to let his younger brother take his place didn't come naturally to him. But it was more than that—it was knowing he was letting down his family—his country.

His stopover in Mont Coeur was to be his last. After he hit the slopes and cleared his head, he planned to return to Ostania to have a difficult talk with the king and queen. It had been put off long enough. Then he would lead a quieter, more productive life.

The SUV slowed as they entered the heart of the resort. Max instructed the driver to pull to a stop outside a ski supply shop. He'd lost his sunglasses at the end of last season and he needed a new pair of shades before hitting the slopes.

Not waiting for his security to get the door for him, he let himself out. He'd just stepped into the narrow road when someone with a camera pointed at him. Max inwardly groaned. It was going to be one of those trips where he was besieged for photos and autographs. Normally it didn't bother him, but right now he had a lot on his mind.

"It's the Prince of Ostania!" someone shouted.

Everyone on the sidewalk turned in his direction.

Quickly his security guards flanked him. None spoke. They didn't have to. The serious look on their faces said they meant business. Being recognized didn't happen all the time. However, it happened more than Max would like.

Security escorted him around the vehicle. He forced a smile as he passed the tourists and then dashed into the shop. He hoped the people wouldn't follow him.

Inside the shop, the walls were lined with snowboards and skies. In the background, "Let It Snow" played. Colorful twinkle lights were draped around the checkout where the workers wore red Santa hats with white pom-poms on the tips.

Figuring it might be easier to search for the sunglasses on his own, he bypassed the people at the checkout who were openly staring. He turned into the first aisle and nearly collided with a pretty young woman. She flashed him a big toothy smile. He intentionally didn't smile, not wanting to encourage her attention. He gave a brief nod and excused himself as he made his way around her.

Ever since he'd met Noemi, no other women had turned his head—not the way she had. And yet, he'd let her get away without even getting her number. He'd thought at the time that he would get over her quickly. That's the way it'd been with the other women who'd passed through his life. But there was something different about Noemi.

She acted tough, but inside where she didn't want anyone to see, there was a vulnerability to her. She'd let him get close enough to gain a glimpse of her tender side. Much too soon, she'd hidden behind a big smile and a teasing comment.

He could clearly recall her beautiful face. Her brown eyes had gold specks like jewels. And when he closed his eyes, he could feel the gentle touch of her lips pressed to his. With a mental shake, he chased those thoughts to the back of his mind.

It didn't take him long to find what he wanted and then he strode to the checkout where the pretty woman was standing, pretending to check out a display of lip balm while she stared at him.

He pretended not to notice as he paid the clerk. All he wanted now was to get to his private chalet and unwind. However, when he pushed open the front door and stepped onto the sidewalk, the crowd had multiplied. Flash after flash went off in his face.

CHAPTER TWO

Maybe shopping hadn't been such a bad idea.

Noemi clutched the colorful shopping bags stuffed full of goodies and headed for the door. She'd purchased some jeans in a bigger size that had spandex in them, making them so much comfier. They fit her a lot like her leggings. She'd pulled on the waistband and was surprised by how roomy they were without being baggy.

She'd also found some loose blouses and sweaters that hung down to her hips. For a while, they would hide her growing baby bump. It wasn't the figure-flattering clothes she normally wore, but it was so much better than what she had before. And she just wasn't ready for maternity—not yet.

As Maria had suggested, Noemi had taken time to do some Christmas shopping, including purchasing two designer sweaters. One for her newfound brother, Leo, and one for Sebastian. She and Sebastian might disagree—heatedly at times—but she still loved him.

With big black sunglasses and a gray knit beanie pulled low, she stepped outside the store and started up the sidewalk toward her car. The snow clouds had passed and the sun shone once more. Up ahead a crowd of people swarmed the sidewalk and spilled out into the roadway. She glanced around, wondering what was going on.

She would love to turn and avoid the crowd, but they were standing between her and her vehicle. And her numerous bags weren't light. She kept moving toward them. Surely the crowd would part and let her through.

She was on the edge of the group when an excited buzz rushed through the crowd. Noemi paused and turned to a young woman who was holding up her cell phone as though to snap a picture.

"Do you know what all the fuss is about?" Noemi asked.

The young woman with dark hair pulled back in a ponytail smiled brightly. "It's the best thing. Crown Prince Maximilian Steiner-Wolf has just arrived."

Noemi had heard the name before, but she knew nothing of the man. It seemed as though she was in the minority as the crowd continued to grow.

Noemi glanced around, curious to see the prince.

The young woman pointed to the shop in front of them. "He's in that store. Right there. Can you believe it? But his bodyguards aren't letting people in."

Noemi felt sorry for the guy. As the face of Cattaneo Jewels, she'd had her fair share of exposure to publicity, but the crowd of people forming around the store was extreme even to her. "And everyone is just standing around waiting for him to come out?"

The young woman gave her a look like she'd just grown a second head. "Well, yeah. Of course."

Noemi nodded in understanding, even though she didn't. Her arms ached from the weight of the bags. She continued to make her way to her car.

"Excuse me," Noemi called out, finding it difficult to thread her way through the crowd.

A cheer rose in the crowd. Then the crowd rushed forward. At last, there was room to walk.

Thud!

Someone ploughed right into Noemi. She lurched forward. In an effort to keep herself upright, she lost her grip on the packages. They fell to the ground in a heap. Her arms waved to the side as she tried to steady herself. Suddenly there were strong hands reaching out, gripping her by the waist.

Once she'd regained her balance, she turned and found herself staring into intriguing hazel eyes. It was Max. Her heart lodged in her throat. What was he doing here? Waiting to see the prince?

"Noemi?" His eyes widened with surprise. And then a smile lifted his lips. "I'm sorry. I didn't see you."

He bent over and started to pick up all her bags. She hadn't realized until then just how many packages there were, but Christmas was her favorite holiday. She had to make sure she bought something for everyone. Maybe more than one thing for everyone—especially her young nephew. It was going to be a difficult Christmas without her parents. And she felt driven to do everything possible to make the holiday bearable.

But right now, her thoughts centered around the father of her baby. And here she'd been thinking she would never see him again. She averted her gaze from him as she knelt down next to him. She scrambled to gather her packages.

"What are you doing here?" she asked.

He scooped up most of the packages and straightened. "I was planning to go skiing."

When she straightened, she had to lift her chin in order to look him in the eyes. And that was a dangerous thing to do because every time she gazed into his eyes, she forgot what she was about to say.

Just then a flash went off. And then another. And another.

"What's going on?" She glanced around as everyone was looking at them. And then the lightbulb went on in her mind. "You." Her gaze met his again. "You are the prince?"

His jaw flexed as his body stiffened. "Yes. I am Prince Maximilian Steiner-Wolf."

Her mouth gaped. Realizing that everyone was watching them, she forced her mouth closed. How was this possible? Was she really that out of touch with reality that she'd missed the father of her baby was royalty?

She had so many questions for him, but they lodged in

her throat. This wasn't the time or the place to rehash the not-so-distant past.

"Come with me," he said.

Not waiting for an answer, he took her hand and led her to a waiting black SUV. With the help of two men, they reached the vehicle without people stepping in their way.

She wasn't sure it was wise being alone with him, not when he still filled her dreams, but it beat being in public where everyone was watching them and eavesdropping. Once inside, she turned to him. She needed answers. She needed to know why he'd kept his title from her. She needed to know so much.

"Not now," he said as though reading her mind. Turning to the driver, he said, "Go."

"My vehicle is back there," Noemi said.

"Don't worry. We'll come back for it. Later."

The driver, as though used to driving through crowds, safely maneuvered the SUV past the sprawling mass of people.

She turned to the window and stared blindly at the passing shops. This had to be some sort of dream. Perhaps she'd fallen back there and hit her head. Yes, she thought, grasping at straws. She'd hit her head and this was all a dream. Because there was no way that she was pregnant with a prince's baby.

"Noemi?" Max's voice cut through her thoughts.

She had absolutely no idea what he was asking her. She turned to him. "What?"

"I asked where you are staying."

"Um…" She thought about returning to her vehicle and decided that Max was right. Later would be better to pick it up. "Take a left at the next intersection."

His dark brows rose. "Those are private residences."

She nodded. Her neighbors were some of the most prominent actors and actresses, athletes and notable figures in the world. Since she'd been coming here all her life, she took it all for granted. But now, seeing it from a stranger's perspective, she realized that it might be impressive. But to a prince? Nah.

He was probably wondering why she lived in such an exclusive neighborhood. Apparently she wasn't the only one in the dark. He didn't recognize her even though her face had been plastered on every glamour magazine as well as television promos for a number of years.

She gave the driver directions to her family's chalet. When they reached the gate to the exclusive community, she put her window down and assured the guard that it was okay to let them through.

"I've never been to this part of Mont Coeur," Max said. "I've always preferred to have my accommodations close to the slopes."

As they passed the large and impressive chalets, she noticed that most displayed Christmas decorations. Some sported a door wreath while others had a bit more. Normally their chalet was the most festive of them all—but not this year. Her father had always taken care of the outside decorations. However, this year Noemi had done it by herself and the twinkling lights weren't quite as spectacular as prior years.

Her palms grew damp as her heart raced. She couldn't relax, not with Max next to her. She didn't know what made her more nervous—the fact that they'd spent the night together or the fact that the man she'd slept with was royalty. When Maria heard this, she was never going to believe it.

He longed to kiss her berry red lips.

The memory of their sweetness taunted him.

Max gave himself a mental jerk. Now that he'd found Noemi again, the last thing he wanted to do was scare her off. What were the chances of them running into each other again?

Slim.

Had she figured out his true identity and planned this reunion? Not possible. He hadn't decided on coming to Mont

Coeur until last night. Even then, he'd only told his trusted staff.

Max gazed over at Noemi. Her posture was stiff and she kept her face turned away. He wondered if the source of her discomfort was from their collision, the run-in with the fans, learning he was a prince or all of the above.

Normally learning that he was the crown prince had women falling all over him. But Noemi had pulled away. In fact, if she sat any closer to her door, she'd fall out. Most interesting. He'd thought they'd both enjoyed their time together.

But it wasn't too late. He still had a chance to find out if there was truly a spark between them.

When the SUV pulled to a stop in front of a luxurious chalet, Noemi said a quick thank-you followed by goodbye. It'd be so easy to just let her go. He'd still have his good memories, but he'd never know what had been real and what had been part of his wishful imagination.

As he watched her head for the front steps, he told his security team to wait for him. He hopped out into the snowy driveway and followed her.

"Noemi, wait."

For a moment, he didn't think she was going to stop. Her hand reached for the doorknob, but then she hesitated. She turned to him but didn't say anything. Her gaze didn't quite meet his. She stood there waiting for him to have his say.

"You didn't even tell me your last name. I don't want to make the same mistake twice." When she sent him a puzzled look, he added, "Letting you get away without knowing your name."

"Oh. It's Noemi Cattaneo."

"Your name. It sounds familiar."

"You've probably heard of our family business. Cattaneo Jewels."

Of course, he'd heard of them. Who hadn't?

"Your family's business has the distinction of handling some of the world's finest and rarest jewels."

"Have you done business with us?"

"Not me personally, but my family has." He was getting off point. "Anyway, I wanted to say..." his Adam's apple bobbed "... I'm sorry. I've handled this all wrong."

"It's not your fault that people recognized you."

"No." He shook his head. "Not that. I'm sorry for before, when I insisted that we keep things casual and not exchange phone numbers." He stepped closer to her. "I've been thinking of you—"

"Don't." She shook her head. "I don't need your pity."

"It's not pity. I—I just handled things poorly before. And I want to apologize."

Her gaze momentarily widened but then she glanced away. "We did the right thing. Our lives are too diverse. I mean you...you have a country to run. And I am... I mean, I have things to do."

He'd never witnessed Noemi nervous before, not that they'd spent a lot of time together. But in the time he'd known her, she'd come across as confident and fun. The Noemi standing before him was different and he wanted to know what had changed her. Why did she avoid looking at him directly?

He is a prince?

How is that possible?

Noemi had so many conflicting emotions flooding her body that she didn't know what to say to him. Part of her longed to fall into his arms and pick up where they'd left off before. But logic told her to tread carefully. Max was a very powerful man. There was no way she was going to blurt out that she was pregnant with his baby. Finding out that he was royalty changed everything. She needed time to think.

"Have dinner with me?" His voice stirred her from her thoughts.

She shook her head. "I don't think that's a good idea."

The hopeful look on his face faded. "Was our time together that forgettable?"

"It definitely wasn't forgettable." The words were out her mouth before she realized she was revealing too much. She'd barely been able to think of anything else these past few weeks since learning she was pregnant.

That wasn't exactly true. She'd thought a lot about him ever since they parted—even before she'd learned she was pregnant. She would wonder what he was doing and who he was doing it with. And she wondered if he ever stopped to think about her.

"That's good to hear," he said. "So we'll do dinner."

She recalled the mass of people waiting for him outside the ski shop. She couldn't even imagine the spectacle they'd make by having dinner in public. It would be an utter zoo.

Though it pained her to say, she uttered, "We can't."

"Sure we can." He smiled like he had all the answers to their problems.

Again, she shook her head. "Everyone knows you're here at the resort. They'll all be on the lookout for you."

"And you don't want to be photographed with a prince?"

She glanced away and shrugged. The ramifications of the photo would be catastrophic once her pregnancy became known. Until she had a plan for this baby, she didn't want to make any more mistakes, especially where the public was concerned.

He laughed. "Do you know how refreshing you are?"

He was amused? Her lips pressed together into a firm line. She didn't know what there was to be smiling about, but then again, he didn't know about the baby.

She lifted her chin. "I don't care to be laughed at."

"I'm not laughing at you." His amusement faded. "I think you're amazing." As though her lack of response went unnoticed, he said, "Most women I've met would fall over themselves to have dinner with me. But not you. Which makes me that much more determined to see you again. In fact, I'm not leaving here until you agree to have dinner—no strings attached."

"Not tonight." She wanted to clear her head—and do an internet search.

He arched a dark brow. "I have the feeling if I let you get away tonight that there won't be another chance for us to get together. You'll always have an excuse. And I can't stay here forever—no matter how tempting that may be."

"I promise we'll do it another time."

"Must I beg, *ma chérie*?"

"You speak French?"

He nodded. "French and Italian as well as English. Ostania is situated near France, Italy and Switzerland. We speak French but it's heavily influenced by the surrounding countries. I could tell you more about my country over dinner."

It wasn't his country that she was interested in learning more about. And they did have much to discuss. Her hand instinctively moved in the direction of her tiny baby bump, but she caught herself in time and lowered her arm to her side.

"If you're worried about privacy, we can have dinner at my condo." A hopeful look reflected in his eyes.

"You're serious, aren't you?"

He nodded. "I've never been more serious in my life."

She didn't miss the part of a wealthy, devastatingly handsome prince begging her to have dinner with him. But as much as she wanted to spend more time with him, there was another part of her that worried about what would happen when he learned of the baby. Would he reject her? Would he reject his own flesh and blood? Or would he try to take the baby from her? The thought of it sent a chill through her.

Proceed with caution.

The only way she would find the answer to any of these questions was if she were to do as he asked and dine with him. Not sure if it was the right decision or not, she said, "Okay. I'll have dinner with you."

He didn't hesitate. "I'll send a car for you at seven."

She shook her head. "I can drive." And then she recalled that she'd left her car back in the village. "Except my car is still in the village."

"I'll send my car. And if you give me your keys, I'll make sure your car is picked up and waiting for you at my condo."

That would be convenient, but it would also make her an easy target for the paparazzi. And she wasn't ready to be a headline on every gossip site.

She checked the time on her phone. "You may send your car for me at…seven fifteen." That should give her just enough time to sort through her purchases to find something appropriate to wear and do an internet search. "Does that work for you?"

Both his brows rose. She wasn't sure if she was surprised that she hadn't fallen all over herself to do as he wanted. If that's what he expected of her, he was in for a surprise. With a baby on the way, she had to stand firm and speak up when necessary.

Max gave a curt nod. "I'll see you then." He turned for his vehicle. A few steps later, he paused and turned back. "Is there anything specific you would like for dinner? Perhaps something you've been craving?"

Craving? Did he know about her pregnancy? She sucked in her stomach. As he continued to stare at her with an expectant look on his face with no hint of suspicion, she realized he'd meant nothing by his choice of word.

She shook her head. "Anything is fine. I'm not a picky eater."

That response rewarded her with another surprised look on his face. Apparently the prince wasn't used to women who weren't picky. She wondered just what sort of women he normally dated, but she resisted the urge to ask.

"I'll pick something special." He turned and walked away.

The desire to run in the house and head straight to her computer was overwhelming, but she restrained herself. She waited until he was inside his vehicle before she let herself in the chalet. With the door shut, her movements became rushed. She threw off her hat and coat before kicking off her snowy boots. And then she took the steps two at a time.

She grabbed her laptop from the desk and threw herself

down on the bed. Her fingertips moved rapidly over the keyboard. Maybe it wasn't right snooping on the internet, but now that she knew her baby's daddy was a famous royal, she had to learn more. From her own dealings with the paparazzi, she knew most of the articles would be fiction or wildly exaggerated. But that didn't stop her from looking—

Noemi's breath caught in her throat as she caught sight of headlines splashed across the screen that were worse than she'd allowed herself to imagine. In fact, with photos to back up the headlines, she wondered if she'd been wrong about Max.

"Twin Blonde Bombshells for the Prince!"

"Prince Maximilian with Woman Number Five in as Many Evenings!"

"The Playboy Prince Strikes Again!"

"Prince Max and His Harem!"

Disheartened, Noemi closed her laptop. She'd thought the night their baby was conceived that they'd shared something special. She never imagined that she was just one more notch on his bedpost. The thought hurt—a lot.

She placed her hand upon her midsection. "What have I gotten us into?"

CHAPTER THREE

Maybe he shouldn't have pushed. After all, he wasn't a man to beg for a woman's company—until now. What was it about Noemi that had him acting out of character? Was it her dazzling smile? Her bewitching eyes? Or her sweet, sweet kiss?

As Max sat at the desk in his bedroom suite, he gave himself a mental shake and tried to concentrate on the plethora of emails awaiting his attention. He checked the clock for what must be the hundredth time. It still wasn't even close to when Noemi was due to arrive. He sighed.

He may not be at the palace, but that didn't mean his responsibilities ceased to exist. In fact, he was beginning to think his parents gave him more than his fair share of work to make sure he didn't stray too far from the business of governing Ostania.

He still had two hundred and seventy-nine unopened emails. He groaned. How was that possible? He'd checked his email last night because he knew he'd be traveling most of today. He'd had it semi under control, but not any longer.

He wished his email was like other people's and full of spam that he could readily dismiss. However, his email was directed through the palace, where it went through stringent screenings. That meant all two hundred and seventy-nine emails would need to be dealt with personally or would require forwarding to someone else with directions.

He worked his way through the emails in chronological order. And then his gaze strayed across an email from his mother—the queen. She didn't email him often as she was a bit exasperated with him. She thought he should be at the palace acting the part of proper crown prince. She had no idea how hard it was for him to act his part because the royal court knew that when the time came, he would not be crowned king.

That role would go to his younger brother, Tobias, who at this moment was being meticulously groomed to step up and assume Max's birthright. He didn't blame his brother. If anything, he felt indebted to Tobias. His brother was the one sacrificing his youthful adventures in order to learn the rules of governing and the etiquette for dealing with foreign dignitaries.

And yet his brother had stepped up to do what was expected of him without complaint. Max would do no less. He checked the time once again and found that he still had close to an hour and a half before Noemi showed up. It was plenty of time to work through some of these emails.

He opened the email from his mother. He didn't know what he expected, but it wasn't the very cold businesslike email telling him the schedule of Christmas events and how he was expected to take on a prominent role in the festivities. He hated pretending to the whole nation that he was something he wasn't—the heir to the throne.

He closed his mother's email without responding because there wasn't anything for him to respond to. There hadn't been one personal word in the whole email. In fact, he would have thought that his mother's personal secretary had written and sent the email except for the fact it had come from his mother's private email that not even her secretary could access.

So the cold, impersonal email from his mother indicated that she thought he'd been gone too long. Or worse yet, she'd been reading the paparazzi headlines—which he might add were wildly exaggerated or utter works of fiction.

He opened an email from his own secretary, Enzo, who stayed on top of everything for him. It sorted his duties into priorities, escalating and FYI items. The only problem was the priorities were now taking up more room than the other two categories. It was definitely time to go home.

Max typed up his response to his secretary, letting the man know how to handle things until he returned to Ostania. And then he moved on to the next official email…

Knock. Knock.

Max granted access just as he pressed Send on another response and deleted the original email.

"Sir, Miss Cattaneo has arrived."

"She has?" How could that be? He'd just checked the time, hadn't he? His gaze moved to the clock at the bottom of the laptop monitor. A lot of time had passed totally unnoticed. "Please offer her a drink and tell her I'll be right there."

He closed his laptop and moved to the adjoining bathroom. He'd meant to clean up before her arrival. He jumped in the shower, not even waiting for the water to warm up.

Five minutes later, with his hair still damp, Max strode into the living room. Noemi was still there. He breathed a sigh of relief.

"I'm sorry about that. Time got away from me." He smiled at her. "Do you need more to drink?" He gestured to her empty glass on the coffee table.

"Actually, yes. That would be nice."

He moved forward and accepted her glass. "What were you drinking?"

"Water."

Water? He didn't know why that struck him as strange. Perhaps he'd become accustomed to serving wine on a date. This was just one more example of how Noemi was different from the other women who'd passed through his life.

He quickly poured water from a glass pitcher. "Here you go."

When he handed over the now full glass, their fingers brushed and, in that moment, he recalled the silkiness of her skin, the warmth of her touch and the heat of her kiss. With a mental jerk, he brought his thoughts back to the present.

His mouth grew dry and he decided to pour himself some cold water. He took a drink and then sat on the couch opposite hers.

He smiled. "It's really good to see you again. I just never expected to run into you here."

She arched a fine brow. "Why? Is skiing only for men these days?"

He inwardly groaned. She just wasn't going to give him an inch. She was angry about the way they'd left things. And that was his fault.

"Noemi, about our time in Milan, I handled things poorly. Is there any chance you will forgive me? And perhaps we can start over?"

"I told you I'm fine." Her lips said one thing but her eyes said something quite different.

"The frostiness in this room is making me think I should go get my ski jacket and gloves."

Her beautiful brown eyes momentarily widened. "It's not that bad."

"Maybe not on your side of the room, but standing over here, it's downright nippy."

A little smile pulled at her lips. It wasn't much but it was something.

"That's better," he said.

She tilted her head to the side. "Why?"

"Why what?"

"Why are you trying so hard when you could have any women you want?" Her gaze searched his as if she could read the truth in his eyes.

"I've thought a lot about you since that night. I've wondered what it might have been like if we'd have had more time together."

"Really?" There was a tone of doubt in her voice.

"Do you find that so hard to believe?"

Her eyes narrowed. "It's the way you wanted it—no strings attached."

"As I recall, you agreed." He wasn't going to take all the blame for the circumstances of their parting.

The frown lines on her face smoothed. "You're right."

At last, they seemed to be getting somewhere. Perhaps they could build on this and get back to where they'd once been—happy and comfortable with each other.

He took another drink of water and then set the glass aside. His gaze rose and caught hers. "Noemi, is it possible for us to start over?"

A noticeable silence filled the room. He knew it was too much to hope that they'd recapture the magic of that special night, but he had to try. With each passing second, his hopes declined.

"Yes, we can try."

Her words caught him off guard—that seemed to be a common occurrence where Noemi was concerned. He would need to tread carefully around her in the future.

"Would you like to eat?" he asked.

Her eyes lit up. "I would."

"Good. I hope you like the menu."

He stepped into the kitchen to let the cook know. Then he escorted Noemi to a table that had been set next to the wall of windows where the twinkling lights of the resort illuminated ski slopes trailing down the mountainside beneath the night sky.

He'd had the cook prepare something basic because he had absolutely no idea what Noemi liked to eat, other than pizza. That's what they'd had in Milan when neither of them felt like dressing and going out for a proper dinner. Since then he'd never been able to eat pizza without thinking of her.

And so, after a Caesar salad, they were served a heaping plate of pasta with Bolognese sauce topped with grated Parmigiano-Reggiano. He didn't have to ask if Noemi approved of it. He tried not to smile as she made quick work of the pasta. It was a quiet dinner as he didn't push conversation, wanting to give Noemi a chance to relax.

When they finished, he noticed there was still a small pile of pasta on her plate. "I take it you had enough."

She patted her stomach. Then just as quickly she removed her hand and a rosy hue came over her cheeks. To say she was beautiful normally was an understatement, but she was even more of a knockout with the rush of color lighting up her face.

"It was amazing. Thank you." She got to her feet. "It was good seeing you again. But I should be going."

He couldn't let her go. Not yet. "Stay. We haven't even had dessert."

"Dessert? I don't have any room left. Not after that delicious meal."

"Come join me." He moved to the couch in front of the fireplace with a fire gently crackling within it. When she didn't make a move to follow him, he said, "Please, give me a chance to explain—about the way we left things."

A spark of interest reflected in her eyes. She moved to the couch. When they sat down, she left a large space between them. He hoped by the time they finished talking that the space would shrink considerably.

"The night we met," he said, "I was captivated by your beauty."

A small smile played on her lips. A good sign. Still, she remained quiet as though giving him room to explain where things had gone wrong.

"The thing was I wasn't looking to meet someone— certainly no one like you. You were like a warm spring breeze on an icy cold night. And the next morning, I received bad news from home."

He hadn't wanted to burden Noemi with the news of his father's collapse. It wasn't like they were in a committed relationship. It had been his burden to carry on his own.

Perhaps he had that in common with his father. Because when his mother had called to tell him of this father's declining health, Max had made plans to fly home immediately.

He had been at the airport when his father called and told him that his mother had overreacted.

His father had insisted he was fine and told Max in no uncertain terms that he would not be welcome at the palace for a pity visit. His father had been so animated on the phone that Max had been inclined to think his mother had gone a little overboard with worry. But that didn't mean his father's lifelong battle with diabetes wasn't taking its toll on him.

Instead of flying home, his father rerouted Max to Spain. It was a diplomatic mission to encourage increased trade between their countries—something Ostania needed.

"Listen, you don't have to explain," Noemi said quickly. "You didn't mean for it to be more than a fling. And that's fine." But the tone in her voice said that it wasn't fine with her.

In that moment, he decided to tell her the whole truth. She deserved that much. "It was about my father. He was ill and my mother was very concerned about his health."

Noemi studied him for a moment. "That's why you were so different in the morning? It was the worry about your father and not regret over spending the night together?"

"Maybe it was a bit of both." When the look of hope faded from her face, he rushed on to say, "I regretted rushing things. I lost my head that night."

She arched a brow. "Do you mean that? You're not saying all this nice stuff just because you don't want to hurt my feelings?"

He shook his head. "I didn't handle the news well. My mother—well, she can be a bit dramatic when it suits her purposes—she made it sound like my father wouldn't last through the day."

Noemi moved to his side. Her gaze met his. "I'm sorry. How is he?"

Within her eyes, he saw caring and understanding. He cleared his throat. "Much better. And quite stubborn."

"I'm glad to hear that—about him feeling better. But why

couldn't you have told me? I would have understood you having to leave immediately."

"I didn't want you to know. I didn't want anyone to know. Telling someone would have made the whole situation real and at the time, I wasn't ready to deal with it."

"And now?"

"Now, I regret how I reacted. I shouldn't have dismissed what we had so readily. I would have liked if we'd been able to keep in contact." He continued to stare at her, wondering if she felt the same way about him.

"That would have been nice." Softly she added, "I thought of contacting you, too."

At last, he could breathe easier. She was slowly letting her guard down with him. He could finally see a glimmer of that amazing woman who'd caught his attention from across the room at the party. He was glad he hadn't given up. He knew if he kept trying that he'd find her.

He resisted the urge to reach out and touch her. He couldn't rush things. He didn't want to scare her off. "I'm going to be here at the resort for the next week before returning to Ostania. I'd like it if we could spend some more time together."

Noemi looked as though she was going to agree, but what came out of her lips was quite different. "I don't think that's a good idea, especially with the press watching your every move."

"I'll take care of the paparazzi. They won't bother us."

"But how?"

"Trust me. I have a lot of experience evading them. So are we good?"

She shook her head. "It's more than that."

He'd come too far to let it fall apart now. "Speak to me. Whatever it is, I'll fix it."

"You can't." She stood and walked to the wall of windows.

He followed her as though drawn in by her magnetic force. He stopped just behind her. Again, he resisted the urge to reach out to her. "Noemi, I know we haven't know each other long, but I'd like to think you look upon me as a friend—someone you can lean on."

She turned to him. "I do—think of you as a friend."

"Then tell me what's bothering you. Surely it can't be as bad as the worry reflected on your face."

"No. It's worse." Her gaze lowered to the floor. "I'm pregnant."

He surely hadn't heard her correctly. "You're what?"

"Pregnant with your baby."

The words knocked the air from his lungs.

He never thought anyone would say those words to him. And now he couldn't believe it was true. At the same time, he wanted it to be real. Torn by conflicting emotions, his body stiffened. What was she hoping to accomplish with such a wildly improbable claim?

CHAPTER FOUR

HE SHOULDN'T HAVE just blurted it out.

And now that it was out there, she couldn't take it back.

This was not how Noemi had envisioned telling Max about the baby. The truth was she hadn't figured out how to tell him this life-changing news. It certainly wasn't something you blurted out, like she'd done. The fact she was pregnant was still something she was trying to cope with. By the paleness of Max's face, he'd been completely caught off guard.

"No." He adamantly shook his head. Then his eyes narrowed on her. "It's a lie."

She refused to squirm under his intense stare. Her mouth pressed into a firm line as she started to count to ten. Her mother had taught her to do this after Noemi had shot her mouth off one too many times in school. Noemi had imagined a lot of reactions but being called a liar hadn't been one.

She made it to the number six when she straightened her shoulders and lifted her chin. "I am not a liar. I'm pregnant and you're the father—"

"Impossible." His voice was adamant as he started to pace.

"Actually, it's quite possible. You're going to be a father in about six or so months."

He stopped and his disbelieving gaze met hers. "Have you gone to a doctor?"

"I have. It has been verified by an official pregnancy test." She could see that he was still in denial. Perhaps she should give him some idea of the changes this pregnancy ha brought to her life. "I've started to grow out of my clothes And I have morning sickness. The doctor says I should sta to feel better in my second trimester."

Max shook his head again. "It must be someone else's—

"It's not." How dare he? What did he think of her? Tha she got around so much that she wouldn't be able to nam the father? "This baby is yours. It doesn't matter how man times you claim it isn't, it won't change the facts."

"You're mistaken."

She crossed her arms and glared at him. "You might b a prince and all, but that doesn't give you the right to talk t me this way. This pregnancy is nothing either of us planned but now that it's happening, we've both got to figure out how to deal with it."

He stepped closer to her. There was torment in his eyes "You aren't listening me. I'm not this baby's father. It's a impossibility."

What was he saying? He wasn't making any sense. Sh hadn't expected him to take this news well, but this was fa worse than she'd been imagining.

She forced her voice to remain calm. "I don't know how many ways I can say this to get you to believe that you an I are having a baby."

He turned his back to her. "You need to go. Now."

"You're dismissing me?"

"Yes, I am."

Her hands clenched at her sides. Her lips pursed as she struggled to control her emotions. "Fine."

Her face warmed as anger pumped through her veins. Di he think it had been easy for her to come here? She quickly gathered her things. Did he really think she would mak something like this up?

She strode to the door with her chin lifted. She refused to slink off into the night. She paused at the door and glance back. Max's back was still turned her way and his postur was rigid.

She tried to think of something to say—some parting shot—but her pride kept her from speaking. And so without a word, she let herself out the door.

Once she was outside, tears of frustration and anger rushed to her eyes, blurring her vision. She blinked them away. She refused to cry over such a stubborn, infuriating man.

She had to be lying.

That was the only possible answer.

Max sent his staff away that evening—even his security. It may have taken a raised voice and an empty threat or two to clear the condo, but he'd succeeded. He needed to be alone.

One hour faded into another as he sat alone in the dark. Noemi's words played on his insecurities and inadequacies—things he'd thought he'd put behind him. He'd only deluded himself into thinking that he'd made peace with losing his rightful place as heir to the throne and the knowledge that he would never be able to father a family of his own. Noemi couldn't have wounded him more if she'd been trying.

Sleep eluded him that night. By the next afternoon, he'd made a decision. Without giving himself a chance to talk himself out of it, he drove to Noemi's chalet and knocked on the door.

When Noemi opened the door, he didn't give her a chance to speak. "Are you ready to admit it?"

She frowned at him. "I already admitted that I'm pregnant. I don't know what else you expect me to say."

He needed to hear her say that she'd made up the whole thing about her pregnancy. He searched her eyes for the truth. He was pretty good at reading people. And he saw nothing but honesty reflected in them. Either she'd talked herself into believing her lies…or she was telling him the truth. But that wasn't possible. Right?

He raked his fingers through his hair. Maybe he needed to come at this from a different angle.

He exhaled an unsteady breath. "Can we talk?"

For a moment, she didn't move nor did she say a word, a though weighing her options.

He couldn't walk away until he made her understand wha she was claiming was absolutely impossible. "Please," h said. "It won't take long and it's important. I've been up al night thinking about what you told me."

He was beginning to think she'd refuse to let him insid when she suddenly swung the door wide open and steppe aside. "Hurry before someone sees you."

He ventured inside. After slipping off his snow-covere boots and coat, he moved toward the great room. Not sur what to do with himself, he stood in front of the darkene fireplace beside the large Christmas tree.

Noemi perched on the edge of the couch. "I know this i hard for you to believe. It was for me, too."

He turned to her. "It's not hard. It's impossible."

"Why do you keep saying that?"

He ran a hand over his unshaven jaw. The stubble felt lik sandpaper over his palm. He'd come here to settle this onc and for all. He couldn't stop now.

"Come sit down." She patted the cushion next to her.

He joined her on the couch, leaning his head back agains the cushion, and closed his eyes. "Some of what I'm goin, to tell you, no one outside my family and trusted member of the court know." He opened his eyes and gazed at her "Can I trust you?"

"I won't tell anyone."

"You already know that I'm a prince, but you might no know that I am the firstborn—the crown prince. Ever sinc I took my first breath, I've been groomed to take the thron of Ostania. It is a small country, but it is prosperous. How ever, when I was thirteen, I was diagnosed with Hodgkin' lymphoma."

Noemi let out a soft gasp.

He cleared his throat. "At that moment, my entire worl stopped. Everything became about my health. I never knew i was possible to become so sick of being sick. Of course, thi was all kept hush-hush. With me being the crown prince, it was decided that it was best that the citizens of Ostania not know about my cancer diagnosis."

Sympathy reflected in her eyes. "That must have been scary for you to go through."

The cancer had been more than scary, it had changed the way he looked at himself. From the time he was little, he'd known exactly who he was, what was expected of him and what his future would entail. The cancer robbed him of that identity.

After the cancer, he'd gone out into the world searching for himself—searching for a new identity. He'd done crazy daredevil stuff, from parachuting to cliff diving to bungee jumping to more responsible endeavors, such as being a diplomatic liaison for his country. Through it all, it still felt as though something was missing from his life.

"I was young. At the beginning, I was certain I could survive anything. And it helped that everyone around me was so positive. But the more aggressive treatments left me extremely sick and my positivity faltered. At one point, I gave up. I didn't think I would live to see my next birthday."

She reached out, placing her hand in his. "I can't even imagine."

"I didn't tell you that to gain your sympathy. I wanted you to realize the intensity of my treatments. I was told it was quite likely I'd never be able to father any children."

He stopped there. He didn't tell her that royal decree stated the ruler of Ostania must produce an heir. That wasn't her problem.

Nor was it her problem that after his treatments were over and the doctors had declared him in remission that the nightmare hadn't ended. The doctors had said he was likely sterile. The palace attentions had turned to preparing his younger brother, Tobias, to become the future ruler of Ostania. Max had to take a step back as his brother replaced him.

"Well, obviously they were wrong." Noemi sent him a

wavering smile. "Because I am pregnant and you are most definitely the father."

He wanted to believe her. But he knew the doctors had been the best in their field. They hadn't told Max and his parents their dire warning lightly. If he was the father, it was truly a miracle. But he didn't believe in miracles.

"I just don't think this can be true," he said. "The doctors said—"

"Stop. I'm telling you it's true."

He stared deeply into her eyes. He wanted so desperately to believe her. But he was hesitant. "I need time."

"I understand."

"We'll talk again." He got to his feet and left. He needed to walk. He needed to think. He needed space.

The stakes were so high. If Noemi was telling the truth, then he would be eligible to inherit the throne of Ostania. He'd be able to assume his birthright. At last, he'd once again feel whole.

The breath hitched in his throat. He hadn't allowed himself to consider it for years. This would change his entire life—his brother's life—if it was true.

CHAPTER FIVE

A RESTLESS NIGHT left Noemi yawning the next morning.

Her first thought was of Max. By the time he'd left, he'd at least been willing to consider that the baby was his. She knew it was going to take time for him to come to terms with the news, especially after being convinced he could never father children.

After a round of morning sickness had passed, she showered. Dressed in the new clothes she'd bought while out shopping the other day, she felt much more comfortable and more confident. Whatever happened next, she could deal with it. After all, she was going to become a mother. Dealing with the unknown came with the job.

Knock. Knock.

Who in the world could that be?

She checked the time, finding it wasn't even eight o'clock in the morning. Perhaps it was Sebastian. But that didn't make sense. He wouldn't knock as he had his own key. Maybe it was Leo. They hadn't had a chance to make him a key. Maybe he'd returned early for the holidays.

Noemi liked the thought of seeing her new big brother again. She'd immediately hit it off with Leo. She rushed to the door and swung it open to find a disheveled Max standing with his hair astray, dark shadows under his eyes and heavy stubble trailing down his jaw.

"Max?"

"I've done nothing but think about what you told me. And I'd like to talk some more."

A gust of wind rushed past him and swept past her, sending a wave of goose bumps down her arms. "Come in."

When he didn't move, she reached out and grabbed his black leather jacket. She gave him a yank toward her. Once he was inside, she swung the big wooden door shut against the gusty wind. She glanced out the window to see if he'd been followed by the paparazzi.

"What are you looking for?"

Max's voice came from much closer than she'd been expecting. When she turned, she almost bumped into him. She tried to put some space between them but her back pressed against the door. She swallowed hard. Being so close to him made her heart palpitate.

"I… I was checking to see if you were followed." She sidestepped around him and moved across the foyer. From that distance, she could at last take a full breath.

"You don't have to worry," he said. "No one followed me."

"How can you be so sure? What if they saw you come here yesterday?"

"After I was spotted in the village, I activated my backup plan."

"Backup plan? What's that?"

"One of my bodyguards is a body double from a distance. The morning after the paparazzi spotted me, he departed Mont Coeur and flew back to Ostania. I and my remaining staff have since switched vehicles and residences."

Noemi arched a fine brow. "Has anyone ever told you that you're devious?"

"I don't know. Is that good? Or bad?"

"In this case, it's a good thing. And here I figured you for the cautious type."

"Cautious, huh? I did pursue you at the party. I don't think anyone would classify that night as cautious."

She turned her head to the side, but not soon enough. She

knew he saw the smile pulling at her lips. "We aren't discussing that night."

"We aren't?"

She shook her head. "No, we aren't." They had a lot more pressing matters to discuss—matters that had apparently kept him awake most of the night. Perhaps the shock was starting to wear off and reality was taking hold.

His bloodshot eyes met hers. "I shouldn't have bothered you so early. I just didn't know who else to talk to."

"It's fine. I didn't sleep well last night so I was up early." She held out her hands for his jacket. "Let me hang that up for you."

After his jacket and boots had been tended to, she led him into the spacious living room. She started a fire while he quietly took a seat on the couch. For a man who wanted to talk, he certainly wasn't saying much.

She left a respectable space between them when she sat on the couch. Even in his disheveled appearance, she couldn't deny that he was devastatingly handsome. And when he lifted his head and stared at her with that lost look in his eyes, her heart dipped.

"How can you look so calm?" he asked.

She shrugged. "I've had time to adjust to the news."

"If we hadn't run into each other, were you ever going to tell me?" His gaze searched hers.

"I wanted to, but remember, I didn't have your last name or your cell number. I didn't have any idea how to reach you."

He rubbed the back of his neck. "That's my fault."

"But it all worked out. It was as if fate made sure our paths would cross again." She paused as her stomach took a nauseous lurch.

Please not in front of Max. Her mouth grew moist and she swallowed, willing herself not to get sick—again.

"What's wrong?" A look of concern came over his face.

Great. So much for hiding it. "It's nothing."

He studied her. "It sure looks like something. You're pale. Is it the baby?"

"In a way." Her stomach lurched again. "I'll be back."

She dashed from the room, leaving Max to come to his own conclusions. She didn't have time to explain.

Was it something he'd said?

He wouldn't know. He'd never been around a pregnant woman. Sure, his mother had been pregnant with his younger brother but Max had only been a kid back then.

Max paced around the living room. Was this really happening? Was he really going to be a father? And if so, how would his family take it?

For years now, Tobias had been learning to be Ostania's new ruler. How would he feel when Max pushed him aside to resume his birthright? Would Tobias be disappointed? Or would he be thankful to have his life back again?

Max honestly didn't know how this news would impact his brother. The truth was that ever since Max's illness and the attention had started shining on his brother, they'd grown apart.

"Sorry about that." Noemi's voice interrupted his thoughts.

He glanced at her. She was still pale, but there was perhaps a bit more color in her face. "Are you feeling better?"

She nodded. "It's just morning sickness. The doctor and books say that it is common and nothing to worry about."

He couldn't see how being sick could be nothing to worry about. "Which way to the kitchen?"

She pointed toward the back of the chalet. "Why?"

"Stay here. I'll be back." He headed for the door off to the side of the large fireplace.

The kitchen was spacious. He glanced at all the white cabinets. Maybe he should have asked a few more questions—like where to find things. But it couldn't be that hard to locate what he needed.

He moved to the cabinet closest to him. He yanked open the doors. He knew what he was looking for and if it wasn't here, he'd go to the store in the village—even if it meant dealing with the crowd of onlookers.

Cabinet after cabinet, he searched. Three quarters of the way through, he opened a door and found exactly what he was searching for—peppermint tea. He set to work filling a kettle and placing it on the stove to heat up.

While it warmed, he searched a little more and located a box of crackers. He placed a few on a plate and turned to set it on the island when he noticed Noemi sitting on a kitchen stool staring at him.

"How long have you been there?" he asked.

"A while."

"You don't trust me?"

"It wasn't a matter of trust but rather curiosity." She eyed the crackers and the now boiling kettle. "Are you hungry?"

"This isn't for me."

"Oh. Well, thank you. But I don't usually drink tea."

"I think you'll like this tea. It should help settle your stomach."

The teakettle whistled. Max set to work steeping the tea. Once everything was ready, he turned to Noemi. "Why don't we take this to the living room where you'll be more comfortable?"

In silence, she led the way and he followed with a loaded tray. He glanced around at the spacious chalet, something he hadn't taken time to do the day before. Nothing had been skimped on in its construction. It had some of the finest details.

"This is a really big place for one person," he said, trying to keep the conversation going.

"It's not mine. It belongs to my parents—well, our family."

"Are your parents here?" He glanced around.

Here he was spilling his guts to her and he didn't even think to ask if they were alone. He wondered how her parents felt about the pregnancy. And then he wondered if Noemi had told them.

"No one is here." Noemi's face once again grew pale as she sat down on the couch.

"What's bothering you?" He sat next to her. "Is it my mention of your parents? If you want me to talk to them—"

"You can't." Her gaze lowered. "They, um…" Her voice grew faint. "They died."

He hadn't seen that coming. "You mean, since we met?"

She nodded as her eyes shimmered with unshed tears. In that moment, he didn't think about right or wrong, he just acted. He moved next to her, wrapped his arm around her and drew her head to his shoulder.

He leaned his cheek against the top of her head. "I can't even begin to tell you how sorry I am."

He didn't know how long they sat there with their bodies leaning on each other. His hand smoothed down over her silky hair. And when he pressed a kiss to the top of her head, he inhaled the berry fragrance of her shampoo.

When she finally pulled back, she swiped at her cheeks. "I'm sorry. I'm not normally so emotional."

"It's okay. You don't have to explain. In fact, you don't have to talk about it." He'd do or say anything to get her to stop crying because he was not good with tears. They left him uncomfortable and not sure what to say.

"Thank you for your shoulder."

"Anytime." He just hoped the next time would come with happier circumstances. "Do you have siblings?" After the words were out, he wondered if it was a safe subject.

She nodded. "An older brother—actually make that two older brothers."

That was an unusual thing to get wrong. He had a feeling there was a story there, but he was pretty certain he'd delved far enough into her life for one day.

For a moment, they sat quietly while Noemi sipped the tea and nibbled on a cracker. Then she turned on the television, letting a morning talk show fill in the awkward silence.

A half hour later during the break in a morning news show, Max asked, "Are you feeling better now?"

"I am. Thank you. How did you know about the tea and crackers?"

He glanced away. "This is what they gave me after my cancer treatments."

"And it worked?"

"Sometimes. If it didn't work, nothing did. I just had to wait it out." He looked at her, noticing the color was already coming back to her face. "Is there anything I can do for you?"

She shook her head.

"Does this just happen in the morning?"

She nodded. "I read that some women get it at any time of the day." Noemi visibly shuddered. "Sounds absolutely horrid."

"Maybe I should go now. I really shouldn't have bothered you so early."

"It's fine. I'm sure you have a lot of questions."

"I really just have one."

She leveled her shoulders and met his stare straight on. "What is it?"

"I wanted to know if you had plans for tomorrow."

Where had that come from? He hadn't come here intending to ask her out, but he could see the benefits. Getting her out of the house, doing something together might smooth out some of the tension coursing between them.

She didn't say anything at first but then she shook her head. "I don't."

"Would you like to do something with me?"

"Are you sure? You probably have other more important things that require your attention."

"There's nothing more important than us getting to know each other better," he said, meaning every word. He couldn't think about anything but Noemi and the baby.

"You don't have to do that—"

"I know. But I want to."

Her eyes flared with surprise.

In the end, they made plans for the following morning to go snow tubing. It was short run meant for kids and adults alike. But right now, he needed to get some work done and then he'd get some much-needed sleep.

"What do you mean, she's pregnant?"

"Shh…" That evening, Max gripped the phone tighter. "I don't need anyone overhearing you."

He was speaking to Enzo, his private secretary and his confidant. He had to tell someone. He couldn't keep this huge—this amazing news to himself. He was going to be a father. His world was about to change.

Enzo's normally monotone voice took on a higher pitch. "But you can't have children—the doctors said—"

"I know what they said, that the possibility was very unlikely. Not impossible."

"Your Royal Highness, do not get your hopes up. This woman is not the first to lie in order to become included in the royal family. Remember—"

"I remember." He'd tried to forget Abree. She'd portrayed herself as everything he could ever want. They'd been happy for three months and then she'd claimed to be pregnant.

When the paternity test was done, he was not the father. The extent of her lies had been devastating for him. But in the process, he'd learned she wasn't the woman she'd portrayed to him. She was nothing like he thought. Thankfully his family never found out how deep her lies had gone.

It was why he'd insisted on keeping his relationships casual since then. Until Noemi. She was different. She didn't seem to care what he thought or what he expected. She did what she wanted. And so far, she wanted nothing from him. There's no way she was lying to him. Right?

Enzo's voice sliced through Max's thoughts. "What is this woman's name? I'll run a background check on her."

Enzo didn't say it, but Max could hear the wheels in the man's mind spin. He wanted to see if Noemi was a liar, a cheat, a scam. He wanted to find every little thing she'd done wrong in her life and prove to Max that she was unsuitable for him. Because Enzo, like his parents, had very definite ideas of how a royal should act and exactly who they should marry.

"I'm not telling you," Max said with finality.

"But, Your Highness—"

"Leave it alone, Enzo."

There was a distinct pause. "Yes, sir."

In time, Max would learn everything he needed to know about Noemi, but it would all come from her. He didn't need a private investigator or a credit report. He was going with his gut on this one. And his gut said he could trust her.

To help alleviate Enzo's worry, Max said, "I will take care of the situation."

"Did you tell her about the necessity for a paternity test?"

Max resisted the urge to sigh. "Not yet."

"What are you waiting for?"

Max didn't say anything. The truth was he didn't know why he was hesitating. He hadn't hesitated when it came to Abree. He'd known from the start that she was lying. He'd insisted on the test as soon as it was safe for the mother and baby.

"Your Highness?"

"I wish you'd just call me Max." He'd never been one for royal protocol. That was his mother's thing—not his.

"That is not possible. You are the crown prince. As such, you deserve the respect due your station."

"And we grew up together. You know me. We played polo together."

"That was a long time ago, sir. And I know that when you don't want to talk about something, you change the subject."

"Don't worry. I'll take care of this."

He didn't want to. He didn't want to do anything to ruin his time with Noemi, but Enzo had a point. He couldn't stand to be played again. And his family deserved to know that their lives were about to be disrupted, once again. This time, though, the disruption would be a good one.

He would talk to Noemi in the morning about the test. Surely she'd understand. Right?

CHAPTER SIX

THE NEXT MORNING, Max decided they should talk first and play in the snow later. The stakes were high and he had to make sure Noemi understood how high.

"Max, what's wrong?" The smile had slipped from Noemi's face. "If you have to cancel our plans, it's okay. I understand."

He shook his head. "It's not that." Max leaned forward, resting his elbows on his knees. "We need to talk."

"I thought that's what we were doing."

"I'm serious, Noemi."

She sighed. "I know."

"We need to talk about the baby and the future."

"If you're about to tell me that you don't want anything to do with the baby, I can deal with it."

"What? No. That isn't what I was going to say."

She gave him a weak smile. "That's good."

"Our child will know me." Max stated it with conviction.

"Okay. Was there something else you wanted to discuss?"

He cleared his throat. "My country dictates that we must provide proof of the baby's legitimacy."

She moved back. "What are you saying?"

Surely she would want her child to be legitimate. Wouldn't she? He'd never imagined that she wouldn't want her child to be a part of the royal family—to be heir to the throne.

"You must have a paternity test done as soon as possible."

"I got that part but why?"

"So we may become a family and the baby will be heir to the throne."

She shook her head. "No."

"What do you mean no?" He got to his feet. Now she was being totally unreasonable. His child had a right—a duty to assume the throne of Ostania.

She got to her feet, straightened her shoulders and lifted her chin until their eyes met. "I know with being a prince and all that you aren't used to hearing the word no, but I'm saying it now and to you. No."

In that moment, his heart sank. He wasn't sure if it was the thought of losing the prospect of being a father and all it entailed, or if it was the realization that once again he'd been lied to by a woman. And not any small lie—but one that was so close to his heart.

It took him a moment to muster up the strength to vocalize the words. He swallowed hard. "Are you saying you lied about the paternity?"

"What?" The expression in her eyes was unreadable. "Is that what you're hoping?"

"No. But if you're refusing the paternity test, there has to be a reason. And the only one that I can think of is you lied to me."

"Or the fact that you totally misunderstood my answer."

He sighed and rubbed the back of his neck. He never knew talking with a woman could be this complicated, but then again, he'd never let his relationships get serious. All his conversations since Abree had been flirting and casual talk about his travels. His whole future had never been on the line.

"Does that mean you agree to the test? It's the only way we can become a family and put the child in line for the throne."

"It means that no matter what is revealed by the test, we are *not* getting married. And I'm not becoming a princess."

He processed what she told him, but he wanted to make sure they were on the same page. "So you're agreeing to the test?"

She nodded.

"But you don't want to be my wife."

"Exactly."

"And the child? How do you expect that to work out? Because if it is my child, I will not turn my back on it."

"I… I don't know how things will work out. I haven't had much time to consider it."

"But you're sure you don't want to be a part of the royal family?"

She nodded. "I already have a complicated family. I don't need another. If I marry, it will be for love and nothing less. And you do not love me."

He wanted to argue with her. But he couldn't lie to her. Sure they'd spent some wonderful time together, but he wasn't ready to put his heart on the line.

He'd been raised to do what was expected of him—to put the needs of the royal family ahead of his own. And he was told from a young age that marriage was a business contract and it had nothing to do with romantic fantasies.

However, Max learned from his time on his own that many people held tight to their dreams of love and happily-ever-after. He didn't know why when so many people ended up with a broken heart. There really wasn't such a thing as love. There was respect. There was friendship. That had to be enough.

His gaze moved to Noemi. A glint of determination reflected in her eyes. He knew there was no arguing with her. He needed to show her that they could have a good life together—even if they didn't love each other.

"It's okay," she said. "Why don't we give it some more time to think through our situation? And then we can figure out what makes the most sense."

At last, they could agree on something. "I think that's a good idea. In the meantime, spend the rest of the week with me."

"I… I don't know."

"I don't know how the future will play out, you know,

with the baby and all, but I think we should take advantage of our relative privacy here at the resort in order to get to know each other better. Because at the very least, I'm going to be the father of your child."

Noemi silently stared at him as though weighing his words. And then she nodded. "You're right. We should know each other better since we'll be linked for life. But I have one condition."

"And that would be?"

"As long as you don't pressure me about the baby and marriage."

He held up his hand as though he were about to take the oath to the throne. "I swear."

Marry a prince...

Wasn't that every girl's dream?

Noemi longed to talk to her mother. What would her mother tell her? To hold out for love? Or be practical and give the baby a mother and father living under one roof—even if they didn't love each other?

She was torn. Both options had their positives and negatives. But what was best for all of them?

At least Max had heard her and was giving them time to figure this thing out. He had no idea how much it meant to her that he valued her opinion.

Noemi tied her hair back in a short ponytail and pulled a white knit cap down over it. She selected her biggest sunglasses and headed for the door. It'd been a long time since she'd gone tubing and she was looking forward to it.

And it was just as she'd remembered. The sun beaming on her face. The cold air filling her lungs. And her racing to the bottom of the hill. The first trip down, Max had won. The second time down, she'd won.

Noemi walked through the fluffy white snow, feeling like a kid again. No responsibilities. No messy family stuff.

It helped that Max hadn't mentioned the M-word again that day. In fact, he'd kept everything light and casual.

She couldn't remember smiling so much.

But she wasn't a child and neither was Max. He was all man—tall and muscled. His eyes said he'd experienced more in life than most people his age, and yet he was able to have fun with her.

"You have to stop this," Noemi said.

The smile immediately fled his face. "What's wrong? Is it the baby?"

She continued to smile as she shook her head. "The baby is fine. It's my cheeks that are having the problem."

"I don't understand."

"My cheeks are sore from smiling so much." She glanced at him. "Speaking of cheeks, are you ever going to shave again?"

He ran a hand over his thickening stubble. "You don't like it?"

She pursed her lips and studied him. "I don't know."

"I'm keeping it temporarily. It's part of my disguise."

With things going so well between them, she had an idea. She didn't know what Max would think of it, but it was something she wanted to share with him.

"Hey, I have a doctor's appointment next week and I was wondering if you'd want to go with me?"

His eyes widened. "You mean for the baby?" When she nodded, he asked, "Is anything wrong?"

"No, it's a regular checkup. They're going to do a sonogram and we'll be able to hear the baby's heartbeat."

"Already?" When she smiled and nodded again, he said, "I'd love it. Thank you for asking me."

She never thought she could be this happy. She told herself this feeling wasn't going to last, but a voice in her head said to enjoy this moment as long as it lasted. When it was over, she'd have the memories to cherish.

And then there was Max, Crown Prince Maximilian Steiner-Wolf, who made her stomach dip every time he smiled at her. Not only did they have fun together, but he'd also been there to comfort her through the morning sickness.

He was so sweet to insist on making her tea. This prince was something extra special.

"Let's go again." She trudged toward the lift.

"Aren't you hungry?"

She shook her head. Okay. Maybe she was a little hungry, but she wanted to go down the hill one more time. And then she had something special in mind for after lunch.

"Please," she begged. "It'll be a tiebreaker."

He sighed. "How can I say no to that pouty look on your face?"

"Yay!" She grabbed his hand without thinking and pulled him toward the line for the tube lift.

Was it possible she could feel the heat of his body emanating through their gloves? Or was it just a bit of wishful thinking? She should let go of him. But it was so much easier to live in the moment and not think about what the future would bring them.

She tightened her hold on him as they slowly moved closer to the lift. "Isn't this the most beautiful day?"

Max looked at her and then glanced up at the sky. "Are we looking at the same sky? It's cloudy."

She breathed in deeply. "I can smell snow."

"You can't smell snow."

She nodded. "Can too. It smells fresh and crisp." She inhaled deeply. "It smells like snow."

He smiled and shook his head. "If you say so."

When his gaze connected with hers, her stomach dipped again. "I do."

"Next," the attendant said. He waved her forward.

With great reluctance, she let go of Max's hand. She didn't know why that connection should mean so much to her. It wasn't like they were in love or anything.

They were friends. Nothing more. Well, not quite. They were going to be parents to a little, innocent baby. That was a connection unlike any other. They had to continue to get along for the child. That was the most important part. She didn't want her child growing up in a stressful environment where the parents always argued.

At the top of the small hill, she waited for him to join her. Once they were side by side in their respective tubes, she turned to him. "First one to the bottom gets to pick what we do this afternoon."

"You think you're really going to beat me?"

"I know I am." She took off down the hill.

"Hey…" His voice got lost in the breeze as the first few snowflakes started to fall.

She laughed as the tube glided down over the dips. This was one of the best days of her life. And for the first time since learning she was pregnant, she felt everything was going to work out. She didn't quite know how, but she believed it would work out for the best and her baby would be happy.

She reminded herself not to get too wrapped up in the prince. They were just friends. There were no strings attached. But the harder she tried to resist his charms, the more she fell for the sexy prince.

She tempered her excitement with the knowledge that the people she loved eventually let her down. Max would eventually let her down, too—whether he meant to or not.

CHAPTER SEVEN

"You cheat."

Max didn't mind losing the race to Noemi—not at all. But he liked teasing her and keeping the smile on her face. She had the most beautiful smile with her rosy lips and it lit up her brown eyes.

"I do not," she said emphatically. "I can't help that you're slow."

"I am not."

There had been nothing slow about his attraction to her at the party that now seemed a lifetime ago. There was nothing slow about the rush of desire that came over him every time she was close by. And there was nothing slow about his yearning to care for her and their unborn child.

They'd just finished lunch in the ski lodge in a private room away from any curious eyes. He worried his beard wouldn't be enough to keep him from being recognized. And he knew he'd stand out if he wore a hat and sunglasses throughout their meal.

And now it was time for him to ante up for losing the tubing race. "So what do you have in mind for the afternoon? Please tell me it isn't skiing."

Her eyes twinkled with mischief. "Well, now that you mention it, skiing doesn't sound so bad—"

"Noemi, you really should be careful—"

"I never would have guessed you'd be a worrier."

"I don't worry. I'm just being cautious. There's a difference."

She shook her head. "Anyway, I've decided to give it up until the baby is born. Better safe than sorry."

"Thank you. So, what did you have in mind for this afternoon?"

She wiped the corners of her mouth with the white linen napkin and pushed aside her empty plate. "I was wondering if you would want to do some shopping with me."

"Shopping?" It was definitely not something he would have suggested. And it was not something he would enjoy. In fact, it was one of the last things he wanted to do. A dentist appointment sounded more appealing.

Noemi frowned. "I can see you don't like the idea."

He'd have to work harder in the future to keep his thoughts from reflecting on his face. "Not at all." He forced a smile. He knew how to be a good loser. "What are we shopping for?"

"I thought we could look at some baby stuff."

Baby stuff? He had absolutely no idea what that would entail. "Where do we have to go?"

"It's right up the road from here. What do you think?" The hopeful look on her face was too much for him to turn down.

"I think we should go. I'll call my driver."

Once the bill was paid, they were out the door. Max's car and two bodyguards were waiting for them. They were quickly ushered into the village, where upscale shops carried most anything you could think of to buy. And there in the heart of the village was a baby boutique.

The boutique was small but that didn't detract from its appeal. Pink, blue and white checked nursery bunting adorned the window, while in the center sat a bassinet, some stuffed animals and itty-bitty clothes. Noemi grinned with excitement. Maybe this surprise baby thing wasn't all so bad. And then her gaze slipped to Max, who opened the shop door for her. No, definitely not so bad at all.

Inside, the shop was brightly lit and filled with pastel colors of every shade. In the background, children's music played. A saleswoman approached them with a smile and offered to assist them, but they waved her off, saying they were just there to look around.

After the woman returned to the checkout, Max turned to Noemi. "We are just looking around, aren't we?"

Noemi shrugged. "It would be so hard not to buy something. It's all so cute. Don't you think?"

It was Max's turn to shrug. She could tell he was trying hard not to be moved by what this shopping trip meant to their future. In less than six months, they were going to have this tiny baby in their arms. He or she would be relying on them for everything. The enormity of the responsibility didn't escape her—in fact, it downright scared her. She'd never been responsible for another human. What if she messed up?

When she'd first learned she was pregnant, she'd considered adoption. She'd quickly dismissed the idea. That's what her parents had been forced to do with Leo and they'd regretted it ever since. She didn't want to be separated from her child. Her hand instinctively moved to the ever-so-slight bump in her midsection. She was already in love.

As she perused a pink, yellow and white dress that looked like it was made for a fine china doll, she couldn't help but feel people staring at them. When she lifted her head, she noticed a young woman had joined the older saleslady at the checkout. She was staring at them. Noemi slipped her sunglasses on and pulled her cap down so it covered all her hair.

"Maybe coming here wasn't such a good idea," Noemi whispered.

"It's fine. My security is by the door. Nothing will happen."

"I think we should go." She worried her bottom lip, but as she looked around this time, she didn't notice anyone staring at them.

"Just keep shopping. Everything is fine."

Perhaps he was right. After all, he was far more familiar with fame than she was. Once off the runway and with her heavy makeup removed, she wasn't easily recognized as the face of Cattaneo Jewels. That used to bother her. Once upon a time, she'd longed for fame.

She used to wear her runway makeup and finest fashions every time she went out. She'd wanted the attention that she failed to get at home. Where her family was concerned, everything had been about Cattaneo Jewels while her opinions were disregarded—while she, as a person, was disregarded.

But ever since she'd learned she was pregnant, her parents had died and Leo had entered her life, being recognized and asked for her autograph had lost its appeal to her. She was learning that there were far more important things in life.

Noemi fingered through the selection of baby clothes. The outfits were all so tiny and adorable. But at this point, she didn't know if she was having a boy or a girl. That would make buying things difficult. But that didn't stop Noemi from leisurely strolling up and down the aisles, feeling the ruffles and placing a pair of booties on her fingertips.

She glanced at Max. "Do you want to know if it's a boy or girl? You know, at the sonogram?"

"Can they tell this soon?"

"I don't know but we can ask." She had a baby book back at the chalet. Maybe it would tell her.

He glanced at the booties dangling from her fingertips. "Can you believe they'll be small enough to wear those?"

"I hope so. Or else I'm in really big trouble." She smiled back at him before turning back to the itty-bitty clothes.

"You're going to be a fantastic mother."

She turned to him and lifted her chin in order to look him in the eyes. "Do you really think so?"

"I do." There was no hesitation in his voice and his gaze did not waver.

"At least one of us thinks so."

His voice lowered. "Trust me."

His gaze lowered to her lips and lingered there. The heat

of excitement swirled in her chest before rushing up her neck and warming her cheeks. He was considering kissing her. And even though they'd already spent the night together, everything had changed since then.

His desire for her, was it real? Or was it fleeting? She didn't know. And to be honest, she didn't know what she wanted it to be. She stepped back.

"Oh, look." She rushed over to an entire display of stuffed animals. There were yellow ducks, green frogs, purple hippos, brown monkeys, polka-dotted inchworms and a whole assortment of other creatures. "Aren't they adorable?"

"Why don't you pick one out?"

She shook her head. "I don't think so."

"Why not?"

"Because I couldn't pick just one. They are all so cute."

"Then I will buy them all for you."

She turned to him, hoping he was joking. He wasn't. "Max, you can't."

"Sure, I can. Watch me."

As he went to make his way to the checkout, Noemi reached out and grabbed his arm. "Wait. You're not being reasonable."

"Of course I am. You like them all. Your smile lit up the whole room. I like when you smile like that. I'll buy the stuffed animals so you'll keep smiling."

When he went to pull away from her hold, her fingers tightened on his black wool coat. "Seriously, you can't. What would I do with all of them?"

He paused as though giving her question some serious thought. "Decorate the nursery?"

"There wouldn't be any room left for the crib or changing table."

"I hadn't thought of that. Maybe the baby will have two rooms. One for the practical stuff and one for the fun stuff."

Noemi's smile broadened. "Something tells me you'd actually do that."

"Sure, I would."

"How about, for now at least, we pick out just one stuffed animal for the baby?"

"One?"

She nodded and then turned back to the display that spanned the whole length of the back wall. "What do you think? A puppy? A kitty? A turtle?"

He shook his head. "I shouldn't pick it out. You're the one who fell in love with them."

"So you're making me do the hard job?"

"Just this once."

She didn't argue. It was a tough job, but she was up to the challenge. Then her eyes scanned the top shelf. Each plush creation called out to her. This definitely wasn't going to be easy.

But she was thoroughly excited to pick out their baby's first stuffed animal. It would be a keepsake. A stuffed animal that hopefully her child would still have when they were all grown up. Something to measure the time of her child's life—when they looked at it, they would remember their earliest childhood memories. Her eyes grew misty. She blinked repeatedly.

Oh, boy, were the mommy hormones kicking in full gear. She'd never been this sentimental in her life. But everything was different now. She was different, but she didn't feel as though she was done changing yet.

The purple snake she skipped over. That was an easy decision. She also crossed off anything pink or blue. Knowing her luck, she'd pick the wrong color.

She didn't know how much time had passed when she heard Max ask, "Do you need some help?"

She shook her head. "I've got this."

She had it narrowed down to a teddy bear, a lion or an elephant. She was tempted to take all three. But then how would she decide which was her child's first stuffed animal? She had to wonder that if something this simple was giving her such great pains to decide, how would she ever make the bigger decisions concerning her child?

Her stomach tightened as she realized the lifetime of responsibilities facing her. And with her parents gone, she wouldn't have anyone to turn to with her questions and doubts. But then she looked over at Max, who was trying so hard not to look bored. At least she wouldn't be all alone with this parenthood thing. Something told her Max would always be available for his child.

She glanced back at the three stuffed animals in her arms. And she knew right away which one to pick.

"Close your eyes," she said.

"But why?"

"Just do it. Please."

Max sighed. "Okay."

She waited until he'd done it and then she stuffed the other animals back on the shelf. She turned back to Max and said, "Okay. Hold out your hands."

A little smile pulled at his lips as he did what she asked.

She placed the animal in his hands. "Okay. You can open them now."

He opened his eyes and lifted his hands closer to his face. "You picked out a purple lion."

She nodded and smiled.

"And how did you decide on him?"

"I wanted our child's first animal to be something special. The lion will remind them of their father. A lion is king of the jungle, just as you are king of a great nation. The lion is also strong and protective of those he cares about."

"And that's how you see me?" His gaze studied her.

"That's how I see you as a father. Or rather a father-to-be."

She'd dodged that question. Her heart sped up when she thought of herself belonging to him—of him belonging to her. Realizing her thoughts were gravitating toward dangerous territory, she shoved them to the back of her mind.

Max studied the lion as though pondering her words.

"Shall we go?" she asked.

He glanced up at her with a puzzled look. Had he been so deep in thought that he hadn't heard her? Could her words really have affected him so deeply? Not wanting to make a big deal of it. She repeated her question.

"Sure," he said.

When she reached out for the lion, she noticed the booties in her hand. She wasn't sure what to do with them. She should probably put them back. After all, she could pick out all that stuff once the sex of the baby was determined—

"Get them." Max's voice cut through her mental debate. She glanced down at them. They were so cute. "Okay."

Noemi followed Max through the narrow aisles to the checkout. All the while, Noemi was admiring her finds. It wasn't until they were at the register and the items were on the counter that flashes lit up the room.

Max turned his back to the store window and pulled her to his chest, shielding her from the probing cameras. What were they going to do if they came inside?

"Oh, my," the older saleslady said.

"Isn't this great?" the younger woman said, all the while her fingers moved rapidly over her phone.

If Noemi was a betting person, she'd hazard a guess that the young woman had alerted the paparazzi to the prince's presence in the shop. And then reality started to settle in— they were in a baby boutique. The whole world was about to know that she was baby shopping with the Prince of Ostania. She inwardly groaned.

"I'm sorry about this," the prince said softly. Over his shoulder, he said to the salesclerk, "Is there a back way out of here?"

The older woman gestured to the back of the shop.

"Come on." With the stuffed animal and booties left behind, Max took Noemi's hand and rushed her out the back while his bodyguard led the way.

But where was the other security guy? There had been two of them. She glanced around but didn't see him anywhere. How strange.

As they ducked out the back door into a single-lane alley, she realized the other man had gone off to get their vehicle.

They scrambled into the black SUV with tinted windows and set off down the alley just as the photographers rounded the corner. More flashes went off, but it was all right. The back windows were so heavily tinted that it was doubtful they would get a usable photo.

It wasn't until they were away from the press that her muscles began to relax. She leaned her head back against the leather seat. What had just happened?

CHAPTER EIGHT

"I'M SORRY."

Max kept repeating those words the next morning at Noemi's chalet. It was earlier than they'd intended to meet up, but he knew she was already up because she'd texted him, canceling today's plans to go snowmobiling.

He didn't need anyone to tell him the reason for the cancellation. The paparazzi had once again messed with his life. Before it hadn't mattered so much, but now it was jeopardizing his future.

His phone had been ringing since last night, but he had yet to speak with his mother or Enzo. Apparently they'd been apprised of the headlines. He needed time to make a plan before he spoke with either of them.

Noemi turned away from him, hugging her arms across her chest as she sat on the couch in her gray pajama pants and a silky pink robe. Her hair was yanked back in a pony-tail holder and her face was pale. "You really shouldn't have come over. I know you have plans."

"Those plans included you. And I needed to check on you." He also had some more bad news to share with her, but he wasn't quite ready to spring it on her just yet.

"I'm fine." Her complexion said otherwise.

"I should have thought more about going into the village." The truth was that he hadn't been thinking about much of anything yesterday except for making Noemi happy. "With our ability to avoid the paparazzi on the ski slopes, I'd hoped they'd grown bored and moved on to another story—another town."

Noemi lifted her gaze to meet his. "Did you really think that would happen?"

"I guess I've grown accustomed to them being on the fringes of my life. Perhaps I got too careless. And I'm sorry you got caught up in the middle of all of it."

There was a definite pause. "It's not your fault."

"You might not feel that way when I show you this." He pulled his phone from his pocket.

"What is it?" Worry lines marred her beautiful face.

It killed him to be the one to cause her such distress. "I'll let you see for yourself."

He pulled up the headline and photo before handing it over to Noemi.

"Crown Prince to Daddy!"

Beneath the headline was a photo of him in the baby boutique. And standing just behind him was Noemi. But her head was turned and the view of her face was partially obstructed by his shoulder. Her ski cap and sunglasses also added to her anonymity.

Below the picture, the caption read, *But who's the baby's mama?*

Max hadn't been surprised to find it in the headlines today. The only thing to surprise him was the fact that Noemi's identity was still a mystery. And that's the way he wanted it to remain.

With great reluctance, he handed over his phone. Immediately Noemi gasped. Her face grew pale. An awkward silence ensued as she read the article summarizing his life and his eventual ascension to the throne.

Over the years, the paparazzi had written many false stories about him, from him eloping to him abdicating his crown to him joining a professional rock band. None of them had even been close to true. But this story, it hit too close to home for his family to ignore. It would change so much for everyone. And so he needed to return to Ostania immediately.

He didn't want to do that without Noemi. But would she go with him?

She handed his phone back to him. If her face was pale before, now it was a pasty gray. And then without a word, she darted out of the room. He didn't have to ask; he knew the morning sickness had returned.

His body tensed as frustration swept through him. He had to do better in the future. It was his job to protect his family and see to their well-being. If he couldn't care for the mother of his child, how was he ever to look after an entire nation?

It was then that he decided no matter what it took, Noemi would go back to Ostania with him. In that way he could see to her well-being. And while they were there, they could make plans for the future—their future. Because somehow—someway—he intended to marry Noemi.

This couldn't be happening.

Noemi's heart pounded. Ever since the run-in at the boutique, she'd realized the fantasy of her and Max living an ordinary life had been nothing but a dream. They weren't ordinary. She was an heiress and he was a crown prince. It meant that neither of them would have any privacy—now or ever.

Right now, she needed her stomach to settle. She sat on the cold tile floor of the bathroom and leaned her pounding head against the wall. She thought the morning sickness was behind her, but the stress gave her a headache that started her stomach churning.

There was a tap on the door. "Noemi, are you all right?"

She supposed she had been gone for a while. Usually her morning sickness wasn't this bad. She must look quite a sight, but she knew Max wouldn't leave until he was certain she was all right.

"You can come in."

The door slowly opened. Max stood there with a worried frown. "You don't look so good."

"Thank you. That's what all women want to hear."

"I'm sorry. I just meant—"

"I know what you meant. I was just giving you a hard time."

He moved to the sink, where some fresh towels were laid out. The next thing she knew, he sat down next to her and gently pressed a cold washcloth to her forehead.

"Maybe that will help."

The coldness was comforting—so was having Max by her side. She didn't say it, though. It wasn't good to encourage this relationship unless she was ready to share her life with the world. Yesterday proved that. She didn't want her baby to be fodder for headlines.

And then a worrisome thought came to her. "Did the press follow you here?"

He shook his head. "Do you think I would intentionally do that to you?"

"No. But that doesn't mean it couldn't happen accidentally."

"They've been camping outside the gates of the community where I am staying. Thankfully it has guards. One paparazzo did sneak onto the grounds, but he was quickly dealt with. I was able to sneak out in the back of a neighbor's car covered with a blanket. They didn't even notice me. They were intent on watching my SUV."

She breathed a little easier. "Thank you." Feeling a bit better, she removed the cloth from her forehead. She got to her feet. "Sorry about that."

"You don't have to apologize. I can't even imagine all the changes your body is going through right now. And then this thing with the paparazzi doesn't help matters."

"At least they don't know who I am."

"Yet."

"You mean they aren't going to give up until they find out what you were doing in the boutique?"

He nodded. "They can be like a dog with a bone. Relentless."

"How do you live like that?" She thought she'd had it bad,

but her notoriety was miniscule compared to his. For the most part, she could pick and choose when to engage with the press, but Max didn't have that choice.

He cleared his throat. "Some would say it is something you are born into—something that comes along with the job of being royal. Others would say it's a privilege to have access to the world. I don't know what I'd say. Right now, it is a curse. But I also know from watching my father over the years that the press can be used for good things. I'm just sorry that you're caught up in the middle of all this."

"And that's why I want out." She'd wrestled with this decision a large part of the night. She hadn't realized that she'd made the decision until the words popped out of her mouth.

Max didn't say anything at first. It was as though he wasn't sure he'd heard her correctly. But then his eyes grew darker, like that of a stormy sky.

"You want out of what? Having our baby?"

"No." She crossed her arms. "How could you think that?"

He rubbed the back of his neck. "What am I supposed to think?"

"I want out of this." She waved her hand between the two of them. "I want you to walk away. There's nothing tying you to this baby. No paper trail. I haven't told anyone."

"But you forget the one very important tie—I am the baby's father." His mouth pressed closed in a firm line as the muscle in his jaw twitched.

She turned away from him and pressed her hands against the cool granite of the sink counter. "But if you don't tell anyone, no one will know. We can each go our separate way."

Even though she had turned her back on him, his image was there in the mirror. She couldn't tell what he was thinking, only that he wasn't happy. Well, neither was she. This was not the way she wanted things to work out for herself or her child. But they had to be realistic.

Creating a scandal wouldn't be good for their baby either. She didn't want people pointing their fingers at their child and whispering. She didn't want paparazzi hiding behind bushes and springing out, scaring their son or daughter. She didn't want her life to be any more of a three-ring circus than it already was—even if it meant sacrifices had to be made.

"I'll let you finish up in here." His tone was even with no hint of emotion.

She knew he wasn't that calm—that detached. But he strove to hide it well. It must be something about being born a royal. Her family was not that restrained—that in control.

When the bathroom door shut, Noemi pressed a hand to her stomach. "Well, little one, it looks like I've really made a mess of things now."

CHAPTER NINE

SHE WANTS OUT.

Max knew what she was really saying was that she wanted away from him—away from all the baggage that came with being the crown prince. But what she seemed to fail to realize was that was impossible. That little baby within her was the heir to Ostania. But more than that, Max couldn't walk away from his responsibility to the baby—to Noemi.

They were in this together whether they liked it or not.

He moved to the kitchen, where he grabbed some crackers and brewed some tea. He took the food back to the living room to wait for Noemi. He had to return to Ostania right away and he was still determined to take Noemi with him. He wasn't going to leave her alone to deal with the press by herself. But how was he going to convince her that going with him was for the best?

A few minutes later, Noemi returned to the living room. Her eyes widened when they met his. It appeared she hadn't expected him to hang around. The other men in her life must not have been as determined to keep Noemi in their lives. It was their loss and his gain.

"I got you some crackers. Maybe they will help." He gestured to the plate and cup on the large coffee table.

"You really didn't have to—"

"I wanted to."

She sat down and sipped the tea. "I'm surprised you're still here."

"Did you really think I would leave without straightening things out between us?"

"I thought that's what we'd done." Her gaze met his. "It's
best for everyone if we just part ways now."

He didn't believe her. "Is that what you really think?"

Her gaze lowered. "It is."

Why was she being so stubborn? Surely she didn't believe
that she was saying. She was scared. The paparazzi could be
intimidating. And he supposed she might be intimidated by
his position—though most women had the opposite reaction.

Still, he had to get through to her. He had to jar her out
of this fantasy that she could just erase him from her life. It
wasn't going to happen. He wouldn't let it.

"Noemi, I'm not going anywhere. We're in this together."

She shook her head. "I'll be fine on my own."

"But will our baby be fine without a father?"

Her gaze was still lowered. "Lots of children are raised
by a single parent."

"And most don't have a choice. But you do. Our child can
have two invested parents."

"But at what cost?" Her gaze at last met his. "My pregnancy will become a front-page scandal. It'll be all over the
television and internet. And they'll call it our love child.
Our illegitimate heir. Or worse."

"Do people still say illegitimate?" he asked in all honesty. "I don't think it will be the scandal that you imagine."

She shook her head. "You aren't going to change my
mind."

Oh, yes, he was. Somehow. Some way.

He had one last plan to bring her to her senses. It was with
tremendous trepidation that he said, "Are you better off having lost your parents?"

Immediately the pain reflected in her eyes. "That's not
the same thing."

"How so? Don't you think our son or daughter will wonder why their friends have both a mother and a father, but

they don't? You don't think it will hurt them? You don't thin
they will grow up with questions?"

For an extended moment, silence filled the room.

Perhaps he'd been too tough on her. But he just couldn'
let Noemi delude herself into thinking that exiling him fror
her life was for the best. It wouldn't be good for any of them
Least of all their child.

"All right," she said, "you've made your point. But I don'
see how this is going to work out."

It was time to get to the reason for his visit. "I have t
leave today for Ostania."

"Because of the article about us at the baby boutique?"

"Partly." He had a lot of explaining to do with his family–
especially his brother.

"Then there's no rush to figure this out." The worry line
on her face eased a bit.

"I want you to come with me."

"To Ostania?"

He nodded. "Have you ever been there?"

She shook her head as she reached for the crackers. "I'v
always wanted to visit. It looks like such a beautiful coun
try, but I've just never had the opportunity."

"So this is your chance. Let me show you my world. I
will be better than sitting here while the paparazzi scour th
area for the mysterious woman in the photograph."

She didn't say anything at first. He took that as a posi
tive sign. The longer she was quiet, the more confident h
became that she would accompany him to Ostania.

Just then, her phone chimed. She frowned as she read th
text message. She responded. Once she set her phone aside
she glanced at Max. There was still a hint of worry writ
ten on her face.

"Is everything all right?"

She sighed. "It was my brother Leo. He was letting m
know that he has flown back to New York."

"So it's just you in Mont Coeur?"

She nodded. "Until Christmas."

"Then there's no reason for you to stay here alone." Feeling that she might need a little more encouragement, he said, "You can do as much sightseeing or as little as you like. You can consider it a vacation. And we'll be able to get to know each other better."

"But won't you be busy with your duties?"

He would be. He wouldn't lie to her about it. This baby would mean so many things would change. He would be taking on a lot of responsibility that previously had been given to his brother. He had many things to learn about governing a nation.

"I will be busy. It's unavoidable. But I promise you'll have plenty to do. Every amenity is at the palace. And there will be a car at your disposal should you want to go anywhere."

She finished the last cracker. "You make it sound like a relaxing trip to a five-star spa."

"It can be if that's what you'd like."

A look came over her face as though she'd just recalled something. "I can't go. I have a doctor's appointment."

The one where he was supposed to hear his son or daughter's heartbeat and see their image. A pang of regret hit him with the force of a sledgehammer.

"You can't miss that."

A look of relief came over her. "I agree."

"But you could see the doctor in Ostania." When she started to shake her head, he said, "Sure you can."

"It's not that easy. I can't just go strolling into a new doctor's office."

"I can put the doctors in touch with each other. Or I can fly in your doctor."

"You know how to exaggerate a house call."

"I'm a prince. There's a lot I can do. Trust me."

She fidgeted with the hem of her shirt. "You aren't going to let this go, are you?"

He shook his head. "If you stay here, so do I."

"But your family—"

"Will have to wait. This is more important."

"I'm not ready to face your family and discuss the baby. We…" she waved her hand between them "…need to figure things out before we tell people."

"I agree." By the widening of her eyes, he could see that his response surprised her. "For the moment, we'll keep the fact that the baby is mine between us."

They sat there quietly staring at each other. If she was trying to find another reason not to go on this trip, he would continue to find ways to allay her worries. He would do whatever it took to ensure the safety of the mother of his baby.

Noemi expelled a sigh and pressed her hands to her hips. "If I do this—if I go with you—I have to return to Mont Coeur for Christmas as my family has some matters to sort out."

"Understood." It sounded like she'd just agreed to travel to Ostania with him, but he wanted to be absolutely certain. "So you'll accompany me?"

She nodded. "I just need to get packed."

"Do you need help?"

She shook her head.

"I'll wait here." He sat down and pulled out his phone. "Just let me know if you need anything. And don't lift the suitcase. I'll get it."

She didn't say anything else as she turned for her room. He couldn't tell if she was angry or just resigned. He hoped with a little time and some rest that she would see this arrangement was for the best.

Had she made the right decision?

Noemi smothered a yawn. It was too late to change her mind as the private jet soared above the puffy white clouds. Part of her said that she should have stayed back at the chalet and hibernated until the press gave up their search for the mysterious woman in the photo. But another part of her wasn't ready to let go of Max—of the dream that their baby could be part of both of their lives.

There was something special about him. It was there when

he smiled at her and made her stomach dip. And there was the way he looked at her that made her feel like she was the only woman in the world. And then there was his gentleness and kindness.

Not that she was falling for him or anything. She refused to let herself do that. She'd agreed to fly to Ostania because it was best for the baby to have parents who were good friends—who could work together to raise a happy and healthy child. Nothing more.

Noemi continued to stare out the window as the plane descended, preparing to land at the private airstrip somewhere near the Ostania palace—at least that's what Max had said when he'd told her to fasten her seat belt. Even though the sun was sinking low in the sky, she was able to make out the palace. The sight captured her full attention. This was where Max lived? *Wow!*

Even from this height, it looked impressive with its blue turrets and white walls. She couldn't even imagine calling this place home. It looked like an entire village could fit within its walls and still have some extra room for visitors.

With so much space, it made her wonder why Max had felt the need to leave here for so long. What had he been running from? Was it his parents? Were they overbearing? She hoped not. Second thoughts about this trip started to niggle at her.

Nestled in the jagged snow-covered mountains, she had no idea where they were going to land. But the plane kept descending and soon a small clearing came into view with a runway. All around the cleared airstrip was snow. It certainly wasn't large enough for a commercial jet. In fact, it seemed rather short—

The wheels touched down with a jolt. Her fingers tightened on the armrests. She closed her eyes and waited. They would stop in time. Wouldn't they?

"Are you okay?" Max asked, drawing her from her thoughts.

As the plane rolled to a stop, she expelled a pent-up breath. "Yes. Um…why?"

"It's just that you've been quiet the entire flight."

She shrugged. "I just have a lot on my mind."

"I understand."

Did he? Did he know how hard this was going to be for all of them? And what was his family going to say when they heard about the baby? But then again, they probably already heard the rumors that had been in the newspaper.

"What about your family?" she asked.

"What about them?"

"They must have heard the gossip. Are you going to confirm their suspicions that the baby is yours?"

He shook his head. "Not until you're ready. They know after my cancer treatments that children are unlikely. They'll easily dismiss the story as nothing but fiction."

She hoped he was right because this pregnancy was becoming more complicated with each passing day.

They were ushered into a waiting black sedan with the flags of Ostania waving on each front fender. She received surprised looks from everyone she met, but none of them vocalized their thoughts. It would appear Prince Max didn't make it a practice of bringing women home with him. She took comfort in the knowledge.

The car moved slowly over the snow-covered road. Noemi told herself the poor road conditions were the reason her stomach was tied up in knots. It had nothing to do with wondering if Max's family would like her or not.

Max reached out, placing his hand over hers. "Relax. My family is going to love you."

She turned a surprised look at him. How had he known what she was thinking?

"I don't know. I'm not royal. In fact, I don't have a clue how to address your mother and father."

"Don't make a big deal of it."

She sat up a bit straighter. As the car drew closer to civilization, she grew more nervous. "I'm serious. What do I do? Curtsy?"

Max laughed. It was a deep warm sound and it helped calm her rising nerves. "I don't think that will be necessary."

"But I need to do something."

"How about a slight bow and a nod of your head?"

"Really? Because I don't want to do anything to offend them."

Surprised reflected in Max's eyes. "You really care that much?"

"Shouldn't I?" Even if they weren't Max's parents and the grandparents of her baby, she'd want to make a good impression. After all, they were king and queen. Wait until she told Stephania and Maria about all this.

Their car approached a small village that was nestled in a valley while the palace sat partway up the mountain in the background. The palace glowed like a jewel as floodlights illuminated it in the darkening evening.

But down here in the village, rooftops were covered with snow. And in the center of the village was an enormous Christmas tree. It soared up at least two stories. And it was lit with white twinkle lights. The branches were dusted with snow. It was simple and yet at the same time, it was stunning.

Noemi longed to stay here in the village. There was nothing intimidating about it, unlike the palce. As the car slowly passed through the center of the village, all the pedestrians turned. Men removed their hats and covered their hearts while the women waved. With the tinted windows, they couldn't make out who was in the back seat but they waved nonetheless. Noemi resisted the urge to wave back.

"Do they always do that?" she asked, curious about Osania and its people.

"Yes. And under different circumstances, I'd stop and greet them."

And then Noemi felt bad. "You won't stop because of me."

"Correct." He didn't elaborate.

He didn't have to. She already knew her condition was changing their lives. What would his family do when he told them about the baby? Would they demand they marry?

Her body stiffened at the idea of a marriage of convenience. If she ever married, it would be for love and nothing less.

But she was pregnant with the prince's child. A royal baby could change things. Would they try to force her?

No. Of course not. It wasn't like she was a citizen of Ostania. They had no power over her. She glanced over at Max as he stared out the window. He wouldn't let his parents force them into anything that they didn't want. She trusted him.

That acknowledgment startled her. She'd never really thought about it before, but she did trust him. That was the first step in a strong friendship, right?

Max turned to her. "Did you say something?"

"Um, no."

"If you have any questions, feel free to ask. I'll try to answer them or I'll find the answers."

She had a feeling he wasn't talking about their unique relationship but rather her magnificent surroundings and the history of the palace. "Thanks. I'll keep that in mind."

As the palace drew closer, she practically pressed her face to the window as she tried to take in the enormity of the structure. She gazed up at one of the towers and couldn't help but think of Rapunzel. Her hair would have been so long to reach the ground.

She smiled at the memory of the fairy tale. But she couldn't help it. She felt as though a book had been opened and she was about to step into the pages of a real-life fairy tale. And she had absolutely no idea how it was going to end. Her stomach shivered with nerves again.

"Relax. My parents aren't that bad."

"That bad?" Her voice rose a little. "You really know how to put a person at ease."

Max sent her a guilty smile as he took her hand in his. "You know what I mean."

"Uh-huh. Sure. They are going to hate me."

Max squeezed her hand. "It will be fine. I'll be right next to you the whole time."

Her stomach grew uneasy. *Oh, no. Not now.* She reached for her purse and pulled out a packet of crackers.

Max frowned. "Maybe this wasn't such a good idea. I thought I'd be rescuing you from the stress of the press, but it appears the thought of my family is just as bad."

She quickly munched on a couple of crackers.

"Is it helping?" Max gave her long hard look. When she nodded, he said, "Maybe I should have some."

"You're nervous?"

"Let's just say my father might be king of the nation but my mother runs the family. She has definite ideas of how things should work and this thing between us won't fit neatly into her expectations."

Noemi reached for another cracker. "I knew it. She's going to hate me."

"Would you quit saying that? It's just going to take a bit of adjusting on everyone's part."

"Especially when you tell her that we're not getting married."

This time Max didn't say a word. Not one syllable. He turned his head away as the car pulled to a stop in front of the palace.

With great reluctance, Noemi stuffed the remaining crackers back in her purse. Then she ran a finger around the outside her lips, checking for crumbs. The last thing she needed was to meet the king and queen looking a mess. But she had a feeling they'd be more interested in her relationship with Max than her appearance. And then a thought came to her.

"You did tell them you were bringing me, didn't you?"

CHAPTER TEN

ONCE AGAIN, MAX didn't say a word. He continued to star blindly out the window. He hadn't told anyone about Noem accompanying him home. Not his mother. Not even Enzo.

Telling them about Noemi would involve questions— questions he wasn't ready to answer. So maybe he'd failed to disclose a couple of things to his parents about his return— a couple of big things. But who could blame him under the circumstances?

It was such a tangled mess. And in the end, his family would insist on an immediate paternity test followed by wedding, and that last part was a sticking point with Noemi He had to handle this very carefully or she would bolt. And he couldn't let that happen.

"Max, you did tell them, didn't you?"

Before he could answer, both of their car doors swung open. He let go of her hand as he stepped out of the car. When he turned toward the palace, Enzo was standing there, and next to him was the queen. *Oh, boy!* She didn't normally greet him at the door.

Max straightened his shoulders and moved to Noemi's side. He presented his arm to her, in proper royal fashion and escorted her up the few steps to the sweeping landing.

"Your Highness." He nodded in recognition of his mother's station—etiquette was something his parents had instilled in both him and his brother from a young age.

"Maximilian." The queen continued to frown at him. "It's bout time you came home."

She was the only one to call him by his formal name. Not ven his father, the king, called him that. But his mother was ll about pomp and circumstance. He rarely ever saw his nother with her hair down, literally or figuratively. When e became ruler, things would change—they would be less igid. But all that hinged on Noemi...

Not only did he have to sire an heir, but that heir must eside within the palace and be groomed from birth to take ver the reins of the Ostania. There was no room for a mod-rn arrangement of partial custody or holiday visitation. His hild must remain here in Ostania with him. And he already new Noemi would balk at the idea.

His mother's frown deepened. "What is that mess on your ace?"

He smiled, knowing his mother abhorred beards. "I hought I'd try something different."

"Well, you're home now. Please shave." The queen turned o Noemi. "And who is this?"

Oh, yes, where were his manners? It was just that being ome again after being gone since last Christmas had him bit off-kilter. His relationship with his mother had always een a bit strained. He got along with his father so much etter.

"Mother, I would like to introduce you to Noemi Catta-eo of Cattaneo Jewels." He turned to Noemi. "And this is ny mother, Queen Josephine."

He noticed the surprise reflected in Noemi's eyes when he nentioned her family's business, but that's how things were lone within the palace. People weren't just recognized for vho they were but what they represented. And Max knew is mother had commissioned a few special pieces from Cattaneo Jewels.

The frown lines etching his mother's ivory complexion ased a bit. "You are related to the owners?"

Noemi nodded. "My parents...started the business. An now, erm, my brothers and I run the business."

The queen's eyes widened. "How truly interesting. I' like to hear more later." Then his mother turned back to him "You did not mention you'd be bringing a guest."

"I didn't?" He knew how to play his mother's games a well as she. "I thought I had."

"No. You didn't." She turned to Enzo. "Did he?"

"Not that I recall, ma'am. But the phone connection wasn the best. Perhaps I missed it."

Max couldn't help but smile at Enzo's attempt to play th impartial party. The man practically had it down to a fin science. When Enzo's gaze caught the slight smile on Max' face, the man refused to react. However, Max would be hea ing more about this later.

"Mother, it's cold out. Shouldn't we go inside?"

The queen hesitated for a moment. Max knew his mothe didn't like to be pushed around or have something pulle over on her. She liked to know things before everyone else

And when she found out what was afoot, he honestl didn't know if she'd be overjoyed with the prospect of grandchild that no one ever thought was possible or if she' be outraged that his wild lifestyle had led to a child out o wedlock, to a commoner no less. With his mother, anythin was possible. But when the time was right, the first perso he had to tell was his brother—Tobias's life was about to b turned upside down.

At last, his mother nodded and turned for the door. It wa then that Max glanced over at Noemi. Her face was pal and drawn as she wore a plastered-on smile. He thought th first meeting with his mother had gone rather well consider ing. But perhaps he should have taken time to warn Noem that his mother wasn't the warm and fuzzy type. The quee loved her sons. He never doubted it. But she kept her feel ings under wraps.

He clearly recalled awakening after his cancer surgery The room had been dim and he had been a bit disoriente first. He hadn't moved while gaining his bearings. And en he'd heard the soft cry of someone.

He recalled how his mother been leaning near him. Her ead had been resting on his bed with her face turned away. nd then she'd said a prayer for him. He'd never been more uched in his life—well, that was until he heard Noemi tell im that he was going to be a father. Those were the two ost stunning moments in his life.

He understood that his mother had been raised to keep n outward cool indifference. But he wanted more for his fe—for his child's life. He needed his child to never ques- on his fierce love for them.

his had to be some sort of dream.

This just couldn't be real.

The grandmother of her baby was a queen. Noemi's stom- ch quivered yet again. And from all Noemi could gather, he woman didn't like her and they didn't even know each ther yet. Panic set in. Noemi didn't even want to think about vhat the woman would say when she learned of the baby. Maybe it was best that she never did.

That was it. Noemi would leave right away. She just had o get Max alone. Surely he had to see that coming here was mistake. She didn't know one thing about royalty. Sure, he'd done an internet search when she'd been alone at night, ut she hadn't found much insight. Certainly nothing to pre- are her for this.

Once inside the palace, Noemi stopped in the grand foyer. he breath caught in her throat as she took in the magnifi- ent surroundings. The tiled floor glimmered as the lights rom the enormous crystal chandelier reflected off it. The iles were laid in a diamond pattern of sky blue and black tile.

To either side of the very spacious room were twin stair- ases with elaborate wrought-iron bannisters with gold hand- ails. Her attention was drawn back to the center of the room vhere the chandelier hung prominently. It must have been t least four meters wide with a thousand individual crys-

tals. And straight ahead were four white columns with gol
trim. In the center was a large window and between the sid
columns were archways leading to other parts of the palace

Off to the side stood a stately Christmas tree. Noem
craned her neck as she looked up at the star at the tippy top
She'd guess the thing stood at least thirty feet tall. *Wow*
And she'd thought the twelve-foot trees that her father use
to get for the chalet were tall. They were nothing compare
to this tree.

The royal Christmas tree was adorned with white twin
kle lights. And the decorations were of white porcelain. Al
looked to be painstakingly positioned on the tree. They n
doubt had professional decorators take care of all the detail

At the chalet, the decorations on the tree had been col
lected over the years. Some were handmade by her and Se
bastian. Other ornaments were from vacations or represente
special moments in their lives. Each of her family's orna
ments held a meaning whereas this palace tree, though mag
nificent, didn't seem to bear the weight of the memories an
sentiments of Max's family.

For some reason, that made her sad. Surely there had t
be another tree somewhere in the palace where they hun
their treasured ornaments. Right?

"Noemi?" Max sent her a strange look, jarring her bacl
to the present.

"Yes. Sorry." Heat rushed to her cheeks as she realize
she hadn't been paying attention to what Max was saying.

"This is my father, King Alexandre."

The king? She swallowed hard. What was she suppose
to do? Bow? Curtsy? Her stomach took that moment to be
come queasy once again. She wished she could reach in he
purse and pull out the remaining crackers, but that woul
have to wait.

Not sure what to do, she bowed. "Your Majesty."

She hoped she'd got it right. When she straightened, th
king drew closer. He was smiling, unlike his wife, who kep
a serious look on her face.

The king held out his hand. He was going to shake her hand? She didn't know that kings did such a thing.

He continued to smile at her. "It's so nice to meet one of my son's friends."

"It…it's nice to meet you, too."

He released her hand. "A friend of Max's is a friend of mine."

"Thank you." Was that the right response? Honestly she'd met a lot of rich and famous people, but none of them had ruled their own country. And none of them had been Max's parents. And like it or not, she wanted to make a good impression. So far she hadn't impressed the queen, but she was doing much better with the king. That was at least a step in the right direction. Maybe she wouldn't rush back to Mont Coeur…just yet.

"Have you known my son long?"

"We met a few months ago," Max said.

His father glanced at him and Max grew silent.

Noemi wasn't sure how his father would take to hearing his son was partying it up so she said, "We met via some mutual friends. And we immediately hit it off."

"Immediately?" Max asked.

She turned to Max, not sure what to say.

"As I recall," Max continued, "you weren't so easily swayed to give me a chance."

"I, uh…" What was he doing? Was he trying to give his father a bad impression of her?

"Relax," Max said, "my parents can respect your selectiveness. And since you didn't recognize me, I was just one of your many admirers."

Heat rushed to her face. She felt as though her face were on fire. If Max was trying to smooth things over with his father, he wasn't doing a good job. She wished he would stop speaking.

"He's not serious," Noemi said, clarifying things. "We started to talk and soon we became friends."

"Friends?" Max wore an amused look. When she turned

a pointed look at him, he said, "Yes, friends. We've been enjoying the snow. And I thought Noemi would enjoy seeing where I lived."

His father was still smiling, but she could see the wheels in his mind turning. He was wondering what exactly was going on between them. Were they just a casual thing? Or was it something more serious?

She didn't have any answers for him because she didn't have any answers for herself. Only time would tell how things would play out for them and the baby.

"Well, we are glad you've come for a visit," the king said. "Isn't that right, Josephine?"

There was a pause before the queen spoke. "Yes, it is. And someone will show you to your suite so you can settle in while we speak privately with our son."

"Thank you for having me," Noemi said, realizing that she'd been dismissed.

As she glanced to the left, she noticed a staff member waiting for her at the bottom of the steps. She turned back to find the king and queen walking away.

"Don't worry," Max leaned over and whispered in her ear. "Everything is going to work out. I'll catch up with you in a bit."

Noemi hoped he was right. So far she was pretty certain coming here was a mistake, even if his father had been very nice to her. And what were they doing now? Talking about the scandalous headlines? Discussing her pregnancy?

She wondered if she should insist on being a part of the conversation if it was going to be about her. When she paused and glanced over her shoulder, they were gone now—down some long hallway or behind some closed door. Maybe it was for the best that she hadn't caught up with them.

She continued up the steps. The thought of lying down for a bit sounded so appealing. She had never been this tired in her life. Usually she was a bundle of energy. But not lately. This pregnancy was taking a lot out of her.

And then there was her uneasy stomach. Her hand reached

or her purse, anxious to retrieve the crackers, but then she returned her hand to her side. There was no way she was going to trail cracker crumbs through the palace. She'd waited this long, a little longer wouldn't matter.

All the while, she wondered what Max's parents were saying. She knew she needed to trust Max, but being here in his palace, it changed things. It drove home the power and wealth of Max and his family.

He should tell them.

He wanted to. Max couldn't wait to shout it from the towers that he was going to be a father. But he knew Noemi wasn't ready for the pressure or expectations that would bring to her life. For now, he had to protect her.

His country was steeped in archaic traditions, as were his parents. Max didn't agree with most of those traditions, but he wasn't in a position to change them—not yet. For now, he had to go along with what was expected of him, producing an heir and providing a paternity test. When he became king—when his authority could not be disputed—then he could implement changes.

Max stepped into the library and stopped, finding that it wasn't just his parents that wanted to speak to him. There were the two highest members of the royal cabinet as well as Enzo and their public representative. This felt more like the beginning of an inquisition than a homecoming.

From the doorway, he took a moment to really look at his parents. His mother looked much the same. She still had a trim figure, and she had no gray hairs but he had a feeling she had them discreetly covered up. His father, on the other hand, looked older and frailer. His face looked weathered and his eyes were dull. He was sicker than he was willing to admit.

The king stepped forward. "This is the woman, isn't it?"

Max sent him a confused look. It was like he'd stepped into the middle of a conversation and everyone expected him to know what had been said. He refused to be put on

the defensive. He'd been in that awkward position too man
times in recent years.

"The woman?" he asked.

"Don't do this." His mother stepped up next to his fa
ther. "I know we've given you a lot of freedom after your..
your illness. Perhaps in hindsight it was too much freedom
It wasn't like we turned a blind eye to your activities. Bu
honestly, the headlines have been getting worse and worse
And now you bring home this girl—"

"She's not a girl. She's a woman. And her name is Noemi."

The queen crossed her arms over her proper navy-and
white linen dress. "I suppose she's the one who claims to
be pregnant?"

"Since when did you start believing the headlines? You
know what the doctor said. I can't father any children."

The angry look on his mother's face deflated. "So it's no
true? There's no baby?"

"Whatever they printed in the paper is nothing but make
believe. There's nothing serious between Noemi and me
We're...friends. She's really nice. I wish you would give
her a chance."

The queen eyed him carefully. "She's important to you?"

He had to be careful here. "She's a good friend. And she'
been through a lot lately. I want this visit to go well for her."

His statement only increased his mother's curiosity. "Been
through what?"

"Darling, leave Max alone." The king spoke in a conge
nial tone. "He is home just like you wanted. Let's not rush
him back out the door."

His mother hated it when they ganged up on her. "Am I
not allowed to be curious about my son and his friends?"

"Of course," the king said. "But you don't have to make
it sound like the inquisition."

His mother's eyes lit up as she glared at his father. "Fine
You deal with this. And when it blows up in our faces, it'l
be on you." And then she turned back to Max. "Make sure
you shave before dinner."

And with that his mother turned and left the room along with the other dignitaries. The door made a resounding thud.

His father shook his head before turning back to Max. "Your mother, she means well. She missed you. I wish you wouldn't stay away for such extended periods."

"I'm sorry, Father. It's just—"

"Easier. I know."

Max nodded. That's what he loved most about his father—his way of understanding him. Whereas his mother was fierce in her love and need to protect the family, his father was the opposite and let his love flow freely and without restriction. For being two opposite types, Max was impressed by the way his parents were able to make their marriage work and last.

"However, I agree with your mother. This woman, she is more than a friend." When Max went to dispute the claim, his father raised his hand to stop him. "Perhaps you don't even see it yourself. But you will. Trust me. It's in the way you look at her and the way you speak of her. However, I'm not so sure she feels the same way as you. So please be careful."

It was no wonder his father was the king. He could see straight through a situation to the heart of the problem—just as he had done now with Max and Noemi.

When his father was called away on urgent business, Max headed for the steps leading upstairs. He wanted to make sure Noemi was comfortably situated. As he walked, his father's words kept rolling around in his mind. Was it that obvious that Noemi wasn't into him?

And if that was the case, what did he do about it? Separate the mother from the child? The thought turned his stomach. There had to be a better way. Pay her to stay here with him and the child until their son or daughter was grown? Again, he didn't like the idea. What did that leave him? To make her fall in love with him?

Max paused outside her door. He swallowed down his thoughts. He didn't want her to sense his inner turmoil. He had to keep it all inside until he figured the best course of action for all concerned—especially their baby.

Knock. Knock.

"Come in." Noemi's voice was faint.

He opened the door and found Noemi sitting up on th
bed. Her face was pale and she didn't meet his gaze. H
pushed the door closed and rushed to her side. He knelt dow
in front of her. "Are you all right?"

She nodded. "I felt a little wiped out and I closed my eye
for a few minutes. I guess I fell asleep."

"I didn't mean to wake you."

"It's okay. I don't want to sleep the evening away or els
I won't sleep tonight."

"Dinner will be at seven. Will you be up for it?"

She mustered a smile, but it didn't quite reach her eyes
"I'll be fine. By tomorrow, I'll be good as new."

Somehow he didn't quite believe her. The stress of th
press compounded by his mother's cold welcome couldn'
have helped Noemi's pregnancy. He was going to have t
do better. He wanted Noemi to enjoy this visit. He wante
her to fall in love with his country—their child's birthright

"What would you like to do this evening?" he asked. I
it was within his power, he would give her whatever sh
wanted.

"Would you mind if we didn't do anything?"

That didn't sound like much fun, but he understood tha
she was tired after their earlier travels. "Not a problem." An
then he had an idea. He checked the time and then turne
back to her. "We have a little time before dinner, how abou
I give you a tour of the palace?"

She perked up a bit. "That would be nice."

"Would you like to change now or after the tour?"

"Change?" She sent him a puzzled look.

"For dinner." His mother insisted on formalities, eve
when it was just the family…and a very special friend.

Worry reflected in her eyes. "Exactly how dressed up d
I need to be?"

"Don't worry. If you didn't bring anything to wear fo
dinner, it'll be fine."

"Of course I brought dressier clothes." She frowned at him. "I do know my way around society, you know."

That was true. She was a Cattaneo. He had worried for nothing. He nodded in understanding. "The men will be wearing suits. So a dress, if you have one, will work."

"I do. I'll change first. That way if the tour takes longer than imagined, I won't hold dinner up while I'm changing."

"Great idea. I'll go and change, too." He ran a hand over his beard. "I guess I'll shave, too. Kind of a shame. It was starting to get past the itchy phase." And with that he was out the door.

Was his father right? Noemi didn't act like the other women who had passed through his life. They were all too eager to be near him, to kiss him, to touch him.

Noemi wasn't that way. She was reserved. And though in part that should be a relief to him, there was another part that worried that she truly wasn't into him—that all they'd ever have was that one night. And that just wasn't enough for him.

CHAPTER ELEVEN

ACTING ALOOF WAS hard work.

Noemi assured herself that playing it cool was the best way to go. Being here at the palace and after meeting the queen, Noemi was certain she and Max didn't belong together. They came from totally different worlds.

And then she had the worst thought. The queen already seemed not to care for her. When the queen learned of the baby, what if she decided, with them being unmarried, that it would be best to have the baby sent away—put up for adoption—like her parents had been forced to do with Leo?

Noemi's imagination had a way of getting away from her. It was only when she reined it in that she realized an adoption would never happen. She and Max were in a totally different position from her parents. Noemi and Max weren't kids. They didn't rely on their parents for food and shelter. They could make up their own minds.

It was just her nervousness from being here. She glanced around the room. It was large with high ceilings and gold trim work. The landscape paintings on the walls were stunning. She moved closer to them. Each painting contained bright-colored wildflowers. In one painting, the wildflowers were part of a big field with blue skies and puffy white clouds overhead. In another painting, the flowers were next to a pond with a white swan. And the last painting was of the wildflowers with the palace in the distance.

Her initial thought was to move to the window next to her

bed to look out and search for the beautiful wildflowers, but in the next instance, she recalled that it was Christmastime and the ground was covered with snow. It would be many months before the wildflowers were to bloom again. And by the time they did, Noemi would have given birth to her baby and she would not be welcome at the palace.

Still, she couldn't resist glancing out the window. As she peered out the window, her mouth gaped. Max had his very own ice skating rink.

"Wow."

This place was just mind-blowing. It was more a private resort than a home. As she stared down at the ice, it beckoned to her. She'd been skating since she was a kid and she loved it. She wondered if Max knew how to skate.

Realizing that she was losing track of time, Noemi turned from the window. Her gaze scanned the room searching for her luggage. The suitcases weren't sitting on the floor. In fact, they were nowhere to be seen. How could that be?

Perhaps they were in the bathroom. She moved to the adjoining bath. The room was practically the same size as her bedroom. And on one wall was a line of cabinets. Was it possible they were in there?

She opened the first door and found it empty, but the second door she opened revealed her clothes. Someone had taken the time and trouble to hang her things up. That was so nice of them. She would have to remember to thank them.

She examined each of her dresses, trying to decide which one the queen might approve of. By the time she'd gone through them all twice, she was no closer to a decision. In the end, she picked a little black dress. It wasn't too flashy. And it wasn't too casual. And most of all, it wasn't too tight around her rapidly expanding midsection.

Not too bad. She glanced at her image in the mirror. *But not too great either.*

She couldn't help but notice the paleness of her face. And were those dark circles under her eyes? She sighed and turned back to the bed, where she'd scattered her things while searching for some concealer.

She'd learned long ago how to make herself presentable in a rush. When she was rushing from the stage to an after-party, there wasn't much time to waste. And when photos were being taken at the parties to distribute to the press, she had to look her best. After all, she was the face of Cattaneo Jewels. It was important to her to do her duty for the family business. She took her responsibility seriously. But perhaps she'd rushed too much today because she couldn't find her elusive makeup.

She didn't know why she was a ball of nerves. It wasn't like her. She was normally confident about her appearance. But that extra two or three inches on her waistline was knocking her confidence. At least that's what she kept telling herself. It had nothing to do with the fact that Max had been keeping a respectable distance from her.

His only interest appeared to be in the baby she was carrying. She tried telling herself that was a good thing. A baby was enough of a complication in her life. She didn't need a prince to mix up her world further. But it didn't keep her from wanting more.

By the time Max rapped his knuckles on her door, Noemi was dressed, her hair was straightened into a smooth bob and she'd at last located her makeup. It wasn't until she looked in the mirror that she realized she'd forgotten her jewelry, which she found ironic as she was now an owner of an international jewel company.

She yanked open the door. "Did you know there's a great big ice skating rink out there?"

Max laughed. "Yeah, I knew. If I'd have known you would get so excited about it, I would have brought you here much sooner."

"It's just that we never got to ice skate back at Mont Coeur." And then realizing that if they didn't hurry they'd be late for dinner, Noemi added, "I hope this dress is all right."

"All right?" His gaze skimmed down over her, warming her skin. "You look amazing."

The heat moved to her face. "Thank you."

She couldn't help but notice his clean-shaven face. Was it possible he looked more princely now? The black suit that spanned over his broad shoulders and cloaked his sculpted biceps looked quite dashing on him. A black tie and white shirt obscured her view of his chest with the smattering of curls that she so fondly remembered.

Realizing that she was letting her thoughts get away from her, she jerked her gaze back up to meet his. "And you're looking rather amazing, too." And then another thought came to her. "Does your family dress formally for every meal or is it just dinner?"

"For breakfast and lunch, it's casual. But my mother insists people dress for dinner. I take it your family isn't so formal?"

She shook her head. "My parents were casual at home. They…" Her voice caught in the back of her throat. She missed them so much. "They were more concerned about getting the family together than anything else."

"It sounds like your family is very close."

Her thoughts turned to her brothers. One was growing more distant by the day and the other one she was hoping to get to know. Not quite the definition of closeness.

She noticed Max watching her as though waiting for an answer. She swallowed down the lump of emotion. "We used to be—at least I thought we were."

But was that truly the case? Had she only seen what she wanted to? After all, her parents had lied to her all her life. The acknowledgment stabbed at her heart. That was not the definition of a close family.

Her thoughts turned to her baby. She would do better by it. She wouldn't lie to it. Never about the big stuff. And she'd listen to him or her—really listen.

"Noemi?"

She blinked. And then she glanced up at Max. Deciding

to turn their conversation back to a safer subject, she said, "Perhaps after this evening, I could eat in my room."

Max's brows drew together. "Why would you do that? Is it my mother? If so, I'll have a word with her. She can come on a bit strong."

Noemi shook her head. "It isn't her." Although his mother's disapproving stare did make her uncomfortable, Noemi wasn't one to back down. "If you must know, I don't fit in most of my dresses any longer. They don't hide my expanding baby bump."

A slow smile pulled at Max's tempting lips. "Is that all?" When she nodded, he said, "Then tomorrow we shall take you dress shopping and you can pick up anything else that you need...or want."

"But do you think that's wise?" When he sent her a puzzled look, she added, "You know, after the paparazzi spotted us at the baby boutique in Mont Coeur."

"Let me worry about the paparazzi."

Who was she to argue? She already had her share of worries. "I just don't want to be a bother."

"That's an impossibility." He smiled at her—a genuine smile, the kind that lit up his whole face including his eyes.

Oh, boy, is he handsome.

Her stomach dipped. No man had ever made her feel that way with just a smile. She'd have to be careful around him or she'd end up leaving her heart in Ostania and that wouldn't be good for either her or the baby.

Max checked the time. "Shall we go? We have just enough time to visit a couple of rooms before we are expected in the great dining hall."

"So this isn't going to be a small intimate dinner in the kitchen?" Somehow facing the queen in a more relaxed setting seemed so much more appealing.

Max shook his head. "I'm not even sure my mother has ever been in the kitchen. I know my father has as I would run into him when I was a kid in the middle of the night searching for a snack."

Noemi smiled. She liked the fact that the king was so

much more approachable. Now if only she could find a way to win over the queen. She wondered if that was even possible.

Max once again presented his arm to her. She really liked his old-world charm. Whoever said that manners were outdated hadn't met Max. He made everything relevant.

Her gaze moved from his clean-shaven face to his extended arm and then back again. Without a word, she slipped her hand in the crook of his arm.

She couldn't deny the thrill she got from being so close to him—from feeling the heat of his body emanating through the dark material. Her heart picked up its pace. It'd be so easy to get caught up in this fairy tale… A snowy palace and she the damsel on the crown prince's arm as they set off on an adventure.

"Where shall we start?" she asked Max.

"I thought we'd start with the public rooms."

"Public rooms?"

"Yes, those are the rooms where the royal family entertains."

"I'm intrigued. Lead the way."

She pushed aside thoughts of dining with his mother. At least, she tried to push the worries aside. Still, it was difficult. She'd never had anyone instantly dislike her. She tried hard to get along with everyone. Maybe she hadn't tried hard enough with his mother. Yes, that was it. She would try harder.

"Is something bothering you?" Max's voice jarred her from her thoughts as they descended the grand staircase.

"Why?"

"You're quieter than normal."

"Sorry." She glanced around the grand foyer. It was spacious enough to have a formal ball right here. "I can't believe this place is so big."

"It's great for playing hide-and-seek."

"Really?" She turned to him, finding a serious look on his face. "You really played in here."

He nodded. "When we were young, my brother and I could spend hours playing hide-and-seek. Why do you seem so surprised?"

"Because this is a palace." She glanced over at the oriental vase beneath a large mirror. "Everything in here is breakable and must cost a fortune. It's more like a museum than a playground."

He smiled. "Maybe to you. To my brother and me, it was home."

"Was home?"

Max shrugged. "I guess I've been away from here longer than I thought." He pointed to the left. "Shall we go this way?"

She gazed up at the priceless artwork on the walls. "Sounds good to me. This place is absolutely amazing."

Max chuckled. "My mother would approve."

So she needed to compliment his mother. Noemi tucked away this nugget of information. They toured a lot of the rooms on the main floor, including a red room with portraits of Max's ancestors. Some of the paintings were very old. The outfits they wore were quite elaborate, both for the men and the women.

And then Noemi came across a portrait of a baby in a christening gown. It was the eyes that drew her in. They looked so familiar. "Is that you?"

"Yes. One day it will be replaced by a formal portrait after the coronation with my crown, scepter and cape."

It drove home his importance and how Max was so not like any of the other men that she'd ever dated. One day he would rule Ostania. She couldn't even imagine what it would be like to carry such an enormous responsibility. And here she was struggling with the demands of caring for one baby whereas he would be responsible for millions of lives.

As she continued to stare at Max's baby picture, she wondered if that was how their baby would look. Would it be a boy and the image of his father? Or would it be a girl?

Noemi glanced around the room to make sure they were

alone and then lowered her voice. "Do you want a son? Or a daughter?"

Max's eyes momentarily widened. When he spoke, it was in a hushed tone. "To be honest, I hadn't given that much thought. Just finding out that I'm going to be a father has been quite a shock."

"But if you had to choose, would you want a son or a daughter?"

Max looked as though he were giving the question some serious thought. "Would you be upset if I say I don't care as long as it's healthy?"

She smiled. "No. I like that answer. I feel the same. I will love this baby no matter what."

"Me, too."

"The thing worrying me is that I don't have a clue what I'm doing. So I bought some baby books. They tell me what to expect at the different stages."

"Maybe you should loan me those books when you're done."

Her gaze met his. "You'd really read them?"

"Of course I would. I keep telling you, we're in this together."

"You don't know how much I want to believe you." And then she realized she'd vocalized her thoughts.

His head lowered to hers. Ever so softly, he said, "Then believe this."

He pressed his lips to hers. In that moment, she knew how deeply she'd missed his touch. As his lips moved over hers, she couldn't remember the reason she'd been holding him at arm's length. She was certain it must have made sense at one point but not any longer.

Her hands rested against his chest—his very firm, very muscular chest. His kiss teased and tempted her. As a moan built in the back of her throat, she slipped her arms over his shoulders and leaned her body into his.

Knock. Knock.

And then someone cleared their throat.

Noemi jumped out of Max's arms. Heat scorched her cheeks. *Please don't let it be the queen.*

"Yes, Sloan," Max said.

"Your Highness, I was sent to let you know that dinner will be served in fifteen minutes."

"Thank you."

And with that the butler turned and disappeared down the hallway.

Noemi wasn't sure how to react. When she turned back to Max, he was quietly chuckling. She frowned. "I don't know what you find so amusing."

He sobered up. "Absolutely nothing." His eyes still twinkled with amusement. "Shall we continue the tour?"

"Are there more rooms on this floor to see?"

Max nodded. He led her down the hallway to the throne room with two massive chairs with carved wood backs and red cushions. Behind the chairs was the family's coat of arms. And then there was a library, but not just any library. The room was enormous. The bookcases soared so high on the wall that there was a ladder to reach the upper shelves.

"Do you think your family would mind if I borrowed a book or two while I'm here?" She liked to read at night. It relaxed her and was something she looked forward to in the evenings. "I was in such a rush to get packed that I didn't think to grab any of mine."

"Help yourself. This room doesn't get utilized as much as it should." He glanced at the gold clock on the console behind one of the couches. "Shall we head into dinner? I can show you the rest of palace later or perhaps tomorrow."

"Yes, let's go." The last thing she wanted was to upset his mother by being late for dinner.

"That hungry?"

"Something like that." Right now, food was the last thing on her mind.

Max stepped in front of her. "Before we go, I want to reassure you that I have not forgotten about your doctor's appointment. In the morning, we can make some phone calls and if worst comes to worst, I'll fly you back to Mont Coeur for the day."

"You really would, wouldn't you?"

"I'd do anything for my family."

Before she could say a word, he kissed her. It was just a brief kiss but enough to make her heart skip a beat.

As Max took her arm to lead her into the dining room, he leaned in close to her ear. "Don't worry. Once my mother gets to know you, she's going to really like you."

"I hope you're right." Though Noemi doubted it, that didn't mean she wouldn't try to make a good impression.

His parents and brother were already at the other end of the long narrow room. The dining table was bigger than any she'd ever seen. It could easily seat two dozen people.

Noemi leaned close to Max, catching a whiff of his spicy cologne. For a moment, she forgot what she was about to say. All she could think about was Max and how easy it would be to turn into his arms and kiss him again.

"Noemi?" Max sent her a puzzled look. "Are you all right?"

"Um, yes."

He guided her across the room. The family stopped talking and turned to them. Noemi's stomach shivered with nerves. Her gaze met the king's. He sent her a warm smile. The queen didn't smile but she didn't frown either. Noemi chose to count that as a positive sign.

"So you're my brother's girlfriend?" Tobias asked.

Noemi's gaze moved to Max's younger brother. He had blondish-brown hair like his brother. Tobias was an inch or so shorter than Max. But he wasn't as reserved as Max. In fact, he was free with a smile that made his eyes twinkle. He wasn't as handsome as Max but he'd be a close second.

He took her hand in his and kissed the back with a fluttery kiss. She was so caught off guard that she didn't have time to react. It took a moment for her to realize her mouth was slightly agape. She quickly pressed her lips together.

"It's so nice to meet you, Prince Tobias." And then because she wasn't sure how to greet him, she did a slight curtsy and dipped her head.

When she straightened, Prince Tobias shook his head. "Relax. It's only us here. Please tell me my brother doesn't make you curtsy to him."

Max cleared his throat. "That's enough, Tobias."

"That's right, Tobias," the queen spoke up. "Please remember your manners."

Noemi wasn't sure if the queen was coming to her defense or if the queen didn't like the lack of proper etiquette.

The queen turned to her. "I hope you found your room adequate."

"It's quite lovely." *Lovely? Really? That's the best you can do.* "Thank you so much for having me. Max—erm, the prince has shown me around the palace and it is breathtaking. I especially love the library."

The queen's eyes widened. "You read?"

Noemi smiled and nodded. She was at last making some headway with the queen. "I read every chance I get." Not wanting to let go of this first legitimate connection with the queen, Noemi said, "I find biographies fascinating. And I enjoy historical accounts."

Before the queen could say more, dinner was announced and everyone moved to the table. Noemi was relieved to see that they were all seated at one end of the table. She didn't want to have to shout the entire length of the table in order to make dinner conversation.

Max hadn't warned her that dinner would be quite so lengthy. It had six courses and it was not rushed. The family for the most part was like any other with each person catching the others up on what was going on in their lives. However, they were more reserved than her family as there was no joking, teasing or laughing. Still, the meal was more relaxed than she'd been expecting.

And so she made her way through the whole evening without any problems with the queen. Maybe the need to rush back to Mont Coeur wasn't necessary after all. She really was curious to learn more about Max's home.

Noemi turned her attention to Max as he discussed the possibility of purchasing a new horse with the king. And her other reason for wanting to stay might have to do with those kisses he'd laid on her. What did they mean? And where would they lead them?

CHAPTER TWELVE

PERHAPS HE'D BEEN hoping for too much—too soon.

The next morning, Max had been summoned to a cabinet meeting to bring him up to speed on everything he'd missed during his time away. The only problem was his mind kept straying to Noemi.

Though dinner the prior evening had gone without a hitch, it had still been reserved with Noemi left out of most of the conversation. He hadn't realized until then just how important his family's acceptance of Noemi was to him. But what was even more important was Noemi feeling comfortable around not only him but also his family. How else would she consider raising their child as an Ostanian?

All was not lost yet. He still had a chance to win her over. And if she felt up to it, he planned to show her some of the charms of Ostania.

"I have to go," he told his mother and father, as well as the royal advisors. He'd promised Noemi that they'd sort out her doctor's appointment.

"Go? Go where?" his father asked.

"This is important," his mother chimed in. "You can't just disregard your royal duties. I know that we've given you a lot a leeway—"

"Perhaps more than we should have," his father finished his mother's sentence. "It is time you quit chasing women and partying. It's time you take your position in this family seriously. You may not end up as king, but that doesn't mean you won't have an important role to fill."

Max noticed his father didn't look quite right. His complexion was paler than at dinner the prior evening and there were dark circles under his eyes. Max couldn't help wondering how long his father had looked this way. Things had definitely changed in the time he'd been away. It appeared that he'd been gone too long.

"I understand," Max said. "I will do more. But right now, I have a guest."

"Right now, you have work to do," the queen insisted. "Your guest can wait."

His mother was right. He needed to do more to alleviate some of the burden from his father's shoulders. And to be honest, Noemi with her morning sickness wasn't up for much until her stomach settled. He checked the time. He had at least another hour before she'd want to go out. They could arrange for the doctor's appointment before they left the palace.

"Just let me make a phone call." Then on second thought, he didn't want his family to overhear his conversation. He settled for jotting out a note and sending it with one of the staff. He didn't want Noemi to think he'd forgotten her.

Noemi smiled.

For the first time in a while, she didn't feel like utter rubbish. Now that she was settling into her second trimester, the doctor said the morning sickness should start to abate. Apparently her doctor had been correct. *Thank goodness.*

She'd actually slept well and had some energy. She couldn't wait to go explore Ostania. So when there was a knock at the door, she rushed over and opened it with a smile. The smile slipped from her face when she realized it wasn't Max.

A man in a dark uniform handed her a white folded paper. "This is from His Royal Highness Prince Maximilian."

She accepted the paper. "Thank you."

With a curt nod, the man took a step back. He turned and headed down the hall. She wondered why Max was sending her a note instead of showing up in person. She hoped that nothing was wrong.

Apologies.
    Unavoidably delayed. Will catch up with you ASAP.
Feel free to make use of the library.
Max

She was disappointed he couldn't join her. She realized she'd been missing him more than she probably should. In fact, he'd been on her mind since the prior evening when he'd escorted her back to her room after his family had coffee. She'd been hoping for another kiss but it hadn't happened.

She wondered if all the royal dinners took close to two hours. Or was it something special because she was there? Then she realized it was more than likely due to Max's return.

Either way, it had gone far better than she ever imagined that it would. Max was charming. His brother was entertaining, almost comical at times. His mother, though still reserved, was more cordial and even gave her some reading suggestions regarding the history of Ostania. And though the king was far quieter at dinner than he had been when she'd first met him, all in all it had been a good evening. Maybe the royals weren't all that different after all.

Max's invitation to explore the library more fully was an invitation that she couldn't pass up. Bundled in a bulky sweater—without being situated near a roaring fire, the palace was a bit on the chilly side—Noemi made her way to the library without getting lost. But even if she had, there was so much staff around that someone would have pointed her in the right direction.

When she reached the library, the sun was poking through the stained-glass windows, sending a kaleidoscope of colors throughout the room. She didn't know the room with its floor-to-ceiling shelves could look any more appealing, but the touch of color made it seem...well, magical.

She moved to the closest shelf and started reading the titles. When she found one that intrigued her, she pulled it out to examine more closely. It wasn't until she strayed across a book the queen had recommended that she was hooked. Noemi knew the book wouldn't include Max but it would be about his ancestors and her baby's ancestors. She wanted to know as much as she could.

She carried the book back to her room to read while waiting for Max. She moved to a couch near one of the windows and settled in. The more she learned of Max and his life here in Ostania, the more she wanted to know about the country. She opened the leather-bound book and started to read. However, every couple of minutes her gaze moved to the doorway. How much longer would he be?

As chapter one turned to chapter two, then three, she had to wonder what was keeping him. He hadn't hinted about the cause of his delay in the note. Had something happened? Had he changed his mind about spending the day with her? Had he realized that she didn't fit in here?

As though he sensed her worries, Max appeared in the doorway. She immediately closed the book and got to her feet. She smiled but he didn't return the gesture.

She approached him. "What's wrong?"

"Why should there be something wrong?"

She shrugged. "I...um...it's just that you look like you have something on your mind. If it's me—"

"It's not. Don't ever think that." He paused as though gathering his thoughts. "I'm just sorry for being late. I hope you didn't get bored."

"Actually, I found this very informative book about the history of Ostania. Do you think anyone would mind if I keep it here until I finish reading it?"

He shook his head. "Please borrow whatever books appeal to you."

She placed the book on her nightstand. "I think just this one for now."

"To make up for being late, I have a surprise for you."

It was then that she noticed he was holding his arms behind his back. "Did I tell you that I love surprises? I always hoped my parents would throw me a surprise party with all my friends from school."

"I take it they didn't?"

She shook her head. "They were always too busy with the company."

"Would you like me to throw you a party?"

She studied him for a moment. "You're serious, aren't you?"

"Is there any reason I shouldn't be?"

She smiled at him and shook her head. "I'm past the age of longing for a surprise party, but I think I'll do one for our son or daughter. What do you think?"

"As long as you include cake, balloons and a pony, they'll love it."

Her smile broadened as they talked of their child's future. "I think the only thing that will capture their attention will be the pony."

"You might be right." A serious look came over his face. "Will you continue to work after the baby's born?"

"I'd like to." She'd been rolling this around in her mind for some time. "But I plan to step down as the face of Cattaneo Jewels."

"Really?" His eyes reflected his surprise.

She nodded. "I've been thinking about this for a while."

"What will you do? Take another role within your family's business?"

She shook her head. "I don't want to work with my brother. He…he doesn't take my opinions seriously."

"You have plenty of other career choices."

"I'd like it to be something meaningful like…like head up a foundation…or champion a worthy cause."

"I'm sure whatever you settle on will definitely benefit from your attention."

"I hope you're right." Her gaze moved to his arm that was still behind his back. "So what's my surprise?"

"Are you sure you still want it?" He sent her a teasing smile. "Are you sure you're not too old for a surprise?"

"I'll never be that old." She reached for his arm, but he stepped back out of her reach. "Show me."

He was still smiling. "After this big buildup, I hope you aren't disappointed with them—"

"There's more than one?"

He nodded and then he held out the purple lion and the white booties.

"You got them?" She accepted the gifts. "But how?"

"I have my ways. And I knew how important they were to you."

In that moment, Max left a definite impression on her. No one had ever done something so thoughtful for her. Her eyes grew misty. *Stupid hormones.*

"Thank you."

"You're welcome." He closed her bedroom door. "Are you ready to make some very important phone calls?"

The doctor's appointment. "Yes, I am."

She talked to her doctor in Mont Coeur and then Max spoke with a local doctor he said could be trusted. In the end, the sonogram would be done in Ostania two days from now. It was arranged for after office hours to aid their privacy.

"Now that that is all settled, would you like to go visit the village?"

"I would." Already dressed in a bulky sweater and her black tights, she was ready to go exploring.

Lucky for her, she'd remembered her black knee-high boots along with her long-sleeve black hooded coat with gray faux fur trim. And so a few minutes later, she was settled in the passenger seat while Max sat behind the steering wheel.

"I didn't know you knew how to drive," she said, surprised to find him so at ease behind the wheel.

"The security staff doesn't like when I drive, but I don't like being escorted everywhere I go."

She glanced in the side mirror. "Isn't that your body-guards behind us?"

"Yes, but at least I have a little distance from them. I can talk on the phone without being overheard or I can turn up the stereo as loud as I want without them frowning."

"So you aren't a perfect prince after all?"

"Perfect prince?" He laughed. "You do remember how we met, don't you?"

"Oh, I remember." She lightly patted her belly. "I'll never forget it."

For a while they road in a comfortable silence. She hadn't seen this playful side of Max since they'd arrived in Ostania. He always looked as though he was carrying around a great weight. She didn't realize until that moment how much she'd missed this part of him—the dreamy smile on his face— the way his eyes sparkled when he teased her. Maybe today would be more entertaining than she ever imagined.

"What are you thinking?" Max asked.

"What makes you think I have something on my mind?"

"Because you have that devilish look in your eyes."

"Devilish look? No one has ever accused me of that before." She leaned her head back on the seat as a smile played on her lips. This was the best she'd felt in a very long time. "Why, Prince Max, is this your attempt to flirt with me?"

Max maneuvered the small car into a street-side parking spot. He cut the engine and then turned to her. He rested an arm over the top of her seat. "I don't know. Is it working?"

With his face so close, her heart started to pound. "Do you remember what happened the last time you flirted with me?"

"I do." His face was so close now that his breath tickled her cheek. "In fact, I can't forget it. You've ruined me for any other woman."

She knew he was just having fun with her, but it didn't stop her from lowering her gaze to his lips. The truth was she hadn't been able to forget about their night together either or her desire for a repeat. It filled her dreams at night and tantalizing images swooped in during the day, stealing her train of thought. The way he kissed her made her feel like she was the only woman in the world. And when his fingers stroked her cheek, as they were doing now, her heart skipped a beat.

She leaned toward him as he gravitated toward her. They met in the middle. There was no hesitation. Both kissed as though they needed the connection as much as they needed oxygen.

His lips pressed hard against hers. She opened her mouth to him and their tongues met. Her pulse quickened. Her hand reached out to him, wrapping around the back of his neck and stroking up through his thick hair.

Mm… Each kiss was better than the last. She released the seat belt, wanting to get closer to him. If only they weren't in a car—

Tap. Tap.

Noemi jerked back. Her eyes opened and glanced around, finding the men in dark suits on either side of Max's car.

"Sorry they startled you." Max settled back in his seat. "It's their protocol when we're in public. They were letting me know that the vicinity is safe for me to exit the car."

"Oh. I felt like a teenager getting busted making out in the car."

He smiled playfully. "So you were that kind of girl?"

"Hey." She lightly smacked him on the shoulder. "I didn't say I did it. I said… Oh, never mind. I shouldn't have said anything."

"Yes, you should. I like learning these things about you."

"Really?" Somehow it just struck her as surprising that a royal prince would be interested in her rather boring life.

He nodded. "Why wouldn't I be? I find you fascinating."

"You're the fascinating one. A prince who escapes the confines of the palace to live a wild partying lifestyle."

"Maybe. Maybe not."

"Maybe not?" He'd piqued her curiosity. "What aren't you telling me?"

Max hesitated. "Never mind. We should go explore the Christmas market."

And with that he alighted from the car. She joined him on the side of the road. Without a word, he reached for her hand. With the sun out, it warmed the air ever so slightly, making it unnecessary for gloves. His fingers wrapped around hers.

She knew she should pull away, but she didn't want to. It felt right to have her fingers entwined with his. The more time they spent together, the more it seemed as though this was how they were meant to be—together.

She glanced up at him. "Aren't you worried about the press?"

He shrugged. "This is Ostania. And more so this is Vallée Verte. These people have known me all my life. They are, shall we say, protective. So when the press comes sniffing around, they make sure they are not welcome. As a result, the press doesn't come here much."

She could see why the townspeople would feel an allegiance to Max. He was kind and thoughtful to everyone, even those he didn't know.

And so they strolled through the village and had a leisurely lunch at a bistro with a hot cup of soup and a warm sandwich. Noemi's appetite kept growing and so did her waistline. It was one of the reasons for the sonogram a few weeks early.

After lunch, they strolled to the Christmas market. Noemi found something to buy for each of her family members. This Christmas was so important. It was the first without their parents and it was the first with Leo. She desperately wanted her brothers to come together, but she feared control of the family business would drive a permanent wedge between them. And she would never have a close family— like she used to know.

Her gaze moved to Max as he checked out some Christmas ornaments. Technically he would be her family, too.

The baby would form a lifetime connection between them. But what would that look like?

In that moment, a little girl bumped into her.

"Hi there," Noemi said.

The girl must have been about four or five. She peered up at Noemi with tears in her eyes. Noemi looked around for the girl's parents but no one appeared to be with her.

The girl started to move away.

Noemi ran after her. She stepped in the girl's path. "Where is your mommy?"

The girl's gaze frantically searched the market. "I... I don't know."

Noemi felt bad for her. She glanced around for Max, but he was some ways away with his back to them. She couldn't just let the little girl run off alone—not even in Vallée Verte.

Noemi knelt down. "Can I help you find your parents?"

The little girl shrugged. Tears in her big brown eyes splashed onto her chubby cheeks.

"My name's Noemi. What's yours?"

"Gemma."

"Well, Gemma, it's nice to meet you." She didn't have much experience with children. She supposed she'd better learn quickly, seeing as in just a handful of months, she'd be a mother. "Come with me." She held out her hand.

The little girl hesitated.

She couldn't blame her. She didn't know Noemi at all. "I promise I won't hurt you. I just want to help you find your parents."

The little girl slipped her cold hand in hers.

"Do you have gloves?"

Gemma shrugged.

Noemi spied a bit of white sticking out of the pockets of the little girl's bright red jacket. "There they are."

She helped Gemma put on her gloves.

"I'm hungry," the little girl whined. And by the looks of her, probably tired, too.

"Okay." Noemi glanced around. There were a lot of food

booths in the Christmas market. "We'll get you some food first and then find your parents. They have to be around here."

As Noemi made her way toward Max, she asked the vendors if they knew the girl. None of them did. The parents had to be frantic. But where were they? If this was her baby, she'd be standing on a table, yelling so everyone could hear her.

"Noemi?" Max's gaze moved from her to the little girl. "Who is this?"

"Max, meet Gemma. She is lost. We're trying to find her parents." Noemi noticed that he had some food in his hand. "Are you going to eat that?"

He glanced down at the pastry. "You can have it."

Though it did look tempting, she said, "It's for Gemma. She's hungry."

Max knelt down. "Would you like this?"

The girl hesitated but eventually accepted the pastry. She took a bite. Then another.

While Gemma enjoyed the food, Max turned to Noemi. "We'll give her to one of my security men. They'll make sure the authorities find her family."

Gemma tightened her hold on Noemi's leg. The girl looked up at her with pleading eyes.

Noemi's protective instinct kicked in. "Can't she stay with us? You know, until we find her parents?"

Max's brows furrowed together. "Noemi, how do you expect to find them?"

She'd been giving this some thought. Her gaze met Max's. "I have an idea but I'll need your help."

"What do you want me to do?"

"Can you lift Gemma onto your shoulders?" When he nodded, Noemi knelt down next to Gemma. "The prince is going to pick you up so you can look over the crowd for your parents. Is that all right?"

Gemma cupped a hand to her mouth. "He's the prince?"

Noemi smiled and nodded. "He is. Can he pick you up?"

The girl sent Max a hesitant stare and then shook her head.

he girl clutched Noemi's leg. Noemi's heart went out to her. he couldn't imagine how scared the girl must be.

Noemi smoothed a hand over the girl's head. "It's okay. Ve're just trying to help you."

Gemma glanced at Max again, but she didn't release Joemi's leg.

Noemi mouthed to Max, *Say something.*

Max sent her was puzzled look. He mouthed, *What?*

She mouthed back, *Anything.*

Max cleared his throat. Who would have guessed Max vould be nervous around a child? She wondered if he would e that nervous with their baby.

Max knelt down next to the girl. "Hi. My name's Max. Vould you like to be friends?"

Gemma shrugged, keeping a firm hold on Noemi's leg.

Noemi intervened. "Gemma, he's a really good friend of nine. You can trust him. I promise." When Gemma didn't essen her hold, Noemi continued, "And I'll be right here with ou the whole time. He'll just pick you up for a moment to ook for your parents. And then he'll put you back down." he paused a moment to give the little girl a chance to think bout it. "You do want to find your parents, don't you?"

Gemma slowly nodded.

With Max kneeling, he held out his arms to Gemma. The irl let him lift her.

This interaction made Noemi eager to meet her own child. he wondered if it would be a girl or boy. Should she find ut soon? Her gaze moved back to Max, trying to imagine im with their child.

"Do you see them?" Max asked.

Gemma shook her head and then she reached her arms ut to Noemi. The girl was so sweet. The parents must be o worried. Noemi took the girl in her arms.

Max leaned over to Noemi. "Don't worry. We'll make ure she gets back to her parents."

It was then that Noemi noticed the policeman approach-ng them. He must have been patrolling the area when one

of Max's guards flagged him down. She wasn't the onl
one to notice the man's approach. The girl's arms tightene
around Noemi's neck.

"It's okay," she said to Gemma. Then she turned to Max
"I can't hand her over. She's already scared enough."

"They are better equipped to handle this." Max pleade
with his eyes. "Noemi, this is for the best."

Max turned to speak with the officer, explaining the situ
ation. The officer assured Max that he would return the chil
to her family. The officer moved to Noemi and reached fo
Gemma.

"No…" Gemma tightened her grip to the point where
was uncomfortable for Noemi.

"Stop." Noemi stared at the officer. There had to be
better way to do this. Then her gaze strayed across the con
cerned look on Max's face. "Just give me a moment."

"Noemi…" Max frowned at her.

"Just wait." She rapidly searched her mind for the bes
way to reunite this little girl with her parents.

The policeman stepped away and spoke into his radio.

Noemi's gaze searched the market. There were a numbe
of people in this part of the market, but none appeared t
be looking for a lost little girl. A band playing folksy musi
was situated in the center while food vendors and artist
had tents along the edges of the market area where they dis
played their goods.

Noemi got another idea and took off.

"Noemi, where are you going?"

She waved at Max to follow her. She rushed over to th
band that was on a little stand. When the band members no
ticed the prince approaching, they stopped mid-piece. Wit
a flustered look, they got to their feet and bowed their head
at the prince.

Max greeted them and told them what a marvelous jo
they were doing. And then Noemi asked them for a favor. Th
four older men were more than happy to accommodate he

With Max and Gemma next to her, Noemi stepped up to the microphone. "Excuse me."

Most of the crowd wasn't paying attention. Noemi placed her fingers between her lips and blew. The high-pitched whistle brought silence over the marketplace. Everyone turned her way.

"I'm sorry to disturb your afternoon but we have a bit of a situation. This little girl has been separated from her parents, are they here?" She scanned the crowd, searching for frantic parents to come rushing toward the stage.

There was no movement. No frantic parents.

And then she had another thought. "Please help me reunite the little girl with her parents. Everyone who has a cell phone, please pull it out. If you all start texting on your social media accounts, hopefully word will make it to Gemma's parents. Use #HelpGemma. Thank you."

When no one moved, Noemi turned to Max. She whispered, "You do have cell phones in Ostania, don't you?"

Max laughed, a deep rich sound that warmed her insides. "Yes, *ma chérie*. We have cell phones and the internet."

Noemi sighed. "Thank goodness." She glanced at the people who were still motionless and staring at them. "Why aren't they doing anything?"

Max looked at her. "Excuse me." When she stepped aside, he moved to the microphone. "Please, help."

All it took was two words from Max in order to spur people into motion. She glanced at him and sent him a small smile—a hopeful smile. This was going to work. It had to work—for Gemma's sake.

Max moved away from the microphone. "Now what?"

"We wait. We'll browse the Christmas market and maybe get some more to eat." She turned to Gemma. "Would you like that?"

Gemma nodded.

And then Noemi added, "Your parents will find us. Just wait and see."

Max sent her a reassuring smile.

She set Gemma on the ground and took her small hand in her own. Then Noemi turned to Max. "Why do you keep looking at me like that?"

"Because I've never seen this side of you."

"What side?"

"The assertive, take-charge mode. You are quite impressive. And you think fast on your toes. You would make a good leader."

"Leader?" She couldn't help but smile. Not letting his words go to her head, she said, "I'm helping a lost child. Nothing more."

"I think you're capable of far more than you give yourself credit for."

She didn't even know if she would make a good mother. She had so much to learn and no parents to turn to for advice. A rush of pregnancy hormones hit her. Doubts about her ability to be a good mother assailed her. What if she messed up her kid? What if she was the worst mother ever?

"Hey, relax." A concerned look came over Max's face. Apparently, her worries were reflected on her face. Max placed a reassuring hand on her shoulder. "I didn't mean to upset you. I was just trying to help."

Noemi shook her head. "It's not you."

"Then what is it?"

She shook her head. "Nothing."

But inside she was a ball of nerves. She didn't even know what she was going to do for a job if she walked away from modeling. Sebastian had made it clear she wasn't welcome in the family business except as a silent partner. She recalled how her parents were hard on him while growing up and how he'd done his best to shield her.

Noemi wondered if that's what he thought he was still doing—protecting her. Sometimes habits were hard to break. And now with Leo joining the company, she would definitely be in the way.

Her whole future was one big question mark.

CHAPTER THIRTEEN

MAX GLANCED OVER at Noemi with her hand wrapped around Gemma's. They'd stopped at a stand where handmade toys were displayed. He was captivated with the way Noemi's face lit up as she talked to the little girl.

He could so easily imagine her with their own child. And after witnessing her strong protective instincts today and her caring way with Gemma, he had no doubt Noemi would make a remarkable mother.

"Shall we eat?" Max asked. He'd spotted a stand where they offered a variety of food that didn't involve sugar.

Gemma turned to Noemi as though trying to decide if she would agree or not. When Noemi agreed, Gemma smiled and nodded her head.

It was remarkable how the little girl had taken to Noemi so quickly. But then again, he'd been drawn to Noemi from across the room without having spoken one word to her. And it went beyond her outward beauty. There was something in her smile and a genuine kindness in the way she dealt with people. Everyone around her seemed to enjoy her company. Even his mother was beginning to thaw around Noemi. And that was saying a lot.

After the food had been presented, the vendor refused to take Max's money. This wasn't the first time something like this had happened. And though Max was touched by the offer, he knew these people couldn't afford to freely give away their goods—nor should they be expected to. And so

he mentioned to his bodyguard to make a note of their name
and then they would be generously compensated later.

As the three of them ate their selection of croissants and
meats while sitting on a bench off to the side of the market
Max noticed that Noemi was busy on her phone. He wondered what had her so preoccupied that she'd barely eaten
any of her food. But then he noticed she was following the
hashtag for Gemma.

"Relax. We'll find her parents."

Noemi slipped the phone back in her purse. "Don't make
promises you can't keep."

"This is one promise I intend to keep."

The urge to lean over and give Noemi a reassuring kiss
came over him. It was so strong that he started in her direction before he caught himself. This wasn't the place for
a public display of affection. Suddenly he was anxious to
head back to the privacy of the palace.

"I'm sorry," Noemi said.

Lost in his thoughts, he wasn't sure what she was referring to. "Sorry for what?"

"I'm sure you have more important things to do than sit
here with us."

The truth was that he did have a meeting with the royal
cabinet. They wanted to discuss options to pump up a slug-
gish economy. At first, the subject hadn't interested him. It
had sounded dry and boring. But after spending this time in
the village with the very kind and generous residents, he was
anxious to do what he could to improve their lives.

However, he wouldn't just leave Noemi to deal with
Gemma. He could already sense the strong bond forming
between the two. If the police tried to remove the child before the parents were found, he knew there would be a scene.
And he didn't want that for Noemi or Gemma.

"I have nothing more important than being here with you."
Did that sound as strange to her as it did to him? He never
talked that way.

Noemi rewarded him with a smile. "Thank you. I'm certain Gemma's parents will turn up soon."

And then there was a commotion off to the side of market. Both of Max's bodyguards and the police officers stood between him and the commotion. The excited voices were getting louder as though approaching them. Max's body stiffened.

Once as a child, his family had come under attack from an angry and disillusioned person. They had blamed the king for all their personal problems and had tried to harm the royal family. Since then, loud commotions in public spots put Max on guard.

He got to his feet and motioned for Noemi and Gemma to remain where they were. When he spoke to his guard, the man said he didn't know what was going on.

Max was about to call in additional security for Noemi when a man and woman appeared in front of the police. The woman had tears in her eyes and the man was speaking so quickly that it was hard to catch what he was saying.

And then Gemma rushed forward. "Mama! Mama!"

That was all the confirmation Max needed to move aside and let the girl by. Gemma rushed into her mother's arms.

In the end, it came to light that Gemma had been anxious to see the Christmas market, but her parents had some shopping to do first at the local shops on the other side of the village. Gemma had slipped away to visit the market, but then couldn't remember how to get back to her parents. Gemma had learned a valuable lesson and had promised her parents never to do something like that again.

"Thank you so much," Gemma's father said to Prince Max.

"It's not me you should thank." Max turned to Noemi. "She was the one that thought of using social media to locate you and reunite you with your daughter."

With a watery smile, the mother profusely thanked Noemi. And though Noemi looked uncomfortable with all the attention, she accepted the kind words graciously.

And then out of nowhere Gemma pulled away from her mother and gave Noemi a big hug. Noemi asked if they could have their picture taken together. When Gemma and her parents agreed, Max pulled out his phone. He noticed that he had three missed calls on his phone. His absence had not gone unnoticed. This trip into the village had taken much longer than he'd imagined. He dismissed his thoughts of what would face him back at the palace and used his cell phone to snap a picture, promising to forward it to Noemi.

Max's bodyguard, Roc, stepped up next to him and spoke softly near his ear. "You are needed at the palace right away. It's an emergency."

That word was never thrown around lightly. The hairs on the back of his neck raised. Max nodded and then waited until there was a pause in the conversation between Noemi and Gemma's parents.

"Noemi, I must go back to the palace."

Noemi's smile faded. "We were just going to finish touring the remaining shops."

He felt bad that their day had been interrupted. He lifted his phone and checked his missed phone calls. To his surprise, only one was from the royal cabinet and the other two were from his mother. His mother didn't make a phone call unless it was important. The emergency must be personal. His father?

None of this concerned Noemi and she wouldn't have anything to do back at the palace while he was dealing with his mother. He wanted this trip to be enjoyable for her. And so far, it hadn't gone quite as he'd planned.

"Why don't you stay here and finish touring the village?" he said to Noemi before he leaned over to his bodyguards and instructed one of them to stay with her.

"Really? You don't mind?" Noemi looked unsure about the idea.

"Not at all." Liar. He did mind. He longed to spend more time with her. "I'll meet you later for dinner."

"It's a date."

He liked the sound of a date. It gave him something good to look forward to. "Roc will be staying with you and escorting you back to the palace."

"But that's not necessary—"

"It's nonnegotiable." The lift of her brows told him he'd misspoken. He'd never felt so protective of another person. The rush of emotion had him coming across too strongly, "I just want to make sure you don't get lost or anything."

Her face took on a neutral tone. The smile on her face returned. "I don't think that will happen. It's a little hard to miss the palace on the hill. It kind of stands out."

He smiled, too. "I guess you have a point, but this way you'll have a ride back whenever you're ready to go. It's a long walk. Trust me. I know from experience."

"Thank you. That would be nice."

He definitely had to make sure to take a lighter approach when the protective instinct came over him. "You're welcome."

She had no idea how much he wanted to stay there with her. He didn't care what they toured, he just wanted to be around her and bask in the glow of her smile and listen to the musical sound of her laughter. He was hooked on Noemi. And it was a dangerous place to be should she decide life in Ostania wasn't for her—he couldn't leave now or ever again. He had to prepare to rule a nation.

Back at the palace, the bright cheery decorations seemed to mock him.

Max was torn between duty to family and duty to nation. On top of it, he was greatly concerned about this emergency. The butler instructed him to go upstairs. It was his father and the doctor had been called.

Max rushed to his father's bedchamber. He'd stayed away for too long. He'd made his father carry the brunt of the weight of caring for a nation all on his own and it had been too much for him.

His mother stopped him in the hallway. "Maximilian, slow down."

"But Father...how is he?"

"The doctor is in with him." His mother didn't say it but she was very worried.

"What happened?"

His mother gazed up at him. In that moment, it was as though she'd aged twenty years. "It's your father's diabetes, there've been complications. His kidneys—they aren't functioning well."

Max raked his fingers through his hair. He knew about his father's diabetes. His father had had it most of his life, but it had always been under control—until recent years. But Max had no idea it was this bad. "Why is this the first I'm hearing of it?"

His mother frowned at him. "Because your father refused to let anyone tell you. He said you needed time to recover from those years of dealing with...with your illness." His mother never could bring herself to say the word cancer. "Your father said everything would be all right and there was no reason to worry you or your brother. But over time, it's getting worse."

"So Tobias doesn't know either?"

With tears shimmering in his mother's eyes, she shook her head.

The door to the bedroom opened and the doctor exited. Max stepped up next to his mother. He had so many questions. He needed to know just how serious this situation was and what he could do to make it better.

The doctor held up a hand to him. "The king just wants the queen right now. Please wait here."

In this instance, the doctor trumped royalty. His mother disappeared into the room and the door closed. Max was left alone—on the outside, looking in. His head started to pound as question after question came to him. How did he let himself become this disconnected with his family?

He had to do better. How was he ever going to make a

ood father when he couldn't even stay on top of the family
embers he already had?

He turned around to start pacing when he noticed his
rother sitting at the far end of the hallway. Tobias was sit-
ng with his head in his hands.

Max approached him. He took a seat and searched for
omething comforting to say. It wasn't easy when he was as
orried as his brother looked. "Hey, it's going to be okay."

Tobias shook his head. "No, it isn't."

"Do you know something I don't?" Considering Max
idn't know much at this point, it was quite possible.

Tobias ran his forearm over his face. "They've been talk-
ng about Father stepping down."

"From the throne?" Max never imagined his father would
ver agree to such a thing.

Tobias nodded. "I… I can't do it."

"Sure you can."

Tobias's eyes were wide with worry. "No, I can't. This
hould be you. You should be taking over."

Max searched for the right words to comfort his brother.
You're just worried. Everything will seem clearer tomor-
ow."

Tobias shook his head. "I don't know why they make such
big deal of having an heir. Look at you. You're calm. You
an handle this stuff."

Max raked his fingers through his hair. "They've been
orking with you. You know how to run the country."

Tobias got to his feet. "I don't want to!"

Max stood. He placed his hands on his brother's shoul-
ers. "Okay. Calm down."

"How am I supposed to do that? Our father is sick. Very
ck. I'm too young for all of this. I… I'm not the right per-
on."

Max knew how to comfort his brother. But was it the
ght time to mention the baby? Things with Noemi were
ill unsettled.

But he never imagined his father's health would have

declined this drastically. Max's gaze searched his brother's bloodshot eyes. He'd never seen his brother so scared. Not since Max had cancer. It was so wrong for his brother to be this upset when he could help alleviate some of his worry.

"Tobias, you can stop worrying about shouldering Papa's responsibilities."

"What?" Tobias's gaze searched his. "Of course I can't. You know this. I'm the spare heir."

"Tobias, listen to me." Max glanced around to make sure they were alone. Then he turned back to his brother. "I have something I need to tell you."

Tobias turned to him. "If it's bad, now isn't the time."

The thought of his baby brought a smile to Max's face. "It's not bad. In fact, it's good news. Really, really good news."

"Well, don't just stand there. Share."

"You can't tell anyone this. Okay?"

His brother nodded.

Max lowered his voice. "Noemi is pregnant. I'm going to be a father."

"You are?" Confusion flickered in his brother's eyes. "But how? The doctors said that isn't possible."

"I know. But it's true. She's pregnant." A smile pulled at Max's lips. "Miracles do happen."

"Why haven't you told anyone?"

"It's complicated. Noemi and I are still getting used to the idea."

"Are you sure it's yours?"

Max nodded. "Definitely. But as you can imagine, it wasn't planned." He pleaded with his eyes. "Please don't say anything to anyone. The situation is delicate. Noemi and I haven't decided how to handle this. I told you this so you wouldn't worry so much. This will all work out."

"I hope you're right."

So did he. There were still so many unknowns about his father's health, the state of the country and what Noemi planned to do next. But right now Max surprised himself y stepping up to the plate to help—could it be that preparing for fatherhood was preparing him for taking over the responsibility and care of his country?

CHAPTER FOURTEEN

IT JUST WASN'T the same.

Not without Max.

Though Gemma and her family were the nicest people Noemi missed Max. She assured herself it was because they were becoming good friends. Nothing more.

Noemi returned to the palace to find another note in her room from Max. Excitement coursed through her body when she read his handwritten note telling her to meet him in the blue room at six thirty. She glanced at the clock on the mantel. That wasn't far from now.

Her gaze returned to the note. The blue room? She didn't remember visiting it on her tour of the palace. She wondered if this dinner would go better with his mother. She'd been a bit friendlier at their last meeting. Noemi hoped their relationship would continue to improve since they would play some sort of role in other's lives once the baby was born.

Noemi rushed to the wardrobe and flung open the doors. She shouldn't have stayed in the village for so long, but for the first time since her parents had passed away, she had that sense of family—of belonging. The residents of Ostania were so friendly and welcoming.

Her gaze scanned over the selection of dresses she'd bought in the village. Red—too daring. Black—already wore the color. Green—too short. Silver—too casual. Why had they all looked so good when she'd picked them out?

A bit of blue lace called to her. She pulled out the dress

ong lace sleeves led to a modest neckline. But the blue chif-
on skirt was short. Too short? But she was out of options.

She wore her hair loose and swept off to the side. She took
xtra care in applying her makeup, not putting on too much.
he looked in the mirror and knew she wouldn't fit in this
onservative household. If Max was hoping she'd change,
e was in for a reality check. Max would have to accept her
he way she was. Not that she needed his acceptance or that
f his family's. She wasn't princess material.

With a second and then a third glance in the mirror, she
ssured herself that she hadn't forgotten anything. Then she
et herself out the door. It was time to go find the blue room.
he didn't want to be late.

In the hallway, she glanced around for someone to ask
irections. She looked up and down the hallway, but there
vasn't anyone around. How could that be? There were al-
vays people going here and there with their arms full of
leaning supplies or fresh linens, but when she needed them,
one were about.

She recalled Max saying that all the public rooms were
n the first floor and so that's where she would start. Al-
hough in a palace this size, it would take her all evening to
earch the rooms.

At the bottom of the steps, she peeked in the first room.
There was no one in it. The next was vacant and the walls
vere red. And so she continued down the hallway, check-
ng each room.

When she stepped into a room with cream walls, she
ound it wasn't vacant. An older woman, with her white hair
p in a bun and wearing a black uniform, looked over from
vhere she was drawing the curtains.

The woman turned to her and gave her appearance a quick
once-over. "May I help you, ma'am?"

"I was looking for the blue room."

The woman's brows momentarily lifted. "Ma'am, the blue
oom is in the west tower on the second floor."

The woman went on to explain how to get there and

Noemi appreciated it because she never would have foun
it any other way. There were so many hallways and door
ways that a person could easily get lost in here. Noemi re
sisted the urge to ask the woman for a map.

When Noemi reached what she hoped was the right towe
she poked her head inside the doorway. It was then that sh
noticed a candlelit table near the windows. She took a ste
into the room. "Max?"

"Over here." He was standing in front of the window
wearing a dark suit and tie. He looked like he'd just walke
off the pages of some glamor magazine. And the way h
looked at her made her knees turn jelly soft. It was all sh
could do to stand up.

"I… I had a little trouble finding you. I hope I'm not late.
She glanced around, looking for the rest of his family.

"You're right on time. And sorry. I totally forgot to pu
directions in the note. I was distracted."

"Where is everyone else?"

"Everyone else?"

"Yes." When he sent her a puzzle look, she added, "Yo
know, your family."

"They aren't coming. This is a dinner for two."

It was then that her gaze moved to the table set for two
There were candles and flowers. "What is all this?"

"Just an apology."

"Apology? For what?" She couldn't think of anything he'
done wrong. In fact, he'd been quite charming.

"For abandoning you today. I wouldn't have left if I didn
have to. I hope you know that."

She nodded. "Did everything work out for you?"

He didn't say anything at first. "It went as well as coul
be expected."

She approached him. "That doesn't sound so good." Sh
stopped when she was in front of him and lifted her chin unti
their gazes met. She could see storm clouds of emotions re
flected in his eyes. The meeting must have been much wors
than he was anticipating.

"What is it?" she asked. "You can talk to me."

"You'd really be interested in hearing about state business?"

She nodded, wanting to be included.

And so Max started to fill her in on how the country's economy was being jeopardized by their insistence on following tradition. Ostania mainly exported agriculture goods such as vegetables, trees and seeds. They had some of the most exotic seeds in the world. But their insistence on relying on one form of export was making the global reach limited and in some cases it was shrinking.

Noemi looked at him thoughtfully for a moment. "So what you need is to broaden your country's expertise?"

He nodded. "But you seem to be the only one to really get this concept. The cabinet is insisting that this is merely an economic hiccup—a blip in the economy."

"But you think it's much more?"

"I do."

She took a sip of ice water as she considered his problem. "Have you considered retraining your people?"

"This country and its people are steeped in archaic traditions—whether they make sense or not. Most people won't consider changing the way things have always been done."

"Then start with the young people. These are the ones that strain against tradition."

"I've thought of that but once the progressives leave Ostania for higher education, they don't return."

"And that's where you're losing your country's most valuable resource. Have you considered opening your own university?"

A light of interest shone in his eyes. "And then we could gear the curriculum toward the future of Ostania."

"Something like that."

"You are brilliant. I will start plans for a university as soon as I am king. No." He shook his head. "It can't wait. This must be started immediately."

She loved being able to contribute to a solution that would

help the country. And she loved it even more that Max too
what she had to say seriously.

He smiled at her, but he didn't say anything.

Feeling a bit conspicuous, she asked, "Why are you smil
ing?"

"It's nice to have someone who gets what I'm saying."

She relaxed and smiled back at him. "And it's nice to hav
someone listen to me and take what I have to say seriously.

A look of concern came over his face. "Who doesn't tak
you seriously?"

"My family. Sometimes it's like I'm not even there. The
talk right past me."

"I understand."

"You do?" He was probably just saying that to be nice
"But you're a prince, everyone must listen to you."

He shook his head. "After my infertility diagnosis, I be
came invisible as they rushed to groom my brother to as
sume the crown. It got so bad that I felt I... I just couldn'
stand feeling so inadequate."

Her gaze met his. "You really do understand. I'm just s
sorry for all you've gone through. And here I am complain
ing and what I've endured is nothing compared to you—"

"Don't do that. Your pain is no less important."

His words meant so much to her. "I became the face o
Cattaneo Jewels by default. My family didn't know wha
else to do with me."

"I thought you were the face of the line because you
beauty is absolutely stunning. Men can't help but stare at you
And women wish they were you. And by wearing Cattaneo
Jewels, it's the closest they'll ever get to your amazing looks.

Noemi's mouth gaped. He surely hadn't meant all that
She forced her lips together. Had he? Because no other ma
had ever swept her off her feet with merely his words.

As though he could read her thoughts, he said, "Don'
look at me like that. You have to know it's true. But there'
so much more to you to admire, such as your generous hear

and your smarts." He reached out, covering her hand with his. "I think we could make a great team."

She didn't know if he meant romantically or professionally, but either way, her heart beat faster as she gazed into his eyes. What would it be like to be his partner? The thought appealed to her on every level.

Just then a server entered the room carrying a tray of food. Noemi and Max pulled apart and her hand became noticeably cold where he'd once been touching her. The server placed the food on the table and quietly left.

Max pulled out a chair for Noemi. "I hope you don't mind that I chose dinner."

"I'm sure whatever you picked will be good."

They started with onion soup topped with sourdough bread and gruyere cheese. She had to admit that it was the best she'd ever had. The soup dishes were cleared and a plate of hardy greens with a lemon and garlic vinaigrette was placed before them.

Once Noemi finished her salad, she said, "I'm going to be too full for the main course."

"You're going to need all the energy you can get for what I have planned this evening."

Was he hitting on her? Suddenly her mind filled with images of them upstairs putting her king-size bed to good use. His lips pressed to hers. His hands touching her... She jerked her runaway thoughts to a halt. The heat of embarrassment rushed up her neck and set her cheeks ablaze.

"Noemi, are you okay?"

Not able to find her voice, she nodded.

And then a smile eased the worry lines on Max's face. "Did you think I was planning to have my way with you?"

"Are you?"

He laughed. That wasn't the reaction she was expecting. Was the thought of making love to her again that preposterous? A rush of emotions had her eyes growing misty. Before the baby, she wasn't the wishy-washy type. She blinked repeatedly, refusing to give in to her pregnancy hormones.

Suddenly a look of dawning came over Max's face. "Hey, I didn't mean anything by that thoughtless comment. You already know how much I enjoy making love to you. I thought I made that quite clear. But if you'd like me to remind you—"

"No." The response came too fast and too loudly. They both knew she was lying. She stared into his eyes, seeing that he was being perfectly honest. "I… I'm just feeling a little emotional right now."

"I've read that about pregnant women."

"You've been reading about my pregnancy?"

He nodded. "You had a good idea about learning as much as we can before that little guy—"

"Or little girl."

He smiled. "Or little girl gets here. Anyway, I will try to watch what I say in the future. Are we okay?"

She nodded. "But you never said what you had in mind for this evening."

"That's right. I didn't."

"Well…"

"It's a surprise."

The server returned with the main course, *pot-au-feu*. Noemi inhaled the inviting aroma of the beef and vegetable stew. It was perfect for a cold winter evening. She gave it her best effort but she couldn't finish all of it.

She pushed the plate back. "I'm sorry. I am so full."

"Does that mean you don't want some bubbly and dessert?"

"First, I can't have bubbly—"

"You can if it's sparkling grape juice."

She smiled at his thoughtfulness. "Do you think of everything?"

"No. But I try. I want you to enjoy your visit to Ostania."

"It's really important to you, isn't it?"

He nodded. "So dessert can wait." He got to his feet and held his hand out to her. "Shall we go?"

She placed her hand in his and stood. "Go where?"

His eyes twinkled. "You'll see."

She followed his lead as they made their way toward the rear of the palace. By the back door, he stopped. On a chair near the door sat a white box. Max picked it up and held it out to her.

"What's this?" She loved presents. Her parents always made sure there were plenty of presents under the Christmas tree. "An early Christmas present?"

"If you want it to be."

While he continued to hold the box, she removed the gold tie and lifted the lid. Inside were a pair of white ice skates. Her gaze moved from the present to Max. "You got me skates?"

He nodded. "Do you like them?"

"Yes. But I didn't get you anything." She had no idea he was planning to give her anything. "It's not Christmas yet."

"I wanted to get a jump start on the holiday."

And then she noticed her coat resting on the back of the chair. "What are you up to?"

"Put on your coat and you'll find out." He paused and his forehead creased as his gaze skimmed over her short dress. "On second thought, would you like to change? It's cold outside."

She glanced down at her exposed legs. "I'll be right back."

Noemi took off for her room, all the while trying to remember her way back to this spot. When she reached her room, her cell phone rang. She considered ignoring it as she was anxious to get back to Max. But then she checked the caller ID. It was Leo.

"Hey, Leo. Is something wrong?"

"No. I'm just checking in. Are you still in Mont Coeur?"

"After you left, I decided to take a little trip, but I will be back for Christmas. You're still planning to be there, right?" When the only response was silence, she said, "Please, Leo. This is really important to me. I want to get to know you. We're family and we should spend our first Christmas together."

"Okay. If it means that much to you—"

"It does."

They chatted a few more minutes while she located her leggings and then shimmied into them. With a promise to see each other next week, they ended the call.

Noemi dashed out the door and down the hallway, hoping she didn't get lost. And then she came upon Max texting on his phone while he waited for her. He lifted his head and smiled. Her stomach felt as though a swarm of butterflies had taken flight within it.

They both put on their coats and headed outside. It was then that she noticed the ice skating rink had been lit up with thousands of white twinkle lights. She hadn't recalled noticing the lights before. Was this another detail Max had seen to? The lights reflected off the ice and made the snow on the sides look like a million sparkling diamonds.

She turned to him. "You did all this?"

"The ice skating rink was already set up. It's part of our tradition."

"But the lights. I don't remember seeing them the other day. It looks…" She paused taking it all in. "It looks magical."

It looks romantic. Just like the dinner.

"I have to admit that I did have the lights put up. I noticed in Mont Coeur that you like Christmas lights."

"I do. I love them."

They moved to the edge of the skate rink and laced up their skates. Max knelt in front of her and made sure her skates were tied properly. When he stood, he held his hand out to her. She placed her hand in his and let him help her to her feet.

"Come on. I'll show you how to skate." Max stepped onto the ice.

How did he get the idea that she couldn't skate? She thought of saying something but resisted. She decided to let him take the lead. She enjoyed the touch of his hands and the nearness of his body.

"Don't worry," he said. "I've got you. I won't let you fall."

Maybe she should fess up about her ability to skate. "You don't have to do this—"

"But I want to. There's so much I want to share with you."

She was pretty certain they were no longer talking about skating. As she continued to stare deep into his eyes, she said, "I'd like that."

"Do you feel steady on the skates?"

She nodded. "You really want to show me, don't you?"

"Yes. We'll take it slow. Take a step. Another step. And then glide."

She did exactly as he said. She could so clearly imagine him being a good parent and patient teacher with their child. They continued around the rink slowly. After the second pass, Max picked up the pace a little.

"You're doing great." He smiled at her. "Instead of being a prince, perhaps I should become a skate instructor."

"You're looking for a career change?" She knew he wasn't serious, but part of her wondered if he was just an ordinary citizen whether their lives would mesh.

"Maybe." His voice cut through her meandering thoughts. "What do you think? Want to give me an endorsement?"

"I don't know how much help I would be. Anybody would be excited to skate with a prince."

"I'm not so sure about that."

She gazed up at him, noticing the smile had fled his face. "I am. You're an amazing man. You're thoughtful, sweet and strong. This country is lucky to have you."

His gaze probed hers. "And how about you? Do you feel lucky to have me in your life?

Back when they'd collided on the sidewalk in Mont Coeur with the crush of fans, her answer might have been different. But since then she'd learned the tabloid headlines were not accurate. Max was nothing like the sensational gossip.

"Yes, I'm lucky. And so is our baby." She meant every word.

On the fourth loop, Max said, "Would you like to try it on your own?"

"Do you think I should?"

"Go ahead. I'll be right here." And then he let go of her hands.

The cold seeped in where he'd once been holding her. She took a step, getting her bearings without his steady grasp. It had been a few years since she'd been skating, but as she took one step after the next, it all came back to her like riding a bike.

She moved past Max. The cool air swished over her face and combed through her hair. She picked up pace and soon she was gliding over the ice.

When she looped back around, she found Max standing there staring at her. She did a spin and came to a stop in front of him. A look of surprise came over Max's face. She couldn't tell if that was a good or bad sign.

"You know how to skate?"

She nodded. "I've been skating since I was a little girl."

"But I didn't think you did."

"You didn't ask. And you were so sweet about it. I... I didn't want to ruin the moment. I hope you're not mad."

He shook his head as he moved closer to her. "What else don't I know about you?"

"My parents loved the holidays. They loved skiing, but they would indulge my passion for ice skating." Talking about her parents filled her with deep sorrow and regret.

Max skated in front of her and took her hands in his. "What's wrong?"

Noemi pulled away from him. She clasped her hands together. The mention of her parents brought back a barrage of memories—some of them good but then there was their final conversation.

"Noemi, what's wrong?" The concern rang out in Max's voice. "If I said or did anything wrong—"

"No. It's not you. It's me." She skated to the edge of the ice.

He followed her. "I don't understand." He took her hand

nd led her to a nearby bench. "I hope you know that you
an talk to me about anything."

She gazed up at the twinkle lights. "When I found out I
vas pregnant and I didn't know how to contact you, I vis-
ted the Cattaneo Jewels headquarters in Milan. Not having
nyone to turn to, I told my parents I was pregnant. They
idn't take it well. They made me feel like…like I'd let them
own. It was terrible."

"I'm sorry. I should have been there. I never should have
valked away from you that morning without knowing your
ull name and your phone number. If I could go back in time
nd change things, please believe me I would."

"I would change that, too."

Max's head dipped and his lips caught hers. It was a quick
iss but it said so much. His touch was a balm upon her heart.

Noemi pulled back. She needed to get this all out. "While
was at my parents' offices, I was handed a piece of mail. I
lidn't know it at the time but it wasn't meant for me—it was
ntended for my mother. We share the same initials. Anyway,
opened it and found a letter from my brother Leo. At the
ime, though, I didn't know I had another brother. He was
vriting to my mother to agree to meet his biological parents."

Max reached out and placed his hand on hers. "That must
ave been quite a shock."

She took comfort in his touch. "It was devastating. I hate
o admit it, but I didn't take it very well. I just didn't under-
tand how my parents could keep such an important secret
rom Sebastian and me."

"Noemi, you don't have to tell me this if it's too painful."

She shook her head as she attempted to get her emo-
ions under control. She swallowed past the lump in her
hroat. "Sebastian and I never had a really close relation-
hip. With him being older and not sharing the same inter-
sts, he never had time for me. And then to learn that I had
nother brother—a brother that my parents kept a secret—
t hurt. A lot."

"I can't even imagine what that must have been like."

"When I took the letter to my parents and confronted them about Leo, we argued. I couldn't understand how they could have been so hard on me when they'd also had an un planned pregnancy. I…" Her voice faltered.

"Noemi?"

"I told them I never wanted to speak to them again." She swiped at a tear as it slipped down her cheek. "And…and a few days later, they died in a helicopter crash on their way to meet Leo." One tear followed another. Her voice cracked with emotion. "Now I can never take back those words. I can never tell them that I'm sorry. That I love them."

"Shh…" He pulled her to him and held her until her emotions were under control. "Your parents knew you didn't mean it. They loved you. They wanted to find their other son because the bond with a child is stronger than anything, and they died united in their love for one another and for their family. And that's what I want—I want to unite our family."

And then without another word, Max lowered his head and caught her lips with his. Her heart fluttered in her chest. There, beneath the starry sky and twinkling lights, a prince was kissing her. This had to be a fairy tale.

His arm slipped over her shoulders, pulling her to his side. She willingly followed his lead. As his mouth moved over hers, deepening the kiss, she let go of the reasons this wouldn't work between them. For this moment—this night—nothing seemed impossible.

When he pulled back, he ran his fingers over her cheek. "You're cold. We should go inside."

She hadn't noticed the cold. Snuggled to him, she was quite warm. But she was in absolutely no mood to argue. "If you think that would be best."

"I do."

He made quick work of switching back into his shoes. He told her to wait and he'd be right back. He disappeared into the palace. She had no idea what he was up to. It was a night of surprises.

Noemi finished switching shoes and was just about to step

nside the palace when Max swung the door open. He had nothing in his hands, but he wore an expression that said he had something planned.

"What did you do?" She stepped inside.

Max shrugged his shoulders and feigned a totally innocent expression as they headed toward her suite of rooms. "Nothing."

Just the way he said it told her that he was most definitely up to something.

"Max?" She couldn't help but smile. Being with him made her happy and she didn't want it to end. "Just tell me."

"Why do you think I did something?"

"Because this night, it has been amazing. And…" She stopped on the landing and turned to him. "I don't want the evening to end."

This time she lifted up on her tiptoes and pressed her lips to his. The kiss was brief, but there was a promise of more— oh, so much more.

When she pulled back, she took his hand and continued up the steps. His thumb rubbed over the back of her hand, sending the most delicious sensations throughout her body. Was it just a prelude to something more?

'Thank you for tonight," she said, as they headed down the long, quiet hallway. "It was the most amazing evening."

When he spoke, his voice took on a deep timbre. "And it's not over yet."

A shiver of excitement raced over her skin. "What do you have in mind?"

"We haven't had dessert yet."

That wasn't what she'd been thinking of, but she was curious as to what he had planned. "What is dessert?"

"You'll see." He swung her bedroom door open.

Max gestured for her to go first. The lights were dimmed. nside was a table with two tapered candles, whose flames flickered. She moved to the table. There was a bowl full of plump strawberries and a bowl of whipped cream. Off to the side was an ice bucket with a bottle of sparkling grape juice and two flutes.

When she turned to Max, he closed the door and approached her. "I hope you like berries."

"I love them." She loved everything. Most of all, she loved that he'd gone to so much trouble for her. "But how did you get them in the winter?"

He smiled. "Being a prince does have its advantages."

"It does, huh?" She turned, picked up a strawberry and dunked it in the whipped cream. She turned back to him and held out the berry.

He bit the berry. Then he did the same for her, only she moved at the wrong moment and some whipped cream ended up on the side of her mouth. When she moved to clean it Max brushed her hand aside. He leaned forward and licked the whipped cream from the side of her mouth. Then his tongue traced around her lips.

A moan escaped her lips. The dessert was so very sweet. And she wasn't thinking about the berries and cream. This was going to be the best night of her life.

CHAPTER FIFTEEN

THE NEXT MORNING, Noemi woke up with a smile.

Her hand moved to the other side of the bed. The spot was empty and the pillow was cold. But Max's imprint was here. And when she rolled over, she could still smell Max's intoxicating scent on the linens.

When her gaze strayed across the time on the clock, she groaned. It was after nine. She'd slept in. No wonder Max wasn't around. She was being a total slacker and yet there was nowhere she had to be until lunch. That's the time she'd agreed to meet Gemma's mother. They were going to grab lunch in the village and then visit the local botanical gardens. She was told it was decorated for Christmas and quite a sight to behold.

She slipped out of bed and rushed through the shower. She was certain that she'd missed breakfast, but she hoped she could grab something to tide her over until lunch. Her stomach growled in agreement. This pregnancy stuff had certainly increased her appetite.

Wearing another pair of leggings and a long flowing top, she rushed back into the bedroom to find Max at the table with a covered dish sitting opposite him. He paused from flipping through a manila folder full of papers to give her his full attention.

"Good morning, beautiful. I wanted to make sure you got something to eat." He set the folder aside.

Heat rushed to her cheeks. "Why didn't you wake me up?"

"You were sleeping so soundly. I didn't want to disturb you."

"I would have gladly woken up." She leaned forward and pressed a quick kiss to his lips. When she pulled back, she noticed the worried look on his face. "What's wrong?"

Max forced a smile on his face but it didn't ease the worry lines. "I can't spend the day with you. I'm sorry."

"It's okay. But you'll still be able to make it to the doctor's appointment this evening, won't you?"

"Nothing could keep me away."

Noemi breathed a little easier. She was worried about the baby for no particular reason other than she'd just read a chapter about all the potential complications of pregnancy. Once she saw the baby and heard its heartbeat, she'd feel much better.

"Then stop feeling bad," she said. "You'll be there for the important part."

"Being with you is important, too. I asked you here so that we could spend more time together. And now I have to bail on you. Again."

"Stop. I'm not upset. See." Noemi pointed to the smile on her face. "I'm good. I'm great. In fact, I have plans for today."

"You do?"

She nodded. "I'm planning to meet up with Gemma and her mother. We're going to visit the botanical garden. There's a Christmas display."

He stood and took her in his arms. "I was planning to take you there. I think you'll be very impressed with the display."

"I understand about you not being able to go, but I will miss you."

"It won't be long until we're together again for your doctor's appointment. Just a few hours. I promise."

He leaned down and pressed his lips to hers. Her heart pounded just like it had when they'd kissed for the first time. Something told her that no matter how many times he kissed her, it would always be special—like the first time.

The day would have been a lot more fun having him along.

t was the first time that she acknowledged just how much she enjoyed Max's company. If his goal had been for them to grow closer, it was definitely working.

But what would happen when this fantasy vacation ended?

Max couldn't get the images of Noemi out of his mind.

Kissing her.

Holding her.

Their night together had been better than the first time. It had bridged the distance between them. It had Max even more determined to make her his princess.

And then there was Noemi's growing baby bump. Now, as they stood in the examination room of the doctor's office, Max was filled with this sense of awe over the baby followed by a wave of unconditional love. In that moment, it really drove home the fact that in just a few months he would become a father.

And what would happen when it came time for Noemi to return to Mont Coeur? Each day they were growing closer, but would it be enough to convince her to stay? How else could he convince her that they could make this work? That he would do whatever it took to make her happy—

"Max?" Noemi's voice jarred him out of his thoughts. When he sent her a puzzled look, she said, "The doctor wants to know if you have any questions before we begin the scan."

Max shook his head.

As Noemi leaned back on the exam table, she gave him another strange look. It was as though she wanted to probe further, but she thought better of it in front of the doctor. Dr. Roussel had been around a long time—long enough to deliver his brother and himself.

However, the man was one to stay on top of technology, which was why Max trusted him with caring for Noemi and their baby. The doctor was also known for his discretion.

After the doctor squeezed some gel on Noemi's expanding abdomen, he ran a wand over her skin. Max watched everything intently, making sure nothing went wrong. Somewhere along the way, Noemi's hand ended up in his as they watched the monitor.

"There is your baby." Dr. Roussel pointed to the screen.

The breath caught in the back of Max's throat. That little white smudge on the screen was his son or daughter. He would never again say he didn't believe in miracles.

Max smiled brightly and then looked at Noemi. "Are you crying?"

She looked at him. "You are, too."

With his free hand, he felt the dampness on his cheeks. And so he was. But they were tears of joy.

"This is the head." The doctor pointed it out. "And this is the spine. And…"

The doctor's voice faded away as he continued to study the monitor. Then he grew quiet as he moved the wand. For the longest time, the doctor didn't say anything. He studied the image this way and that way. And then he started to take measurements.

Max looked at Noemi, whose joy had ebbed away and was replaced by a frightened look. So he wasn't the only one?

"Is something wrong?" Noemi asked.

Max couldn't find his voice because he was too busy praying that his son or daughter was all right. He was even willing to make a deal with God for the baby to be healthy.

"Everything is all right." The doctor turned to Noemi and smiled. "Your baby is healthy. I'm just checking something that might explain your rapidly expanding waistline and increased appetite."

Max's gaze caught Noemi's. She looked hesitant to relax. The doctor was being cryptic and that was not reassuring.

"Doctor—"

Dr. Roussel waved him off. "I just about have it." He moved the wand a little bit. "Yes, it's just as I suspected."

"What is it?" Max asked, staring at the monitor, not sure what he was seeing.

"It's this right here." Dr. Roussel pointed to an image. "And this right here." He pointed to another image.

"What is it?" Noemi's voice was a bit high-pitched.

Dr. Roussel turned with a reassuring smile. "Those, my dear, are your twins."

"Twins?" Max felt a bit light-headed. His legs felt rubbery. He was glad there was a stool beside him. He sank down on it.

"Yes," the doctor answered. "See here." He pointed to the monitor. "That is baby number one's heart beating. And that is baby number two's. I'll turn on the speaker."

They heard one heartbeat. It was a strong whoosh-whoosh sound. The other heartbeat was softer. The doctor assured them that was natural.

When Max looked at Noemi, her face was wet with tears. He leaned over to her and kissed her gently on the lips. "You are amazing."

"Twins." Noemi's voice was filled with awe. "Do you know if we're having boys or girls? Or one of each?"

As the doctor wiped the gel from her abdomen, he said, "I'm afraid it's too early for anything definitive, but they should be able to tell you at your next appointment."

Max felt as though this was part of some sort of dream. Twins. That seemed so unreal. Sure, there were twins on his mother's side of the family, but he never thought it was a possibility because he wasn't supposed to have children in the first place.

When they were ready to go, Dr. Roussel handed them some paperwork and photos. "Here are pictures from the scan. They are both the same. One for each of you." And then the doctor said to Max, "Your parents are going to be so happy. This is the kind of news they could use right now."

Noemi sent him a puzzled look as Max had yet to find a good time to tell her about his father's condition or the fact that the king had been put on the organ donor list. And there was a more selfish reason. Telling her would make it real. Everything in his life was changing at once and he was having problems keeping his footing.

He would tell her everything, very soon.

* * *

The following morning, Max found himself stuck in another cabinet meeting. All his plans for Noemi's visit were ruined. And yet he couldn't turn his back on his responsibilities. Maybe it was the worry over his father's condition or learning he was about to be a father of twins, but he wanted to pitch in.

"Your Highness?" A royal advisor peered at Max over the top of his spectacles.

Max had lost track of the conversation about the sudden dip in Ostania's economy—a problem that could have a devastating effect for everyone in the nation if it wasn't dealt with swiftly. The whole cabinet was in the meeting, including his brother, Tobias. The only empty chair was his father's.

"Why are you looking to me for the answers?" Max asked, feeling as though he was missing something. "You should be talking to my brother."

"With your father under the influence of medication, his heir needs to make the decision."

Max glanced around the room. "And we all know that is Tobias."

"Do we?" the elder advisor asked.

He knew. Max's gaze moved around the room from one person to the next. The whole cabinet knew Noemi was pregnant. Max's body tensed. This wasn't good—not at all. Noemi wasn't prepared for what was to come.

And there was only one way the cabinet could know about Noemi's pregnancy. Max turned an accusatory stare at his brother.

Tobias cleared his throat. "I need to speak with my brother in private. Can you give us the room?"

The elder advisor looked as though he was going to protest when Tobias gave him a very stern look, silencing the man's words.

Once all the people had moved to the hallway and closed the door, Tobias turned to Max. "You need to tell them."

"Tell them what?"

"About the baby. That you are the legitimate heir to the throne."

Max shook his head. "No."

"Max—"

"I said no. It isn't the right time."

"I don't understand. I would think you'd be shouting this from the palace towers for all the world to hear. You aren't having doubts about the baby, are you?"

"The baby happens to be twins—"

"Twins?" Tobias smiled brightly. "That's awesome. Twice the babies to spoil."

Tobias gave him a hug and clapped him on the back. Max longed to tell everyone the great news but he had to be patient and so did his brother.

"Wait until you tell Mother—"

"Slow down. Noemi isn't ready for all that. She's still getting used to the idea of us and now she has to adjust to the idea of twins."

"Well, I have something to admit." Tobias at least had the decency to look guilty. "The cabinet knows."

"I thought as much." Max frowned at his brother.

This couldn't be happening. He'd been waiting for the right time to make the announcement. This wasn't it. But if the news was out, he could help run the country. He could lift the burden from his father and brother. He would talk to Noemi later. He'd fix this…somehow.

CHAPTER SIXTEEN

SHE NEEDED TO find Max. She couldn't wait.

After checking with everyone she passed in the palace, Noemi finally got his whereabouts from the butler. She had big news; the babies had moved. It was the first time she'd been able to feel them. It was the most amazing experience. And she needed to share it with Max.

She rushed down the hallway, glancing in each room that she passed. Max was going to be so excited. The babies were getting bigger.

And she was growing closer to Max all the time. She could talk to him and he listened. Just like in the village when Gemma had been lost, he'd listened to her.

Max was everything she could want in a man. He was thoughtful and caring. Maybe they could be more than co-parents. Her heart fluttered at the thought of him taking a more prominent, more romantic role in her life.

As such, she wanted to invite him back to Mont Coeur for Christmas. She wanted him to meet her brothers. She knew it might not be the smoothest of holidays and she would feel so much better if Max was there next to her.

As she turned the corner, she found a group of men standing in the spacious hallway. The voices echoed in the hallway. And then someone said Max's name.

Noemi paused next to a large potted palm plant. Something just seemed off to her. Max was nowhere to be seen

nd yet they were talking about him. It was probably noth-
ng, but still she stayed in place.

"Prince Maximilian told Prince Tobias that we'd have
o wait a couple more weeks before they can do an in-utero
est to confirm the parentage of the baby. Once it's legally
onfirmed, we can proceed with plans for Prince Maximil-
an to take over the throne. At last, it will be the way it was
upposed to be all along."

"And the prince? Is he certain this is his baby?"

"He said he needs the test to be sure. The sooner, the
etter."

Noemi's heart sank the whole way down to her black
eels. Her word hadn't been good enough for Max. She
noved until her back was against the wall. She needed the
upport to keep her on her feet.

All this time he'd had doubts.

Once again, her words didn't carry any validity.

Her heart felt as though it was being torn in two. She'd
ever felt so devastated—so angry. Tears pricked the back
f her eyes, but she blinked them away. Giving into her
motions would have to wait. She had things to do now. She
vouldn't stay where her word meant nothing.

The sound of a door opening had her glancing up.

"Gentlemen, let's continue the meeting. My brother and
would like to discuss the best way to make this transfer of
ontrol once we have the test results."

It was Max's voice. And he'd just confirmed what the
nen had said. The breath caught in her throat. She didn't
nove. She just couldn't face him now. She was afraid she
vould say something that she couldn't take back. And no
natter what she was feeling in this moment, she had to think
f the babies.

The men were moving away from her. When at last the
oor snicked shut, Noemi blew out an uneven breath. It was
s if she were waking up from a dream and reality was so
arsh.

Her feet started to move, retracing her steps. She had to

get away. She had to make sense of all this. The kisses. The steamy looks. The dinners. Were they all just some ploy? Did he feel nothing for her?

Her head started to pound. Her steps came faster and faster. She forced herself to slow down. She didn't want any one to think that something was wrong. She didn't want t explain that she'd made an utter fool of herself—falling for a prince with nothing but power on his mind.

Everything would work out.

Max rotated his shoulders, trying to ease the kink in his neck. The meeting with the cabinet had been long and at times contentious. But in the end, it was best that the news of the twins was out. He was able to lift a lot of stress off his younger brother and he was able to fill in for his father who had just started dialysis.

Now it was time he talked to Noemi. Everything they'd arranged in the meeting hinged on her agreeing to do a paternity test. Otherwise, the bulk of responsibility would be thrown back at his brother and that just wasn't fair—not when Max was in the position to do the right thing.

But first, he needed a hug and a long tantalizing kiss. Just the thought of holding Noemi in his arms again had him moving faster up the steps until he was taking them two at a time.

When he reached her bedroom door, he rapped his knuckles on it. Then he opened the door and stepped inside, expecting to find Noemi. She was nowhere to be seen.

He checked the time. It was going on seven in the evening. Would she be in the village this late? Maybe Gemma's family invited her to dinner. It wasn't like he expected her to sit around, waiting for him.

He was about to turn and leave when his gaze strayed across an envelope propped up on the nightstand table. Was that his name on it? He took a step closer. It was.

A smile lifted his lips. He imagined there was a love note inside. The idea appealed to him. He'd never had anyone

rite him a love letter before. Warmth filled his chest—a
eeling he'd never known before Noemi. She'd brought so
many amazing firsts to his life.

With his hopes up, he stuck his finger in the top of the
nvelope and ripped. He slipped out the piece of paper. He
ouldn't wait to see what it had to say.

Max,

*I've gone back to Mont Coeur. I know that you've
told everyone about the twins and I'm not willing to
go along with this. You only have your own interests at
heart—not what's best for me or our babies. I refuse
to be a "silent partner" in both my own and our twins'
lives. Please don't follow me. I need time to think. I'll
send you updates on the babies.*

Some of the words were smudged as though tears had
meared the ink.

How had this happened? How did she know when he'd
ist found out about his brother spreading the news? Had
obias said something in front of the help? Even so, they
ere usually so discreet.

He gave himself a mental shake. It didn't matter how she
ound out. It only mattered how he got her back. If he could
peak to her, she would understand. Wouldn't she?

CHAPTER SEVENTEEN

HOME SWEET HOME.

Although Noemi didn't feel the comfort that the luxur[] chalet normally gave her. In fact, she'd barely slept the nig[] before. That morning, the sun shone brightly, reflecting o[] the snow, but it didn't cheer her up.

Noemi didn't bother turning on the Christmas lights. Sh[] wasn't in the mood to be jolly. She hadn't had morning sic[] ness in quite a while, but right now her stomach was sou[] and her head pounded.

She couldn't believe she'd been so wrong about Ma[] She'd thought he was such a nice guy. She'd thought tha[] the news sources had gotten him wrong. He wasn't out fo[] himself—he cared about others. Boy, had she been wrong[]

Knock. Knock.

She wasn't expecting anyone. When she'd arrived las[] night, neither of her brothers were here. Christmas wasn[] until next week. Maybe Leo had arrived early. After all, thi[] was now his home, too. And maybe it would be better not t[] rattle around this big place by herself.

She swung open the door and the words of greeting stuc[] to her tongue.

Max stood there with red roses in hand. Flowers weren[] going to fix this problem.

"You shouldn't be here." Noemi attempted to close the doo[]

Max stuck his foot in the way. "I flew all this way. Won[] you even hear me out?"

She let go of the door and walked into the living room. Maybe it was best to have it all out now. Behind her, she heard the door close followed by approaching footsteps. She moved to the other side of the room and turned. She leveled her shoulders and crossed her arms. And then she waited.

"I…uh…brought these for you." He held out the roses. When she didn't move to take them, he placed them on the wooden coffee table.

When he straightened, his gaze caught hers. She refused to turn away. She hadn't done anything wrong here.

"Aren't you going to say anything?" he asked.

"You're the one that flew here after I told you I needed time. It's up to you to talk."

Max slipped off his coat and then rubbed the back of his neck. "You shouldn't have just left. If you'd waited and talked to me, we could have worked it out."

She shook her head. "No, we couldn't."

"You're overreacting."

"No. I'm not. I know what I heard."

He held up his hands in surrender as he sank down on the couch. "I didn't come here to fight with you."

"Then why did you come?"

"To tell you that I want you—" He stopped himself, shook his head and then started again. "I came here to *ask* you to be by my side as I ascend to the throne."

Not I love you. Or I'm sorry.

Noemi shook her head. "I don't want our children to be used as some bargaining chip to give you an easy path to the crown."

Max sat straight up. "That's not what I'm doing. There's been a lot going on at the palace—things I haven't told you. It's important that the babies are tested as soon as it's safe and then I can assume my position as the heir to the throne."

"You aren't listening. This isn't all about you. There's also the babies and myself to consider. Or don't we count?"

"Of course you do. And if you would just hear me out, you would understand how important the test is."

He was so focused on the throne and that blasted test tha he wasn't hearing her. He was acting the same way as he family—making her a silent partner in her own life. How had she missed seeing this before?

Her heart ached over the future they wouldn't have. Sh drew in a deep steadying breath. "Do you know what hur the most?" She didn't wait for him to say anything. "It that after the loss of my parents—the loss of my mother— I thought that I'd finally found someone that I could cou on. Someone I could lean on. Someone who'd listen to me.

"You did. I'm here for you." His eyes pleaded with her.

She shook her head. "Not when your sole focus is becom ing king. Now, please go."

Max got to his feet. He looked at her. His mouth opene but no words came out. And then he turned and walked ou the door.

Noemi didn't know whether to be relieved that he'd le without a fight or hurt that he'd given up on them so easil

CHAPTER EIGHTEEN

HE WASN'T GIVING UP. He was regrouping.

Max strode back and forth in the condo he'd rented for the night. On this trip, he'd broken with protocol and traveled alone. He needed privacy in order to fix what he'd broken.

He walked away the night before because they both needed to catch their breath. He hadn't expected such resistance to the idea of her coming back to Ostania and having the babies tested. He thought she liked it in Ostania. She had been making friends.

He continued to pace.

He was not giving up.

And that was something new for him. After his cancer diagnosis, he gave up. And yet he went into remission and since then he'd been deemed cured. And when he was told he couldn't have children—he couldn't live up to his birthright—he'd given up and left Ostania, left the palace life. This time when things weren't going his way, he refused to give up—to walk away.

He realized how much he wanted to stand up and take responsibility. He wanted to help his country. And at the same time, he wanted his family. He wanted Noemi.

He was being torn in two different directions. In that moment, he acknowledged that he couldn't live without Noemi and the twins. If he had to, he'd give up his claim to the throne.

He grabbed his coat and raced out the door. He had to tell Noemi that he chose her. He would always choose her.

The fresh snow from the night before slowed him down as he maneuvered his rented vehicle. Max stepped on the gas pedal harder than he should have and the back end fishtailed. He lifted his foot off the gas until the car straightened out. His back teeth ground together as he smothered a groan. He just wanted to get to Noemi as fast as possible. The longer this thing festered, the worse it would get.

Each second that passed felt like an hour. He wanted to tell Noemi that he chose her—that he loved her. It was the first time he'd been brave enough to admit it to himself. It was true. He loved Noemi and those babies with all his heart.

At last, he pulled to a stop in front of her chalet. He jumped out of the car and then realized he'd been in such a rush he'd forgotten to turn off the engine. Once he silenced the engine, he jogged to the front door.

Max pushed the doorbell once. Twice. Three times. "Noemi! Noemi!"

He paused and waited. Nothing.

She had to be here, didn't she? Surely she wouldn't have left. Would she?

His hand clenched and he pounded on the door. "Noemi, please. We need to talk."

Still nothing, but he sensed she was listening to him.

"Noemi, please open the door." He placed his palm against the door and lowered his head. "Noemi, I love you."

He heard the snick of the deadbolt. He lowered his hand and took a step back, not wanting to crowd her. And then the door swung open.

Noemi stood there. There were shadows under her eyes. And her face was devoid of makeup. Her hair was pulled back in a haphazard ponytail. And she was wearing a baggy T-shirt with some pink leggings. He wasn't the only one who'd had a bad night.

She stood there. Silent.

"Noemi, may I come in?"

"Do you really think that will change anything?" Her eyes said that she didn't think it would.

It was okay. He had enough faith for both of them. "Yes."

To his surprise, she stepped back and swung the door wide open. He brushed off the snow from his coat and hair and stepped inside. He deposited his coat on a chair in the foyer and then followed her to the living room. Noemi sat down and he did the same, leaving a respectable space between them.

He couldn't help but notice that once again all the Christmas lights were dark. He knew how much she loved the holiday. This told him that she wasn't all right with the current circumstances either.

Max turned to Noemi. She was staring down at her hands as she fidgeted with the hem of her shirt. This wasn't going to work. He needed her full attention.

He knelt down in front of her. "Noemi, I've made a mess of all this. And I'm sorry."

Her gaze lifted. "You are?"

He nodded. "And I want you to know that I didn't tell the royal cabinet about your pregnancy. But I did tell my brother. I know I shouldn't have. It's just that he was so upset and scared when he heard how sick our father is. I didn't think, I just reacted. Later, he went behind my back and told the cabinet."

"Wait. What's wrong with your father?"

Max drew in a deep breath and told her about his father's diabetes and the kidney damage as well as his father waiting for a new kidney on the organ donor list.

"So you told your brother because you were comforting him?" When Max nodded, she asked, "You didn't tell him because you wanted to reclaim your position as next in line for the throne?"

Max shook his head. "I wouldn't have done that."

"But it doesn't change the fact that the babies are the key to you having everything."

"I've done a lot of thinking—a lot of soul searching. And

I've come to a decision." He drew in a deep steadying breath. "I love you."

"You do?"

He nodded. "And I don't want to live without you. If need to choose, I choose you. You and our babies."

"You'd walk away from your birthright—from the crown?"

"I would if that's the only way I could have you in my life."

CHAPTER NINETEEN

HER HEART HAMMERED.

He was saying all the right things.

Noemi struggled to find her voice. She couldn't hear her thoughts for the beating of her heart. He'd picked her. He wanted her. He loved her.

She swallowed hard. "I love you, too."

Noemi leaned forward and pressed her lips to his. Max moved to sit on the couch and pulled her onto his lap. They kissed some more. She wondered if he could feel the beating of her heart. It felt as though it was going to burst with love.

When she pulled back, she slipped onto the couch cushion next to him. She rested her head on his shoulder. She knew they couldn't leave things like this. She couldn't expect him to walk away from his heritage for her. In the end, they'd both be unhappy.

"Noemi, do you think your parents would have been pleased that you and I—that we are together?"

"You mean because you're a prince?"

"No. Because I love you so much. I didn't know it was possible to care this much for another person."

Noemi's chest filled with the warmth of love. "I think my parents would have approved of you. I wouldn't have given them a choice. I can't live without you either. I love you very much." Before he could say anything, she momentarily pressed a fingertip to his lips, causing his brows to rise. "And I could never ask you to give up your claim to the throne. You are a wonderful leader, caring, compassionate and determined. You will make an excellent king. But you have to know that I'm done being a silent partner. If we do this…" she gestured to him and her "…then I need your assurance that you won't take me for granted." When his lips parted, she held up a finger to once again silence him. "And I need to know that you'll hear me when I speak and you'll take my opinion into consideration."

She looked at him expectantly. He arched a questioning brow and she smiled. "Yes, you can speak now."

"See. I do know how to listen. And I promise we will be in this life's adventure together—as equals. What you say matters to me, whether it's to do with our relationship, our children or the running of the country."

Her heart swelled with love for this most amazing man. "How did I get so lucky?"

His thumb caressed her cheek. "I'm the one that's lucky."

Max moved away. She thought he was getting ready to kiss her, but instead, he got up from the couch. What was he doing? He moved to the foyer. Where was he going?

"Max?"

"Stay there. I'll be right back."

Seconds later, he rushed back into the room. He was smiling—a great big smile that lit up his eyes. He stopped in front of the Christmas tree and turned on the twinkle lights. "Come here."

Her pulse picked up its pace. "Max, what are you up to?"

"Just come here." He held one hand behind his back as he waved her over with his other hand.

Her heart pounded with a blend of excitement and anticipation. "If you have an early Christmas present, you have to wait. I don't have any presents wrapped for you."

"Just come here. Please." His eyes pleaded with her.

Without another word, she moved from the couch and joined him next to the tree. It was then that he dropped down on bended knee. Her eyes filled with tears of joy. Was this really happening?

He took her hand in his. "Noemi, I love you. I've loved you since that first night when I spotted you across the room. I never believed in love at first sight, but you've turned me into a believer. And I can't imagine my life without you in it."

She pressed a shaky hand to her gaping mouth.

He moved his hand from behind his back. And there, nested in a black velvet box, was a stunning sapphire engagement ring. Noemi knew from her tour of the palace that the ring was in Ostania's royal colors.

"Noemi, will you please be my partner—because we'll decide everything together—be my lover—because I could never ever get enough of you—and be my wife—because I want to spend every single day of my life with you?"

After a lifetime of being relegated to a silent partner and not having her thoughts or feelings heard, Max had presented her with a proposal she couldn't turn down. Hand in hand, heart to heart, they would step into the future as equals.

She didn't hesitate. "Yes." Tears of joy raced down her face. "Yes. Yes."

Max stood up and pressed his lips to hers.

CHAPTER TWENTY

THE STAGE WAS SET.

The Christmas tree twinkled and carols played softly i
the background.

Noemi glanced around the great room at Mont Coeu
Evening had settled on the resort and Max had started
fire. It crackled and popped in the large fireplace, castin
the room in a warm glow.

She couldn't help but miss her parents. Her father had al
ways taken charge of the fireplace and her mother had mad
sure there was something delicious to eat. Family gathering
had been a highlight for her parents. Family had been impor
tant to them. And now it fell to Noemi to pull her brother
together—she just wondered if that was even possible.

And what were they going to say when she revealed he
news? Leo, well, she didn't think that he would feel one wa
or the other as they were still getting to know each other.

But Sebastian, he was a different story. Not so long ag
she thought she knew how he'd react, but over the past yea
he had grown rather distant and then with their parents
deaths, he just wasn't acting like himself.

Max approached her. He placed his finger beneath he
chin, lifting her head until their gazes met. "What's the mat
ter?"

"Why does something have to be the matter?"

He lowered his hand. "Because I know you. And you'r

orried. Are you afraid your brothers won't take the news
f the baby well?"

She continued to stare into Max's eyes, finding strength
n his gaze. "Sebastian and I haven't been getting along very
ell lately. I just… I don't know how he's going to take the
ews."

"Would it be easier if I wasn't here? You know, so you
ould talk to your brothers one-on-one."

She reached for his hand and squeezed it firmly. "I want
ou right here next to me." And then a thought came to her.
Unless you don't want to be here."

This time he squeezed her hand. "There's no place I'd
ather be."

It was only then that she realized she'd been holding her
reath, awaiting his answer. "Have I told you lately how
uch I love you?"

"Mm…it has been a while. Almost a half hour."

She grinned at him. "How could I be so remiss?"

"I was worried you might have grown bored of me."

"That will never happen." She lifted up on her tiptoes
nd said in a soft, sultry voice, "I'll show you how much I
ve you later."

"Can't wait."

She pressed her lips to his. Her heart picked up its pace.
here was no way that she'd ever grow bored of him. He
as her best friend and her lover. He was her first thought
n the morning and her last thought at night. If someone had
ld her that she could be this happy, she never would have
elieved them.

Someone cleared their throat.

Noemi reluctantly pulled away. Max smiled at her, letting
er know that this would all work out. She ran her finger
round her lips, drew in a deep breath and turned.

Sebastian's dark gaze met hers. She couldn't read his
houghts. She supposed she should have given him a bit of
heads-up about Max.

"Sebastian, thanks for coming. I'd like you to meet Max."

She'd intentionally left out the part about Max being a crown prince. She didn't want to overwhelm her brother all at once.

After the men shook hands, Noemi realized that he was alone. "Where are Maria and Frankie?"

"I… I don't think they're going to make it."

Before she could delve further into Maria's absence, the doorbell rang. That must be Leo. She would have to make sure to tell him that this was his home as much as theirs and there was no need for him to ring the doorbell.

She rushed to the door and swung it open to find that her brother wasn't alone. Standing next to him was a beautiful blonde with a warm smile.

"Come in." She glanced at Leo. "You know you don't have to ring the doorbell. This is your home, too. I hope that one day it will feel like it."

"Um…thank you." Leo's gaze moved to Sebastian and the smile faded from his face.

Not ready to deal with the tension between her brothers, she helped them with their coats and then walked them into the great room. Noemi turned to the woman with Leo and held out her hand. "Hi. I'm Noemi. Leo's sister."

"Nice to meet you. I'm Anissa. Leo's, um, friend."

"Girlfriend," Leo corrected, placing his arm around her slender waist.

"Welcome. I hope we'll get to be really good friends."

Just then the doorbell rang again. Noemi cast a glance over her shoulder at Sebastian. He moved toward the door and Noemi turned back to the get-to-know-you conversation going on between Leo and Max.

A few seconds later, she glanced back at the front door to see Maria and Frankie had arrived. Noemi smiled as she'd missed Maria and her nephew dearly. But seeing as Sebastian and Maria were having a hushed conversation, she didn't want to intrude. She really hoped those two would be able to patch things up.

A couple of minutes later, Sebastian, Maria and little two-year-old Frankie joined them in the great room. Noemi

uldn't hold back any longer. With a big smile pulling at
r lips, she rushed over to them.

"Hi." She gave Maria a quick hug. Then she knelt down
front of Frankie. His eyes were big as he glanced around
e large room at all the people he didn't know.

"Hey, Frankie," Noemi said, trying to gain his attention.
hen his gaze met hers, she said, "Can I have a hug?"

Frankie sent his mother a questioning look.

"It's okay," Maria said.

That was all it took for Frankie to release his mother's
nd and let Noemi draw his little body to her. "I'm so happy
u're here. I've missed you tons."

He pulled back and returned to his mother's side.

Noemi straightened. Her gaze moved to Maria, noticing
e worry reflected in her eyes. "That goes for you, too."

Maria glanced in Max's direction. "I take it things are
ing well with you."

Noemi couldn't hold back an enormous smile. "Better
an I could ever imagine."

"I'm so happy for you." The smile on Maria's lips didn't
ach her eyes.

Noemi moved back to stand next to Max. He placed his
m over her shoulders. And then he leaned close. "Are you
re you want to do this now?"

She smiled up at him. He knew how nervous she was
out her brothers' reactions—most especially Sebastian's.
e nodded at him.

"Noemi," Sebastian said, "why did you call us all here?
it the attorney? Does he have news for us?"

She shook her head. "This isn't about the will."

"Then what is it about?" Sebastian's gaze moved to Max
d then back at her. "You know I don't like guessing games."

Maria elbowed him and he quieted down. But it was her
other's stormy look that he gave his wife that worried
emi. Instead of things getting better for these two, they
peared to be getting worse. Maybe when her brother heard
r good news, he'd relax some, knowing that she wouldn't

be bothering him about the business any longer. She clu~
to that hope as her brother hadn't been himself in a while

"Maybe we shouldn't be here," Leo said, meaning hi
and Anissa.

"Of course you should," Noemi said. "You are my broth
as much as Sebastian is. Our separation as kids was a ho
rible mistake, but I hope going forward that there will h
no distance. Because I'm going to need all of you." Whe
her brothers got worried looks on their faces, she said, "I
nothing bad. I promise. I… I'm pregnant. You're going
be uncles." And then glancing at the women, she adde
"And aunts."

For a moment, there was silence as everyone took in th
news.

Noemi's heart pounded. "And we're having twins."

Sebastian was the first to approach her. He had a serio
look on his face and she wasn't sure what he was going to sa

"Are you happy?" he asked, in the same manner that the
father would have asked.

She smiled at him. "I've never been happier."

He studied her face for a moment as though to make su
she was telling him the truth. And then he put his hands o
her shoulders. "Then I am happy for you, too. Congratul
tions."

He pulled her into his arms and gave her a tight hug—
something he hadn't done since they learned of their paren
deaths. She was so thankful that this time it was good nev
that had brought them together.

When Sebastian released her and backed away, Leo stepp
up to her. "You do know that I have no idea about children
how to be a cool uncle, right?"

She smiled and nodded. "I think you'll figure it out.
fact, I'll insist." She reached out and hugged him. At firs
he didn't move. His body was stiff and she thought that h
was going to resist, but then he hugged her back.

When they pulled apart, Noemi moved to Max's side. Sl

placed her hand in his, lacing her fingers with his. "Do you want to tell the rest?"

"You're doing fine."

Just the fact that he was standing there with her filled her with such happiness. All she needed was this right here—the people she loved. She needed to pinch herself to make sure this was all real, but she resisted the temptation.

"First, I should probably introduce Max by his proper name. I'd like you to meet Crown Prince Maximilian Steiner-Wolf. He is the heir to the throne of the European principality of Ostania."

Everyone's face filled with surprise. It felt so strange introducing him as a prince, as he was just Max to her. She really hoped his title and position wouldn't make a difference to her family.

Noemi drew in a deep breath and then slowly expelled it. "And he has asked me to marry him."

Maria said, "You'll be a princess."

"Wow," Anissa said in awe.

"Yes, she will," Max spoke up. "She will be the most beautiful and compassionate princess. And I couldn't be luckier. I promise you that I will do my best to make her happy."

Sebastian's gaze moved between her and Max. "So you're moving to Ostania?"

Noemi nodded.

Max spoke up again. "I'm afraid that my duties are increasing and after Christmas, I will need to spend the bulk of my time in Ostania. I'm sorry to take your sister away from you all, but you will always be welcome at our home."

"Don't you mean your palace?" Maria asked.

Max nodded. "Yes. And trust me when I say it has a lot of guest rooms."

"Guest rooms that I expect all of you to use regularly," Noemi said. "Wait until you see this place. It's so beautiful. And they have great skiing. But I wanted you all to know that we will be here for Christmas. It'll be a family Christmas just like Mama and Papa would have wanted."

It would take time, but slowly they were coming closer together—just as their parents always wanted.

EPILOGUE

Five months later
Ostania Palace

"It's a boy."

Max exited his wife's birthing chamber to carry his new-born son to the library, where the king, queen and his brother waited. He couldn't stop smiling. He'd never been happier.

Everyone oohed and aahed over Prince Leonardo Sebastian, named after Noemi's brothers. And after the decreed paternity test had been done a month ago, his son was now third in line for the throne. And when his sibling was born, they would be fourth in line.

"He's absolutely perfect," the queen declared with a big smile. And, to Max's surprise, she began to speak in baby talk to his son. His mother really did surprise him at times.

His father was doing much better after his transplant surgery. In the end, Tobias had been a perfect match and had given their father one of his kidneys. Both had come through the surgeries with flying colors.

"How's Noemi?" the queen asked.

"She's exhausted and resting before baby number two arrives. She came through Seb's delivery like a real trouper."

"Your Majesty?" came a voice from the doorway.

Every head in the room turned.

"Yes?" the king said.

The nurse looked a bit flustered. "I need Prince Max."

She turned to Max. "The next baby is about to make its entrance into the world."

Max felt torn. His son was still in the queen's arms and she didn't look as though she planned to give him up any time soon.

"Go," the queen said. "I need a little time to get acquainted with my grandson." And then she turned back to the baby. "Your father acts like I've never been around a baby before."

Max didn't have time to argue with his mother. The baby should go back to the medical staff to be cared for before being passed around the room. Max turned to the nurse. "Will you take my son to the nursery?"

The older nurse smiled at him. "It would be my honor."

That's all Max needed to hear before he tore off down the hallway. He couldn't believe his blessing. Not that many years ago, he'd wondered if he'd live or die. And now he had the most loving wife and instead of being sterile, he'd fathered twins. It just proved that you never knew what was right around the next corner. You could never give up believing that there was something better—something amazing awaiting you if you just kept looking.

Max entered the chamber to find his wife groaning. He rushed to her side, taking her hand in his. He wished she didn't have to go through the pain. It didn't seem fair. But she didn't complain. She didn't yell at him like he'd read in some pregnancy blogs.

"You're doing amazingly," he whispered in her ear. "I love you." And then he kissed the top of her head.

In just a couple of minutes, the room filled with the loud cry of a baby.

The doctor held up the baby and smiled. "Your prince has a very healthy set of lungs."

"Yes, he does." Max smiled as his vision blurred with tears of joy. And then he turned back to his wife, who also had happy tears in her eyes. "You make beautiful babies."

"We make beautiful babies," she corrected.

"Yes, we do." He leaned down and kissed her lips.

Once again, Max cut the umbilical cord. The baby was cleaned up, wrapped in a blue blanket and handed over to his mother. Prince Alexandre, named after his grandfather, grew quiet as he gazed up at his parents.

Max's heart grew two times larger that day. He didn't know it was possible to love this much, but Noemi showed him each day that miracles really did come true.

* * * * *

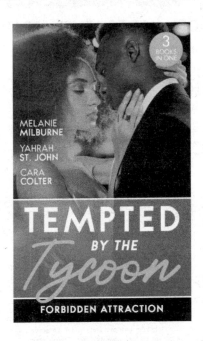

MILLS & BOON

THE HEART OF ROMANCE

A ROMANCE FOR EVERY READER

MODERN

Prepare to be swept off your feet by sophisticated, sexy and seductive heroes, in some of the world's most glamourous and ro locations, where power and passion collide.

HISTORICAL

Escape with historical heroes from time gone by. Whether your pa for wicked Regency Rakes, muscled Vikings or rugged Highlande the romance of the past.

MEDICAL

Set your pulse racing with dedicated, delectable doctors in the hig sure world of medicine, where emotions run high and passion, co love are the best medicine.

True Love

Celebrate true love with tender stories of heartfelt romance, from rush of falling in love to the joy a new baby can bring, and a focu emotional heart of a relationship.

Desire

Indulge in secrets and scandal, intense drama and plenty of sizzlin action with powerful and passionate heroes who have it all: wealth good looks…everything but the right woman.

HEROES

Experience all the excitement of a gripping thriller, with an intens mance at its heart. Resourceful, true-to-life women and strong, fea face danger and desire - a killer combination!

To see which titles are coming soon, please visit

millsandboon.co.uk/nextmonth

JOIN US ON SOCIAL MEDIA!

Stay up to date with our latest releases, author news and
gossip, special offers and discounts, and all the
behind-the-scenes action from Mills & Boon...

 @millsandboon

 @millsandboonuk

 facebook.com/millsandboon

 @millsandboonuk

might just be true love...

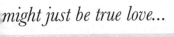

MILLS & BOON
MODERN
Power and Passion

Prepare to be swept off your feet by sophisticated, sexy and seductive heroes, in some of the world's most glamourous and romantic locations, where power and passion collide.

Julia James

Heiress's
PREGNANCY
SCANDAL

MILLS & BOON
MODERN

Jennie Lucas

Chosen as the
SHEIKH'S ROYAL
BRIDE

MILLS & BOON
MODERN

Kim Lawrence

A WEDDING
at the
ITALIAN'S DEMAND

MILLS & BOON

Sharon Kendrick

The
SHEIKH'S
SECRET BAB

Eight Modern stories published every month, find them

millsandboon.co.uk/Modern

MILLS & BOON

Desire

Indulge in secrets and scandal, intense drama and plenty of sizzling hot action with powerful and passionate heroes who have it all: wealth, status, good looks…everything but the right woman.

GET YOUR ROMANCE FIX

Get the latest romance news, exclusive author interviews, story extracts and much more!

blog.millsandboon.co.uk